I0831871

THE MYSTERIOUS HAND

Also Available from Valancourt Books

GASTON DE BLONDEVILLE
Ann Radcliffe
Edited by Frances A. Chiu

CLERMONT
Regina Maria Roche
Edited by Natalie Schroeder

THE MYSTERIOUS WARNING
Eliza Parsons
Edited by Karen Morton

THE VEILED PICTURE
Ann Radcliffe
Edited by Jack G. Voller

THE ITALIAN
Ann Radcliffe
Edited by Allen W. Grove

GLENARVON
Lady Caroline Lamb
Edited by Deborah Lutz

THE IMPENETRABLE SECRET, FIND IT OUT!
Francis Lathom
Edited by James Cruise

THE DEMON OF SICILY
Edward Montague
Preface by Jo Beverley

Gothic Classics

THE

Mysterious Hand;

OR,

SUBTERRANEAN HORROURS!

A ROMANCE.

THREE VOLUMES IN ONE.

BY

AUGUSTUS JACOB CRANDOLPH.

INTRODUCTION AND NOTES BY

CASPAR WINTERMANS

Ordina in guisa
Gli umani eventi il ciel; che tutti a tutti
Siam necessari, e 'l più felice spesso
Nel più misero trova
Che sperar, che temer.

Kansas City:
VALANCOURT BOOKS
2008

The Mysterious Hand by Augustus Jacob Crandolph
First published by A. K. Newman in 1811
First Valancourt Books edition, April 2008

Library of Congress Cataloging-in-Publication Data

Crandolph, Augustus Jacob.
The mysterious hand, or, Subterranean horrours! : a romance : three volumes in one / by Augustus Jacob Crandolph; introduction and notes by Caspar Wintermans.
p. cm. – (Gothic classics.)
ISBN 1-934555-36-3 (alk. paper)
I. Wintermans, Caspar. II. Title. III. Title: Mysterious hand. IV. Title: Subterranean horrours.
PR4518.C135M97 2008
823'.7–dc22
2007049125

Published by Valancourt Books
Kansas City, Missouri

Composition by James D. Jenkins
Set in Adobe Caslon Pro

10 9 8 7 6 5 4 3 2 1

CONTENTS

INTRODUCTION

For Jan Keijser, director of the Avalon Press, maker of beautiful books

Thomas Frognall Dibdin was a budding author of twenty-one when at a dinner party given by a friend his attention was fixed by one of those present, a middle-aged man with dark eyes and yet darker whiskers who, seated next to the host, in a loud voice discoursed on literary themes. Dibdin's neighbour whispered in the youth's ear that this person, the cynosure of all eyes, was 'an Editor of one of the *Reviews*,' and Dibdin was deeply impressed.

The table once cleared, the conversation turned to the influence of critics.

'Sir,' said the editor to Thomas, 'their influence is inconceivable. I am one of that *corps diplomatique*. I know a young man, at this moment, who has a volume of poems in the press. I know it will be sad trash; and I am whetting my critical knife to cut it to pieces the moment it sees daylight.'

Dibdin nearly fainted, for he, too, had a volume of poems in the press. He ventured to protest he could not understand how his fellow-guest was looking forward to slate a book he had not seen and which might contain lyrics that were actually quite good.

'Poh! young man,' said the critic, 'I see clearly you know nothing of the world. There are at this moment six unfledged authors begging and praying for a good word from me.'

Dibdin stood aghast, 'not less at the insolence of this critical dictator, than at the meanness of those young spirits who could "beg and pray" for his commendation.'[1]

The encounter took place in London in 1797, and if we look at magazines which were then published, such as the *Monthly Review*, the *Anti-Jacobin Review* and the *Monthly Mirror*, we shall find that many of their contributors resembled the critic whom Dibdin had met. They took pleasure in demolition, especially of novels; and it cannot escape observation that the fair sex in particular were dealt with in an exceedingly harsh way—but then the critics did not like to see the fair sex emerge from obscurity anyhow. 'When a woman will, perversely, exchange the needle for a pen,' declared one of these wig-wearing, clay-pipe smoking lords of creation, 'our duty directs us to attend to the *performance*, not the *sex*, of the writer.'[2] In an age that we perhaps suppose treated women with courtesy, critics more often than not took off the gloves. 'To tell [this female] that she can write well, were to deceive her in an eminent degree,' a gentleman proclaimed in a review of *The History of Lady Emma Melcombe and her Family*. 'It were to resemble the *cruel kindness* of a parent who indulges his children in their untoward humours, and who even allows them to proceed in their error till they are wholly beyond the reach of check or control. We will act more generously by the Lady in question. We will tell her that her novel, in point of style and grammar, abounds with faults.'[3] When 'A Farmer's Daughter in Glocestershire' published *Virtue in Distress; or, The History of Miss Sally Pruen, and Miss Laura Spencer* a reviewer peevishly remarked that she would, 'surely, be much better employed in plying the churn-staff than in brandishing a goose-quill; in the first of these occupations she could hardly fail of doing *some* good; in the latter, she must certainly expose herself to ridicule, perhaps even among the rustics of her father's neighbourhood.'[4] And the authoress of a Gothic novel was advised, if she wrote for amusement, 'to take some pastime that may not be so public; if she write from necessity we are truly sorry for her, since the proceeds of such a work [as *Sherwood Forest; or, Northern Adventures*] must afford a very scanty supply.'[5] Praise from reviewers was, indeed, so rare that one can understand that Sarah Ann Hook, whose debut had been recommended by the *Monthly Mirror*, could not resist the temptation of quoting part of its eulogy in the preface to her second novel.[6]

Many authors did their utmost to avert the stings of criticism by adopting a self-deprecating attitude towards the self-styled 'grave Reviewers.'[7] Agnes Maria Bennett apologized beforehand for 'the many errors in point of diction and grammatical propriety with which *Juvenile Indiscretions* will be found to abound,' adding that 'those errors are female ones.'[8] Regina Maria Dalton (subsequently Mrs. Roche) went a step further by imploring the critics 'to disregard this humble tale'—*The Vicar of Landsdowne; or, Country Quarters,* her first work—, for it was not, she said, 'worthy of your high attention. [...] Permit it, I entreat you, to pass by in unheeded insignificance.'[9] Other novelists, Augustus Jacob Crandolph among them, were anxious to obtain permission from the high and mighty to inscribe their books to them, hoping that the reviewers would restrain themselves on finding that the Duchess of X or the Countess of Y had deigned to accept such a dedication. Yet even a distinguished patron could not always blunt the edge of the critics' weapon.[10]

There were also writers who refused to grovel and

fawn, who reciprocated contempt with contempt. Sophia King, for instance, compared 'the critical ephemera of the day' with those 'little animals, who *live*, by picking the crocodiles' teeth, but are unable to inflict upon it a real injury; to such insects, the nature of reviewers must assimilate; *they* settle like animalculæ on a stupendous map, which they seek to corrupt, as they exist upon it.'[11] Across the Channel, where conditions were exactly the same, Ludwig Franz Freyherr von Bilderbeck admitted he felt inclined to hurl, not a duodecimo, but a folio at the heads of those 'pedants' inveighing against fiction,[12] while in a poem the young Goethe advocated even stronger measures: 'Beat him to death, the dog! He's a reviewer.'[13]

Now why was the critical fraternity around 1800 so strenuously opposed to the novel? I propose to give way at some length to one of the contributors to the *Anti-Jacobin Review*, who, in the course of his article, could not refrain from kicking (without mentioning his name) the shins of Matthew Gregory Lewis, author of *The Monk*.

> Our readers, we think, must have frequently observed that a very small proportion of our pages is dedicated to Romances and Novels; nor is our conduct, in this respect, the effect of accident, but of design. Were we anxious to pay particular attention to such publications, it will easily be granted, that we should seldom be in danger of wanting employment. But this department of writing is, in general, so miserably and contemptibly executed, as to be altogether undeserving of criticism. To the genius, indeed, of a Fielding, of a Smollett, of a Richardson, and of a Radcliffe, we bow with respect; though even to the fascinating productions of these authors we have many objections, which we cannot,

at present, afford time to state. But the worthless trash which, year after year, comes forward to load the groaning shelves of our circulating libraries, and the toilets of our fine ladies and gentlemen, we should think sufficient, and more than sufficient, to give an intolerable surfeit to the most voracious appetite for nonsense and folly. Of such publications, indeed, nonsense and folly are, not unfrequently, the most innocent ingredients. Our novels are often intentionally filled with poison of the most destructive kinds; with sedition, irreligion, and the grossest immorality. It is, accordingly, owned, and deeply lamented, by all persons of sober and benevolent minds, that no one cause has contributed more to corrupt both the principles and the practice of our youth than the infected food so plenteously prepared for them by those literary cooks who profess to deal in the article of novels. No man who has read or thought on the subject can be ignorant how necessarily the ruin of a state is produced by a general depravity of morals; and it will be readily acknowledged, that nothing can have a more fatal influence on the morals of a people than eradicating from the minds of the female sex, those sentiments of purity, delicacy, and fidelity, which constitute the brightest ornaments of their character, and which, in better times, they were taught to consider as their honour and their pride. The mischief which, in view of the matter, has been produced by the universal and inextinguishable passion for the reading of novels, it would baffle the most skilful arithmetician to compute. [...]

For tainting the imagination, and corrupting the heart, of an innocent young woman, no surer method could be devised than putting into her hands those pernicious volumes which dress out vice in the garb of pleasure, and of which the object is, by luscious descriptions of such scenes and situations as are inconsistent with chastity, to excite propensities sufficiently apt to rise of themselves. In consequence of this diabolical device, many thousands of amiable and interesting objects, who might otherwise have been the ornament and delight of elegant, or of useful society, are annually plunged into misery ineffable, to their own perdition, and the disgrace of their friends. [...]

It may be said, we are aware, that, in these observations, we have given only the gloomy side of the picture; and that a very great majority of these volumes, which are denominated Novels, are calculated to inculcate strict maxims of duty, or, at least, to communicate harmless amusement. We most willingly allow that many of them are intended to have these effects; for this line of writing is certainly not monopolized by those whose aim is to debauch the age. Yet we have our doubts whether *moral* novels are those most generally sought after and perused. We are greatly mistaken if *Sir Charles Grandison* has ever so universally, and with so much avidity, been read by our fine gentlemen, or even by our fine ladies, as a late publication, the most pernicious, perhaps, which, during the whole course of the last century, issued from a profligate and prostituted press. Our readers will know that we allude to a production, the work of a certain senator, who, instead of acting up to the dignity of the honourable character with which he was invested, appears to have been ambitious of attracting the notice of posterity as a pandar for the stews. [...]

Supposing, however, that all our writers of novels were as able as Fielding, and as moral as Richardson, we should still regret their amazing multiplicity; for no species of reading can be less improving, or, to speak more accurately, more detrimental. It is observable that those who have long accustomed themselves to this meagre kind of nourishment, come very generally, at last, to lose all relish for more substantial food. [...] Such a course of reading is, very generally, attended with disagreeable

> consequences. No employment whatever more directly tends to relax the tone, and destroy all the useful energies, of the mind. It hardly ever fails, when long persisted in, to generate a habit of lifeless inattention to every serious study and pursuit; so that they who indulge in it are completely disqualified for the acquisition of any kind of valuable knowledge, and sink into a despicable frivolity of character, which makes them equally useless and ridiculous. We have known many instances of well educated men, distinguished originally both by natural abilities, and by laudable industry employed in improving them, who, afterwards, addicting themselves, almost exclusively, to the reading of novels, disappointed every reasonable expectation which had been formed of them. They not only lost courage to erect the superstructure for which, in their youth, they had laid a promising and solid foundation; but they suffered the foundation itself to be demolished. They gradually forgot what they formerly learned; and their minds became, at last, so feeble as to be terrified at the prospect of application or exertion, however small. Our readers, we are confident, will readily recollect among their own acquaintances, various examples of a similar kind. We cannot, therefore, help very seriously wishing that this unprofitable, or rather, this dissipated manner of spending their time were less common than it is.[14]

When reading these strictures on the novel one is reminded of the condemnation, in much the same terms, of that other scourge of the times, masturbation.[15] There were clearly many around who were deeply suspicious of pleasures mental and physical; who wanted to exert a strong control on young folk in general and on girls in particular. To such authoritarians the craze for novels posed a very real threat, instilling, as it supposedly did, 'a detestation of all prudential advice, impatience of controul, love of imaginary liberty, and an abjuration of all parental authority.'[16] It was also pointed out that the 'contagion' of reading undermined the class system, spreading as it did through all ranks, servant-girls 'now talking as familiarly of swains and sentiments as the accomplished Dames of genteel life.'[17]

Sarah Bennet (subsequently Mrs. Sheriffe) did not lose her temper when in the preface to her second romance, *Correlia, or, The Mystic Tomb* (1802), she pointed out that far from corrupting the rising generation, modern novelists instilled in their readers a love of virtue and a detestation of vice, thereby contributing towards 'the so much talked of *perfectibility* of our being.' And there is nothing reprehensible, she went on, in '[whiling] away the tedious hours of convalescence, [detaching] the aching mind from scenes of *real* uneasiness, or [cheating] of its length the winter evening' by reading a good yarn. Romance writers, therefore, are not the foes but the friends of mankind.[18] It was a spirited defence, full of good sense, which one hopes was not without some effect.

Elsewhere in Europe strong action was taken to curb the vogue; in Austria a censorship of novels was introduced in 1810, the works of Ann Radcliffe and Walter Scott even being put on the index by the killjoys of Vienna.[19]

In certain quarters the prejudice against fiction persisted well into the twentieth century. Thus the puritanical mother of Sir Edmund Gosse (1849-1928) barred the Waverley novels from the house: 'they were, she said, not true; and a lie is an abomination.'[20] An anonymous subscriber to *The Academy* went in 1909 at those 'erotically-inclined ladies [who] let their emotions run riot through page after page and chapter after chapter, in a manner that makes the decently-minded reader look anxiously around for a disinfectant' as well as those publishers 'who cater for the most depraved tastes by blatantly advertising these works in terms that should call for the active intervention of Scotland Yard.'[21] And the father of the historian Joachim Fest (1926-2006) blamed Joachim's aunt Dolly, a librarian, for lending one of her nephews a novel by the future Nobel Prize laureate Hermann Hesse. Novels, Herr Fest maintained, are for housewives and kitchen-maids who have nothing better to do.[22]

But to return to the days of King George III. On the whole the efforts of the *Monthly Mirror* et al. to stop the spread of the novel were spectacularly unsuccessful, and by thundering against the books issued by 'that ingenious person who has given the name of wisdom to the forge of folly'[23]—that is, William Lane of Minerva Press fame—they unintentionally merely heightened the pleasure the aficionados derived from those delightful little volumes, for a fruit that is forbidden seems the more succulent for that very reason. Incidentally it should be remarked that, contrary to what is often asserted, novels were devoured by males as much as they were by females. 'I myself,' says Henry Tilney to Catherine Morland in *Northanger Abbey*, 'have read hundreds and hundreds. Do not imagine that you can cope with me in a knowledge of Julias and Louisas.'[24] We may be fairly certain that both Henry and Catherine would have been delighted to make the acquaintance of yet another Julia, Miss Julia Bolton, whose adventures at home and abroad were set forth by Augustus Jacob Crandolph in *The Mysterious Hand; or, Subterranean Horrours!* [*sic*], a three-decker issued in January 1811 by Anthony King Newman, who had recently succeeded William Lane as proprietor of the Minerva Press.

The novel, surely one of the most curious to have been published by the fiction-factory of Leadenhall Street, ran into three editions, at least if we can believe what the title-page of the French translation tells us.[25] The author is at pains to point out that he is not giving rein to his imagination when recounting the vicissitudes of the 'sylph-like' Julia and her beloved Theodore whose 'Grecian nose' serves as an indication of his 'nobleness': 'I describe nothing but what has happened. As I live I tell no falsehood'—which fools no one, of course; the designation *A Romance* that follows the book's title cheerfully contradicts these asseverations. All this is a ploy, a contrivance of make-believe which lies at the basis of the fun of telling, and reading, a story.

The question 'Who was Augustus Jacob Crandolph?' may be followed by another, 'Was there ever a person bearing that name?' James D. Jenkins informs me that the name Crandolph is not so much rare as non-existent, and our author is called 'Randolph' in both the *Biographical Dictionary of the Living Authors of Great Britain and Ireland* (1816) and *The English Catalogue of Books 1801–1836* (1914). It is possible that the printer of the Minerva Press misread the author's name. Such mistakes occurred. The prolific Mrs. Meeke was called 'Meek' on the title-page of her first novel, *Count St. Blancard; or, The Prejudiced Judge* (1795), while Regina Maria Roche must have been annoyed to see herself called 'Maria Regina Roche' on the title-page of *Nocturnal Visit, A Tale* (1800), which shows that authors were not always able to correct the proofs of their works. Crandolph (or Randolph) certainly did not see the proofs of his book, or he would have corrected a glaring misprint in the third line of his motto taken from Metastasio's opera libretto *Adriano in Siria*.[26] Subsequent editions of the novel might have been expected to have borne the author's correct name; but no copies of these have been located, and the French translation, said to have followed the third edition, ascribed the book to 'A.J. Crandolph.' Further to complicate matters, the Parisian bookseller and publisher Pigoreau refers to our author as 'Grandolphe.'[27]

So is 'Crandolph' a pseudonym? Are we to believe the novelist when he claims to have lived 'threescore years and twelve'? His spelling, which we have retained, is certainly old-fashioned. Are we to infer from his dedication to the Princess Mary, the future Duchess of Gloucestershire and Edinburgh (1776-1857), one of the King's sixteen children and subsequently Queen Victoria's favourite aunt—are we to infer from it that he moved, or had once moved, in the highest circles? Was it economic hardship which made him take up the pen? In the fourth chapter of the third volume there is a reference to shivering authors scribbling in their garrets who have to face 'the insolence of booksellers, the severity of criticks' and who yet persevere, for 'they must dine.' Crandolph morbidly announces at the end of his romance that nothing now remains for him but to prepare for another world. Did he indeed die soon after the delivery of his manuscript? No novel ever appeared 'by the author of *The Mysterious Hand*,' yet we cannot doubt that it won applause from the public, nor need we wonder that the book should have attracted the attention of such an industrious translator as René-Jean Durdent, about whom we know more than about Crandolph or Randolph.

Durdent was born in Rouen in 1776 and first set out to

be a painter. He became a pupil of the celebrated Jacques-Louis David and travelled to Rome to pursue his studies there, as did most aspiring young artists in those days; but realizing that he lacked the requisite talent as well as a true vocation, he exchanged the brush for the pen and turned author and translator, providing French versions of works by Monk Lewis, John Palmer, and Sophia Frances. Durdent wrote for his daily bread and did not mind extolling the restored Bourbons in his poetry after having waxed lyrical about Napoleon when the latter had been in charge. His translation of Crandolph's novel, published in three volumes by J.G. Dentu under the title *La Main mystérieuse, ou les Horreurs souterraines*, appeared in November 1818,[28] about half a year before Durdent died 'in a state bordering on misery.'[29] Alcoholic excesses are said to have hastened his end.

A review of the novel seems not to have appeared, and modern criticism has not said much about the book, Maurice Lévy merely remarking he had 'never been able to hold *The Mysterious Hand* in [his] own, unmysterious ones except for a few hours in the British Museum.'[30] But Frederick S. Frank entered in some detail.

> The exquisite Gothic title of this forgotten shocker is far more titillating than the actual pace of the plot, which is sluggish and uncertain. [...] In Crandolph's long and obscure Gothic, the terrible hand reaches after many maidens in the dark but never quite seizes. The hand belongs to a defrocked Capuchin who hides in a cavern near his former monastery. Into this unlikely abyss comes a series of Gothic maidens looking for exactly the sort of adventure in the dark that the mysterious hand extends. All of Crandolph's gropings are quite inferior

> to the use of the hand in [Mary Anne Radcliffe's] *Manfroné* [or, *The One-Handed Monk*].[31]

Elsewhere Frank changes the cavern where the monk hides into 'the subterranean darkness of Mortmain Castle,' and adds:

> A Gothic novel is certainly entitled to have an absurd or outrageous premise as the basis for terror. But a truly gripping Gothic is also required, even within the bounds of a fantastic premise of action, to offer some artistic consistency by developing its characters logically (howsoever mad) and making its plot coherent (howsoever strange). *Manfroné* and *The Monk* do just this, but *The Mysterious Hand* does not.[32]

So—are we resurrecting a novel that is a failure? Good heavens, no. Professor Frank differs from the critics of the *Monthly Review* and the *Anti-Jacobin Review* in one important aspect. They disliked the Gothic novel, but at least took the trouble to read what they condemned. Frederick S. Frank is supposed to like the Gothic novel, but *he* never held *The Mysterious Hand* in his own, mysterious or unmysterious ones, not even for a few minutes. There is no defrocked Capuchin in the book, hiding either in a cavern or in the vaults of a castle, and there is no bevy of girls looking for excitement in his company. All this has sprung from the imagination of Professor Frank who for reasons best known to himself was anxious to give the impression he had read the book. Nor is this the only instance of his inventing plots and passing judgment on works he has never seen. He does it again and again.[33] This practice, to use a phrase of Montague Summers, is scarcely indicative of serious scholarship. And it is rather unwise, for one is always found out.

Far from being sluggish, *The Mysterious Hand* is a fast-paced thriller. Only the description of the interior of the castle of St. Uldrich in the third chapter goes on a bit, as the author concedes. The novel is a fine example of the 'hard-boiled' Gothic that features one of the most remarkable of villains, Count Egfryd, who, interestingly, is acknowledged even by the hero to be 'irresistible' (to ladies, that is). Theodore himself deviates from the path of virtue by becoming 'criminal' (in other words, has sex) with a woman who (unbeknown to him, it is true) has the blood of her husband on her hands. Such behaviour is altogether exceptional for a fictional hero of the time and would certainly have been condemned by the reviewers who, it may be remembered, deemed the gaming habits of Ann Radcliffe's Valancourt to be 'unnatural.'[34] Theodore, who wisely keeps his lapse to himself, differs from other heroes in other respects, too. None of his dashing young colleagues entertain the slightest doubt, as he does, about the wisdom of marriage—wondering if he should bring any more children in a world that is already over-populated. His objections against capital punishment, which he pronounces in the dock when, in an episode that prefigures the detective story, he finds himself charged with murder, ring quite modern as well, while it is amusing to note that it was his writing a negative review of a volume of Count Egfryd's poems which brings about his persecution by the villain in the first place.

Miss Julia Bolton allows herself slightly more freedom than the heroines of her time, placing 'her light and elastic figure, by a magical movement,' upon Theodore's lap, 'her lips'—*her* lips!—'involuntarily [approaching] his, [receiving] and [returning] the sweetest of kisses,' and this *before* the wedding bells have rung out. It is true that her erotic dreams are the result of some unspecified drug put by the Count in her *bouillon*, but the fact that she has these dreams at all shows that our author went further than most of his contemporaries when dealing with matters sexual. No doubt the august niece of the Princess to whom *The Mysterious Hand* was dedicated would not have been amused by Crandolph's romance; but for those who like this sort of thing this is, certainly, the sort of thing they like. Enjoy!

CASPAR WINTERMANS
The Hague

December 14, 2007.

ABOUT THE EDITOR

CASPAR WINTERMANS is a Dutch author and scholar. Much of his work has centred on Lord Alfred Douglas, poet and lover of Oscar Wilde; his biography of Douglas has so far appeared in three languages and was made into an award-winning documentary film, *Two Loves*. A passionate lover of the English, German and French Gothic Novel since the age of seventeen, he will be editing a series of *romans noirs* for Valancourt Books, including books by Elisabeth Guénard, Baroness Brossin de Méré and Charlotte de Bournon, Countess de Malarme, while *Un scandale belle époque: L'Affaire d'Adelsward à travers la presse parisienne* is to be issued by Valancourt Books later this year.

The editor would like to thank Joan Navarre and Jean-Claude Féray for their help and advice.

NOTES

1 Thomas Frognal Dibdin, *Reminiscences of a Literary Life* (London: John Major, 1836), I, pp. 182-184.

2 *Monthly Review*, August 1791, p. 465.

3 Ibid., May 1787, p. 448.

4 Ibid., March 1772, p. 264.

5 *Anti-Jacobin Review*, August 1804, p. 398. The novel in question was by Mrs. Villa Real-Gooch.

6 Sarah Ann Hook, *Secret Machinations* (London: R. Dutton & C. Chapple, 1804), I, vi-vii. In the course of her novel the author makes the following observation: 'I do believe [men] feel and know the pre-eminence given to us by Nature, and nothing but a jealous fear prevents their benefiting by our abilities; and most men of penetration and discernment have a far higher opinion of women in general, than they are willing to acknowledge' (II, p. 268).

7 *Anti-Jacobin Review*, September 1800. p. 27: 'The romance of "the Mysteries of Udolpho" hath been long received, as a first-rate production: and its merits have not been too highly appreciated. It was the reputation of this work, which, at length, induced us to *honour* Mrs. Radcliffe's "Italian," with our attentive perusal:—so may we be allowed to express ourselves. For we, grave Reviewers, very seldom look into novels or romances for any other purpose, than to discover and point out their moral tendency, and offer to the sex our serious admonitions; which, we fear, are, for the most part, unavailing.'

8 [Agnes Maria Bennett], *Juvenile Indiscretions* (London: W. Lane, 1786). I, i-iii.

9 Maria Regina [*sic*] Dalton, *The Vicar of Landsdowne; or,*

Country Quarters (London: Printed for the Author; and sold by J. Johnson, 1789), I, vii-viii.

10 See the *Monthly Review*, March 1787, p. 266, on *Lord Winworth; or, The Memoirs of an Heir* (London: Allen, 1787): 'Dedicated to her Grace of Devonshire—and with that noble lady's permission too! Is it possible?—Those who read these memoirs, and also are acquainted with the good sense, and cultivated taste, of the Duchess of Devonshire, will be staggered by this assertion; yet here it stands, printed in the title-page; and who shall disprove it?—We hope, however, that the author's next production (if he resolves to follow this exhausted trade) will be more worthy of her Grace's approbation,—and of *ours*.'

11 Sophia King, *The Fatal Secret, or, Unknown Warrior; A Romance of the Twelfth Century, with Legendary Poems* (London: Printed for the Author by G. Barnard, 1801), ii-iv.

12 [Ludwig Franz Freiherr von Bilderbeck], *Die Urne im einsamen Thale* (1799) (Leipzig, [no publisher's name given], 1800), IV, p. 6.

13 'Schlagt ihn tot, den Hund! Es ist ein Rezensent.' *Goethe Werke.* Erster Band. *Gedichte – Versepen* (Frankfurt am Main: Insel Verlag, 1977), p. 35.

14 *Anti-Jacobin Review*, December 1804, pp. 424-426.

15 See Thomas W. Laqueur, *Solitary Sex: A Cultural History of Masturbation* (New York: Zone Books, 2003).

16 'Eusebius,' 'On Reading Novels.' *Gentleman's Magazine*, November 1797, p. 912.

17 Ibid., April 1793, p. 294.

18 [Sarah Bennet], *Correlia, or, The Mystic Tomb.* (London: Lane & Newman, Minerva Press, 1802), I, ix.

19 See 'Die Zensur englischer und französischer Erzählliteratur in Österreich 1815-1848,' in: Norbert Bachleitner,

Quellen zur Rezeption des englischen und französischen Romans in Deutschland und Österreich im 19 Jahrhundert (Tübingen: Max Niemeyer Verlag, 1990), pp. 52-93. The censors were in particular opposed to the *Ritter-, Räuber- und Schauerromane* which were supposed to engender superstition and coarseness.

20 Montague Summers, *The Galanty Show: An Autobiography*. With an Introduction by Brocard Sewell (London: Cecil Woolf, 1980), p. 229.

21 Letter to the editor headed 'Feminine Fiction,' signed 'A Reviewer.' *The Academy*, 3 July 1909, p. 283.

22 Joachim Fest, *Ich nicht. Erinnerungen an eine Kindheit und Jugend*. 2. Auflage (Reinbek bei Hamburg: Rowohlt Verlag, 2006), pp. 128-129.

23 *Anti-Jacobin Review*, September 1803, p. 96.

24 Jane Austen, *Northanger Abbey*. Edited with an Introduction and Notes by Marilyn Butler (London: Penguin Books, 2003), p. 103.

25 'Traduit de l'anglais sur la troisième édition.'

26 My grateful thanks to Giovanbattista Brambilla for identifying Crandolph's quotation.

27 Alexandre-Nicolas Pigoreau, *Petite Bibliographie biographico-romancière, ou Dictionnaire des romanciers* [...], (Paris: Pigoreau, 1821), p. 210.

28 The title-page gives 1819 as the year of publication, but the *Bibliographie de la France, ou Journal général de l'Imprimerie et de la Librairie* announces the book on 28 November 1818. Copies of Durdent's translation are at the Bibliothèque nationale in Paris (where the first volume is missing) and at the library of the Château d'Oron, Vaud, in Switzerland.

29 *Journal des Débats*, 2 July 1819. Dr. Hoefer, *Nouvelle biographie générale* [...] (Paris: Firmin Didot frères, fils et Cie,

1868), xv, p. 444, gives the date of Durdent's decease as 30 June 1819.

30 Maurice Lévy, 'English Gothic and French Imagination: A Calendar of Translations, 1767-1828.' In G. R. Thompson (ed.), *The Gothic Imagination. Essays in Dark Romanticism* (Washington State University Press, 1974), p. 150.

31 Frederick S. Frank, 'The Gothic Romance: 1762-1820.' In Marshall B. Tymn, *Horror Literature: A Core Collection and Reference Guide* (New York/London: R. R. Bowker Company, 1981), pp. 58-59.

32 Frederick S. Frank, *The First Gothics: A Critical Guide to the English Gothic Novel* (New York and London: Garland Publishing, Inc., 1987), p. 62.

33 A few examples may suffice. In the volume edited by Marshall B. Tymn (pp. 77-78) Frank mentions some novels by Elisabeth Guénard, baronne de Méré. His account of *Les Trois moines* is fairly accurate, but then Montague Summers gave a summary of its plot in *The Gothic Quest: A History of the Gothic Novel* (London: Fortune Press, 1938, pp. 247-248). *Les Forges mystérieuses ou l'Amour alchimiste* is described by Frank as a work 'that mixes magic potions in subterranean settings. [It] tells the story of a deadly elixir and an equally deadly desire to possess eternal love by bartering away the soul.' Not so; the book is a picaresque novel whose impoverished hero makes gold in his laboratory. To call *Les Capucins, ou le Secret du cabinet noir* 'a genuine and powerful *roman noir* that strongly imitates the suspenseful procedures surrounding the mysterious black veil of Udolpho [...], an outstanding example of the Radcliffean strain in French Gothic fiction,' clearly shows that Professor Frank did not read this book either, for it features no veil and bears no resemblance whatever to the works of Ann Radcliffe who would have dismissed it as immoral French trash. And *Le Château de Vauvert, ou le Chariot de feu de la rue d'Enfer* does not have 'flaming chambers, ectoplasmic tapestries, and a staff of ghoulish caretakers who transmit their business of licentious

persecution with Gothic gusto.' Let us finally look at what is said about William Frederick Williams' *The Witcheries of Craig Isaf* (1805 [i.e. 1804]) in *The First Gothics* (p. 423). 'Williams set his romance in the troubled reign of William Rufus (1087-1100), the son of the Conqueror. His throne is threatened by a fictitious, Macbethian usurper who is spurred on to his crimes by the false prophecies of the witches. He is also implicated in the eerie murder of the King during a hunting foray [...], a ready-made event for the enterprising Gothic novelist.' This, again, is pure invention. William Rufus's murder is not recounted at all in the novel. The red-haired monarch plays no part in the story; it is not even set in his reign (whatever Montague Summers may say on p. 175 of *The Gothic Quest*), but in that of Henry I!

34 *Monthly Review*, November 1794, p. 281.

PUBLISHER'S NOTE ON THE TEXT

The Valancourt Books edition follows the first edition of 1811, published in three volumes by A. K. Newman of London. In accordance with Valancourt Books' policy of editorial restraint, no attempt has been made to modernize or regularize spelling or grammar. Internal inconsistencies have been retained (for example, the dual usage of terror/terrour, horror/horrour, music/musick, etc.) Spelling of names is sometimes irregular as well (as in *Count Egfryd*, *Count d'Egfryd*, *Count D'Egfryd*). Since for the most part these inconsistencies pose no difficulty in comprehending the novel, they have been retained to preserve the flavor of the original. Many words, particularly foreign names and titles, are italicized haphazardly; this too has been allowed to stand, with the exception of '*the grave*,' the name of the subterranean prison. In the first edition, it occurs both italicized and roman, but to avoid confusion, the phrase has been italicized throughout for this edition. Finally, although obsolete spellings such as 'chace,' 'chearful,' and 'chesnut' have not been altered, a few obvious typographical errors have been silently corrected.

James D. Jenkins

January 29, 2008

THE

Mysterious Hand;

OR,

SUBTERRANEAN HORROURS!

A ROMANCE.

IN THREE VOLUMES.

BY

AUGUSTUS JACOB CRANDOLPH.

> Ordina in guisa
> Gli umani eventi il ciel, che tutti a tutti
> Siam necessarj, e 'l più felice spesso
> Nel più misero trova
> Che sperar, che temer.

VOL. III.

LONDON:
PRINTED AT THE
Minerva-Press,
FOR A. K. NEWMAN AND CO.
(Successors to Lane, Newman, & Co.)
LEADENHALL-STREET.
1811.

Facsimile of the title-page of the first edition (1811)

The Mysterious Hand

Volume I

TO

HER ROYAL HIGHNESS,

THE PRINCESS MARY.

MADAM,

WITH much of the anxiety of an author, and all the attachment of a subject, I dedicate to you these volumes. They are your's, Princess, as a tribute to real excellence, from admiration the most sincere.

Blessed with seclusion and tranquillity, I court not, I desire not popularity. My ambition aspires to a nobler prize, and your acceptance of my labours is the great and only object of my wishes.

As the Daughter of our beloved Sovereign, my loyalty to you is an obligation; and as the model of my heroine, this dedication is, perhaps, a duty.

But the resemblance of the good and gentle Julia is not that of person. There are charms which her's does not possess.

May I call this production mine? Did you not inspire it? and, without your approbation, must it not perish? I shall, therefore, dare to hope that it will be rescued from oblivion. The laurel that emerges out of darkness and the earth, from the sun receives its being, and by the sun it is preserved.

THE AUTHOR.

November, 1810.

THE

MYSTERIOUS HAND.

CHAPTER I.

Non era l'andar suo cosa mortale;
  Ma d'angelica forma; e le parole
  Sonavan' altro, che pur voce umana.

....

E pur tante bellezze, e sì pregiate
  Altro non sono, che un' opaco velo,
  Con cui dell' Alma la beltà velate.

....

——————When she speaks,
  The air, a chartered libertine, is still;
  And the mute wonder lurketh in men's ears,
  To steal her sweet and honied sentences.

Mr. Bolton was a widower, and Julia was his only child. These pages shall relate their story. Never was there a worthier man than Mr. Bolton. Nature had bestowed on him a sound head and a feeling heart, and fortune, not less liberal, had gifted him with a large estate. His age was fifty-two; goodness beamed in his countenance, mildness attended his every motion, and equanimity marked his every look. Envied by the worldly, esteemed by the virtuous, loved by his friends and blessed by the poor, Mr. Bolton was, nevertheless, unhappy. The loss of his wife, who had died about a year before the period when this history commences, left an impression of sadness on his mind that no fortitude could assuage, no time remove. In addition to which, his darling, the delight of his heart and the pride of his age, his beloved Julia, had, in consequence of her mother's death, been attacked by a nervous complaint, that threatened to decline into a consumption. This was the opinion of the most eminent physicians in London.

Shocked to the very soul by the alarming information, he hastily prepared, under their advice, to seek a southern climate, and court continual diversion for her by an incessant change of scene.

Julia, melancholy and depressed, prepared for her travels with little of the ardour of a youthful mind, and few of the brilliant expectations of a sanguine disposition. Happily, her dejection was not constitutional. Arrived in France, the novelty of her situation, and the rapidity of her journey, gave a new current to her thoughts, and speedily arrested the progress of her disease.

Miss Bolton's education had led to the useful rather than the ornamental. She was well-bred, but she was far from being all-accomplished. She had still much to learn, and she had yet, as a young lady should have, to take from him whom her heart and her father should select, that impression of character, those manners and those habits, which were to perfect her as a woman. Alive to every gentle impulse, the docile Julia had been instructed from her infancy to obey and to oblige. She was too thin to be perfectly beautiful, but being feminine almost to timidity, and graceful even to elegance, with elasticity in her step, and chearfulness in her countenance, it was not possible to see her with indifference, or to know her without admiring her. She possessed playfulness of wit and ductility of temper, quickness of perception and solidity of understanding: no vanity deformed her innocence, and no affectation disguised her simplicity. Her articulation was distinct, her delivery was correct, and her voice, to say that it was sweet, would not express its excellence; it was that varied and perfect melody which proceeds from clearness of sound, delicacy of accent, and tenderness of intonation, united in the human organ, and breathing truth, eloquence and animation. Like the strains of fairy musick, fancied by some poets, it engaged the ear with a gentleness so winning, with a harmony so unusual, that to hear this interesting girl was to experience a pleasure not less rare than it was refined. Such were the father and his daughter.

They travelled through France in a manner suitable to their fortune and their habits, displaying no ostentation, but presenting unequivocal marks of wealth and respectability. Every where they were received with distinction, and treated with flattering attentions, but no where did they remain longer than three or four days. Mr. Bolton willingly sacrificed his love of rest and quiet to promote the health of his daughter, and she, with juvenile volatility, readily consented to be whirled with rapidity, and without intermission, from one town to another.

In the latter end of May they arrived at Bourdeaux. Here they purposed to remain for a few weeks. It was manifest that Julia's health was restored. Her father saw that there no longer existed a necessity for velocity of movement, and he gladly availed himself of this opportunity to indulge in repose. In truth, he had not, since his wife's death, been less unhappy than he was at present. She on whom he doted, she on whose welfare his existence depended, was now out of danger. Now he could look at her with satisfaction. The hue of health overspread her cheek; the smile of content played upon her countenance.

CHAPTER II.

Fortune, dont la main couronne
Les forfaits les plus inouis,
Du faux éclat qui t'environne
Serons nous toujours éblouis?

....

Trovasi ancor chi per sottrarsi a' numi
Forma un nume del caso, e vuol, ch' il mondo
Da una mente immortal retto non sia:
Cecita temeraria! empia follia!

....

Why, I can smile, and murder while I smile,
And cry content to that which grieves my heart;
And frame my face to all occasions:
I'll play the orator as well as Nestor;
Deceive more slily than Ulysses could;
And, like a Simon, take another Troy;
I can add colours even to the cameleon;
Change shapes with Proteus, for advantages;
And set th'aspiring Catiline to school.

Truth shall govern my pen, simplicity shall guide my narration. No tale of impossibility shall stain my veracity, and never shall I be convicted of falsehood. If I write a book that may amuse, I intend that it shall likewise instruct. If any of the characters I describe shall appear uncommon, the incidents incredible, or the situations romantick, let me not be blamed. I deserve no reproach. Nature in the innumerable movements of her admirable mechanism, in the perpetual revolutions of her immense empire, occasionally produces events that are unaccountable, and beings that are monstrous.

The Count Egfryd at this period lived in Bourdeaux, where he possessed a magnificent hotel. The Count had attained his thirtieth year. His figure was well proportioned, his face was sensible and regular, and in his whole appearance there was a striking air of dignity. His ancestors had been for ages noble, and his fortune was of princely extent. Impenetrable dissimulation, and a serenity that no accident could disturb, were peculiarly his. He was deep in design, vitious in his propensities, bold in the execution of plots, inventive in resources, persevering and indefatigable. With an assumed frankness that might deceive even the eye of penetration, a mildness that never deserted him, and a chearfulness that was constitutional, he possessed the polished graces of a refined courtier, and the intellectual advantages of an excellent education. His speech was fluent and his style elegant. The subtlety of his mind, aided by early habits of metaphysical disquisition, gave him a decided advantage in the art of persuading: but he seldom argued. His habits were voluptuous and dissipated, and the gratification of his revenge was with him an important consideration. His indulgences often partook of cruelty, and his pleasures not infrequently led him into the perpetration of crimes. But to him cruelty and crime were indifferent. He was an atheist. He had already offended against the most awful of the commandments of his Maker, and against the most solemn laws of society. He never felt remorse, and he was incapable of fear. To gratify a trifling wish he would not have hesitated to commit any atrocity, provided he could commit it with security; and of two pleasures equally grateful to him, one simple and innoxious, the other attainable only by vice, he would have preferred the latter. What I have drawn is but a faint sketch of the diabolical Egfryd; but in the course of these pages, enough will be narrated to convey with accuracy his detestable delineation. He was married, and he had one child.

An acquaintance that soon ripened into intimacy was formed between our English travellers and this family. Julia was charmed with the easy address and insinuating manners of the Count. He appeared to her the most accomplished man she had ever seen, the most ingenuous, the most noble. She observed with surprise, that the serenity of his manner, and the gentleness of his tones, had the power of banishing all agitation from the minds of those with whom he conversed: that every commotion of the passions instantly subsided at his approach, and that it was impossible to feel constraint in his presence. In her estimation he was the true model of a perfect gentleman; nor, could his depravity have been subtracted, was she much mistaken.

He, demon-like, saw the impression that he made on a female, essentially different from all those whom he had seen before, and incomparably superior to every other he had known. Already he plotted her ruin; already he indulged a deadly passion, that had for its object her total and irremediable destruction. Mr. Bolton thought of his new acquaintance with little less respect and admiration than his daughter. His unsuspecting and guileless nature yielded involuntarily to this libertine's dangerous attentions, and in his society the good man experienced and submitted to the fascination of grace united to gaiety, unstudied politeness, modest eloquence, and knowledge that seemed little short of inexhaustible, and forgot the existence of his grief.

The Count had a castle on one of his estates in the neighbourhood of Bourdeaux: it was called the *Chateau de St. Uldrich*, and it afforded the happiest specimens of that species of architecture which is denominated Gothick. It was in truth a beautiful and magnificent fabrick. Thither he and the *Comtesse* invited the father and daughter, who consented to remain there for a month.

Having arrived at the *chateau*, Julia employed two whole days in traversing the galleries and the apartments, in admiring the numerous decorations of the building, and interrogating the Count and her father upon the more prominent objects of her curiosity. In another chapter I shall give a description of the *chateau*, by which it will appear, that her admiration was not the wonder of infancy or ignorance, but a just tribute to real excellence.

Julia, however, had time and inclination to devote the third evening after her arrival to the duties of friendship. The following letter to the earliest of her acquaintances, which, by accident, came lately into my possession, will serve to shew the state of her mind at this time.

"MY DEAR ELIZA,

"AT length I have an hour to myself—that hour shall be your's. You will expect, in the first place, I know, to hear something about my health. Know then that I am quite well. Such rattling, such flying as I have had! I thought I should like travelling, but it far exceeds my most sanguine expectations. Though the days are now long, I think each of them infinitely too short. I have been in one continued bustle since I left England. My papa bids me be composed, and Ellen requests me to leave every thing to her. It is all in vain. I cannot be quiet. But don't suppose that I am become industrious since I saw you; on the contrary, I am sorry to tell you that I never work, and I cannot read. How can I work, read, draw, or play, or any thing else while we keep moving about so? But now that we are to remain in one spot for some weeks, I will try to do some good.

"Oh! Eliza, I have so much to tell you, much, that I don't know where to begin. Shall I tell you first of Theodore? (so my father calls *Monsieur Dalbert.*) No, I did not see him till we arrived at Bourdeaux. Shall I commence with the *Chateau de St. Uldrich?* or shall I——? My dear Eliza, you must excuse me. I know not what I am saying, doing, thinking. But come, I must mention something.

"You must know then that when we arrived at Bourdeaux, my father went to pay his respects to the *Marquise de Narsey;* she visited me the next morning, and in the evening we all went to the theatre to see a new piece. This new piece, you must know, was the prettiest thing I ever saw; and so my father and the Marchioness thought. He, who, you know, is so curious, inquired the name of the author—and who should this prove to be but *Monsieur Dalbert!* But who is *Monsieur Dalbert?* Why, my dear, his father was General Dalbert's son, that was disinherited by him for marrying a poor Frenchwoman. The General being our friend and neighbour in England, my father took some trouble to find out the author, and he invited him to dine at our hotel.

"I had expected a nasty, pedantick, self-sufficient fellow, and therefore took no great pains at my *toilette.* I was sitting behind the drawing-room door when he entered, and only think of my surprise on seeing, instead of the person I had pictured to myself, one of the handsomest and most elegant young men I ever saw. He accosted my father in English, and addressed me in the same language, with that air of ease and politeness that we do not frequently see in England. You see I already assume the airs of a traveller.

"In his countenance and accents, there was a charm that I cannot describe to you. I soon found he had spoken English merely in compliment to us, for insensibly we all in a short time conversed in French. I don't know how it was, but every time that I spoke, or that he looked at me, I felt a something of embarrassment, together with a faltering of my speech, that I am not accustomed to. A more polite or agreeable man, however, I never met. But enough of Mr. Dalbert. No, one word more—he has, my dear Eliza, without exception, the finest black eyes, the whitest teeth, and the prettiest hands I ever saw. The epithet that best applies to him, I think, is *interesting*. Nobody can be more free from that lively gesticulation which Frenchmen generally possess than he. He is, as they say, *sans façon*. He is uncommonly tall; I am sure he is above six feet; and, to complete his picture, he is very brown, and very thin; he is, besides, perfectly well made. Poor fellow, he has for years supported his mother and himself entirely by the labours of his pen. I understand his mother is at present in the country. My father thinks him one of the best writers of the present day; and certainly that dramatick piece we saw was admirable. I should tell you there is a calmness about him, mingled with a slight portion of melancholy, that would please you infinitely. But shall I never have done with this man?

"We have met with another charming man, the Count d'Egfryd. But he is married. He and the *Comtesse* are excessively attentive to us. I don't know how we shall be able to repay all their civilities. The Count is one of the most amiable men in the world—but the *Comtesse*, between you and me, I don't admire with enthusiasm. Her manners and disposition are diametrically opposite to mine, and therefore we shall never be called the inseparables. However, nothing can exceed her politeness or attention. We are now at their castle, about ten miles from Bourdeaux. It is a Gothick building, but such a building! No, never did you see any thing half so handsome. But it is very late, and I am getting sleepy. Good night, and believe me your sincere friend,

"Julia Bolton.

Chateau de St. Uldrich."

Theodore Dalbert, after the departure of Mr. Bolton and Julia from Bourdeaux, was melancholy and uneasy. He felt depressed without knowing why, and thought of his English friends at one time with affection, at another time with regret. His studies no longer amused him. He could not sit at home. He could not remain abroad.

In this mood he was entering the narrow street in which was his humble habitation, on the second day after the departure of his friends, when, as he passed by a dark passage, a man, muffled in a large coat, suddenly darted on him with a stiletto, and aimed a blow at his breast. Theodore, most fortunately, had a book within his coat, through the leaves of which the instrument pierced even to his skin. But for this the blow must have been mortal. It was intended to be so.

The assassin had not time to repeat his attack. Swift as lightning, his intended victim caught and disarmed the murderous hand and with his *parapluie* warded off a similar blow from a second ruffian, who now advanced.

The first, Theodore, though alarmed, rushed on with irresistible vigour, and pierced with the stiletto that had been a moment before directed against himself. The wretch dropped with a groan, pouring out his heart's blood. The contest now was more equal; it was between two men, each armed alike. Theodore, accustomed to fencing from his infancy, immediately saw the mode of fight he should adopt; this was to retreat, and to defend himself till his adversary should give him an opening; accordingly he did so, and in less than a minute his foe, wounded, prostrate, and disarmed, lay before him. Curious to know the motive for such an outrage, he conducted the miscreant to his apartment, dressed his wound, and having made him sit down, considered with attention his countenance and person.

A figure more uncouth, or a face less human, can hardly be conceived. The former heavy, shapeless, and gigantick; the latter black, lowering, and malignant. His eyes alone would have rendered him diabolical; small, dark, and unsteady, their squint was never to be caught; sheltered by jaw-bones of brutal projection, and brows of preternatural and gloomy exuberance, they shot their felon glances with ominous obliquity. His lips, which were never closed, displayed a cavern not to be surveyed without disgust, and were extended in swollen masses from one ear to the other. His nose was broad, flat, and rough. His ears, raw and discoloured, seemed monstrous excrescences of flesh, rather hanging from than growing to the head, with a weight that sunk them to the shoulders. His cheeks displayed numerous eruptive marks of gross intemperance, and his forehead was wrinkled into a thousand folds, and every fold contained a frown. His skin was foul and sallow. His hair was black and crispy. He had the stutter of habitual and designing falsehood, and his voice was deep, hoarse, and savage. To look at the monster without horror was impossible; to meet him in a lonely place without feeling alarm, was to be superior to the weakness of fear.

Such was the person to whom Theodore, with a composed countenance and with mild accents, addressed himself. And here, as well as on future occasions, I shall take the liberty granted to all historians, of rendering into the language which I employ, what was originally uttered in another tongue—"What has happened this night," said Theodore, "or any thing I now say, the thought of your companion lying dead, or the recollection of my clemency, will have no effect on you. I will not prosecute you, because my principles forbid my becoming an accessory in taking away the life of any one; and if you were to be tried you would be executed. My principles I shall not explain to you. It is probable you would not understand me. All I require of you is to tell me what induced you to attempt my assassination. What injury has any one to accuse me of? Who employed you? Who and what was your companion? Who are *you?* and what benefit were you to reap from my death? Speak with confidence and candour. By my honour I will never reveal what you shall communicate to me this night, without your permission."

The man, at language so unexpected, looked surprised and incredulous. A momentary expression, resembling the sneer of contempt, passed across his brutal visage. He coughed, hemmed, raised his shoulders, scratched his nasty head with one hand, the other he drew across his nostrils, elevated his frightful eyebrows, awkwardly endeavoured to give to his feeling of security some appearance of gratitude, and shook the apartment by the vulgar motion of his enormous feet, which, as he sat, danced with lively action on the floor.—"Sir," said he, "I know not of any harm you have done, nor any enemy of your's. All that I know is that I was to get a thousand livres,* and my companion as much more, if we despatched you."—"From whom?"—"I know not, Sir."—"Who employed you?"—"I don't know, Sir."—"Don't know!"—"Why, Sir, the story I have to tell you is a queer one. I will tell you, because it is impossible not to trust you; and because I can invent no tale at present that would impose on you. My employer is unknown to me. I can't even guess who he is. He gives me my orders in such a way that I can never discover him, and he pays me so well that I never disobey him. Besides if I did, I should never be employed again, and it's not improbable but that I should be murdered for my pains."

"In such a way that you can't discover him! explain yourself."—"Oh! if I knew him, it would be the best day to me I ever saw. By threatening to *peach* I could have any sum of money, for I'm sure he's woundy rich. I was a smuggler, please your honour, at Toulon, and I had got some little reputation, I believe, though I say it, for my spirit. But that's neither here nor there. I had been more than once in prison, but I need not lose time in telling you about that. It is now about fourteen months since I got a letter in an odd sort of hand; I believe I have it about me; I will show it to you. Let me look for it. It will explain all this here business. Aye, here it is."

---

* About £50 Sterling.

Saying this, he produced from an old pocket-book a dirty piece of paper, which with some difficulty Theodore read. It was to the following effect—"Gaspar Pontgebre, I have seen you, and I know your character. You are poor. Become my agent, and you shall never want for money. Inquire every Friday at the post-office of St. Marc for any letter directed to you. Whatever you shall be enjoined to do in the letters you will there receive, execute with promptitude and precision. I now enclose you four hundred livres* as an earnest of my generosity. Indiscretion or disobedience will cost you your life. You shall never be employed without receiving a gratuity. Some of my commands will require the agency of two persons. On Sunday next at two you will meet Conrad D'Aufrine at the *cabaret* with the green door, near the convent of Dominicans, *Fauxbourg du Plendey*. He is an Italian, and a bravo by profession. He will wear a red waistcoat. I shall instruct him how to know you. Accost him, and ask to see my letter to him. Show him this. Do what I shall in that point out, and on the Friday after you shall have performed those orders, you will find a letter for you in the office with five hundred livres."†

"Dark and horrible scheme! Did you meet this Conrad?"—"I did, Sir. He it is who now lies dead in the street. We did many a job for our unknown employer, and were always handsomely paid. The last required of us you will read in this letter, which I received yesterday."

He now produced a letter, which was in the handwriting of the unknown. It ran thus—"Gaspar Pontgebre, a young man, named Theodore Dalbert, lives on the first floor of the house No. 23, *Rue St. Sulpice*, in Bourdeaux.

---

* About £20 Sterling.

† About £25 Sterling.

He is an author. He wears black, is twenty-five years of age, six feet high, brown and thin, with dark hair, black eyes, and straight nose. He is handsome. His deportment is grave and dignified, and his countenance mild and engaging. I hate him. Watch him, know him, murder him. I enclose two hundred livres.* You shall have two thousand† more, to be divided between you and Conrad, on the Friday after I shall have learned your success. Be particularly attentive to this order. No command you ever received was half so important to me. Dare to disobey. Dare to tamper with him. Dare even to whisper your employment, and inevitable destruction shall overwhelm you. I shall pursue, I shall find, I shall strike; no power shall protect, no flight preserve you. Know, miscreants, that with respect to you I am omnipotent. But know, likewise, that if you obey me but a little while longer, a happy independence shall certainly await you." Theodore shuddered as he read this infernal scroll, of which the writing was evidently disguised.

"You see, Sir," said the assassin, "what danger I run in showing you these letters, but as for his threats, I don't care that for them," snapping his fingers. "He thinks to frighten me into silence, but I can tell him, that but for his presents this would have little effect. Conrad and I were thinking, no later than yesterday, of publishing something about his commissions, in order if possible to discover, by means of any attack that should be made upon us, some clue by which to find him out. But Conrad thought we played a surer game in holding our tongues, and Conrad was a clever fellow."

"Well," said Theodore, "I thank you, friend, for your

* About £10 Sterling.

† About £100 Sterling.

information. I told you I should never reveal your secret without your permission. I never will; but I am not without hopes that you will give me leave. Humble as I am, I undertake to procure for you a decent maintenance, and to ensure your safety. It behoves every man to unfold if possible an atrocious mystery of this kind, and you more than all others, having been the instrument employed. It is a reparation you owe to society. I would willingly abstain from another argument. I know it is ungenerous to allude to favours bestowed; but on this singular occasion permit me to remind you of the debts of gratitude you owe to me. Pay this debt. Bind me to your interests for ever. Confer a favour on me. Absolve me from my promise, and suffer me to keep these letters."

"As to the matter of this, do you mind me," replied the murderer, "I don't well understand what you be about, not I. I believe you are what they call a mighty good kind of gentleman, and all that; and only I am not in the habit of liking people, I should perhaps approve of you hugely; but you are somehow softish, I observe, with submission, and I must thank you for my letters, and to hold your tongue if you please, as you promised. If you was to go for to talk about this, it would be after bringing an old house about my ears, and therefore I must wish you good night."

He folded up his letters and was going.—"There is one question I would ask you," said Theodore, "before you go. Has your employer communicated to you any mode by which you may convey information to him?"—"Convey information to him? aye, that he has. The second letter I ever got from him told me how I was to send any message to him I might have to communicate, and, sure enough, it is a comical method. You have heard of the *Place de Sable*,

Sir?"—"That deserted place among the marshes. I know it."—"It is commanded by all the back windows in the market-place, you know, perhaps."—"It is."—"Well, Sir, when I have any thing to say, I go to the *Place de Sable*, where being knee deep in mud, I am sure to meet nobody. With a long white pole in each hand, and standing on a spot described to me, I give my message by certain signals pointed out in a letter of instructions I received for that purpose. I am sure that, provided I do this on Sunday, at twelve o' clock, my employer is looking at me—reading me, I might say. But as there are a thousand windows, through any one of which he may look, and a thousand hills about, on any one of which he may be placed, it is impossible to guess where he actually is. Besides, when I have any thing to communicate, I must, the night before, shoot three rockets from my house; one at ten, one at eleven, and one at twelve o'clock."—"Merciful Heaven!" exclaimed Theodore, sinking into a chair, "such a contrivance!"—"Good night, Sir," said the ruffian abruptly, who now retired as fast as his wound and its attendant pain and weakness would permit him, and shut the door.

Merciful Heaven! repeated Theodore, what superlative and unprecedented art! What horrible villainy! But am I, who, under all circumstances, have been the champion of innocence, and the assertor of virtue, to be initiated involuntarily into the black and hellish mysteries of guilt and treachery? Am I to learn a dark and dangerous transaction, and keep it secret? Am I to become the confidant of an assassin? Am I to know a conspiracy which threatens the happiness and security of society, and not reveal it? Shall I not become in the estimation of the virtuous, a conspirator myself? Shall I not, by a mistaken discretion, save the guilty and expose the innocent to destruction? Alas! such is my situation, that to perform a problematical duty, I should be guilty of a positive crime. Can I tell what I have heard this night without becoming the accuser of that assassin? and can I accuse him without exposing him to publick execution? To death? But who has a right to rob any man of life? What society, however numerous, has authority to do so? Every wretch that expiates his crimes at the tree or on the wheel, is in my opinion a victim to cruelty and prejudice. Human life is inviolable. The abstract reasoning of philosophy demonstrates this to the enlightened mind, and the practical experience of publick justice proves it to the ignorant. Not only has society no right to take away the life of any of its members, it is even guilty of impolicy, not to speak of barbarity, in attempting it.

Oh Beccaria,* Beccaria! When will thy mild and admirable system be understood by the besotted multitude? When will thy enlightened book be read by the rulers of the earth? Gaspar shall never be accused by me. Mercy prohibits it. But for the sanguinary laws of this country, I might have stepped forward between him and his victims, but here in France it must not be. Gaspar, I will keep my promise. Not a word of this transaction shall issue from these lips, or be written by these fingers. With respect to myself, and to ensure my own preservation, what must I resolve? I am in danger of ruin and assassination. I am detested by a monster, who hesitates to perpetrate no crime however atrocious, and whose interest it now is to murder me. Be it so. Shall I for this sacrifice my independence, my peace of mind? Shall virtue and innocence for ever yield to vice and violence? Forbid it, magnanimity, forbid it Heaven! I will live as usual, walk out as usual, and trust to Providence and this arm for my preservation. So saying and so thinking, the proud and virtuous Theodore went to bed and slept till morning, and no sentiments of anger or of fear disturbed his repose.

At one the next day the Count Egfryd waited on him, and invited him to the *Chateau de St. Uldrich* in so polite and kind a manner, that he knew not how to refuse. Unknown to him, or in spite of him, a wish to be near Miss Bolton predominated in his breast, and he accepted the invitation.

CHAPTER III.

———Usciro in un gran prato; e quello
Avea nel mezzo un grande, e ricco ostello.

....

Mais, ô Dieux! qu'est-ce que je vois?
Que de prodiges à la fois!
Quelle merveilleuse structure!
Je me trompe, ou l'art envieux
Semble vouloir en ces beaux lieux
Le disputer à la nature.
N'est-ce point un enchantement?
Qui m'impose agréablement?

....

How reverend is the face of this tall pile,
Whose ancient pillars rear their marble heads,
To bear aloft its arch'd and ponderous roof,
By its own weight made stedfast and immoveable,
Looking tranquillity!

THE territory of *St. Uldrich* lay in the province of Guienne. It was an estate belonging to Count Egfryd, and had been possessed by his ancestors for many centuries.

This estate had, with a nobleness of design which has never been exceeded, and a magnificence of execution which has seldom been equalled, been converted by its present proprietor into one beautiful, immense demain.

At some distance from the *chateau*, but concealed from it by a thick plantation of chesnut trees, was a Dorick temple. It was intended for study, and it contained an extensive library. Its architecture was chaste and classical. The acclivity on which it stood was adorned with the choicest productions of the forest, which were disposed in appropriate combination and with peculiar taste. Beyond this, in a valley, was a grove of cypress; in the midst whereof, in all the solemnity of shade and silence, was a remnant of antiquity, for ages distinguished by the name of the Monument. This monument, the remains of a simple chapel, was contained within the enclosure of an old and ruined cemetery, in which the humbled observer was struck with awe and astonishment at the view of an immense pile of human bones, the accumulated spoil of ages, and the awful reproach of worldly vanity. The monument contained a mutilated inscription, by which it appeared that it had been erected to preserve the memory of the *Sire Urien d'Egfryd*, who died in 1249. The last three lines were still legible. They were in barbarous French, and they ran thus:

> "*Preez pur li en bon manere,*
> *Ke Jesu pur sa paisun*
> *De phecez li done pardun.*"

The meaning of which was, that the passenger should pray earnestly that Jesus, on account of his passion, might pardon the sins of the deceased.

The demain was, throughout, replete with picturesque

effect, and admirably and most judiciously adapted to the Gothick architecture of the *chateau* that it surrounded, and the inartificial grandeur of the circumjacent districts.

Here was no *edginess of bank*, no *whiteness of water* unrelieved by trees, no insipid straightness of walk, no tasteless regularity of disposition. Here were no mechanical clumps, no velvet slopes, no mathematical quincunx; but on every side nature in her most beautiful attire. Here the gardener and the florist had exhausted their industry and their invention. In one place the fairy scenes of juvenile and innocent delight, in another the wild and fantastic pictures of Arabian romance; here the peaceful occupations of simple swains, and there the terrifick and alarming appearances of tremendous precipices and impetuous cataracts, alternally enchanted and astonished, delighted and confounded the senses and the imagination.

Water was sometimes heard to pour its rapid waves in passages under ground, and at other times a gentle stream, within flowery borders, was seen to flow in silver currents with a thousand little circuits through diversified and delicious meadows.

A hermitage not encumbered nor perplexed by false ornaments, the collection of which would appear artificial, though each might be natural, such as disciplines, sculls, beads, and hour-glasses, invited the romantick rambler with its severe yet captivating simplicity, to renounce the tumult of a treacherous world, and to taste happiness, unadulterated by no excess, and distributed by no intrusion, within its peaceful recess.

In another quarter, along the craggy edge of a rocky mountain, inhabited by goats and deer, a rude paling had been erected to prevent the unwary peasant from tumbling down the precipice. Between this edge and a neighbouring cliff, a long and narrow rustick bridge, of one arch, offered to the terrified beholder a passage frightfully high and alarmingly slight. Under the bridge a torrent rushed with irresistible violence, and on the top of the cliff a grotesque cottage had been constructed, which seemed to totter on the verge of destruction. Nor were there wanted to complete the scenick beauty of a landscape so varied, the rich and magnificent effects of statues, fountains, marble basons, and balustrades; together with *jets d'eau*, a large collection of exotick plants and animals, blocks of ancient ruins, and various remains of sculpture.

The *chateau* itself had been built by Albert d'Egfryd, a native of St. Maurice in Switzerland, and an ancestor of the present *Conte*. The prospects from it were grand and extensive. There was much of wildness, and a little of rudeness in some of the views. There were tracts of naked rock. There were abrupt hills, and there were uncultivated heaths. But there was likewise much wood, much water, and an infinite diversity of surface.

The waters of the Garonne were to be seen at a distance, apparently motionless. Boats of pleasure and vessels of trade floated on its surface. Villas and plantations adorned its banks, and into its silver bosom the humble Dordogne might be observed to pour without cessation its tributary stream. On another side the city of Bourdeaux and the sea of Gascony were discernible. Distant mountains closed the scene.

The *chateau* had been built according to the principles which distinguish what is often called the latter Gothick, an order of building that even the partisans of Greek simplicity must think well adapted to the picturesque scenery, and mountainous wildness of the surrounding country. This, whether well or ill-founded, was the opinion of the present Count d'Egfryd, who thought the various sculptures indicative of ancient superstition, which were dispersed through the several parts of the edifice, and the innumerable relicks of feudal independence, and the trophies of victory, both in the field and chace, which his ancestors had honourably obtained, and which were profusely scattered through the apartments, were, if not ornamental, at least allowable. The mind was, unavoidably, led to associate with them atchievements of chivalry, feats of courage, habits of virtue, and the observance of religious duties. Nor did he apprehend a charge of an application of false ornament, in combining with the antique and arabesque decorations of ruder times, what Grecian elegance has taught us in the fine arts, what modern science can supply to increase and heighten our comforts, and what Parisian luxury has devised to please the eye, indulge the touch, or promote voluptuousness.

After passing through an ancient arch-way, the remains of a fortified watch-tower, and in which might still be perceived the loop-holes, out of which the besieged shot their weapons, and the apertures, known in architecture by the term machicolations, through which they poured boiling water and scalding pitch on the besiegers, a long, broad and winding avenue appeared. This avenue conducted through a thick wood of lofty trees to the front of the *chateau*, which was in an extensive and rocky plain, though partly concealed from the view of those approaching, by several widely-spreading oaks, that had now resisted the rage of three hundred winters.

The front, still retaining a few specimens of barbarous fortification, and presenting to the view numerous ornaments of Runick invention, was grand, and perhaps sublime. Huge balusters, an embattled top, with deep mouldings, grotesque vases on the pilasters, some pinnacles nobly emerging, straight parapets, and cupolas much resembling Ottoman minarets, all tended to give it the appearance of extreme age, massy strength and venerable solemnity. A whimsical but not unpleasing application of some politer decorations, such as Roman eagles, Persian statues, and cariatides, which appeared in several parts of the structure, served at once to gratify the eye and amuse the mind.

The *chateau* was built of a reddish freestone, which contributed no small portion of romance to its character; and it was of a height to excite wonder, if not to injure proportion. A noble flight of white marble steps conducted to the principal door of this baronial palace, and under the *fronton* was the motto, not less haughty than independent, "*Selon mon vouloir et franc arbitre*," in golden and Gothick characters. The door, which was twelve feet in height, and proportionably broad, was placed in a magnificent porch, that gradually diminished as it receded, and of which the sides were adorned with slender columns (of exquisite delicacy and admirable workmanship) forming various arches over head.

The porch led to the grand hall, which was lofty and spacious even to grandeur, and of which the windows were formed of stained glass of every colour, producing an inexpressibly rich effect. The clusters of little shafts, and the intervening mouldings, not less regular than complicated, that supported the glass, gave to the whole an appearance of peculiar lightness and elegance.

Around the hall, the floor of which was one superb mosaick, and of which the furniture was composed of cedar and crimson velvet, there was a number of slender columns surmounted by arches, filled up from the spring to the summit with beautiful tracery work. In the windows the stained glass presented several pictures chiefly chosen from the Pentateuch. In one place was seen Moses in the rushes, saved by Pharaoh's daughter. In another the murder of Abel; and in a third place the attempted seduction of Joseph by Potiphar's wife. There were some subjects of these paintings founded on the traditions of the Swiss. Among the rest was the famous story of William Tell, and a delineation of the victory gained in 1315 at Morgarton, over Leopold, Archduke of Austria, by the inhabitants of the three forest towns, headed by Hugo, surnamed the Haughty, the first Count of the house of Egfryd.

Here Hugo appeared, compared with those about him, of gigantick size, mounted on a fiery charger, and with his two-handed sabre cutting off the head of Rupert of Gascoigne. Hugo's horse was completely enclosed with steel armour, which protected even his ears. Thousands of plates seemed rivetted together to form the impenetrable covering.

Hugo himself carried an iron helmet surmounted by a plume of black feathers. His equipment was complete. At his left were a javelin and battle-axe, and at his right a hatchet and a lance. These were so artificially disposed, that neither his nor the horse's movements seemed in the least degree impeded by them. His legs and feet were defended by greaves, his face by a beaver, his thighs by cuisses, his hands by gauntlets, his arms by brassets, his back by a *guard de reine*, and his breast by a gorget, and over all these he wore a surcoat of cloth of gold, embroidered with armorial bearings. From the front of his saddle was suspended that sort of shield termed a *rondache*, and to his greaves were attached enamelled spurs, the rowels of which were several inches in diameter, and formed of large spikes. Rupert, whose head he was cutting off, was equipped with a *haubergeon* or shirt of mail, which, though steel, availed not against the mighty force of Hugo's arm.

These pictures could not be touched; approach to them was denied by the height of the windows, and therefore, minute criticism being impossible, it was probable that they appeared to have more merit than perhaps they really possessed. Be this as it might, their effect was striking in the extreme.

The sides of the hall, and the columns that surrounded it, were adorned with sculptures, in the Saracenick style, of various military engines: and here might be seen, in marble, every kind of armour and every instrument of war, known to our ancestors, and, among the rest, in proper arrangement, and copied with infinite exactness, the ancient war-chariot, armed with hooks and sithes, mangonels, tripgets, and war-wolves, all engines for throwing stones, scaling-ladders, moving castles, and battering boats. Here likewise were to be seen bows, slings, standards, casques, spears, pikes and targets; and with these were interspersed, in capacious disorder, some grotesque figures playing on different instruments of music.

The fire-place in this great hall was an immense hearth, on which nothing but wood was burned, and round which the inhabitants of the *chateau* frequently sat in winter. It was decorated with a variety of sculptures, and several pieces of mosaick, representing the tools of masonry known in the fourteenth century, and the sacred implements used in the Romish church. Here were trowels, hammers, rules and plummets; and here were likewise fonts, bells, sprinklers, mitres, canopies and organs. Over the fire-place was a painting on copper of an immense size, by the celebrated *Francesco Albano*,* of a prospect in Switzerland. In this painting the master had, with admirable skill, introduced nearly all the scenery of the *Pays de Vaud*, from the Lake of Geneva to those of *Yverdun* and *Morat*. Mont-Jura, which separates it from *Franche-Comté*, was to be seen at a distance, and even a portion of the desolate and sterile *Le Chablais* was introduced, to contrast with the rich plantations and exuberant vegetation of the foreground. To match this picture, one of equal size, at the opposite side of the hall, represented the grand tournament held by Philip the August on the plains of Picardy.

The hall that I have been describing, was lighted at night by sundry lamps, held in the hands of bronze statues, and it led to a noble banquetting-room, the windows of which were lancet-shaped, and of which the floor was a *chef d'œuvre* of art. It was a mosaick pavement of a square shape, with a deep border of the richest pattern. Mouldings of different colours surrounded the border, within which was described a purple circle. In the four angles formed between the circle and the border, were represented a ship, a horse, an eagle, and a stag. Within the circle was a representation of Attila, king of the Huns, attended by Walamir the Ostrogoth, and an army of Scythians, consecrating the sword of Mars. Pagan superstition had given a divine origin to this famous sword, which was here seen on the top of an immense altar, or rather pile of faggots, round which the blood of numberless victims taken in battle, formed a broad and dismal current.

The sides and columns of the banquetting-room, which was furnished in blue and gold, were still more superbly ornamented with sculpture than those of the hall. Its roof was composed of the segments of six several spheres, the whole forming a steady support to the superstructure.

On each of these segments was painted a chosen classical piece. On one was represented the story of Vertumnus and Pomona,* with four boys playing around them, being allegorical representations of the seasons. On another were the three Graces sacrificing to Hymen, and Cupids presenting different emblems of love. On the third was Venus introducing Helen to Paris, and around them were various symbols of joy, happiness, and constancy. On the fourth was Andromache, attended by the Trojan matrons, invoking Minerva for the safety of Troy. On the fifth was Medea delivering the soporiferous herbs to Jason, by means of which he was to overcome the Dragon, with allegorical representations of Fame, Victory, Peace and Plenty. And on the sixth were Minerva and Apollo entreating Jupiter to send back Justice to the world, that she might restore the golden age, and Jupiter's refusal.

It was scarcely possible to resist the sentiments of enthusiasm that this banquetting-room excited. Recollections of chivalry and romance were inseparably associated with it. Here, thought Julia as she entered it, have knights and ladies often assembled. Here the young warrior, cased in steel, and vowing eternal fidelity, knelt to his mistress, who, placing a ribbon or a bracelet round his neck, bade him acquire glory and deserve her. How often, said she, have these walls resounded with the haughty tones of independent barons! How often have they echoed the amorous and the heroick strains of feudal minstrelsy! How often reverberated the direful clangor of opposing arms!

Between the hall and the banquetting-room was the

grand staircase, on which no less art had been bestowed than was conspicuous in the rest of the building. The oak that had been employed in its construction was now almost black with age. Every other part of the *chateau* was in an equal style of splendour, and beautified with ornaments in no wise inferiour to those that have been described.

The chapel, which lay in a retired part of the building, was, like most other Gothick places of worship, formed in imitation of a grove of trees. In this intention the architect had perfectly succeeded. Its floor was a tessellated pavement of black and violet-coloured marble. Over the altar was a monumental shrine, enriched with a multiplicity of delicate decorations, and a prodigality of florid spire-work. The choir, the screen behind the altar, the oratory, the episcopal throne and the tabernacle, were in the same laboured and complicated style. The canopy of the last was of massy silver.

The great eastern and western windows spread their marble ramifications in profuse variety, and were embellished with pictures of St. Jude with a club, St. James the Less with a fuller's pole, St. Simon with a saw, St. Paul with a sword, St. Thomas with a lance; and various subjects from the Apocalypse.

To produce the illusion of a grove, the columns of the chapel (that were thickly planted along the nave and aisles), though small, were split into delicate clusters of slight marble rods, which rising in pointed arches, twined, and doubled, and convolved, with endless intricacy and apparent fragility; and at length terminating among spindling pinnacles and innumerable branches, were finally lost in the nice lace-work of the lofty and variegated roof.

About the centre of the chapel were some larger columns, having ribs and bosses on their sides, and faced with a circular series of zig-zag indentations. Round the smaller ones a spiral groove passed from the bottom to the top, while a delicate net seemed to overspread the whole.

The sides of the chapel were adorned with what architects term the embattled frette, with various escutcheons of arms, with foliage and animals, and here and there with a *mezzo-relievo* of some devout ceremony. The little light that entered was coloured by the stained glass through which it passed, and a sacred and mysterious gloom hung on every object within this consecrated place.

The whole was regular, beautiful and solemn, and never, perhaps, since the days of Druid devotion, was there a spot better calculated for the offices of religion, which more happily accorded with sentiments of piety, or which more powerfully excited holy awe and enthusiastick veneration. The *chateau*, in all its other parts, was abundantly extensive, perfectly commodious, minutely elegant, and eminently grand.

As when a prince described in some fairy tale, after wandering for many days in quest of adventures, through sterile and uninhabited tracts, discovers, on a sudden, a magnificent palace and delicious gardens, created for his gratification by the magick power of his tutelary necromancer; so with little less surprise, and with nearly as much pleasure, our travellers first viewed the *chateau* and its demain. They felt an indescribable emotion of wonder, admiration and delight; to which, in the mind of the innocent Julia, was added a mingled feeling of enthusiasm and tenderness, for Julia was young, pious and sentimental.

CHAPTER IV.

La tendre hypocrisie aux yeux pleins de douceur:
Le ciel est dans ses yeux, l'enfer est dans son cœur.

....

A lover's eyes will gaze an eagle blind,
A lover's ear will hear the lowest sound,
When the suspicious head of theft is stopt.
Love's feeling is more soft and sensible
Than are the tender horns of cockled snails.
And when love speaks, the voice of all the gods
Makes Heaven drowsy with the harmony.

....

Benedetto sia 'l giorno, e'l mese, e'l anno,
E la stagione, e'l tempo, e'l ora, e'l punto,
E'l bel paese, e'l loco, ov' io fui giunto
Da duo begli occhi, che legato m'hanno.

E benedetto il primo dolce affanno,
Ch' i' ebbi ad esser con Amor congiunto;
E'l arco, e le saette, ond' i' fui punto;
E le piaghe, ch'infin' al cor mi vanno.

I FEAR I have been tedious in the foregoing descriptions, but I live retired from the world, and know little of the publick taste. Judging of others feeling by my own, I have indulged in a minuteness, which, were I younger, I should not probably have hazarded. Old age is prone to verbosity; but let me not be charged with a wish to enlarge my history by useless digression. In this respect I shall never err intentionally. My book, without any extraneous matter, will be, perhaps, too bulky to be terminated by me; "My soul," in the words of the Scripture, "draweth nigh to the grave." The finger of death beckons to me, and the awful summons must be obeyed; but if allowed to breathe for a few months longer, I shall, I hope, be able to complete my task. I have now lived threescore years and twelve, Ah! within this period what vicissitudes have I not experienced, what pains have I not felt, what sorrows borne, what miseries endured! And how few have been my pleasures, how short my comforts! The retrospect presents a black and melancholy picture of hopes disappointed, misfortunes unmerited, kindness ill requited, and labours unrewarded. And shall I now be accused of that meanest of offences—book-making? At the base thought my ancient blood pours in rapid currents to these furrowed cheeks, and my feeble limbs tremble with indignant agitation. No, I write from a principle of duty, from a feeling of justice, and from a hope of being useful. Never, never could I lend my name or my pen to cheat or to deceive society, under the promise of amusement or instruction.

It may be necessary to explain the motives that induced the Count to invite Theodore to the *chateau*. It seems Mr. Bolton had benevolently projected a plan for the author's advancement in life, which, to be carried into effect, required an interview with him. The plan was to take Theodore with him to England, where his appearance, joined to Mr. Bolton's expostulations, might soften, if not remove the resentment of the grandfather, General Dalbert. In order to prevent any objection that pride, or a spirit of independence might start against accepting favours from a stranger, Mr. Dalbert was to be invited to finish the education of Julia, and to become her father's secretary at two hundred pounds a-year. On these terms it was hoped he would not object to enter into their family. So intent was the worthy man to execute this project, that he determined to revisit Bourdeaux on the fourth day after his departure from it. There was no possibility of diverting him from his purpose, nor of frustrating it. Mr. Bolton must see Theodore, and Julia must accompany her father.

Their crafty host, sensible of this, and apprehensive lest some accident might delay their return to the *chateau*, undertook, with apparent good humour, to effect the desired meeting, without rendering a departure from St. Uldrich necessary. What was more easy? It was only to bring Theodore thither, which, the Count protested, nothing but forgetfulness had prevented him from attempting before. To this he added, with seriousness and an air of self-conviction, that a man endowed with more estimable qualities than *Monsieur* Dalbert he had never known. Some other expressions of kindness and esteem followed, that left not a doubt on the minds of his auditors of his regard for their favourite.

The Count had met Theodore at Mr. Bolton's in Bourdeaux, and had with a jealous eye observed Julia's partiality to him.

In Egfryd's malignant heart this were sufficient to excite animosity; but another and more irritating motive existed, one that touched him in the tenderest point; one that wounded both his weakness and his pride.

This was a severe *critique* written and published by Mr. Dalbert, on a collection of the Count's poems that had appeared anonymously. The *critique*, though just, possessed little mercy. It convicted the author of temerity and phlegm, and proved him to be utterly destitute of poetical genius. Theodore, who wrote for subsistence, neither inquired nor cared whose work he reviewed, and by writing what he knew to be true, he hoped that he had violated no duty. But the Count, feeling all the rage of an unsuccessful and insulted author, vowed vengeance against the critick, and had actually identified Dalbert as his castigator when he met him at Mr. Bolton's.

Hating him with more than ordinary rancour, he had treated him with more than ordinary attention, and Theodore, won by the manner, and flattered by the kindness of the treacherous Egfryd, lamented the *critique* as the most unfortunate act of his life, secretly hoped he was not suspected to be the author of it, and solemnly resolved never to write another.

The failure of the attempt to assassinate had now aggravated the hatred of the Count to a degree nothing short of abomination. What! was he the employer of those assassins? Ah! who but he could have planned, with such precaution and ingenuity, so iniquitous a scheme? He it was who employed Conrad and Gaspar as the blind and wicked instruments of his hatred and his revenge. Cruel and perfidious man! never before did human depravity wield an engine so efficient or so atrocious as this of thy invention.

He had not yet determined what method he should next adopt to continue his murderous hostility. He therefore wished to have Theodore at the *chateau*, lest the late event should act on his prudence or his timidity in such a manner, as to cause him to remove himself far from Bourdeaux. The miscreant, moreover, desired to learn from him the particulars of Conrad's death, as no communication was to be made by Gaspar for some days. For all these reasons the Count invited Theodore to the *chateau*, as has been mentioned.

During their ride he artfully turned the conversation on duelling, and the modes of gratifying revenge practised in different countries. This necessarily introduced the subject of assassination. Theodore declared that any act of this kind was cowardly and villainous in the extreme, but the other exhausted the epithets of reprobation to express his horrour of the practice. He then, with a seemingly unintentional transition, mentioned the circumstance of a body having been found mortally wounded in the city. He described the wound, and the man, and the place where he had been found, and with a glance saw enough to convince him of the hand that had directed the blow; but with all his art he could not satisfy his curiosity further.

He soon afterwards expatiated with earnestness and eloquence on the charms of Miss Bolton. By this he hoped to obtain from his artless and unsuspicious companion some unguarded declaration. He was not mistaken. The name of Julia called forth all the attention and awakened all the animation of Mr. Dalbert, who spoke of her with the softened tone, with the faltering accents, with the decisive admiration of vehement passion. Never was woman so fair, never creature so feminine as Julia. His looks betrayed the feeling, his language the exaggeration of love. "These," said he, "are the sentiments of my reason. I speak of her in the coolness of my judgment. To her extraordinary endowments, and not my partiality, is to be attributed the warmth of my language. Love for her I ought not and I do not feel."—"And why not?" interrupted the insidious Count. "What inequality exists between you but that of property? I hate and despise the narrow and selfish principle, which inculcates a respect for wealth. I say it without flattery, I think you, *Monsieur* Dalbert, in every respect qualified to deserve her."—"Ah!" uttered Theodore with a lengthened sigh, and the carriage stopped.

It would be curious to pursue the Count's reflections during this conversation. The honest unstudied words of his companion were doubtless in his sophisticated mind translated into the brutish language of the cold and sensual materialist. Every human action, every human sentiment, considered through the clouded prism of atheistical perversion, loses its brightness and its beauty, and presents only the indistinct and dusky outline of selfishness.

Mr. Bolton received Theodore with the affectionate cordiality of a parent, Julia saw him and blushed. He, suspicious of his own sentiments, and doubtful of his resolution, determined to assume a distance and coldness of manner towards her, which, when they now met, he practised for the first time. She, unconscious of the motives that operated on his mind, and hurt by what she considered marks of indifference, was silent and unhappy. She endeavoured to call to her recollection any thing she had said or done, that might have occasioned this change in the only man she had ever seen whose friendship she desired. But her endeavours were vain. At times she would catch his eye fixed on her with an expression of earnest admiration, and on these occasions, inexperienced as she was, she felt and thought that she was not hated by him. This consciousness frequently tinged her cheek with an unbidden rose. At other times, when she spoke, so fixed and undivided was his attention, that he seemed as it were to suspend his respiration, lest even his breath should rob him of any portion of the sound. To reconcile these observations with his formality and reserve when he chanced to speak to her, and with his apparent unwillingness to speak to her at all, baffled the powers of her sagacity. Now she feared he disliked her; but this supposition, though afflicting while it continued, never disturbed her long. Again she hoped he loved her, and while this opinion predominated, she was the happiest of human beings.

Julia, innocent as she was susceptible, never for an instant entertained a suspicion that she was herself in love; and though she was sensible of lassitude and restlessness in the absence of Theodore, and of tranquillity and content in his presence, yet it never occurred to her to investigate the actual situation of her heart; nor, if she had, would she perhaps have ascertained the truth. But an accident occurred shortly after his arrival, which fixed the sentiments of each unalterably, and so strongly, that it was impossible for either to doubt any longer the existence of a mutual attachment.

He had entered the Dorick library, where, listless and absent, he sauntered about, casting his eye over the maps and at the titles of the books, but it was an eye of vacancy. He was thinking of Julia. Suddenly a cry of distress reaches him. It is hers, and near to him. It proceeds from an open gallery close to where he stands. The eagle soaring over her nest, and seeing her callow young in danger, darts not with greater velocity for their defence, than Theodore now to preserve Miss Bolton. She had wished to read a book on an upper shelf, and one of the library ladders being already raised to it, she had mounted. She was employed in reading this book, as she stood on the ladder, when Theodore entered, but by some accident it had slipped and fallen, and she with it. She was frightened and stunned, but not hurt.

Theodore took her up. His countenance expressed an undissembled and affectionate kindness of inquiry, and his action was dexterously rapid. There was no seat near them, and she was pale and speechless. He placed her at a window. He supported her agitated frame with one hand, with the other he took hold of hers.—"You are not much hurt, I hope?" said he softly and tremulously. "My God, how you tremble! Ah! be composed. But I feel no less alarm than yourself. Dearest Miss Bolton, let me have the pleasure of recalling your scattered spirits, of hearing from you that you are not injured."

Unconscious of what he did, he at the same time pressed her hand to his lips. A flame unknown to him before darted through his bosom. The tremour of timid love shook his frame. His dark intelligent eyes gazed with unutterable tenderness on her sylph-like form. Her face was overspread with a blush of the deepest red. Her heart beat impetuously; she tried to speak, but her accents, mild as the evening breath of infant zephyrs, expired in their own sweetness on her balmy lips. With a motion, compared with which the finger of a doting mother passed along the dimpled cheek of her sleeping infant is harsh and sudden, she attempted to withdraw her hand. A timorous and inquiring glance, not less quick than a sunbeam shot through the etherial void, informed her of the ardour and the perturbation that prevailed in the manly countenance which was still fixed on hers. Love and happiness, timidity and respect, gave to it a character that caught her imagination and touched her sensibility. Their situation was new to each, and interesting to both.

"Mr. Dalbert, pray," murmured she in a voice scarcely audible, and the attempt to remove her hand was renewed—"I—." He, urged by hope, led by passion, or influenced by fear at an action, the grace and delicacy of which were such, that to the coarseness of common feeling it would not have communicated the intention to remove her hand, threw himself on one knee. His was not a common feeling: the touch of love is a mysterious conveyance of soul: the sphere of sensation improves as it expands from brute perfection even to the confines of intellect: the grossness of the material root, of the physical centre, becomes gradually less base and more subtle, as the circle of refinement enlarges towards the empire of mind, until at length it volatilizes into absolute spirit and perfection. At this action, if action it may be called, that was rather the sensitive hesitation of a disordered temperament, Theodore, no longer master of his conduct, threw himself on one knee.—"Have I had the misfortune to offend you, adorable Julia?" said he. "You see before you the most enraptured, the most miserable of mortals. From that fatal moment when I first saw you, I have felt a passion till then a stranger to me. In vain have I since struggled to suppress a sentiment that I knew would embitter my existence, but each succeeding day has strengthened my attachment and confirmed my misery. Yes, loveliest of women, I confess, and I am proud to confess, that I feel for you a sentiment more pure, more exalted, than any that man has hitherto ever known; a sentiment of inextinguishable and unexampled love. Banish me from your presence. Kill me with a frown; but I must love you." His manner precluded the possibility of doubting his sincerity, and he again dared to press his lips upon her hand, and to squeeze it within his. At the same moment a tear of tenderness, distilled by the alchemy of love, from ardent and unsophisticated passion, dropped on it with a heat that penetrated to her soul, a moisture that softened her to the heart.

If she had been before disturbed, her agitation now became excessive. She had lately felt hesitation, she at this instant trembled with apprehension. By education and by habit led to the rigid that rejects, rather than the liberal that allows a slight personal familiarity, her prejudices all whispered to her to affect scorn or indignation, but her incipient attachment, her complexional sensibility, her artlessness and her inexperience, were antagonists too potent against prudery and pride, against the stupid formalities of ceremony, and the doubtful dictates of decorum, which with feeble effort struggled in her mind.—"Mr. Dalbert, it seems to me," said she with a graceful confusion, "that is, I—I think we are both very foolish. Will you permit me to consider whether or not I have been hurt? I am really so confounded with the ladder and you, that I hardly know what I am doing or saying."

Her blush which had, at first, overspread her whole countenance, and which was as much a confusion of the senses as a motion of the blood, was now confined to her cheeks. The blueness of her eyes was less concealed by their jealous lids, and again she stood self-collected, smiling with the sweetness of youthful Hebe.* Theodore relinquished her hand and was about to answer, when the entrance of the *Abbé Le Flos*, the librarian, terminated their conversation.

CHAPTER V.

———My conscience, sick,
No quiet knows. Crimes heap'd on crimes, present
A horrid group.

....

E vede l' hoste, e tutta la famiglia,
E chi a finestre, e chi fuor ne la via,
Tener levati al ciel gli occhi, e le ciglia,
Come l'Eclisse, ò la Cometa sia.

....

Un carro apparecchiossi, ch' era ad uso
D'andar scortendo, per quei cieli intorno.

....

E ch' aguzzar conviengli ambe le ciglia
S' indi la terra, e'l mar, ch' intorno spande,
Discerner vuol.

THE European, travelling, indolently secure, through Hindostan or Bengal, looking with delight at the spreading beauties of the rising sun, and inhaling the odorous freshness of an eastern morning, while a fierce and famished tiger, couched within a neighbouring thicket, glares a baleful look and prepares unseen to spring upon him, is as little apprehensive of his fate, as Theodore was of the danger that now awaited him. A deep and deadly hate filled the breast of the hypocritical and ferocious Count. His thoughtless victim lay defenceless within his grasp. The poisoned bowl, the murderous stiletto, the thousand horrid shapes in which inventive violence can picture the ghastly image of death, passed in quick succession and perpetual recurrence through his cruel mind. But his was not ordinary revenge, and as much as he exceeded common villains in atrocity, so much the closer resemblance was his vengeance to assume to demoniacal malignity. To inflict death were mercy, to rack with corporeal suffering were lenient compared with the torture that was conceived in the hellish imagination of the specious smiling Count Egfryd.

The powers of his mind great and comprehensive, the resources of his fortune princely and almost inexhaustible, his caution and his courage, his ingenuity and his craft, were all to be employed on this barbarous conception. He had suggested to his victim the possibility of an alliance with Miss Bolton, and he endeavoured, with unceasing and dexterous insinuation, not only to excite in his breast the passion of love, but to inspire him with the hope of a union with her. When this passion should be fixed, which it now was, and this hope encouraged into confidence, then was he to snatch the unsuspicious Theodore from all his joys, to place him in sad and solitary captivity, to taunt him with the degraded situation and criminal submission of the partner of his soul, to display the triumph of seduction in the debasement of the virtuous Julia, and to leave him in hopeless misery, the wretched inhabitant for life, and a protracted life, of a loathsome dungeon.

To effect this the Count already possessed such means as never before were had by man—such means as effectually barred the remotest possibility of detection—and such as, were the supernatural power of Satan his, could not be rendered more efficient.

The animosity of the Count towards Theodore was not such as malice or injury produces among the generality of mankind. It was a loathing, an antipathy, that rankled in his heart, inflamed his impatience, and gave to his mind the raging and restless fever of the damned; not unmixed, however, with ebullitions of diabolical joy as his projected vengeance ripened towards execution. He envied him for his success as an author. He despised him for his poverty. He abhorred his virtues, and he dreaded the effect of his person and manners on Julia. To be criticised, to have the edifice of his literary labours dismantled and demolished, were cause enough for his inextinguishable hatred, but to this to add the intolerable presumption of becoming his rival and preventing his most poignant pleasure, was to incur the thunders of his utmost wrath. Denying and not believing the existence of his immortal soul; despising the blessed doctrine of a future state; he saw in death only the natural and necessary termination of animal functions, and in life he sought for nothing but what contributed to his personal gratification.

Utterly indifferent to him was the fate of all the rest of his species; their happiness gave him no satisfaction, their misery excited no commiseration, their death produced no concern, no remorse. Selfishness alone governed his conduct. To this might be ascribed all the actions of his life. He affected amiable manners, because the respect and affection of his acquaintances and relations were necessary to his happiness. He laboured in literary composition, because this was the basis on which he strove to erect the structure of his posthumous fame; and fame he sought, because his vanity was indulged by hoping that his name would be handed down to the latest posterity. He was led to intrigue by irresistible temperament; but every object of his passion had been invariably destroyed by him. Their ruin seemed as necessary to his depravity, as their favours to his propensities.

The gratification of his revenge was with him a principle of inflexible severity. No injury, no slight, had he ever received, that he did not remember, and that he did not punish; no submission could soften, no contrition appease his vindictive temper; and even in the course of his soft and sedulous attentions to the unhappy victims of his lubricity, every mortification, every invective, every frown, delays, disappointments and oppositions, were all treasured in his deep and retentive memory, though he should smile with seeming inattention, or soothe with apparent humility, and were all followed by an inevitable and dreadful retribution. He carried on a secret warfare against mankind. No moral tie bound him, no kindred relations influenced him; he lived for himself alone; but he knew that the open indulgence of his appetites was incompatible with the regulations of society, and that therefore it would not be allowed. For this reason he hated social order and all its members, for who could have a community of feeling or interest with him, with an atheist, a being who would have sacrificed half his fellow-men to ensure a pleasure or obtain security?

His opinions, his faith, his wishes being all proscribed, he was necessarily a creature of imposture and mystery. He was virtually an outlaw, and every human being whom he saw, he considered as a minister of justice or a foe, whose duty or whose interest it was to expose his machinations and to punish his misdeeds.

Alas! what is man! this unhappy being, from perverseness of constitution, from profligacy of habit, and from duplicity and fraud long practised, seemed to have entirely lost the character of our nature, and was a rare and horrible example of the effect of passions indulged, and depravity unrestrained.

To such an enormity of vice had his lust of pleasure, his indulgence in unsanctioned gratification, his detestation of moral restraint, all joined to an acute sensibility of shame, carried him, that he now no longer considered any woman worth the conquest, any object worth fruition, where the one was not separated from him by propriety, law or honour, and the other inhibited by nature, justice or humanity. His native pride, the stubbornness of his character, the freedom of his education, all revolted against restriction, all prompted to an infraction of commandment. The laws of God he derided, those of man he despised, and his turbulent disposition, his active mind, found employment and indulgence only in vitious, inhuman and abominable pursuits.

People of virtue, sons of benevolence, daughters of purity, respectable matrons, and constant husbands, frown not with disapprobation, look not with incredulity—such is the history of delinquency; and be assured that in the progress of criminal pursuits, a love of wickedness is invariably acquired, and that the concluding service of vitious repletion requires the horrible seasoning of impending infamy and danger. It is thus with needy villains, with irresolute, and shallow, and silly reprobates; but what must be the accumulated horrours of moral perversity joined to consummate deceit, matchless intrepidity, superiour talent and untarnished reputation! Count Egfryd was in truth the most dangerous of mankind.

It may rank among the phenomena of ethick philosophy, that great mental endowments should be found conjoined with extreme flagitiousness, but I am a narrator of facts, and trouble myself little about the surprise or disbelief of others. Count Egfryd was such as I have described him. Though a married man, he indulged for Julia a passion, compared with which every other attachment he had felt before was weak and transient. He burned, he expired for her. He determined that she should fall, and that Theodore should perish; but the fate of the latter was delayed for a short time by a slight indisposition which confined him to his chamber: meanwhile, the innocence of the former was to be exposed to a new and dangerous experiment.

Plain people think only of simple means to effect their purposes. It is for the bold, and great, and wicked, to hazard extravagant enterprizes, and exhibit the resources of daring novelty. The Count above all other men possessed eccentricity of project, and fancifulness of speculation. They well agreed with the darkness of his character. Neither in his motives, his actions nor his ends, was he to be read; and in proportion as his plans were extraordinary and incredible, he considered them well laid. That which his active mind projected against Miss Bolton will support this assertion.

In the whole circle of scientifick enterprize, there is no victory over ignorance and inertness so admirable or so curious as that of aeronautick navigation. It is an invention beyond the compass of the human intellect. The experiments of Montgolfier* were at this period the subject of universal wonder and inquiry. The Count was among the first who improved upon the original idea by filling a silken globe, not with smoke, but with a gas as elastick as common air, yet considerably less heavy. The consequence of employing a globe so filled is, that being specifically lighter than the same bulk of the atmosphere which surrounds us, it rises in it until it arrives at the region where the air about it is nearly of the same degree of rarity with the gas. If the globe be made very large, it is clear that it will be able to lift to a great height a weight attached to it.

The Count's experiments proved a constant source of interest and amusement to the visitors at the *chateau*. He, always original, and always wicked, determined to convert his last improved balloon into an instrument for the seduction of Miss Bolton. However whimsical or absurd this may appear to the unsophisticated mind, such, nevertheless, was his intention. Herein he was prompted chiefly by the difficulty he experienced in finding opportunities to speak to her alone.

Besides this young lady, her father, and Mr. Dalbert, there was other company at St. Uldrich. The Marquise de Sagoné, and her daughter; the Vicomte du Gressy; the Chevalier Le Paing; Madame la Baronne Monesier and her daughter, and the old Bishop of Autun. There were the Count's three unmarried sisters, Le Chevalier d'Arpens, the Abbé Le Flos, and four officers of the French dragoons from Bourdeaux. A more polished or agreeable society was nowhere to be found. Julia, to whom French manners were little known, and French gaiety was always welcome, entered into their amusements with unqualified delight. She insensibly caught the vivacity of her new associates, and was in a short time the very soul of their union. She projected parties of pleasure, and from every such party she banished, by the unaffected chearfulness of her temper, and the playful effusions of her wit, all possible approaches of languor or insipidity. She prattled in French with a foreign, graceful incorrectness, that charmed her auditors; and she often laughed herself at the blunders she committed.

The *Comtesse D'Egfryd*, like many other women of quality in France, had never left the convent in which she had been educated, until her marriage. She was then eighteen, and in accepting the hand of the Count, she had been prompted not so much by partiality to him, as by her impatience of monastick restraint. It might be said that nature had intended her for a coquette, and no education could have rendered her either amiable or constant. A flow of spirits that seemed inexhaustible, and a love of pleasure that was not to be satiated, joined to readiness of wit and fluency of language, rendered her soon the chief favourite of the fashionable and frivolous. Vanity appeared to be her chief foible, but intrigue was, in reality, her ruling passion, and intrigue alone employed all her serious moments.

At once volatile and ardent, her attachments were many and criminal; but she had art equal to her depravation, and she had sufficient address to conceal both. From the world she concealed them, but her husband was not to be deceived. He had read her disposition before their marriage, and her subsequent conduct, which confirmed his opinion of her, neither surprised nor disturbed him. He was indifferent to her person, and while she continued to occupy the station of a woman of distinction, and to preserve the character of a woman of fashion, he cared little if she forfeited the reputation of a woman of virtue.

She was small but well made, and she had the prettiest legs and feet in the world. Her face, though not handsome, was so playful and so intelligent, that without being able to discover a single beauty in it, every one was pleased with its expression. Her manners had little of that elegance which expresses dignity and grace, but they had much of that ease and propriety which an early and a continued association with the French *noblesse* always teaches. With all her chearfulness and all her pleasantry, the *Comtesse D'Egfryd* had never been loved. Her gallants had been men of the highest rank, whom her vanity had prompted her to enroll in her train, and who from complaisance, or mere *besoin d'agir*, had appeared about her for a season; or handsome vacant and dissipated men, whom she herself had dismissed in a few weeks; but the Chevalier d'Arpens, the friend of her husband, was the only individual among all her admirers, who wished to be retained, and whom she wished to retain. He was almost as profligate as the Count, but he wanted his talents and his courage. He was neither so agreeable nor so dangerous. The Chevalier found in the *Comtesse* a mistress to his mind, and from pure indolence he dreaded the trouble of obtaining another. The *Comtesse* saw in the Chevalier a lover, less insipid than any of those she had dismissed, a lover whose attentions to her were pleasing, and whose personal and mental accomplishments were deserving of her admiration.

His age was thirty-five, his person was tall and graceful, and his face regular and handsome. The animation of his black eyes contrasted strangely, but not unbecomingly, with a listlessness in his manner and a languor, that sometimes suggested to those who observed him the ideas of collapse and debility. He spoke but seldom, and he rarely let his eyes meet the looks of those with whom he conversed. He never laughed, and his smile was a grimace practised for the sake of fashion. His words were slow, and without appearing to be studied, were invariably arranged with logical correctness and laconick precision. He spoke just loud enough to be heard by every person with whom he happened to be in company, but no louder; apparently he dreaded the exertion of even uttering a breath unnecessarily. His voice was full and clear. His attitude was seldom varied. Stillness was his characteristick. In his looks, his motions, and his accents, the gentleman was unequivocally expressed, together with absolute tranquillity; and though silent and languid, he never appeared sullen, dull, or gloomy; and unknown to him was every species of affectation. He could be eloquent when he chose; his mind was enriched with varied and copious information; and more than one woman had thought him fascinating. But his propensities, like those of the Count, were vitious and perverse. His passions were violent; he was malignant; he was false; he was vindictive; and, like the Count, the indolent D'Arpens was an atheist.

Every hour increased Julia's intimacy with the Count, her respect for his talents, her admiration of his accomplishments, her regard for his seeming virtues. There was a charm in his tone and manners, an unstudied eloquence in his language, an unction in his address, a softness in his looks, that she could not resist, and which she yielded to with pleasure.

He, irritated at the difficulties that opposed all his attempts to obtain a *tête-à-tête* with her, had recourse, at length, as I have said, to the air-balloon.

The giddy *Mademoiselle De Sagoné*, and the intrepid *Mademoiselle Monesier* had, each of them, already ventured to ascend with him in it to a height of fifty feet. A strong rope that was fastened to it, prevented the possibility of its rising higher. They expatiated with habitual exaggeration, and affected raptures, on the pleasures they had experienced, the sweet sinking of the heart during the ascent, the enchanting prospect from the great height, and the voluptuous softness of the airy motion as they hung suspended. They even assumed some glory to themselves, for an achievement that marked the strength of their minds and the ardour of their curiosity. To other women they left the errours of an illiberal education, and the follies of unfounded fear. The gentlemen, on their part, were prodigal of their praises to the fair aeronauts.

At some moments of emulation, or whim, or volatility, it passed through Julia's brain that she would likewise go into the air-balloon, but the thought always brought with it a shuddering which she could not conquer.—"Ah, Sir!" said she to Mr. Bolton, "if I could but once have it to say that I had mounted in a balloon, how happy I should be!"—"My dearest girl, your ambition, I fear, is too soaring. Nature never intended you for situations that require courage; and though there may be no danger here, yet there is something in an attempt of this kind that might terrify even a man."—"But, Sir," observed the Count, "might we not gratify Miss Bolton without the possibility of alarming her fears? The balloon can be brought as near to the ground as we please, and I can't see why she should not indulge herself, particularly as you would stand at the wheel-work which governs the rope, and would order it to be lengthened or shortened as she should direct."—"It's very true, Count, and if Julia wishes it I have no objection."—"My dear papa, let us go look at it; I will only stay in it an instant, and it shan't be higher than three or four feet from the ground. I wish poor Mr. Dalbert was well enough to look at me." This last expression did not escape the Count. He heard it with a smile, but he treasured it in the black register of his mind.

The balloon was filled with gas, and the boat was only two feet from the ground, when Julia, with a pallid countenance and a palpitating heart, stepped into it with the Count. In a few minutes she lost all her fears, and requested that she might be allowed to rise a few feet. Her father consented. The happiness of his Julia was ever the first of his wishes. By degrees she rose to twenty feet, then to twenty-five, to thirty, to thirty-five, to forty, and even to fifty feet, which was as high as either of the other two young ladies had ventured to ascend. What a triumph was Julia's! What joy filled her little heart! She no longer had any apprehensions, she came down in safety, and it was agreed that she should ascend again, the next morning, before all the world.

The Count, during the remainder of the day, struggled to appear happy and contented. But his turbulent and vitious soul could not endure, much less enjoy, any scene of domestick felicity or virtuous repose. Julia was the divinity that he adored, but his adoration, as inconsistent as it was profane, tended only to her destruction. Her ruin was the object of his wishes, and the employment of his thoughts. His passion for her was equally criminal and uncontrollable. How different from that which animates the bosom of the virtuous lover, who, in all things, studies the happiness and the honour of his mistress! The peace and tranquillity of the gentle Julia were now in danger from a married man, a wicked seducer, who, not more sensual than cruel, sought to subdue her honour and betray her repose, and who preferred the external and inferiour attractions of her person to the more exquisite perfections of her mind.

Ah! innocent and too lovely Julia, the justness of your taste, which induced you to cultivate his acquaintance into intimacy, the goodness of your heart, the candour and the purity of your mind, the sensitive delicacy of your manners, all are but feeble, all, perhaps, insufficient, to guard you from the corrupt designs of a monster, whose riches give him an almost unlimited command over every physical energy of man, and over each of the kingdoms of nature; whose knowledge of the sciences affords all the means possible to human genius to effect his purposes; whose deep and comprehensive understanding contains a mine of invention; whose tumultuous passions are now concentered in one burning wish, that of triumphing over your virtue; who knows no fear of God or man; whose atheistical and atrocious principles prevent the possibility of remorse or hesitation; whose prudence never sleeps, whose arts are inscrutable, and whose character is deemed good and amiable. May the power that watches over unsuspecting innocence, and guards the chastity of your sex, shield you from the impending danger, and conduct your steps from the abyss which now threatens to devour you!

The Count had endeavoured, with sedulous concern, to render the *chateau* at this period the centre of all the refined and elegant pleasures. He lavished his riches and strained his invention to procure attractions and create variety. There was nothing left for delicacy to seek, or voluptuousness to wish, nor was there any thing admitted which the most fastidious refinement could have rejected. Every sense was gratified with as much pleasure as it was capable of receiving, while the mind, excited by curiosity that was never allowed to slumber, was indulged and astonished with the most beautiful specimens of art, the noblest productions of genius, and the richest charms of nature.

But what appeared most worthy of his magnificence, and most strikingly characteristick of his grandeur and originality, was the air-balloon that I have mentioned. It had been constructed under his own directions. It was of immense size, and made entirely of silk. It was painted with the richest colours. A net of purple silk enclosed its summit, and from this net eight ropes of the same substance, and of buff colour, descended to the boat, to which they were fastened.

The boat was exceedingly beautiful. Its exteriour represented a shell of mother-of-pearl, with a broad spiral line of burnished gold. On the shell were represented the birth of Venus, the marriage of Thetis, the death of Ceyx,* and the flight of Helen. Its edges were of the brightest azure, and the seat within it, being a circular sopha, and calculated to receive two persons, was furnished with cushions of lilac velvet. Its sides and bottom were covered with orange brocade, on which was embroidered in silver, Ganymede's ascent from Mount Ida on an eagle, and the story of Prometheus stealing the fire of Heaven. The gold spiral line terminated, at bottom, in a *bouquet*, composed of stained glass appearing to be real jewels, and at top, in a wreath of artificial flowers, which was divided into six parts by the same number of Cupids, each appearing to present to the aeronauts some of the different refreshments suitable to a voyage through the air.

A festoon of silver and yellow fringe hung from the edges of this airy vehicle, and the oars and rudder, which were intended to govern its motion, were constructed of the lightest materials, embellished in the highest style of ornament, and embroidered with butterflies and zephyrs. The swelling sides of the immense sphere itself were decorated with gold and crimson arabesques of the boldest design. From its summit arose a lofty standard, spreading to the wind the armorial bearings of the house of Egfryd on white satin; and its bottom, which was thirty feet above the boat, was painted to represent the celestial mansions, the deities smiling with approbation, and appearing to open their heaven to receive the adventurers from below.

Nothing described by Pagan poets, nothing to be found in Arabian fiction, exceeds or equals the magnificence of this balloon. It pressed against the liquid bosom of nature with a rapidity, a force, a splendour, a sublimity, that baffled all the reasonings of experience, and exceeded all the calculations of probability.

The Count had acquired an admirable dexterity in its management, and was accompanied, the next day, by Julia according to their agreement. Their little flight afforded a safe and rare entertainment. Mr. Bolton guarded the rope below, now ordering the balloon to be wheeled down, and again suffering it to rise. She, disturbed by no apprehensions, was delighted with the prospects her aerial trip afforded, and the emotions it excited. The beauty of the boat, the gentle undulation of its movement, the clearness of the air, the applauses of her friends below, the extent of the view above, the serenity of the sky, the convenience of her seat, in which no motion of the machine, however violent, could disturb her, but above all, the presence of the Count, his placid and dignified deportment, the graces of his conversation and the delicacy of his attentions, soothed her mind to tenderness, courted her attachment to the beautiful and the romantick, and even elevated her sentiments of piety to enthusiasm. She felt resigned and delighted.

Her appearance this morning was uncommonly interesting. Her hair, of the finest flaxen, was negligently secured by a comb, and as she sat in the boat, her head and neck, that appeared above its sides, could have served as a model for the bust of Maia. Her dress was of pink sarsnet, her ornaments were of pearl, and while she slowly ascended from the ground, she might, not unaptly, be compared, for her innocence and her beauty, to one of the virgin saints, when called from this earth to the bosom of their Creator, to exchange terrestrial substance for etherial essence, and who, thus summoned to immortality, may be imagined to float with eager attitude and benign countenance, through our grosser atmosphere, to the regions of celestial bliss.

Arrived to the utmost height that the rope, securing the balloon, would admit, the Count, by a simple contrivance which he had previously arranged, detached the boat from the rope that secured it. The screams of her father and of the other spectators informed Julia of her danger, who attributed to accident what was the result of premeditated fraud and desperate depravity. In an agony of terrour that beggars description, she perceived the balloon rising majestically to an elevation that made her shudder. The colour forsook her cheeks, the sight her eyes.

In vain the Count protested to her there was no danger, in vain he assured her that, by permitting the hydrogen to escape, they should descend gradually in a few minutes. In vain he displayed his activity in a seeming endeavour to liberate the gas, by pulling the string that opened the valve for its departure. They had already mounted to the highest regions of the atmosphere, when, turning her eyes towards the earth which she feared never more to tread, what was her consternation to see it at a depth that took distinctness from every object?

To be suspended by a few cords at such a frightful height: to have no support but a little frail boat, which a thousand accidents might precipitate: to find herself above the clouds in a machine of silk: it was too much for the delicacy of her frame and the weakness of her nerves. How many heroes would, in her situation, have trembled with terrour?—"My God! my God!" cried she in a tone of anguish and with a look of despair, "save me, oh, save me!" She could articulate no more. Her agitated frame sunk lifeless into the arms of the Count, who soon succeeded in discharging as much gas as caused the balloon to descend into a warmer region. Here, with the assistance of salts and other stimulants, he quickly recovered her. The violence of her first emotion having abated, she was able to hearken to his assurances.

The tranquillity of his countenance and the firmness of his manner, tended in a considerable degree to diminish her terrour. He assured her, that, but for the pain her fright occasioned him, this aeronautick excursion would appear the most delightful and interesting adventure of his life. He conjured her to be composed, and, with a persuasive eloquence peculiar to himself, proved, if not to her satisfaction at least to her conviction, that she had never taken an airing in a carriage more secure than the sublime voyage she was now making.—"At my pleasure," said he, "I can rise or descend, and I only wait until we shall arrive over yonder plain, to anchor our little vessel, which I can do with perfect security and without any trouble. How charming to sail, as we do, through the air with extreme rapidity, and not to be sensible of the motion! How grand to float in silent majesty over the lofty habitations of the proud, which appear to our eyes, rendered philosophical by our elevation, as humble as the lowly cottages of the poor! How sublime to take in, at one view, mountains, rivers, plains and cities, and to have our horizon extended far beyond the visual reach of all other mortals! How voluptuous to recline on velvet cushions in mid-air, while we are warmed by a summer sun, and fanned by zephyrs of true etherial origin! Let me," continued he, "prevail on you to banish your apprehensions, believe me they are quite unfounded."

"Oh!" exclaimed she, "let us descend immediately! I am nearly dead with apprehension."—"You will observe," said he, "with what an easy motion we are approaching the plain; in fifteen minutes we shall be on the ground. But I am really vexed to think that your unreasonable fears should deprive us of the most rational enjoyment in nature."—"You speak like a courageous man," replied she, dreading his contempt, "and make no allowance for female timidity: but, in truth, I believe you are right. I am sure we are safe, and you may, if you please, descend more slowly. I have that reliance on your skill that I am persuaded there is no danger, but—"—"With your permission, then," said he, "I will descend less rapidly; and be assured that if I did not know a little delay would contribute to your gratification, which I prize above all other considerations, I should not presume to indulge myself by delaying our debarkation for an instant." As he uttered these words, he took one of her hands in his, and, gently pressing it, he looked at her with tenderness. A blush of modesty immediately suffused her expressive countenance.

His words, his looks, and the pleasure that she always felt when sitting near him, joined to the intellectual luxury which her situation actually afforded, and on which he had eloquently expatiated, tended in a great degree to compose her mind, and to enable her to speak with collected thoughts of the accident that had occurred. Such was her confidence in the judgment and activity of the Count, and such her dread of being despised by him, that she forced herself to appear pleased with her situation, and it was not long till she thought of the circumstance which had given her to the sky, without much terrour, and looked forward to the moment that was to restore her to the earth, without much impatience.

The stillness of the air increased every moment, but still a gentle current wafted them, almost imperceptibly, towards the Garonne.—"Now," said the Count, "we have an opportunity of visiting that romantick little island in the river, which you have heard so often described as the sweetest spot in France. If you permit me, I will navigate you to the very centre of it, and as there are innumerable boats traversing the water this fine day, we can suffer no distress for an opportunity of returning. I undertake to supply you with a collation on the island, and we shall be able, with ease, to revisit the *chateau* before supper. This will add infinitely to the *éclat* of your voyage, and will prove that if, at first, you had any fears, you possessed good sense enough to conquer them. I recommend this to you," continued he, "in the full persuasion that it can be effected with perfect security; and, I assure you, upon my honour, that you cannot possibly oblige me more than by giving your assent."

If there were no other motive, this last assurance of the Count would, alone, have been sufficient to induce her to acquiesce. Accordingly it was determined that they should steer for the island. The wind was favourable, and with the assistance of the oars which the Count made use of, and the rudder which Julia by his instructions governed, they proceeded in a direct and gentle course towards the place of their destination.

The strangeness of her situation, the hurry of her thoughts, and her exertions to appear composed, had deprived Miss Bolton in a great measure of the faculty of reflexion. Nevertheless she regretted her entrance into the balloon more than any other act of her life, and she thought of her father's distress with a feeling of agony; but such was her facility of disposition, such her fear of disobliging, such the gentle pliability of her manners, and such her desire to bestow contentment, that she could not summon courage enough to insist on an instantaneous descent. Besides, her curiosity and her ambition were both artfully played upon by her insidious enemy.

Every moment she appeared more reconciled to her situation, yet still she spoke of the uneasiness which her father would feel during her absence, with concern and alarm; but her companion ridiculed her distress with so much volubility and so much wit, that she was, at length, forced to admit that Mr. Bolton's meeting her at night unhurt, would more than compensate for any anxiety he might suffer until then.

The current of air that had lately wafted them with gentle motion towards the river had now subsided. A youthful writer would say, that the aerial deities seemed to have produced a universal calm, as if anxious to retain an invention that did honour to their empire, and desirous to prolong the stay of their two illustrious visitors by a perfect and heavenly repose: and, perhaps, he would add that the zephyrs, forbid to play upon the bosom and cheeks of the lovely Julia, now slumbered among these charms. She, with a mind now harmonized to the magnificence of the scene, expected with calm submission the moment when the Count should propose to her their descent. Relinquishing his silken oars, and looking with an air of entreaty at his amiable friend, he asked her, and smiled as he spoke, if they should take their collation where they were? She nodded a doubtful, hesitating assent; when, with the rapidity of magick—but here I must pause.

Can I, without repugnance, submit to the painful necessity of describing what my reason contemns, what my integrity detests? Alas! it is my peculiar lot to find my duty and my principles irreconcileably opposed. Who, with more impatience, abhors a deed of darkness than I? Who, with less pleasure, relates a tale of surprise or an incident of puerility? But I must follow the dark obliquities of this monster. I have sworn to paint his infamy in the colours of truth, and I will perform my task. Whether he tries to delude with frivolity or frolick, or to soar beyond suspicion in the flights of romance, I will pursue his wanderings, and detect his machinations. The display of his little and laborious arts, which now follows, will serve as a memorable proof that apparent absurdity of detail, may, by the accomplished libertine, be employed at once to conceal and to promote extreme flagitiousness of design.

Having, as I have said, seduced Miss Bolton into a tacit approbation of an aerial repast, with the rapidity of magick a little table, not visible before, appeared. This table, made of tortoiseshell and ivory, and embellished with imitations of amethyst and topaz, was soon covered with delicious wines and sweetmeats from both the Indies, which with iced creams and lemonade, completed a collation, that from its richness and elegance, the small size, accurate proportion, and comprehensive variety of the service, the neatness of the ornaments, and the convenience and ingenuity of the distribution, might be thought worthy of fairy hospitality. In the meantime a dew of perfumed water (which was contained in a gilt receiver under the balloon, and which could be discharged by pulling a silken string within the boat) sunk in imperceptible drops about the vehicle, while a small organ, concealed beneath the circular sopha, played several of Julia's favourite airs, whose countenance expressed unutterable astonishment and admiration. She tried to eat, and the Count protested that all was much improved in flavour by the voyage to so pure a region. He even declared with vivacity that she looked like the goddess of Love, sipping nectar in the skyey mansions, and tasting the divine ambrosia.

The repast finished, he removed all that had composed it, except some hermitage and a jar of water—"It would be vain to deny," said he, after pressing her to take some wine, "that this aerial excursion of ours was premeditated on my part. I have ravished you from the earth, which is unworthy of you, to transport myself to heaven in your society. I confess myself guilty of a fraud, but it was a fraud dictated by a power that will be obeyed. You see before you a criminal, but a criminal that shall never again offend. If you think him not entirely unworthy of forgiveness, say so before we descend, which will be immediately, and you will make him the happiest of mortals; but if you hearken to your justice rather than to your clemency, then, indeed, shall I be for ever miserable. Yes, fairest and most amiable of women, I confess myself the guiltiest of men, if it be a crime to adore you, and I appear before you the most miserable of wretches if you must condemn me. You know the sincerity, the honesty of my disposition, you know how long I have combated the most ungovernable of passions under the veil of friendship and respect, but you do not know the flames that for some time past have consumed me, the disorder that now preys upon my constitution. Day after day I pass in anxious solicitude, or in society still more intolerable. The bosom of darkness receives my sighs, my pillow is the depository of my tears."—Here sighing and shedding a few tears upon the hand of Julia, which he at the same time offered to press to his lips, the dissimulating Count Egfryd appeared in an agony of conflicting passions.

Julia, at language so unexpected and so alarming, stared with amazement. Her eyes, at once repellent and inquiring, were fixed upon him. Pride, surprise, and trepidation, deprived her for a moment of utterance. She had never before been insulted, she had never before wished to possess the language of reproach, or lamented her feebleness of invective. In her indignation she forgot the adventures of the morning, and even the existence of the balloon. She felt that her situation required decision. She withdrew her hand with instinctive promptitude, and in a tone of dignity and firmness forbade a repetition of the offence. She would have been eloquent, but her thoughts were too tumultuous and too rapid to be expressed with much order.

"Sir, Count Egfryd, is this your friendship? Is your attachment to my father to be shown by your contempt for me? Is your sincerity to be marked by treachery? Your kindness by outrage? You are a married man, the *Comtesse* is my friend, and I am alone; never did I give you cause to suspect my honour or my delicacy, and this, Sir, I must consider a base advantage of brutality over weakness. Politeness may condemn my words, but virtue abhors your action, and though I should even violate good-breeding, still will I assert your turpitude. My God! my God! is it possible you could intentionally have torn me from my father, in order to expose me to this affront! Sir, I hate your purpose, despise your means, and now loathe your presence; and——." —"Miss Bolton, *Mademoiselle* Julia, your pardon for a moment. Be a little less warm. Do not increase our misunderstanding by unnecessary vehemence. It is true I am a married man. It is certain I love you. It is demonstrable that I have encountered trouble and peril to have an opportunity of telling you so. In all this am I to blame? If you are fair beyond the wishes of female vanity; if you are gentle, delicate and attractive, beyond the belief of all who do not know you; if a charm hangs on your lips and attends on your steps, that bewitches every ear and every eye; if a wondrous irresistible fascination encompasses you, and you alone—am I to blame? If I loved you, and were silent and mysterious, I should be pardoned. Loving you, as I do, with unparalleled impetuosity, and with unexampled sincerity, shall I be condemned? For what? For my honesty in declaring the real sentiments of my heart! Away with such injustice! You possess too much ingenuousness."—"Sir, I possess too much pride to listen any longer to such language. I insist on being instantly released from this terrible machine, and on your silence."

The Count, who clearly saw in her manner the annihilation of all his hopes, drew back his hand slowly and contemptuously. His eyes, now almost closed, scarcely deigned to regard the object of his scorn. A half-suppressed yawn decided the haughtiness of his manner. The insolence of his nature, upon this occasion, overcame his systematick and artificial tranquillity.—"Why, Madam, I confess it is very fine, and very interesting, to act the vestal in this heroical strain, but, in truth, I am not accustomed to the harshness of your insular phraseology; and you will excuse me if I do not perfectly understand it. You have a great deal still to learn, I fear, Miss Bolton, and there is one most important accomplishment you seem entirely unacquainted with, that of a graceful submission to inevitable necessity. I saw you an amiable but unpolished English girl. You differed materially from the other females of my acquaintance, and I determined to possess you. Don't frown—I determined to possess you; and my determinations I always accomplish. Consider the man who speaks to you. Look attentively upon him. Reflect on his resources, and acknowledge that resistance were absolutely useless."

"Monster!" cried the terrified Julia. "Let us instantly descend, or my instantaneous precipitation to the earth shall convince you of my courage and my abhorrence." With these words the agonized girl made an effort to lean over the side of the boat. In her look despair and determination were powerfully expressed. The Count, unmoved by her distress, but apprehensive of the effects of her resolution, immediately changed his mode of procedure. Persuasion, he saw, would be fruitless, and sophism unavailing. To entreat her were to exasperate her, and to threaten were only to fortify her opposition. Her death would rob his licentiousness of a victim, and leave his vengeance unsatisfied. And her death, it was manifest, would be the immediate effect of any repetition of insult, of any violence. Any violence! yes, capable of every crime, the horrible libertine dared at that moment to meditate the grossest of injuries.

"Well, well," said he, with well-affected gaiety, and placing himself so as to prevent the threatened effects of her desperation, "I perceive our French gallantries are not entirely to your taste. I therefore, from this moment, relinquish and abjure them; and to convince you, Miss Bolton, of my sincerity and contrition, you shall be instantly gratified in your desire to descend." He then caused a rapid discharge of the gas, and threw out an anchor. The machine quickly descended, and the anchor caught a low rock. The gas still continuing to escape, the boat touched the ground, and the silken globe above, now nearly flaccid, became troublesome to their heads. The Count having helped Julia to land, followed himself; and placing some heavy stones in the boat, he left the balloon to empty itself gradually and sink upon the earth.

Thus were all his intentions defeated. No advantage had he been able to take of her terrour and surprise. No current of air had enabled him to bear her off to a remote province, which was an exploit he had basely projected; and her former good opinion of him was for ever and utterly destroyed. To trace the course of his thoughts, since her declaration of suicide, would be to follow a villain in the unfeeling adherence to profligate principles, and the cool conception of habitual vice. He spared her only to reserve her for miseries, compared with which death would have been a blessing; and irritated by disappointment and defeat, he now swore to himself never to relinquish his hellish enterprize against this unhappy girl, till he had accumulated on her innocent head the united horrours of shame, contempt, and infamy; till he had poured into her guileless heart the poisons of remorse, destruction, and despair. Malignant libertine! but for thee, the flower of virgin innocence would have still blown in tranquil security, defended from every storm, and secure against every blast. It now flourishes in the bloom and pride of youth, and health, and beauty, an object of esteem, respect and love; and shalt thou, ruthless barbarian! pluck it from its stalk, and expose it to wither, faded and despised, without support and destitute of beauty? Shalt thou cause it to droop, a thing of indifference, and soon, perhaps, to perish, deserted and degraded, avoided and abhorred?

When the alarm was given of the rope that secured the machine having given way, several men and horses were sent, with all possible expedition, in the direction that the balloon was seen to take; and immediately on its descent, three servants with as many horses arrived at the spot where it landed. One of the horses was supplied with a side-saddle: this Julia mounted. The Count took another, and they proceeded to the *chateau*, attended by a servant.

On their way home she preserved a mournful and dignified silence. She felt humiliated, and, though released from apparent danger, she felt alarmed. To remain any longer in the *chateau* would be horrible. To quit it instantaneously might be impossible. To acquaint her father with what had happened were to risk his safety. It would be to involve him, perhaps, in an affair of honour with the desperate and merciless Count. To deceive him by any false information, or to withhold from him a considerable part of what she should profess to disclose, was what her pride and her honour equally forbade. To make a confidant of Theodore, and employ him as an agent, were indiscreet in the extreme, if not indelicate, and might even produce a quarrel between him and their formidable enemy. To urge a request to her father that they should quit St. Uldrich, without assigning a reason for their doing so, would probably receive little attention from him. In whatever manner she considered the subject, insurmountable or fatal difficulties presented themselves. The Count, who had an uncommon share of penetration, read the nature of her distress, and discovered her several emotions in the various changes of her expressive countenance.—"We shall soon arrive at the *chateau*, Miss Bolton," said he. "How will you act? Will you exclaim, openly and loudly, against what you think my treachery and dishonour, and thus force me into desperation to justify or support an innocent artifice? Or will you, with magnanimity and good sense, forget an indiscretion which my sober reason abhors, and which nothing but the volatility proceeding from an extraordinary and whimsical situation could produce? I fear neither you nor your father, but I respect you both. I acknowledge the impropriety of my conduct, and I entreat your forgiveness for it. Drive me not to extremities. I feel and I acknowledge, with heartfelt shame, the indignity that my thoughtlessness offered you, and I now supplicate your pardon. Grant me this favour, and never while I live shall I forget your goodness, nor ever again violate towards you the duties of delicacy and decorum. Ah! are the gates of mercy to be closed against me? or may I enter the temple with a fearless heart, and bless the goodness that vouchsafes to accept my confession and repentance?"

To this Julia made no answer. She knew not what to reply. But her silence, and the undecided expression of her features, sufficiently conveyed to her artful companion that he had nothing to apprehend.

Supper had just been served when they arrived. Great was the exultation, and loud were the congratulations at their escape. Our female aeronaut threw herself upon the bosom of her father, and, as he kissed her with rapture, wept bitterly in his arms. He, good man, attributed her tears to her agitation and to her late terrour.

Excessive was the curiosity, and innumerable were the inquiries about their adventures. The Count endeavoured to satisfy the former, and to answer the latter; but Julia requested permission to retire to rest, which, after such an excursion as she had taken, was readily granted.

He then proceeded to relate what had happened, and only omitted two circumstances; one was his detaching the rope that had secured the balloon, and the other his base and ungenerous conduct towards Julia.

Never was an extraordinary story narrated with more propriety or more grace; and never was the Count more instructive or entertaining.

CHAPTER VI.

E fu pur ver, che dal sasso marino
Gittarsi in mar lo vide a capo chino.

....

Danger! whose limbs of giant mould
No mortal eye can fix'd behold,
When forth he stalks a hideous form,
Howling amidst the midnight storm;
Or throws him on the ridgy steep
Of some loose hanging rock to sleep.

....

Environ'd round by deathlike gloom, I hear
Destructive tempests howl, and feel the spot
Whereon I stand trembling beneath my feet
With sad and dreadful quake, denoting all
Perdition can inflict; while o'er my head
Huge fragments loosely hang, upon whose frown
Destructive demons wait.

....

Come on, Sir; here's the place—stand still. How fearful
And dizzy 'tis to cast one's eyes so low!
———The murmuring surge
That on th' unnumber'd idle pebbles chafes,
Cannot be heard so high. I'll look no more,
Lest my brain turn, and the deficient sight
Topple down headlong.

....

Oh! woman, woman! When to ill thy mind
Is bent, all hell contains no greater fiend.

In the territory of St. Uldrich, and between the *chateau* and the sea, lay a mountainous, sterile, unpeopled region. The mountain, at its extremity, abruptly terminated in an immense rocky cliff, at a frightful height above the water. To creep on one's face and look down from it, was an act of courage beyond the powers of ordinary men. The mind revolted from the most distant possibility of falling into such a horrible abyss; the limbs shrunk involuntarily from the audacious attempt, vertigo seized the brain and dizziness the sight.

The cliff shelved inwardly from its top to the bottom, so that a line dropped perpendicularly from it, would, below, be some thousands of feet from its base. The edge of this enormous and immeasurable arch was sharp and bare. A gulph of deadly gloom and dread extent lay below. Everlasting night frowned within the hard, rough, black, tremendous vault, where ruin and desolation seemed to have established their dominion. No human being was so forlorn or so desperate as here to venture. No samphire seeker, no fisherman, no fowler, was to be seen. All was a dreary uniformity of horrour. Pride and intrepidity were annihilated by the sullen magnificence, the appalling sublimity of this awful waste, and man, here, shrunk into littleness, and felt the imbecility of his nature.

The Count, by constitution daring and adventurous, had when a boy practised here those terrifick exploits related of the daring inhabitants of the Feroe Islands. Sitting in the bight of a rope, and holding a long pole with an iron crook at its end, he would order himself to be lowered gradually to a depth of several hundred feet, care having been first taken to make that part of the edge of the cliff on which the rope passed (and which edge was of one continued naked rock) round and polished. The bight on which he sat being loaded with a great weight of lead, he was enabled to keep himself in such a swing, from the commencement of his descent, that even at the depth of three hundred feet, he at each oscillation could touch the surface of the retiring arch, from which pushing himself back with all his strength, a sufficient impetus was obtained to bring him again within reach of it. When he saw a roughness in the rock which might be caught with his crook, he would sometimes fasten himself to it, enjoy the frightful sublimity of his situation for a while (an incalculable weight of ruin impending over him) and then plunge again with unparalleled fearlessness into the unlimited profundity of the abyss.

The mountain boys, with trembling limbs and anxious admiration, would gaze, their eyes half averted, at his deeds, as they lay crouched on the verge of the precipice above: and the mariners of a coasting vessel would sometimes be unwilling witnesses of what I relate, and would, incredulous of such mortal daring, piously and naturally invoke the protection of the saints against the pranks of the flying demon of the rock, for such they thought and termed him.

In winter, when the desolateness of this place, which was emphatically called *the grave*, was aggravated to a degree of indescribable horrour, when the rain fell in torrents, when the tempest reverberated with deafening impetuosity within the infernal arch, when the sea lashed with irresistible fury against its rocky foundations, when the thunder pealed with incessant roar along its frowning sides, when no rays illuminated its tartarean gloom but those of the forky lightning; then would the dauntless boy chiefly delight to play his gambols. Amid the raging of the elemental war, and the seeming ruin of nature, he would swing, fearless and unconcerned, through the chaos, be covered with the foaming waves, be blown about by the angry storms, be scorched by the rapid lightnings:

he, all the time, challenging death and destruction with a defiance, an exultation, that no other being could have dared, or would have felt. While I write my hand shakes, my frame shudders, my blood grows cold; but such was Count Egfryd when a boy.

In the course of his terrible researches, he chanced, one day, to fasten his crook on a projecting point, behind which was a cavity that attracted his observation. It was about one hundred feet below the brink of the precipice. Having drawn himself close to it, he perceived that this cavity sunk and extended into the rock. Before it was a ledge of five feet in breadth and two in depth, affording a standing place. The projecting point on which he had fastened his crook was in this ledge. Possessing as much curiosity as courage, he alighted on it, quitted the rope that he descended by, and left it on the ledge secured by the leaden weight. Romantick as he was then, warm and enthusiastick, what must have been his delight at perceiving an aperture in the face of the cliff, branching into extensive and lofty subterranean passages? For want of light he was compelled to retire without then being able to ascertain either their boundary or their shape. Having resumed his rope, he launched with precipitation from the ledge, pulled the string, which was the signal to his attendants to draw him up, instantly supplied himself with matches, tinder, flint and steel, together with some *flambeaux*, and again descended.

Having landed a second time on the ledge, he struck a light, and with a *flambeau* penetrated a recess, till then unvisited and unseen by mortal. Its mouth, which was about six feet square, and which opened on the sea, was the termination of an avenue of twenty feet long, that gradually enlarged as it receded from the opening, and passing horizontally into the mountain, led to a large lofty cavern of irregular shape and singular appearance. The numerous columns that it contained of fantastical shape, the natural fret-work of its variegated misshapen sides, the irregularities of its grit floor, the whimsical distribution of its sparry ornaments, here in a regular congeries of brilliant crystallizations, and there, in rude and glittering heaps of seemingly ostentatious magnificence, and innumerable stalactites reflecting a thousand splendid colours, formed a spectacle at once grand and extraordinary. The view was closed by a dusky layer of iron ore and a thick stratum of coal.

On continuing his search he found other passages and cavities, some of which were high and capacious. They all bore a striking resemblance to the outer cavern, and through one of them a stream of water of considerable breadth and depth flowed with rapidity. The wonders of these subterraneous recesses were many and varied.

The fervid fancy of the boy was charmed with the scene. It resembled what he had read in fairy tales. He considered himself the sole and rightful proprietor of this terrible retirement, and he resolved never to hazard its loss, or the profanation of its solemn character, by a disclosure of his discovery. Here he could live in solitary state, at least here he should pass his choicest and happiest hours. He had found a treasure, which to be preserved must be concealed. The natural closeness and craft of his disposition enabled him to keep a resolution of secrecy, which, under the same circumstances, no other boy could have adhered to.

Under pretence of sporting, he caused a hut to be erected near the precipice, and by degrees, and without suspicion, he contrived to furnish his newly-obtained possession with a bed, a stove, and other articles of convenience. He had acquired such dexterity and strength in the use of his rope, that he, after some time, required no assistance to be lowered, but, having secured it above, he would slide down to its very extremity and climb it up with perfect facility. When he wished to rest himself, he had learned a method of twisting it about his limbs and body, so as to render any exertion, to prevent him from slipping down, unnecessary, and this at a distance from the sea, which, not even in Feroe, could be reflected on without horrour.

To complete his eccentrick arrangements, he had a strong iron ring sunk and soldered in the rock above, within a few feet of the precipice's edge. To this ring he fastened one end of his rope, and to prevent the possibility of losing the means of ascending, when in the cavern, should the fastening by any accident be untied, for his cautious mind, even then, could guard against the remotest contingencies, he attached a second rope, not visible above, to a projecting flint immediately below the sharp border of the abyss, so that having the end of it on the ledge, he could at all times ascend within a few inches of the brink, and thus scramble up. This was a resource against a misfortune that was barely possible, but a misfortune that cannot be thought on without shuddering; for were he in the cavern without his rope, he must necessarily perish. No sound he could utter would be heard, no signal he could make would be seen, and there, hopeless of all relief, he must have died of hunger.

The young Egfryd had practised in this school of terrour so long, that, at length, the passion of fear in his breast was completely suppressed, if not extinguished. Hither he was accustomed to resort in fits of gloom and periods of despondency, from his boyish days even to the period at which this history commences. He ever found a strange delight in sitting at the cavern's mouth, surveying the horrours of *the grave*, and brooding over the black objects of his wicked mind.

Hither his preposterous vengeance determined to transport the hated Theodore; and here the unfortunate Julia was, perhaps, to end her days. Here had been already, here now existed, a female inhabitant, Marie de Solase. Wretched woman! worthy tenant of such a mansion! Better would it have been for thee, hadst thou suffered the sentence of the law, the death of ignominious torture, for the murder of thy husband, than drag on a horrible existence in these caverns, bereft of every comfort, plunged in the depths of solitude and darkness, and exposed to never-ending misery and despair, than be buried alive as thou art now. Willingly would I avoid the painful task of describing another miscreant; I abhor wicked characters, and I shrink from their portraiture, but her's is a figure in this historical piece that must be given.

Marie de Solase, whose story ranks high in the record of crime, had been the adulterous wife of an advocate in Bourdeaux whom she had murdered. The circumstances were peculiarly atrocious. For this she was sentenced to be broken on the wheel, but her paramour, the Count, who was accessory to her crime, by the agency of Conrad and Gaspar, and by the liberality of his bribes, rescued her from this fate, and had her carried to a spot contiguous to his hut on the precipice. From the hut he saw the two villains conduct her to the appointed place and retire, and when he had satisfied himself that they were out of sight, he went towards her, now overcome with fatigue, and proposed to her to become a resident in the cavern.

She, in momentary dread of arrest and a cruel death, and convinced of the impossibility of escape from a country, where every one knew her, where every one was her enemy, and where all were in search of her, embraced the offer. The Count then tied her to a chair, and lowered this to a sufficient depth by a rope fastened to the iron ring. What her feelings were in this situation I shall not attempt to describe. He immediately afterwards descended himself in his usual way, and having landed on the ledge, pulled by means of a string the chair towards him, and brought her into the recess. He promised to supply her regularly with provisions and other necessaries. He pointed out to her the stratum of coal as an inexhaustible body of fuel, and he instructed her in an expeditious way of catching fish in the running stream.

Why did he take all this trouble? Why? ah! who can account for the perverse aberrations of depravity? Perhaps he intended the cavern as a gaol for the objects of his hatred, and required a gaoler whose cruelty should second his resentment. Perhaps his boisterous passions, his irregular desires, called for the active obedience of desperate vice, or the base submissions of meretricious profligacy. Perhaps his morbid and restless appetites demanded the society, if society it may be called, of the vitious and proscribed; and Marie de Solase was not only submissive, vitious, cruel and proscribed, but beautiful.

Her age might be thirty, and her person was tall, plump and well proportioned. Her hair and eyes were black, and her complexion was of the deepest brown. Her features were regular and handsome, but her look exceeded the powers of delineation. It was that malignant, penetrating, merciless expression, with which the head of Medusa petrified beholders. There was a spirit of enterprize, an extent of talent, a darkness, a depth, an audacity, a hardness in her countenance, that rendered it demoniacal. When she tried to soften its inflexibility and to seduce, it was like sweetening the poisoned bowl, or gilding the pointed stiletto. It was death concealed behind the semi-transparent mask of beauty. Perdition and she were one. She was constitutionally dissolute, but she was susceptible of love, and while she loved, no human attachment could exceed in ardour the passion she professed. She was capable of any sacrifice and any desperation; she could feed upon hope, and exist upon a look: but quick as the transient gleam of a winter's sun, and fickle as the dubious current of a winter's wind, she could desert and loathe the object of her partiality, and pant for the possession of another, to whom perhaps she had never spoken. The Count had the art to make her believe that it was his love for her which induced him to preserve her life, and he had the ingenuity to convince her that there were no other possible means to attain this object, than those which he employed. To rescue her from death he had employed his fortune and ingenuity, and risked his reputation, and to obtain for her a pardon he promised to exert all his interest and activity.

On her side she affected gratitude, but she felt it not; she was incapable of feeling it. With consummate hypocrisy, she feigned submission and content in the dread of losing his protection, on which her miserable existence depended, and in the hope of being enabled to escape to a distant country. Her abilities, her accomplishments, her personal attractions were such, that the Count insensibly became fond of her society, and neglected nothing that could render her wretched situation endurable. But such was his perfidy, such his selfishness, that he determined she should never quit her dungeon. To inspire her with chearfulness, and thereby promote his own gratification, he furnished her with many of the luxuries, and all the necessaries of life. She had musical instruments, drawing materials, a telescope and books; two little dogs, a parrot, a monkey, and a squirrel.

CHAPTER VII.

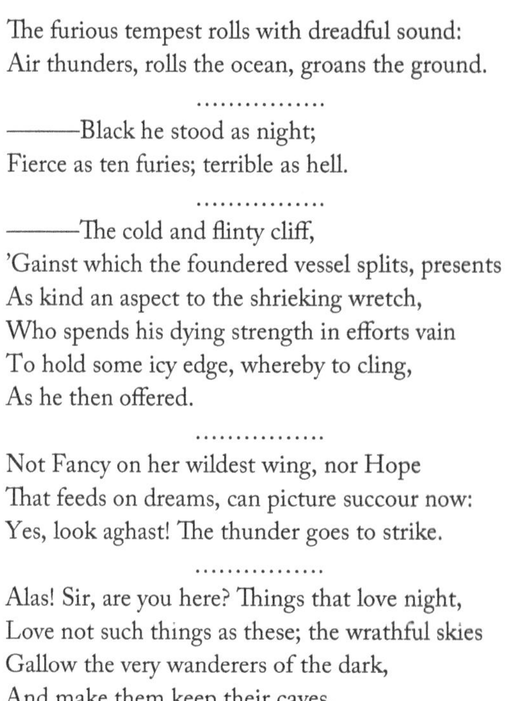

The furious tempest rolls with dreadful sound:
Air thunders, rolls the ocean, groans the ground.

....

———Black he stood as night;
Fierce as ten furies; terrible as hell.

....

———The cold and flinty cliff,
'Gainst which the foundered vessel splits, presents
As kind an aspect to the shrieking wretch,
Who spends his dying strength in efforts vain
To hold some icy edge, whereby to cling,
As he then offered.

....

Not Fancy on her wildest wing, nor Hope
That feeds on dreams, can picture succour now:
Yes, look aghast! The thunder goes to strike.

....

Alas! Sir, are you here? Things that love night,
Love not such things as these; the wrathful skies
Gallow the very wanderers of the dark,
And make them keep their caves.

THE complaint which had confined Theodore to his chamber had left him. He was now able to walk out; and the morning after the adventure of the balloon, he met Miss Bolton at the monument described in a former chapter. He was feeble and pale; she was dejected and sad; each looked at the other with that commiserating air of kind inquiry which soothes the mind and penetrates to the heart. To this was added, on her part, a blush at the recollection of their interview in the library; and on his, a sudden glow of animation and delight from the same cause. Neither had, since that moment, felt indifference or rest. For him, the conflict it produced in his breast, had, in truth, been the cause of his illness. The ardour of his disposition, the quickness of his feelings, and the acuteness of his sensibility, had fixed in his heart an unalterable, inextinguishable love, a love not less merited than it was pure, for the charming Julia; at the same time that the delicacy of his principles determined him to fly from her presence for ever, the disparity of their fortunes being in his opinion an insuperable bar to their union. For her, could she know his talents and his virtues; could she see the manly beauty of his countenance, the graceful proportions of his person; that countenance beaming with soul and gentleness, that person worthy of such a countenance; could she survey his forehead made to command, his Grecian nose indicative of nobleness, his lips so sweet in conversation, his eyes so eloquent and so bright, and the slender symmetry of his tall elastick figure; could she admire the ease of his motions, the elegance of his gait; could she hear a declaration of attachment from such a man; could she recline in his arms; could she remark in him as he embraced her the sensitiveness of irresistible genuine passion; could she know that she was loved by him, and be indifferent? Ah, no! Accident had given to her observation the only object that nature would permit her to regard with affection: the only object, perhaps, in the creation that could be united to her. She felt that there existed between them a reciprocalness of sentiment, a congeniality, that promised and required the most intimate communion of soul. She indulged the delightful reflection of his sincerity and worth, she doubted not the truth of his declaration, the violence of his flame, she believed he was destined for her, and she resigned herself without a struggle (alas! she could not struggle) to the sweetest and most dangerous of illusions.

With faltering accents she inquired after his health; with unfeigned pleasure she heard he was recovered; and with an agitated manner, and manifest confusion, she answered his questions about her aeronautick flight. His embarrassment was not less. He feared to trust his words, lest they should betray his emotions; his looks, lest they should convey his admiration; his tones, lest their softness should indicate his disorder. All he loved was before him, but stern honour prohibited the indulgence of any hope. He was distressed, and for a moment irresolute. Roused, at length, by an effort of pride, he said—"Miss Bolton, we shall soon part, perhaps for ever. To-morrow I shall quit the *chateau*, and as I may not see you again alone, you will excuse me for declaring now that never while I live shall your image be absent from my thoughts; never, never, shall I cease to pray for your happiness. It were——."—"Part for ever! Quit the *chateau*! Mr. Dalbert, you do not mean to leave us so suddenly?"—"Indeed, I must."—"That is unfortunate. I wished to consult you on an affair of some consequence—perhaps I wanted your assistance, but——." Here Julia checked herself. She already repented having said so much. She had intended to keep from Theodore's knowledge the Count's misconduct, but unused to concealment, and betrayed, in part by her confusion and in part by her apprehensions, into an indiscretion, she believed that she ought not now to withhold any part of her communication.—"But you fear to employ me," said Theodore, continuing her speech.—"No, but I fear to give you trouble, and I fear the effects of your warmth."

Having assured her that no affair that concerned her would be considered troublesome by him, and protested that nothing like anger should appear on his part, let the cause of excitement be what it might, she made a disclosure to him of all that had passed between her and the Count. As she spoke a tear of outraged virtue stole gently down her crimsoned cheek, while the high spirit and ingenuous disposition of Theodore broke forth, now in exclamations of horrour, and then in apostrophizing accents of indignation, or appeared in his looks of sympathizing concern, or spoke in the sighs of tenderness that issued from his commiserating breast.

What was to be done? Julia must quit the *chateau*, but Mr. Bolton must not be informed of her motives. There was difficulty in this, and perhaps address and stratagem were requisite. They considered the subject in every point of view, and at length it was determined that, for her greater security, Theodore should remain at St. Uldrich till her departure, and that they both should use every persuasion with her father to continue his tour without delay into Italy.

They went to seek him that moment, and Miss Bolton, in the language of importunity and impatience, urged her suit so strongly, that he consented to depart in a few days; at the same time he hoped, he said, that Theodore would accompany them till their return into England, upon the terms which I have elsewhere mentioned. This was presenting to a starving man a plenteous repast. It was a helping arm extended to a drowning wretch. It was a rich prize in the lottery to a ruined merchant. It was a limpid well to the thirsty traveller of the desert. But Theodore hesitated. He had been solicited before by this good man to do so, but he durst not trust himself near Julia; he durst not expose himself to the influence of her charms, and he dreaded the baseness of a clandestine attachment.

He shook his head, stammered out his acknowledgements and his gratitude, and was preparing to utter an unwilling negative, the conclusive and irrevocable *no*, when casting a look at Miss Bolton's countenance, he there caught a glance, oh! such a glance! What reproach, apprehension and entreaty did it not convey? With what earnestness did it not supplicate, with what softness did it not upbraid! Every fibre in his frame received and confessed the eloquence of its magical expression. His blood rushed in impetuous currents through his veins, and his heart throbbed with violence and transport. His organs of speech acknowledged the wondrous potency of the charm, and he promised all that Mr. Bolton required. In this he acted weakly, perhaps ignobly. I attempt not to excuse him. But I will say that there are few who, in his situation, could have acted otherwise.

What important consequences may be deduced from trivial causes! How curious to follow trifling occurrences to their final effects, sometimes fatal, at other times beneficial! How often does poverty or riches, misery or happiness, death or life, depend on a circumstance apparently unimportant as the flight of a feather!

Julia was fond of birds, and she had, on her arrival at Bourdeaux, purchased two goldfinches, of that variety called cheverel; they were male and female, were quite tame, would answer when called (he Manon, and she

Manette) and even fly upon the finger. They had a nest, formed of fine moss, silk and camel's hair, in the centre of a little glass house, and were, when Julia purchased them, hatching five eggs. In a state of domesticity, the period of incubation is often delayed beyond the natural season. She became so fond of these intelligent, beautiful little creatures, that when she went to St. Uldrich, she took their house and them with her in the carriage; but the male met with an accident there, the second day after their arrival, that frightened her exceedingly. He had gone out of his house, which was always open, and was standing at Julia's window, when a hawk, that the servants kept about the *chateau*, darted on it, and though its mistress flew immediately to its rescue, one of its legs was broken.

Her grief on the occasion was extreme, and she brought the little sufferer with tears in her eyes to Theodore. He looked at the wound and undertook its cure. Her reliance on his humanity and skill was such that she left her favourite with him. And truly the tenderness and attention he bestowed on it justified her good opinion, and far exceeded whatever imperial wealth or despotick power has been able to purchase or extort from venal physicians or trembling attendants. He first restored the fractured bone to its proper situation, and then applied a bandage to keep it straight. To prevent the creature from injuring itself by any exertion, he put it into a cage barely large enough to contain it, and this he would sometimes carry in his bosom, in order to communicate to the poor bird the advantage of kindly warmth. Manon was not insensible of his cares. It would greet his visiting looks with its sweetest notes, and even embrace his finger with the grateful pressure of its bill.

In a few hours after the conversation, in which Mr. Bolton, Julia and he, had, as I have related, agreed on a speedy departure from the *chateau*, a person, not known to Theodore, accosted him, and said that he was sent by Madame Dalbert, his mother, who wished to see him at the village of Du Quesney, on the borders of the territory of St. Uldrich, where she was waiting to communicate to him some affair of importance. Supposing that she had declined approaching the *chateau* from motives of delicacy, as she was acquainted with neither the Count nor the *Comtesse*, and knowing that she had a journey to perform which would bring her through Du Quesney, he immediately departed, on foot, with the messenger, who was a young man of simple appearance, and who remained behind at a respectful distance as they walked towards the village.

Theodore would have taken one of the Count's horses, as he was still weak, but he disdained to be indebted to him for any accommodation. He had entered a village which was shaded by a thick plantation of larch and chesnut trees, when, suspecting no danger, he received from behind a sudden stroke of a loaded stick. The violence of the blow stunned and threw him. It had been given by his treacherous attendant, by whom and Gaspar Pontgebre, who now rushed forward from a thicket where he had lain concealed, the unhappy youth was in an instant bound and rendered incapable of resistance.

In some moments he recovered, in part, the powers of reflection, and was sensible of his extreme danger. He dreaded every evil that human nature may endure, and every outrage that brutal violence may inflict. The perturbation of his thoughts was encreased by the mystery that attended this proceeding, and by the *linguaggio grossalano*, or ruffian dialect of Naples, in which the two miscreants conversed. With the presence of Gaspar he associated the dread of being butchered, and the ideas of mischief, assassination and Count Egfryd. The conduct of this nobleman towards Miss Bolton had rendered him, since her disclosure in the morning, an object of suspicion and abhorrence to the virtuous Theodore, who possessed sufficient penetration to perceive that the attentions bestowed on the father and daughter, the pressing invitations which had led them to the *chateau*, and the ascent of the air-balloon, were all to be traced to the blackest designs. He had already believed the Count capable of any crime; he now recollected the *critique*, and he shuddered to think of the revenge of such a man.

"What! you, Gaspar Pontgebre," (on whose brutal brow at that moment hung treachery and murder) "attack me a second time, after my conduct towards you! surely you do not forget my kindness?"—"Oh, Sir! as to that you acted very kindly to me, I know, but I am only doing my duty now. This handy lad you see here, that knocked you down so neatly, is a new associate that I recommended to my employer. I knew him aboard ship, and was acquainted with his merits. But we are losing time: come this way, if you please, and we can talk as we go on."

So saying he dragged Theodore into a green lane that terminated in a path up the mountain.—"Now, Sir," said Gaspar, "first and foremost take notice, that if we should meet with any person, you must not speak; the first word you utter in that case shall be your last. Look at this machine. It is an air-gun. It contains a bullet that shall enter your heart, if you disobey this order. It makes no noise, and when you fall we shall say you are a madman, whom we are conducting to Deverac-au-parc, and that you have sunk into a fit that you are subject to. Believe me nobody will be very curious to inquire further, or inclined to prevent our carrying you off. Such are my instructions."

Theodore looked at the villain and then at the machine, and raised his eyes to heaven in silent horrour. To address himself to the feelings or compassion of such wretches, he thought would not only be useless, but humiliating. He therefore observed a haughty silence.—"Aye, aye, my master, you may sulk and frown as much as you please, 'tis little we mind you," cried the younger ruffian. They hurried him on so fast, that they soon reached the path and began to ascend the mountain. It was evening, and a lurid sky threatened a tempestuous night. No human being did they meet, no living creature did they see, save a solitary ass that sought a scanty meal among the heath and brambles, some gulls flying with rapid wing towards the south, as if anxious to escape to a less inhospitable region, and a distant *chamois* skipping among the rocks.

Their footing was slippery and insecure, and Theodore, his hands being bound, became soon fatigued. He inquired how much further they were to advance, and what was their object, for he no longer dreaded assassination.—"We have three miles further to go," said the unfeeling Gaspar, "and our object is merely to obey orders. We are assured that you shall never again see the face of man, neither do I suppose you will. I know my employer now so well that I have every confidence in him, and have no doubt of the extent of his power. Do you think I would ever part, you alive, after what passed between you and I in Bourdeaux, and what has happened this evening, if I was not convinced you would be deprived of the power of injuring me by any complaint? No, no, I am not so soft as that neither. We are ordered to leave you near *the grave*, tied to an elm tree that grows there, and to return to the town immediately; and a grave it will be to you, or I am much mistaken." Theodore cast down his head in mute despair.—"To tell you the truth," continued Gaspar, "I did not half like the job. I did not approve of putting myself in your power, do you see, if any accident should occur that would save your life. But there is no passing through this world without running some risk. Besides I have this in my favour, that nobody in Bourdeaux knows my real name or my present residence. My employer I believe guessed what would run in my mind, for in his letter he assures me positively you shall never be seen again, and he never was so liberal to me as on this occasion."

"What!" cried the prisoner, "to that fatal grave! Am I to be tortured in cold blood? Villains, unbind me! never shall I be forced to that scene of horrours! Rather kill me here." Uttering these words, he struggled violently to loose his hands, but without effect. He then threw himself on the ground and would not proceed. The assassins, unaffected by his distress, unmindful of the threats, the promises, the supplications, that he poured forth with the hurried vehemence of a man in extreme peril, and regardless of the resistance that he in vain employed, partly dragged, and partly carried their hapless victim to the dismal tree. To this they bound him.

"What," cried the youthful miscreant to his companion, "if we were to hide hereabouts until we saw who would appear to the prisoner? We should thus have a clue to find our unknown employer, perhaps we should see himself."—"Bless your soul!" said the other, "how silly you are! To arrive here we have climbed a smooth bare rock for the last mile, and besides that, there is no hiding-place hereabouts. It is clear that any body standing there above could command a view of the smallest object for miles all about. It would be a miracle if we succeeded, and it is a hundred to one if we should not perish in the attempt. Our employer, who is at this moment looking at us, perhaps listening to what we say, would certainly murder us; his precautions are wonderful, and the devil himself has not more ingenuity: for my part, I dread him more than I do the devil."—"I believe you are right," replied the other, "so we may as well be going. Good evening, *Monsieur*. Good evening, Sir."—"Oh, cruel men! Surely, surely, you will not, cannot, desert me in this forlorn and savage place? The night already advances, and promises to be inclement. I have been lately ill, and shall I be exposed to the horrours of such a situation, to the imminent and dreadful danger of being devoured alive by wild beasts? Do not, oh! do not, Gaspar, forget the time when I saved your life."—"Good evening, *Monsieur*, good evening," returned that ungrateful monster with a sneer, and he departed with the other.

The winds began to whistle. Darkness soon covered the face of nature. The sable car of night passed with frightful velocity across the canopy of heaven. The ancient tree shook forth abrupt and alarming sounds as it yielded to the hurried blasts. The raging of the sea against the cliff spread over the rocks and mountains the desolating accents of the grave. The howling of distant wolves, caught by the growing storm, strike upon the terrified ear of Theodore. The black clouds discharge their torrents on his unprotected head. The storm every moment increases; the tempest rages; the thunder peals; the lightning strikes.—"God of nature! what duty have I neglected, what crime committed, to deserve this misery? Feeble and exhausted, am I to groan through hours of suffering, incapable of motion, till my murderer comes to plunge me, mayhap, into greater torment? Am I to stand, tied to this stake, till the starved, ferocious animals of the desert scent out their prey, and tear me piecemeal? Almighty Providence! pity my ravings, punish not my presumption. Thy justice is supreme. Thy wisdom is unspeakable." The unhappy youth bent his head, shut his eyes, thought on Julia, and prepared to die.

An hour of torture passed. The inclemency of the weather became yet more violent, and the moon had risen, rendering now to the organ of sight, what had before been only heard or felt. Though the lightnings appeared less vivid, the clouds were more black, and their furious encounters more terribly distinct. Hah! what fearful crash is that? The bolt of heaven strikes the lofty elm. It yields. It splits. The quickness of the stroke, its violence, and a strong sulphureous smell, at once rouse and appal the prisoner. His head and back suffer severe contusions. He would kneel, but his cords forbid the attempt. He offers a pious ejaculation. Terrour has entered his very heart.—"Gracious, incomprehensible, Almighty Being! Thou——." He would have proceeded, but a rude hand suddenly grasped his throat.

"Villain, at length in my power, never shall you escape my hold. Do you know me, creature?"—"Count Egfryd, I expected this."—"Did you so? 'tis well. But did you expect what you are to meet? Know, imbecile, mischievous, pernicious animal, that this is the happiest moment of my life. I have you in my power, and that power is unlimited and to be equalled only by my vengeance. Never did man hate man as I hate you; and this hate I can indulge, can satiate, with absolute security."—"Hate me! Ah! what have I done to deserve your hate?"—"Done! more than your worst sufferings can repay. Much more than murder could requite. But my joy produces delay. We must from this. Come, my critical amorous adventurer, we shall try your fortitude."—With these words the Count placed a board to Theodore's breast, and slipped another between the tree and his back. Having tied both together, and secured his arms effectually, he released him from the shattered elm. In the back board was a hook, and to this a rope being fastened, the ferocious Count pulled the object of his vengeance forward to the precipice. Arrived there, he fastened the end of the rope to the iron ring, and placed the miserable sufferer upon his feet.

The moon shone brightly, but the tempest raged, the thunders rattled, and the blue lightnings still shot their fiery darts across the firmament. The sea, inflamed and foaming, boiled in mountains, and rocked the foundations of the continent. All was visible, but all was aggravated by night. What during the day would have been obscure was now deadly, what had been deep became profound, what suspicious was terrible, what alarming, direful. Each cloud had the blackness of revenge, each wave a shade of death.—"Seest thou this cliff, fool?" said the nefarious Count in a triumphant voice. "Thou knowest it well; thou hast visited it from curiosity, now occupy it from necessity. Exhausted, powerless, thou now shalt be precipitated into the abyss, thence never, never, never, to rise again. Hah, hah, hah, hah!" The fiend at this moment felt the transport of Satan when he ruined our first parents. His laugh made night more dismal, and gave even to *the grave* new horrour.

"Count Egfryd, hear me for one, only one moment. I have already endured more than ordinary torments. I merit not your wrath, nay I deserve your pity. If I cast myself on my knees before you, as I now do, upon this flint, if I prostrate myself at your feet, you may despise me, but you, surely, will not deny me your compassion. A widowed mother depends upon my exertions for her support. Upon my life your happiness depends. Yes, tremendous man, rob me of life, and the canker of remorse will never grant you a moment's ease. The hell you sought and deserved will follow you eternally. My murdered spirit will pursue your steps, and nightly hover over your sleepless couch. You will live wretched and abhorred, and will die unlamented, cursed, and for what? to revenge an imaginary injury. Imaginary it is. I never wronged you. I have esteemed, but I never despised, I have loved, but I never hated you. I criticised your work, it is true, but upon my honour, and by all that man holds sacred, I knew not when I wrote whose work it was. I love Miss Bolton, I confess, but for that am I to blame? could I have supposed that *you* were my rival? Ah! let me conjure you, in this suppliant attitude, as you tender your peace, as you value your safety, as you regard your immortal soul, as you dread the Almighty justice, grant me my life; so may Heaven shower its blessings on your head, and may I sink into everlasting perdition, if ever I whisper to mortal ear a syllable of this transaction! Enjoy, then, the luxury of doing good, and bind me to your service by ties of eternal gratitude."

The cliff, against which the ocean was now vainly expending its fury, was not more cold nor more unmoved than the inexorable Count.—"This last humiliation was necessary to my triumph. Know, changeling, that I defy remorse and hell, that I laugh at your canting about conscience, and that in nature there does not breathe a thing so loathsome to my sight, so offensive to my thought as you. Your promises and your threats I alike deride. You believe in the existence, and rely on the power of your Providence; then why be terrified at the prospect of this precipice? Your terrours give your words the lie. Cease your sneaking supplications. Look at that fathomless abyss. Look!"

The malefactor about to be launched from the tree of justice into eternity; the wretch on the brink of the sulphurous chasm occasioned by an earthquake, and who expects to be swallowed alive at its next convulsion, feels serenity compared with what Theodore now suffered. It was a prospect to petrify the boldest.—"Look into that fathomless abyss, to that thou art condemned for ever. Into it. Away!"—"Oh! oh! oh! mercy! mercy! may God have mercy——" shrieked the agonized victim of cruelty and crime.

His shuddering frame, incapable of resistance, pushed impetuously into the horrid deep, lost the sensations of life before the visitation of death, but lost them only for a moment. Arrived to the length of the rope that connected him with the world, a frightful distance of one hundred feet, his rapid descent received a check so violent, so shocking, that animation returned from the very poignancy of his pain, from the intenseness of his torture. Every bone felt as if it had been broken, every fibre as if 'twere cracked, every muscle as if torn. The blood experienced a sudden revulsion, that took from the springs of life their natural current. His breath failed. The spasms of expiring nature shook his limbs, a sanguine stream poured from his mouth. In this situation, intolerable, unparalleled and indescribable, lashed every minute by the angry waves, and driven by the winds through the infernal vaults of this interminable sepulchre, he remained not long. The evil spirit of *the grave*, the fearless, the inhuman Egfryd, with active intrepidity and devilish exultation, descended to the cavern. The tiger drew his prey into the den, and having removed him to the closest recess of the subterranean abode, chained him to a rock, and removed from his breast and back the boards that confined him. He still appeared dead, but animation was only suspended. After some time he heaved a deep sigh, opened his eyes with a vacant stare, and moved his limbs.

The pains which death had terminated, returned with returning life. Red hot irons applied to the flesh, boiling oil, lashes, pincers, flames, give not greater anguish than that which he endured. It was every where at once, and yet seemed to fly from limb to limb, from joint to joint, from organ to organ, from vein to vein, with a quickness and severity exceeding the experience of all human suffering. He groaned, he writhed, he shrieked.—"He will be very well presently," cried his abominable persecutor. "I must now return to prevent suspicion. With you, *Madame*, (to Marie de Solase) I shall leave the wretch till my next visit, when I will make my final arrangements." He then ascended, and with him took the rope which was mentioned in the last chapter under the name of the second rope, lest Theodore recovering and breaking his chains, should attempt to escape by it; needless precaution! for who but Egfryd could have dared to use it?

Marie de Solase had for some time entertained jealousies of the merciless Count, and suspected him of an intention to trifle with her. The pardon he had promised to obtain for her, she despaired of procuring, and all her entreaties to have her escape to another country effected, he evaded with evident disingenuousness.

She looked on him as her oppresser, she conceived for him a rooted aversion, but her existence depended on his protection, and she was compelled to affect gentleness, gratitude and attachment. The arrival of Theodore was a new era in her captivity. Theirs was a common cause, and the profligate mutability of her nature already marked him as an object of her unworthy passion. She made for him a comfortable bed. She poured cordials into his mouth. She removed his wet clothes. She dried his hair, and she bathed his feet in warm water. The fatigue he had undergone, the agitation he had suffered, and the pains he had endured, had exhausted his strength, and brought on a crisis which in a short time, maugre his pangs of mind and body, terminated in sleep. It was the last effort of nature to preserve vitality.

Marie de Solase meanwhile prepared a nutritious jelly for him when he should awake, corrected the disorder of her dress, heightened the attractions of her person, dried his clothes before a large fire, burned some perfumed pastiles, and hung poor Manon at a sufficient distance from the monkey. It is strange how it survived the rudeness of the treatment its master had received, but the wire of its little iron cage was strong, and had not yielded much to the pressure of the board, and Theodore's coat had protected it in some measure from the waves. The creature, however, was nearly dead with wet and fright, when its new mistress placed it in a warm situation. She gave it water in her thimble, and some thistle seed which dropped from its master's pocket, and which is so well known to be their favourite food, that from *chardon* or thistle, comes *chardonneret*, the French term for a goldfinch. Escaped from his danger, Manon was not long till he rewarded her for her care with one of his sweetest chirps.

"Ah!" cries the incredulous critick, "silly author, what hast thou undertaken? Thy romantick pen having first lifted thee in a preposterous balloon, from which with the utmost difficulty thou escapedest, has now led thee into a cavern more horrible than that of the Cyclops. Thy heroine is in a castle exposed to the outrages of a villain, to whose arts and violence she must succumb; and thy hero is, at the commencement of thy work, placed in a situation from which no human exertion can rescue him. Unity will be injured, probability outraged, and poetick justice violated. Where is thy judgment? Where is thy taste? I pity thy attempt, but it is wretched and will be despised. Thou wilt be forced to close thy tale before it is finished, or thou must be guilty of the absurdity of throwing down the cliff by an earthquake, or of saving Theodore by a miracle. This, or the clumsy resource of placing the Count on his untimely deathbed, where he is to confess all, and to prove the author a miserable dunce."

Criticks, criticks, cease your insulting insinuations. I have, according to the Psalmist, "chosen the way of truth." I describe nothing but what has happened. As I live I tell no falsehood. Faith-worthy witnesses can corroborate my facts. I am past the age of invention; "on my eye-lids," as on Job's, "is the shadow of death," and my character is above the reach of aspersion. A moral principle demands this sacrifice of my repose. My abhorrence of vice and my love of virtue require this narration. For once, throw away your rules and your balances. Learn to estimate works not by calculation and measurement, but by genius, invention and utility. On the last I rely. My personages are uncommon, I know, and the incidents I relate extraordinary. But do I mention any thing that is beyond belief, any thing that is impossible? I said, and I repeat it, that it is my peculiar lot to be the historian of romantick realities, the narrator of seeming fiction. My children, to you I consign the task of vindicating my fame. To you I bequeath the happiness of reaping the reward of my honest labours, of hearing my authority pronounced unquestionable, and of finding my book placed among the authentick records of morality.

But as I must draw scenes of novelty, surprise and horrour, gift me, oh Godwin!* with thy magick pencil. As I must convey the emotions of virtuous hearts in situations of extreme difficulty and danger, and the tempests of rage in the bosoms of the impious and abandoned, teach me, master as thou art, to acquire thy rich and flowing style, and thy matchless powers of description. Who but thou has the talent of embodying fancy, and pursuing moral sensibility through all the intricacies of the human heart? Who but thou can create a new being, invest him with new capacities, and endow him with a refinement and flight of soul that exceed our imitation, and almost demand our worship? Painter of nature! Man of eloquence! grant me a spark of thy genius, a breath of thy expression; so may my cautious finger copy the delicate shading of thy Falkland,* and my fervid words convey a portion of thy St. Leon!*

END OF VOL. I.

The Mysterious Hand

Volume II

THE

MYSTERIOUS HAND.

CHAPTER I.

Divine Foi! dont la puissance
Guide nos esprits à ton gré,
Je me vois par ton influence
Au sein de la Divinité.
Quel éclat!

....

Come then, Religion! Holy, Heaven-born maid,
Thou surest refuge in our day of trouble;——
To thy great guidance, to thy strong protection,
I give my child.

....

The crickets sing, and man's o'er-laboured sense
Repairs itself by rest: our Tarquin, thus,
Did softly press the rushes ere he wakened
The chastity he wounded.————
O, sleep! Thou ape of death, lie dull upon her,
And be her sense but as a monument,
Thus in a chapel lying.

Some days of anxiety and alarm passed after the disappearance of Theodore. Every one regretted him. Every one apprehended that some unhappy accident had befallen him. The Count affected distress; Mr. Bolton was uneasy, but Julia was really unhappy. She sometimes looked at the former with an eye of suspicion, but she was too good and innocent herself to entertain her suspicions long, and he dissembled concern so well, that at length she acquitted him in her mind of any treachery towards this unhappy sufferer.—What can have happened to him? she would say to herself. May he not be detained by some business, or confined by some slight illness? It is certain that no one could have the cruelty to kill him. Perhaps he will come back by and by.—She was restless and miserable. Every moment she would inquire if any tidings of him had been received, if any letter from him had arrived. Alas! there were no tidings; there was no letter. Messengers had been sent in every direction, but no trace of him had they discovered. He was lost. In this state of things she walked pensively into the Gothick chapel, and closed the door after her. She had been educated to respect the forms, and to believe the tenets of the Roman church. She devoutly observed the former and she believed implicitly in the latter.

Had Julia been a heathen, she had, nevertheless, been interesting and amiable; but as a Catholick her virtues became refined and excellent. This religion had converted her persuasion to faith, her affections to duties, her love to devotion, and her piety to adoration. Her chasteness was virginity and her mildness Christianity. She walked slowly towards the altar, and there kneeling down, poured out the unpremeditated effusions of a pious heart.

"Heavenly Theresa!* Benevolent intercessor! Look with complacency on a sinner, and despise not her prayer. Deign to hearken to my supplications, and mediate, I beseech thee, between the divine wrath and Theodore. Help me in my affliction, and preserve him from all danger. Protect him, govern him, lead him in the path of virtue, and give him, ah! give him once again in safety to my longing sight. Grant my prayer, beatified Virgin! who now lookest upon me with an aspect of benignity from thy heavenly abode, and let me not sue in vain!"

The chapel in which this prayer was offered was a place to inspire sentiments of religious fervour, to humble the pretensions of human pride, to extinguish frivolity, and to dissipate the clouds of arrogance and selfishness. A venerable and awful gloom prevailed in every part of it. A deathlike silence reigned throughout. It was an artificial grove, but darker and more retired than that of Dodona.* The dim rays of coloured light that entered it through the variegated casements partook of the austerity of the building. The symbols of revelation, the hallowed signs of Christian mysteries, and the sufferings of the martyrs and of their God, that every where met the eye in this consecrated spot, might awaken sentiments of piety in an apostate, or fill the atheist with terrour. A solemnity, sacred if not supernatural, marked this chapel as the abode on earth of all that man holds reverend. Involuntary respect and lowly humility, and an indefinite inward sense of mystick importance, were inspired by it. It was the quiet mansion of the happy. It communicated with heaven. It threatened hell. Its majestick dome how lofty, how impressive! Its nave and aisles how grand, how rich, how diversified! Its altar how simple, how sublime! How beautiful is the whole, how apparently interminable are its parts!

Man of faith, kneel on that marble; look on that cross, sign of mercy, pledge of salvation! From thence to heaven is a road broad and bright. Angels, in thousands and in tens of thousands, float betwixt, carrying thy prayers to the throne of grace. In those entangled boughs of stone the tutelary saints of fallen man watch over thy safety and join in thy adoration. Beneath that roof of infinite complexity, choirs of happy souls pour forth the harmony of gratitude and love, and offer to thy acceptance a place in joy. Man of faith, beneath those hallowed vaults our enemy is hidden, gnashing his teeth with agony at their happiness, and seeking to seduce thee from righteousness and heaven to the path of utter and everlasting torment. Ah! shun his snares; it is Satan that invites, and if thou hearken to him, damnation will be thy lot.

Julia after her prayers sunk her forehead on her hands, and wept from tenderness and agitation. Relieved by her devotion and her tears, a gleam of joy illuminated her mind, a religious nerve thrilled through her heart, hope filled her bosom, and a pious enthusiasm seized on her imagination. She shut her eyes, clasped her hands with force, and communed in mysterious silence (her swelling lips unclosed) with her beneficent, celestial patroness. Visions of bliss glowed on her mental sight. Rapt, inspired, a holy frenzy lifts her soul, she feels the force of supernal grace. She throws off her grosser frame. She treads the golden paths of heaven. She breathes the living gale of immortality. She is received by her sainted mother and all the blessed who sing joyful hallelujahs. Floods of eternal light burst upon her ravished spirit. She is all purity, all happiness. Her prayer is heard, her Theodore is safe.

Reformation, if properly so called, what hast thou done? Infidelity, what wouldst thou dare? Behold the virtuous, the innocent Julia. Consider her feelings at this moment, and reflect on the purity of her mind. Bethink you of her faith in the efficacy of her prayers. Forget not her reliance on the intercession of her saint, and keep in recollection that she has an absolute conviction on her mind that the sanctified Theresa is present, and attends to her obsecrations. Know that her happiness at this moment surpasses what the ignorant sceptick with all his vanity, or the empty philosophist with all his petulance, is capable of conceiving. That it exceeds what the pompous Pagan in the frenzy of a fallacious faith had ever hoped to enjoy. And shall she be deprived of it? For what? To despise the forms of ancient worship, to scorn the amiable weaknesses of traditionary doctrine, to wrap herself in the phlegm of cold indifference, or yield to the pangs of dumb despair? to see in man and nature matter alone, dull and sluggish matter? To be dead to the poetry of spiritualized devotion, the sentiment of prayer, the feeling of inspiration; to be insensible of the refined and exquisite sensuality of a mystick adoration? To be warmed by no sacred visions, to receive no angelick warnings, to be transported by no supernatural and incomprehensible ecstacies, to trust in no holy and immaterial agencies, to feel her own weakness and the helplessness of her nature, and yet to expect no providential assistance, no protection from above?—No, by Heavens! she shall preserve the religion of her fathers. She shall pour forth her vows in simplicity and love, with familiarity and gentleness, to the patroness of her youth. That patroness will hearken to her prayers and attend at her invitation, will comfort her perturbed spirit, will pardon her venial transgressions, will intercede for her heavier faults, will pour balm into her soul, and whisper consolation and felicity. Divine faith! Happy, thrice happy, they who acknowledge thy supremacy!

Julia with lightened heart and chearful countenance retired from the chapel. Her alarms were quieted, her hopes were revived, her serenity was restored. She had since the adventure of the balloon observed a distant but polite manner toward the Count, and though she now felt herself unsafe and unhappy at St. Uldrich, yet she willingly assented to her father's intention to remain there till they should learn some account of Theodore. The Count for several days never left the *chateau*, his absence he thought might expose him to suspicion, but his mind was a theatre where all the angry and unamiable passions raged. He had overheard what had passed between Theodore and Julia on the morning of his disappearance. He was therefore well aware of her sentiments, and convinced that any endeavour on his part to weaken her principles of virtue or to recommend his infamous suit by argument or sophistry, would not only be treated with contempt, but resisted as well from attachment to another as hatred to himself. Any libertine but himself would under these circumstances, have relinquished his enterprise as chimerical, absurd and impossible, but he resolved to subdue Miss Bolton or perish in the attempt. His pride as well as his profligacy was engaged, and victory must be obtained at any price.

After her devotions she passed the day in tranquillity and resignation, and immediately after supper retired to her apartment. This consisted of a bedchamber and closet; the former was hung with tapestry woven in ancient times in the looms of the *Hotel Royal* at Paris. The subject of it was an attack of cavalry made during the conquest of *Franche Comté* by Lewis the Fourteenth, from a drawing of M. Le Brun, director of the *Gobelins*.* Nothing could be more brilliant than the colours, nothing more spirited than the design. The floor of the room was of marble, and covered with a rich Turkey carpet. The ceiling, which consisted of many segments of arches, was painted with art and taste; the ornaments of the room, together with the bed and the *sultan*,* were of lilac and crimson. The *ruelle** of her bed, according to the French custom, was large and lofty, the *toilette* was superb, and in the closet were placed her harp, her books, her bath, her writing-desk, and a sopha.

She this evening retired unusually early. She wished for privacy and to indulge in the luxury of solitude, and the presence of the Count became every moment more disagreeable to her. In addition to these motives, she found herself unwell. An uneasiness, a nervous agitation, a heat, a heaviness, had seized her. She felt no pain, she complained of no weakness, but she experienced sensations till then unknown to her. Retired to her chamber she placed herself at the window, and tried, by looking at the moon and inhaling the breeze of night, to recover her usual coolness and tranquillity. The stillness of nature at this hour, the clearness of the azure sky, the mild brightness of the luminary, all should have co-operated to quiet perturbation and restore composure. But Julia's restlessness increased. She became sleepy, and yet she was disinclined to repose. Her cheeks glowed with heat, her arms sunk with languor. Her thoughts, at once obscure and active, rested on Theodore. Her fancy, indistinctly fond, yielded him to her closing eyes, and she experienced the disorder or the transport of a vague and wild conception joined to a lively sensibility. She continued her endeavours to rouse herself. She entered her closet. She sealed a letter for England, and seated herself on the sopha with an intention to direct it. The pen fell from her hand. Her heavy lids refused obedience to her will, and closed with resistless force the organ of sight. On the sopha she slept, but so heavily as if she were no more to wake, and in her sleep such dreams seized her unquiet mind as never before disturbed her. So ardent, so tumultuous were they, that her tongue moved in incoherent distraction, and her limbs stretched with involuntary and morbid energy.

But no dream however vivid, no motion however violent, had the power to rouse her from her lethargy. Nay, had force been employed for that purpose, it would not probably have availed. In her ravings the most revolting images presented themselves, but surely the purity of her mind did not, from these unspontaneous wanderings, become less admirable or less immaculate. The intention it is that decides human virtue and human culpability, and at the awful day of judgment, mild will be the accusation against those who have transgressed involuntarily or by compulsion.

Sometimes she would seem to herself to relinquish the sober precepts of her youth, and to smile with thoughtless complacency at the derelictions of propriety; but the remorse that would immediately follow was painful and terrible. Her father, she fancied, offered to conduct her into a scene of repose and happiness, but with a criminal and unaccountable inconsistence, she rejected his assistance, and courted the shocking objects of her dread and danger. Sometimes she would see the Count, hardened in impudence and debauchery, present to her view a front of boldness and libertinism, at the same time that he outraged her ears with the most insulting professions of his odious passion. Pollution, she thought, attended on his touch, and ruin hung upon his eye. Against the presumption of his manner she tried to frown, to shriek, but her muscles refused their office, her rebellious organ denied a sound, and she seemed to suffer a total revolt of her limbs and senses.

At a late hour next day she was awakened by Mademoiselle De Sagoné. She opened her eyes with that feeling of horrour and alarm that a person under the pressure of a heavy calamity, or the sentence of a severe punishment, or stung by an accusing conscience for an atrocious crime, may be supposed to experience when roused suddenly from sleep and a dismal dream. Mademoiselle De Sagoné was a young lively brunette, between whom and Julia there subsisted a great intimacy. At the pressing solicitations of the former, who in consequence of early prejudice never slept alone, they had the day before agreed to occupy the same bed while they should remain in the *chateau.* "Is it possible," said she in French, "Julia, that you passed the night in this closet? I laid down at an early hour in your chamber, thinking that you would soon join me, but from your present appearance I should suppose you did not undress at all. For my part, I have had such a shocking time of it since I fell asleep, and I have been tormented with such horrid dreams, that my head is at this moment ready to split."—" *'Tis so with me,"* replied Julia. *"I have lain here in a sort of trance all night,* and I find a confusion in my thoughts that cannot be described. My stomach, too, is much disordered."—"It is very strange," returned the other; "we must certainly have taken something at supper that disagreed with us." Her suspicion was just. They both had suffered from the same cause, for each had tasted of a *bouillon*, which was intended by the Count for Miss Bolton alone. *Mademoiselle De Sagoné*, being of a robust constitution, felt little immediate injury from it, and she was able in a few minutes to dress for breakfast; but Julia, whose health and frame were delicate, found it necessary to remain in her apartment during the day.

Languid and dejected she endeavoured in vain, when

left alone, to call to her recollection the course of her wanderings, the detail of her ravings. The impression they had left was deep, but dark, and all she knew was that she had been agitated, affrighted, tortured, to a degree and in a manner beyond her waking conception.

What could be the cause of such terrible effects? she asked herself, what had she eaten, what had she drank, that could have occasioned her illness, that could have produced a sleep, a trance rather, so profound, so fearful, so preternatural? Her meditations were indistinct but terrifying. She had heard of the vampire and the hag of night, and she had read of incubus and incantation. Witchcraft and drugs, the philtres of vitious love, and the imps of perdition, opiates, charms, and conjurations, passed in a rapid and revolting series through her thoughts. A deadly fear seized her heart, a cold perspiration bedewed her frame.

Addressing herself to the Virgin, and kissing her golden crucifix, she implored the assistance of Heaven, and besought the protection of that Providence which never forsakes the virtuous. Her faith prevailed. Her mind once more resumed its happy serenity, and when her father visited her, which he did after she had bathed and taken some tea, she was able to speak to him with composure. Her mental disorder gradually subsided. The clouds of her heavy sleep were insensibly dispersed; and the clearness of her intellect was restored.

Mr. Bolton, whose love for his daughter could only be equalled by his paternal attention, with delight observed the amendment in her looks, and remained with her most of the day. She did not venture to quit her apartment till towards evening, when, leaning on his arm, she took a short walk in the demain. The warmth of the air, the quietness of the scene, the presence of her father, the warbling of the birds, and perhaps the languor of her own frame, all contributed to produce that chearful resignation, that luxury of sentiment, which transports humanity to the confines of Heaven. She looked at her father with an expression of attachment and innocence, she thought of his uniform tenderness with gratitude, and a tear of sensibility glistened in each eye. She recollected that awful moment when her pious mother departed for a better world, and she recalled to her memory the last look of Theodore. Buried in these thoughts, and absent in mind, the Count suddenly met them. Beneath his mask of politeness, a feeling of wicked triumph was discernible, while his enquiries about her health were delivered in a tone, and with a look, that brought to her recollection some of the horrours of her dream. She blushed, she faltered, she sunk upon her father, and would have fallen but for his assistance. Having recovered a little, the Count offered her his arm. Leaning on both, her head stooping, and her eyes cast down, she entered the *chateau*, and immediately retired to her apartment.

Mademoiselle De Sagoné, alarmed by what she had suffered the night before in Julia's apartment, determined to lie during her stay at the *chateau*, in the chamber of her mother the *Marquise*. Miss Bolton now, the first time in her life, was apprehensive of sleeping alone; she wished much that Ellen, her English servant, should place a bed in her room, but she dreaded expressing such a wish, lest she should excite a greater alarm in her father's breast respecting her health than what he already felt, and she could not keep Ellen with her without his knowledge. She determined, therefore, to remain alone as usual.

As soon as her father left her at night, she secured the

door more carefully than usual, and with a candle in her hand proceeded to survey every corner of her apartment. New fears and vague suspicions disturbed her mind, producing an excessive and perhaps useless caution. Her closet was wainscotted all round with solid oak, its ceiling was arched with stone, and its floor was marble. The ceiling and floor of her bedchamber were of similar materials, and its sides were covered with tapestry. The tapestry was, she soon discovered, attached by silver nails to a wooden wainscot, which in every part returned a sound of steady solidity, and immovable weight. It was almost certain, then, that there was no place of concealment, no secret door, either in the chamber or the closet. To render her investigation decisive of security, she placed some pieces of furniture, one over another, in the latter, and standing on the uppermost one, she with the end of an iron key, obtained demonstration of the reality of its stone ceiling. It was plaistered and painted, but there was no deception. She next examined her windows, but they were well secured. Her scrutiny was performed slowly and carefully, and it had now employed her two hours; but not yet satisfied, she proceeded to try the roof of her chamber in the same manner that she had proved that of the closet, and in one place she thought a hollow sound was returned.

The part that she thought yielded this sound was one of the many sections of elliptical arches that supported the superstructure. It was painted like the rest, and in no respect differed from them in appearance, but striking it with more force, and comparing the noise with that which was returned from each of the other segments, she had no longer a doubt that there was a vacancy above it. Could any thing be more terrifying than such a discovery? Her sight acquired new sharpness, her hearing new delicacy. She pushed against the suspected spot, but it was immovable. She viewed it, felt it, and it betrayed no deceit, but she sounded it and it was hollow.

The subject painted on it was the apparition evoked by the hag of Endor for Saul.* The ground was black, and along the edge of the witch's drapery, she, at length, by dint of examination, discovered something like a crevice. Having got another candle to assist her sight, Julia succeeded in tracing this crevice through other dark parts of the picture, till she discovered what she considered a door of irregular shape. It was about four feet long and its widest part was about two feet. No eye but that of fear could have discovered it. She next searched for hinges, and found them at one end, when, pushing with all her strength against the other end, it yielded. It is a secret door, it opens.

Julia had no sooner reduced her suspicions respecting it to certainty, than she descended with precipitation to the floor, left her candles on her *toilette*, and flew to her chamber door. This she unlocked hastily, and then rushed into the corridor. All was silent. All was black. She trembled in every joint. Her teeth chattered. Unable to stand, she sunk upon her knees. Whither should she fly? She knew not the way to her father's apartment. She knew not Ellen's room, nor that of her friend *Mademoiselle De Sagoné*. To advance were as terrible as to retreat. To traverse by herself and in the dead of night a gloomy pile of building, to involve herself in the intricacies of its various windings, to lose herself in the labyrinth of its complicated apartments, was horrible in the extreme. To take a candle in her hand and by loud cries awake all its inhabitants was the first measure that occurred to her, but, alas! she wanted courage even to breathe, and were it to save her life, she durst not disturb the universal stillness by the slightest noise. As Julia deliberates, now about to rise from her knees, her head inclined, her hands extended, her mouth half open, a distant sound, like that of a step of a man who seeks to escape observation, reaches her ear. Her heart beats violently. It is a step. It strikes against something in the dark. She wishes to cry "who's there?" but her voice absolutely fails her. She retreats to her room, the door of which still remained open. Her knees knock one against the other. She is nearly dead with fright. With difficulty she enters her room, and as she is about to close the door, the sound of a suppressed sneeze from an adjoining gallery distinctly strikes her ear. A shriek of terrour escapes from her, and she has just force enough left to lock herself in, when throwing herself on the *sultan*, and looking, scarcely alive, at the dreadful door in the ceiling, she remains gasping and motionless, expecting every instant to see it opened by the nefarious Count. She continues to gaze on it for a considerable length of time. Its stirs not. She hears no noise, and her heart by degrees beats with less violence. In this situation Julia remained, vigilant and fearful, till the blushes of Aurora streaked the east. The splendour and the chearfulness of morning revived in some degree her exhausted spirits, and dispelled much of her alarm. She placed herself at one of her windows, still looking at the treacherous door, till, at length, she insensibly sunk into a slumber. From this she was awakened by Ellen. She felt herself little refreshed, but not so ill as she had been the morning before.

She deliberated with herself about the discovery she had made. Should she tell her father of it, and conceal all she knew besides? The only consequence would be, she feared, a change of apartment. Should she disclose to him what had occurred in the balloon, and the terrours of her dream, what mischiefs would she not have to apprehend? His safety might be endangered, and perhaps her own innocence rendered questionable. In short, what evil was there that might not be dreaded from the courage, the arts, and the villainy of the Count? It was a subject of great importance and one that required much deliberation. She could think of no mode of proceeding that was not objectionable. She found herself unable to come to a final determination, and all she could resolve on, for the present, was never again to remain for a night by herself in her present apartment, and to leave the *chateau* as soon as she possibly could.

CHAPTER II.

Era lo loco, ove a scender la riva
Venimmo, alpestro, e per quel ch' iv' er' anco,
Tal, ch' ogni vista ne sarebbe schiva.

....

Qual' è quella ruina, che nel fianco
Di qua da Trento l'Adice percosse,
O per tremuoto, o per sostegno manco.

....

Il giovinetto con piedi, e con braccia
Percotendo venia l' orribil' onde.

Theodore awoke after a sleep of ten hours. He felt violent pains in his head; his chest, back and sides were much contused, and every muscle in his body had a sensation of soreness. He remained motionless for some time endeavouring to collect his scattered thoughts, and to call to his mind the strange and shocking events of the day before. The romantick appearance and uncommon splendour of his grotesque apartment, the extraordinary cruelty that had been exercised on him, and his apparently miraculous preservation were so unlike reality, so far removed from the probable, that for some time he doubted if he were awake, or if all these things were not the illusions of a disordered imagination. He listened with surprise and apprehension to the hollow noises of echoed waterfalls, that for ever reverberated through the subterranean chambers. He moved his eyes to prove to himself that he actually saw. His organ of smelling he employed to determine the fragrance of the air he breathed. He passed his hands over different parts of his body to ascertain that he really felt, and he would have stirred his feet but for a heavy chain that confined them. He is not in a dream, his senses are all awake. It is too true that he is the wretched victim of unprecedented depravity, and that the acute pains he feels are those of unprecedented suffering. He recollects being precipitated into the abyss, and the horrible shock that bereft him of animation. Of all that passed afterwards he is utterly ignorant. As he ponders upon his unhappy situation, and looks with astonishment at the glittering decorations of the cavern, now illuminated with wax candles, the sound of a guitar in a low and plaintive movement, accompanied by a delicate female voice, strikes his ear. It is an Italian air that he had often sung himself. He turns his head to see the musician, and beholds Marie de Solase in an elegant undress standing near his bed-side. She had heightened her natural charms with *rouge*. Her hair of the finest texture and of a glossy black, was turned in an antique wreath and secured by a silver comb. One small foot appeared in a *mule de chambre* of white satin, and her hands and arms, of admirable shape and colour, were gracefully employed upon her instrument.

He who regards the Medicean Venus as the standard of female perfection, would perhaps have thought Marie too fat, but such was the justness of her proportions, such the clearness of her skin, such the springiness of every muscle and the firmness of each swelling surface, that singular and fastidious must he be who could refuse her the praise of beauty. Theodore's pains were for a moment forgotten by him. His eyes were dazzled by the lustre of the object before him. Who can this be? thought he. Whither have I been transported? What am I to suppose? If I were superstitious I should believe that I was under the influence of enchantment, but in truth my senses are still so confused, my mind so bewildered, that I in vain seek to reconcile the horrours of my recollection with the wonders that now engage me. In vain I endeavour to account for my preservation or to develop the mystery that attends it. She, perceiving that he was awake, and reading astonishment in his countenance, suspended her performance and summoned to her features all the tenderness they could assume. "You are here, Sir," said she with counterfeited embarrassment, "a prisoner, and I am appointed your gaoler, but never was gaoler less harsh than you shall find me, or less inclined to inflict the miseries of confinement. Alas! a prisoner myself, I feel too severely the cruelty of captivity not to endeavour to mitigate your affliction." Here she put her handkerchief to her eyes.

"Lovely and amiable apparition," replied Theodore, "I feel that to you I am indebted for life; oh! tell me how I have been conveyed to this brilliant grotto. What have I to expect? what to think? and that my gratitude may not be silent, confirm my opinion that you are the preserver of my being."—"The offices of humanity, Sir," said she, "deserve little praise. You were conveyed hither by your inexorable and merciless foe, the Count D'Egfryd—you were chained by him to that rock, and left speechless and insensible. At the risk of offending him, I placed you, as soon as he departed, in the situation in which you now find yourself, and by continuing my cares I hope soon to see you perfectly restored."—"Oh my God, my God!" cried he, "what a barbarian! His perfidy, his violence, his atrocity, flash across my memory, and with them *the grave:* ah! was I not precipitated into that horrible abyss? how then have I escaped death?"

" 'Twere long to explain this to you now, Sir; another time you shall know all. At present you must take some refreshment that I have prepared for you." With these words she left him. In her absence he endeavoured to rise, but he soon found that he was too weak and too sore to quit his bed. He, therefore, having raised himself a little, sunk back upon his pillow and there remained motionless and patient.

In two days he was much recovered. No invalid could be better attended. Marie was assiduous and tender, and never was nurse more vigilant or kind. Gratitude and admiration on his part, and on hers the artifices of accomplished seduction, rendered them in a short time intimate. Companions in misery, inhabitants of the same dungeon, each fled naturally from the comfortless and forlorn prospect of their unhappy fate, and sought for consolation in the presence of the other. She communicated to him all the arrangements of the Count. His detestable principles, his skill in the use of narcoticks and other drugs. His mode of descent to the cavern, his precautions, his perverse propensities, his inextinguishable malignity. She represented herself as a victim to his libertinism and treachery, aided, as she said, by some infernal philtre, and she bewailed her weakness with such well-acted remorse that Theodore's compassion was powerfully excited.

"Do not," he would say, "my fair and tender friend, do not indulge such unavailing sorrow. You were unfortunate to be exposed to the arts of such a monster, you are unhappy, but who shall dare to call you criminal? shall the delicate and disinterested sensibility of an inexperienced female, shall her amiable credulity, shall the fond and innocent wanderings of her imagination, shall the gentle acquiescence of her manners, her habitual and feminine submission, suspicious of no guile and incapable of energy save in efforts to oblige, shall these virtues be converted into instruments for her seduction by the insidious corrupter, be construed into weakness, or deemed tokens of levity or looseness? Forbid it, Heaven! no, let the hard unyielding disposition of the suspicious prudent matron, the repelling austerity of mortified temperament or inveterate dissimulation, the practised caution of crafty intrigue or dubious character; let unfeeling indifference and masculine resistance, and the bosom of marble from which avarice and vanity have excluded all the soft and kindly feelings, meet the approbation of the silly and prejudiced, and receive the homage of ignorance and stupidity. But truth and compassion, justice and virtue, will ever whisper consolation to contrite frailty, and extend their benign protection to the lovely and weeping penitent. Be comforted, my amiable preserver. Ah! who that knows the Count, but knows him to be irresistible?

Can the tender lamb escape from the rapacious wolf? The chicken from the kite? Be comforted. You have committed no crime, but you have suffered injuries greater than profligacy unaided by the depraved refinement of vitious seduction, could have inflicted. To consider your accomplishments, to behold your charms, and to think of your destiny, the sternest censor would pity, not condemn; and for me, I admire, I respect, and I applaud."

By degrees she suffered herself to be consoled into apparent tranquillity, while Theodore's regard for her every moment increased; but his heart was already engaged. He could not love her, nay, were he without attachment, he felt that he could never entertain for her any sentiment but that of friendship. He reflected on his own disposition and he examined hers, but the cause of this phenomenon he could not discover. His principles were established and his taste was formed. Which of the former was not possessed, in what respect was not the latter gratified by Marie? She spoke, she sang well; her good sense was conspicuous, her manners were correct, and her information was extensive. She hath, thought he, a cultivated understanding and a humane heart, an even temper, a graceful address; what then does she require to render her amiable? Why am I sensible of a disparity between us? In what particular is she deficient, or has nature intended her for a situation in society more refined or more elevated than any to which I could arrive?

In truth he could look, or he thought he could look at her figure with as much tranquillity as if it had been sculptured in marble. He was sensible of its charms, but he was indifferent to them. The regularity and beauty of her face struck him as uncommon and admirable, but from the expression of her brilliant eyes his soul involuntarily revolted. He had been served by her most materially, he had been attended by her most kindly, he was obliged and grateful, and he therefore could not feel antipathy to her; but at her countenance he looked as seldom as politeness would permit. There was that in it which was not only uncongenial and foreign to his nature, but which even filled him with uneasiness. How different was she from Miss Bolton! On Julia's sweet and gentle face he could gaze for hours, and grow fonder as he gazed. Conversing with her, all perturbation was quieted, all unhappiness forgotten. Oh, the delight to look at and admire her, to hear her and forget every other object! Let me return to her for a moment.

She was during his absence truly wretched. Her anxiety for him and her horrour of the Count deprived her of ease, robbed her of rest and comfort, and even injured her health. On the morning after the discovery of the secret door, she had, with Ellen's assistance, fastened it so securely with nails and wooden wedges, that it was no longer to be dreaded. But she would not again sleep alone in this apartment. After much deliberation she invented an excuse for having a second bed removed to it, and Ellen, who was at once resolute and affectionate, became her protector.

But this is a digression. By degrees Marie de Solase recovered her chearfulness. "To you," said she to Theodore one evening when he was nearly recovered, "I am indebted for my present contentment. What magick in your words and presence to cause forgetfulness of shame, happiness so long unknown, and feelings of self-respect! Truth and honour are inseparable from your sentiments, and absolution from you I receive almost as a pledge of divine remission. Ah! how could I support the humiliation of your contempt, the terrour of your condemnation? No, I feel that your regard is necessary to my existence. There is in your character what demands my reverence, and may I flatter myself that now in your looks I see that which may confirm my acquittal? I shall henceforth study to deserve your friendship. Possessing this, my gloomy cavern will appear the abode of felicity and joy: the prospect of my future life will be illuminated with sunshine: no cares will molest, no fears disturb me. And you, the cause of such happy changes, will sometimes, perhaps, testify your approbation by a smile."

They were sitting on a sopha near the mouth of the cavern. The last rays of the setting sun gilt with softened lustre its sparry roof. The sky was variegated with the splendour of the hour, the season, and the climate. A fresh breeze from the sea produced a delightful coolness, and now, for the first time, *the grave* seemed to Theodore to relinquish its horrours for beauty and for pleasure.

All the animation of Marie's character enlivened her countenance. "How little do you know me," said he, "if you suppose I could be insensible to your perfections, or capable of the cruelty of reproach or inattention! It is true that before I saw you I engaged my heart to another, but does this require me to be blind to beauty such as your's, or unsusceptible of the tenderness that you inspire? Ah! too lovely woman, in vain I would struggle to resist your charms. I feel a passion that must be love from its warmth and its force. In the contemplation of that admirable figure, of that commanding countenance, I forget all former impressions, all my present misfortunes, and revel in new and delicious transports. Other women may gain conquests and may captivate, but it is for you alone to strike and to inflame with the first glance. This hand alone were sufficient to thaw the frost of ninety, but to contemplate the numberless beauties of that perfect form, the elastick plumpness of that arm, and that neck, the clearness of that skin, the matchless delicacy of that foot! Ah! in mercy hide those eyes, their lustre is intolerable."

In a fatal moment virtue and Julia were forgotten, and the amiable, the grateful, the unsuspicious Theodore became false and criminal.

Marie de Solase was in hourly expectation of a visit from the Count, and she made such arrangements in the cavern, that when he came he should not perceive any marks of her tenderness or attention to Theodore. She knew that her dogs would always give her intimation of his approach ten or twelve minutes at least before his appearance, and she contrived matters so as that she could, in this short space of time, make the prisoner appear to have no other protection against the hardness of the rock and the cold than a few blankets. The chain which had secured his legs was fastened by a lock, that she had the ingenuity to remove, and she instructed him how to replace it speedily in such a way as that no one could suspect it had been opened. Thus he was enabled to move about his subterranean dungeon, and at night, when there was little danger of a visit from the Count, he would sometimes amuse himself by exploring its recesses.

A frequent subject of his thoughts and of his conversations with Marie was the possibility of escaping from the cavern. To make a rope of all the bed-clothes and other suitable materials, which being secured above might reach to the sea, was the idea that first occurred to him; but this would be, he soon perceived, a vain attempt. To be strong enough to bear his weight it could not be made sufficiently long, as the cavern was many hundred feet above the surface of the water. To attack the Count on his arrival and throw him over the ledge, was another project that presented itself, but this his new acquaintance showed him would be to expose themselves to certain destruction, for who but the Count could, holding only a single rope, swing into the abyss, and climb up by such a perilous, slender and unsteady mode of ascent? The consequence of the Count's death would be that they must both inevitably perish where they were. To make signs of distress, and throw down letters stating their situation, was at one time proposed by Theodore.—"Ah!" said Marie, "so long as I have been here, never did I see a vessel sufficiently near to convey to it a signal from hence, and we might fling down a thousand letters secured in bottles or by any other mode you might devise, every one of which would in all probability be for ever lost among the rocks, and currents, and caves, and whirlpools, of these tempestuous vaults."

"Does no mode present itself," cried Theodore, "by which even the possibility of escape might be obtained? Might not some perpendicular fissure of these rocks be widened and continued even to the light of day?"—Marie shook her head.—"I understand you," said he, "a mass of stone of immeasurable thickness lies between us and heaven. But the stream in the inner cavern, could not that be followed? Who can tell whither it flows? perhaps if I were to try, it might conduct me hence in safety; your deliverance would follow of course."—"You are still too weak to attempt so desperate an enterprize," replied she. "Think of nothing now but the restoration of your strength."—"You are right I believe," returned he with a sigh: but his impatience to escape grew every hour more violent, and the assiduities of Marie became soon little less irksome and disagreeable to him than the gloomy confinement of the cavern.

But her attachment to him was so strong and so disinterested, her endeavours to please were so conciliatory and so flattering, that he could not bring himself for an instant to treat her with distance or indifference. When at times his sense of fidelity gave to his manner an appearance of formality or reserve, the effect on her countenance was sudden and distressing, and she appeared so very unhappy that he more than once accused himself as a barbarian. He thought her an unfortunate interesting woman, who had preserved his life, and who was entitled to every return of gratitude and sensibility. Thus the strictness of his principles and the tenderness of his disposition produced that, which no seduction had otherwise affected.

His thoughts were involved in gloom, he apprehended some dreadful issue to his adventure. Murder in its worst shape and Count Egfryd appeared constantly before him. On Julia he thought incessantly, but he never expected to see her again. His attention to *Manon* he still continued, and while he was employed in cleansing its cage and supplying it with food, he would sometimes, for an instant, lose his wretched situation in the remembrance of those delicious moments he had passed with its mistress. It still formed a point of union between him and her, and now it was the only comfort he possessed.

Theodore had read and reflected much, and his invention was equal to his knowledge. The use to which the species of pigeon, called carrier, had been often applied, was not unknown to him, and it occurred to him that Manon might be employed as a messenger to Miss Bolton. The thought when it struck him filled him with inexpressible joy. The first conception of a new project, though absurd or impracticable, is always delightful. To discover its imperfections or its difficulties requires reflection, and reflection requires time. Meanwhile hope is engaged and the imagination amused. The sagacity of all birds is so great, and their attachment to their young so powerful, that he entertained the most sanguine expectation that the little goldfinch, liberated from its cage, would fly to Manette, be seen and examined by Julia, and be the bearer to her of a billet. He instantly communicated his project to his companion. She, afraid of losing him, and likewise afraid of being apprehended and consequently executed for her crimes, determined to oppose his intention.

"I am surprised," said she, "that you could entertain such a hope; do you suppose that a bird in pain and terrour, and kept from the view of all surrounding objects by your clothes as you came hither, would be able to regain its nest at such a distance? No, believe me it will fail in the attempt, and will perish in consequence of the disuse and forgetfulness of its natural habits. Do not I pray you wantonly sacrifice the beautiful little creature."—"You are ignorant, my friend," answered he, "of the powers of birds. They possess a sagacity or an instinct of which we can form no idea. There are instances of pigeons carrying letters more than a thousand miles, and in trying this experiment I do that which it is possible may effect our release. It may be of service, it can do no harm. Let me therefore have pen, ink and paper."—"No, really," replied she abruptly, "it must not be. I am determined Manon shall remain here."

As she spoke the violence of her temper and the blackness of her character became partly visible. Theodore shuddered as he examined her frown—"Why now, really, *Madame*, you are unreasonable. We are here in a miserable situation. The project I propose may rescue us from it, and yet you oppose it. Do not," added he with a smile, "make me suppose you are a confederate with the Count."—"Suppose what you please, Sir, but in this I must not be opposed."—"Nay, nay, this is foolish. Come, give me pen, ink and paper, and let us finish our ridiculous altercation."—"I will not give you pen, ink nor paper; you shall not write to that impertinent Miss Bolton, nor shall this troublesome bird molest me any longer." These words had scarcely escaped her when she seized the little cage, and with a violent effort threw it out of the cavern. It fell on the extreme border of the ledge. Another inch and Julia's favourite had fallen into the gulph.

Theodore grew pale. He flew to recover it and returned to Marie. Undisguised fury inflamed her countenance. The deformity of her character was legible in every feature of her face. Theodore would perhaps, at this moment, have less regretted her loss than that of Manon. His attention to her had first arisen from a principle of gratitude, and his sanguine complexion had too readily yielded to her seduction; but he now regarded her with aversion. He felt remorse at his own immorality. His seducer was unamiable, indelicate and unfeminine. He had penetrated much of her character, and it filled him with disgust. He was shocked and enraged at her present action. He looked at her with disapprobation and contempt, but he said not a word. He felt that his language would be impolite if not intemperate, and he had sufficient command of himself to resist his inclination to express his thoughts. He put the cage in his bosom, and proceeded in silence and without opposition, for she saw that this would be fruitless, to procure materials for writing. These obtained, he went with a light into the most retired cavity of his dungeon. Marie burned with jealousy, revenge and disappointment.—"You shall repent this," said she as he was retiring. Her menace was terrible. The attitude in which it was delivered, the tone in which it was uttered, the merciless and malignant look with which it was accompanied, might alarm the most courageous. He was moved by it. He felt a dread that he, who was naturally brave, could not explain; a new and complicated mischief, the offspring of perfidy, malice and assassination, appeared in shapeless terrours before his imagination; though indistinct it threatened and it terrified. In this agitated state of mind, but unmoved from his purpose, he sat down and wrote on a small piece of paper the following.

"If this shall reach you I may yet be happy. On this slender chance, alas, how slender! depends my release from a situation shocking to humanity. If you receive not this paper, a captivity without hope must be my wretched lot, aggravated by cruelty, and to be terminated by my murder. But if it reach you, my chains will be broken, despair will no longer fill my bosom, happiness will once again visit me, and again I shall behold you. *If!* Oh sad and dreadful word! Thy coldness freezes my soul, thy uncertainty tortures me with the anxiousness of death. Know, dearest and most respected of women, that your friend, the unhappy Theodore, now languishes in a frightful cavern, from which all escape without your assistance is impossible. The cavern is in the fatal *grave*, about one hundred feet below the iron ring that is at the verge of the gulph near the hut. Hither that monster Egfryd by violence and treachery has conveyed me. Need I say more? Recollect that all escape without your assistance is impossible, and save me.

To Miss Bolton, 28th of June."

This he tied to Manon's foot, and advancing with him to the ledge, he dismissed him on his errand. The poor bird was frightened and undecided. He would have returned into the cavern and his cage, but Theodore scared him away with a handkerchief. At last he mounted and flew speedily out of sight.

Theodore returned to his fellow-prisoner, whose ill-humour he endeavoured, in vain, to remove. She who of late had studied his wants and who had even insisted on the drudgery of washing for him, now with characteristical inconsistency avoided his looks and his conversation, and would not even deign to listen to him. Vexed and uneasy, he left her, and in order to remove himself as far as possible from her, he (being now quite recovered from the effects of the violence lately practised on him) determined to explore the passage in which was the stream of water. This was the only one to the extremity of which he had not already gone.

It was a wide and lofty vault, rugged, black and terrifying. Here the murmuring of the water, echoed from a thousand arches, inspired awe. Here the dampness of the air produced a sensation of chilliness and a smell of unwholesomeness, that nothing but the dread of Marie, or a hope of liberty, could tempt the most curious adventurer to encounter. Having supplied himself with two light boards, and leaving his clothes on the rock, Theodore committed himself to the stream. It carried him a considerable distance in his desperate voyage, and as it advanced became more rapid. At length the increased noise of waves, and of a waterfall not far distant, admonished him to use all his caution. He determined, therefore, to follow the left bank, and to go no farther than it should afford him means of holding by his hands. He threw away his boards as useless, for he had brought them merely to float him down the stream without the trouble of swimming. He now depended entirely on his powers of feeling, for his organ of vision was here quite useless. He was in utter and profound darkness, and he was even ignorant of the situation of the spot from which he had proceeded. But he knew that the left bank would conduct him back to it, though perhaps with considerable delay, obliquity and danger. The stream grew impetuous, but still a lengthened and elevated ledge of the rock afforded him a protection against its force, as it enabled him to keep his head and shoulders above the torrent. He persisted in his rash endeavour, but his body was benumbed by the cold water, and his senses confounded by the strange and deafening noises around him. These noises grew louder, and at the same time, as he followed the ledge, his feet touched a hard substance.

A few steps more and he is on a smooth stone, but it is a narrow shelf of which the sides rise beyond his reach. It is about fourteen inches in breadth. Its edge is sharp, and beneath it at a depth, perhaps unfathomable, he hears a noise of a thousand cataracts, louder than the loudest thunders of the torrid zone, tumbling impetuously, and roaring with infernal violence among the rocky passages below. A spray like a heavy shower of rain falls upon him.

Torrent against torrent, gulph within gulph, horrour on horrour, blackness and solitude, despair and death, interminable extent, incalculable ruin, and a depth to the very bowels of the earth; all that experience can furnish of most perilous, all that the imagination can supply of most dreadful, what man avoids, and what nature hides, were there.

Theodore, astounded and trembling, hastened to return, but the treacherous slate on which he stood, yielding to his weight, sunk into the abyss. He followed it, recommending his soul to mercy, and expecting a frightful and instantaneous dissolution.

By one of those involuntary and instinctive acts practised by all animals in danger, he extended his arms as he was falling, and caught most providentially, a remaining portion of the ledge. The fear of an immediate and horrible death gave him new strength; he not only supported himself, but by his efforts he soon gained a spot of comparative security.

Fully sensible of the imminent danger and the inutility of his enterprize, he proceeded with all possible expedition to regain the first cavern along the left bank. Again he entered the water, again was benumbed, but in a severer manner than before, and ere he had gotten half way, he found that he was utterly unable to proceed further. A convenient place for resting himself fortunately presented itself, and he took advantage of it. It was a hollow in the bank above the water. He climbed into it, and, advancing a few steps, threw himself on the ground. A few minutes rest was all he required. But such was the wetness and incommodiousness of the place, that, notwithstanding his unwillingness to move, he found himself necessitated to enter more deeply into the recess.

He did so. He advanced yet a little further, when the soft impending mass, disturbed by his motions, fell upon him with a mountain's weight, and buried him alive in an untimely and abhorred sepulchre.

It was evening, and the barking of the dogs in the outer cavern announced the Count's approach. Twelve days had now elapsed since his visit with Theodore. He enters and is accosted by Marie with vehemence and precipitation. She, in as few words as it was possible to convey her meaning, told him of the means employed by the prisoner, who she said had broken his chains, to inform Miss Bolton of his situation. Her information was a dagger-blow to Egfryd's hopes and revenge. No sooner did he hear of Manon having been despatched with a letter, and sooner than the information was concluded, than he rushed into the inner cavern, with a cocked pistol in his hand, intending, no doubt, to murder Theodore. But he was not to be found. Being informed of the cause of his absence, the Count looked at Marie with distrust, but staid not to say a word.

Having regained the ledge, he seized his rope, dashed into the abyss, and climbed up the edge of the impending rock. His object was to see Manon (if it should return to its nest) before Miss Bolton saw it. Having this object, he gained the *chateau* with the greatest possible expedition. It was two o'clock in the morning when he arrived there. All was still and pitchy. He immediately provided himself with a dark-lantern and went softly to her door, but this was locked. He then, by a concealed portal in the sacristy, entered a close vault that led to a dark passage. This passage conducted by narrow and winding stairs to that secret opening in the roof of her chamber, which was concealed by the painting of the witch of Endor's drapery. The dark passage was well known to him. He had stolen through it, and into her apartment, on the night of her extraordinary trance, and he would, perhaps, have afterwards repeated the audacious intrusion, but that he discovered she had obtained the protection of Ellen. However, his present object was so important, the danger threatened was so imminent, that he was to be restrained by no such consideration, but to his extreme disappointment and surprise, the mysterious door now for the first time opposed all his endeavours to open it. He employed his strength and his dexterity equally in vain. Frustrated in his intention, he retired and procured a long ladder from a part of the *chateau* that was under repair. He raised the ladder to her windows thinking to enter there, but again he was disappointed, for they were so well fastened on the inside that he could not, with his utmost efforts, force them open. Thus baffled in every attempt he was compelled to retire. What would he not have done, what would he not have dared, to prevent her from seeing Manon?

The poor bird had, in about an hour and a half after it was despatched, flown in at her window and joined its Manette. Julia had just entered her apartment for the night when she heard its notes, which she could well distinguish from those of the other. Her astonishment was equal to her joy. She flew to its nest, welcomed it back with delight, and examined it with tenderness. Its broken limb was the first object of her attention, and the billet at its foot the next. But what was her consternation and horrour on reading it! She instantly ran to her father, showed it to him, mentioned the dangers and the misery she had experienced since her arrival at the *chateau*, the circumstance of the balloon, the alarming discovery of the hidden door in her ceiling, and her sleepless and watchful nights since that discovery; and she implored him, as he valued her safety and the preservation of Theodore, to fly with her that moment to Bourdeaux.

Mr. Bolton did not want energy; he instantly ordered his servants and his carriage, but in such a manner as that the *Comtesse D'Egfryd* should not be apprized of his intention. In half an hour Miss Bolton and he left the *chateau*, and not having time to remove their property, they took the keys of their apartments with them.

When the Count found he could not gain admission into Julia's room through the window, he returned to her door, and impatient of any more delay, burst it open with a violent effort. This done he flew to the little glass house, and there to his dread and confusion saw the hated bird without the billet. The apartment he perceives is empty. He is instantly sensible of all that has happened, but his coolness does not desert him. He calls up Guiscard, his confidential servant, and from him he learns that Mr. Bolton and his daughter left the *chateau* in their carriage, for Bourdeaux, at ten o'clock, attended by their servants.

"Saddle me my fleetest horse!" cried he impatiently. Never before did he feel terrour. His reputation, his consequence, his happiness, his liberty, his existence, all were in danger. Having mounted, he flew rather than rode to Bourdeaux, and was there not long after the arrival of Mr. Bolton. Knowing his hotel, he easily found him, and, with an air of sprightly familiarity, thus accosted him in the presence of his daughter.

"Mr. Bolton, how comes this? Why have you deserted us in this manner? May I indulge the hope that you purpose to return to the *chateau*? And you, *Mademoiselle*, to consent to the flight!"—"Look you, Count Egfryd," said

Mr. Bolton interrupting him, "this volatile manner ill becomes you. Theodore Dalbert must be liberated, and if there are laws in France you shall be punished." The Count, who till now would have confessed nothing, lest he should have betrayed himself unnecessarily, replied coolly and unmoved, "I perceive, Sir, you have learned where Mr. Dalbert is confined, and I can read in your countenance that you believe all that has been written and said against me. I expect, therefore, no favour from you, I require none. I admit that he is a prisoner, and that he became such by perfidy and force. But what is your remedy? You apply to the magistracy of Bourdeaux. They hear you with doubt because they regard me with respect, and with difficulty you gain an order to have the cavern searched. In the mean time you and your agents are exposed to the effects of my power and my vengeance; and when you get the order, should you live to obtain it, how is it to be executed? who will visit the prison in *the grave*, or how can it be entered? Mr. Bolton, you are a worthy, sensible man. Relinquish all prejudice and passion. Attempt no hostile proceeding. Be discreet and silent, and Theodore shall be surrendered. To this I pledge myself; provided that this affair have not already transpired, that you now give me the letter from him carried by the bird, that you engage upon your honour, for him and your daughter as well as for yourself, that you will embark immediately on board a ship that I shall provide to carry you to England, and that what has occurred shall never be disclosed."

Mr. Bolton paused for a while. He was aware of the extreme difficulty that would attend any adverse or publick proceeding against the Count, and he therefore was tempted to comply with the proposal made to him. "I make the engagement you require," replied he after some deliberation; "my daughter and I only are acquainted with your crime. I pledge my honour for the performance of the conditions you prescribe, and I bind myself for Theodore's acquiescence. But he must be liberated before to-morrow night."—"He shall," said the other. Miss Bolton, to hide her agitation, had turned her back on them during this conversation.

The mode of his release was next to be considered. In this Mr. Bolton showed his usual good sense, for he insisted that the Count should not quit him till the moment of embarkation, and in the mean time he despatched a messenger for three or four English seamen from a vessel, then lying in the road, the captain of which he knew. The Count consented that one of these sailors should descend to the cavern, along with him, to assist in restoring the prisoner to liberty; and in return for this it was agreed, on the part of Mr. Bolton, that a female then in the cavern with Theodore, should accompany them to England.

The Count in this proceeding was influenced principally by the dread of a publick accusation, which would expose him to Gaspar's insolence and indiscretion, and which might eventually develop the attempted assassination of Theodore in Bourdeaux, and several other crimes that had till then baffled all inquiry. The means employed to communicate the information to Mr. Bolton from the cavern, were such as no human prudence could have prevented, and the sudden departure of the English visitors from the *chateau* put it out of the villain's power to employ any other mode of proceeding than that which he had adopted; but he already determined to remove from the number of the living all those from whom he had now to apprehend danger or disgrace. These were Mr. Bolton, Julia, Theodore, Marie, and the two miscreants who carried Theodore to *the grave.*

But the compact that I have just mentioned could not be evaded; the English sailors were obtained, the property of Mr. Bolton and his daughter was removed from the *chateau*, and the cavern was visited. Theodore had not perished. Though he had been buried for a moment under a mass of earth, where he had suffered the horrours of a violent and most shocking death, he had, by a sudden and powerful exertion, succeeded, though nearly suffocated, in freeing himself from the enormous burden, and he had afterwards regained the outer recess. He and Marie were liberated, and they with Julia and her father embarked for England.

CHAPTER III.

Nought is there under Heav'n's wide hollownesse
That moves more deare compassion of mind,
Then beautie brought t'unworthie wretchednesse,
Through envie's snares, or fortune's freaks unkind.
I, whether lately through her brightnes blynd,
Or through alleageance and fast fealty,
Which I do owe unto all womankynd,
Feele my hart prest with so great agony
When such I see, that all for pity I could dy.

....

————Mia speranza!
Ah sie pur tu? Pur ti riveggo? Oh Dio!
Di gioia io moro; ed il mio petto appena
Può alternare i respiri. Oh caro! Oh tanto
E sospirato, e pianto,
E richiamato in vano!

THEODORE's delight at gaining his liberty and meeting Julia was unspeakable. She who had lately found herself attached to him by a new tie, that of their common danger, fondly yielded to her now resistless passion, and when together, few were the moments that there did not pass between them some sweet though silent mark of mutual attachment, or some eloquent token of corresponding sentiment. Mr. Bolton's satisfaction at the prospect of his return to England, and at the recovery of his daughter, was unmixed with any uneasiness. It even communicated to his manners a portion of gaiety.

Marie, whose guilty fears were perpetually awake, and whose jealousy of Miss Bolton amounted to aversion, not only never left the small cabin that was allotted to her, but refused the visits of Theodore, who felt himself bound by humanity as well as politeness to offer her every attention in his power. The vessel in which they had embarked was clean and commodious, they had a fair wind, and they proceeded pleasantly on their voyage.

It is not my wish to dwell on minute or unimportant facts. If I ever err in this respect, I err unintentionally, and I would now land my personages in England, without further delay, impatient as I am to enter on the principal event of my history, but for an incident that occurred aboard their ship, not less terrible than it was singular.

In the same vessel was a passenger, an elderly man, who was unknown to every one aboard. His habits were reserved if not suspicious. He seemed to shun all observation, and he never appeared on deck except at night, and then muffled in a cloak. Theodore, whose love of contemplation and study kept him out of bed later than Mr. Bolton and Julia, had sometimes seen him, and had once by accident, without officiousness or inquisitive obtrusion, entered into conversation with him. He spoke like a man of observation, and seemed perfectly acquainted with nautical affairs; but he was not polished, and he neither sought to please, nor did it appear that it was in his power to be agreeable.

They were within two days sail of England. Theodore and the stranger happened to meet for the second time and to converse. They were standing at the side of the vessel looking towards the stars. It was midnight. A smart breeze from the South-west had agitated the sea considerably. The noise of the cordage, the luminous appearance of the water, and the strong smell of the tar, accorded well with their conversation. It was on the subject of navigation. Theodore was listening attentively to the other, who had just pointed his attention to the constellation of the *Greater Bear*, when, by a sudden and vigorous action, he was pushed by his perfidious instructor into the deep. A loud cry escaped him as he fell. The alarm was given, the vessel was put about, ropes, coops and lanterns were hoven overboard. All was bustle and exertion among the few seamen who were on deck, and no one was more active than the murderer. But he had taken care that their endeavours should be useless, for as Theodore was falling, he had hooked a leaden weight to his coat, to prevent him from rising to the surface of the water. For two hours they stopped the vessel's course as much as was in their power, and employed such means as experience could teach to save or find him, but all in vain. The account given by the assassin was that Mr. Dalbert had seated himself on the gunwale, and had in consequence of the tossing of the vessel, suddenly fallen over, and the villain pretended to be so exhausted by his exertions, and so shocked by what had happened, as to be unable to remain any longer out of bed.

In the morning what was the grief, what was the horrour of Mr. Bolton and of Julia, when they were told of the dreadful accident? She heard the doleful tale and was struck with speechless misery. The coldness of death froze every avenue of her heart. She sunk into her father's arms, dumb as despair, motionless as a monument. The wretch who had perpetrated the crime affected illness, and never rose till their arrival in England, and then he contrived to land without being suspected, and without being seen by the other passengers.

Mr. Bolton having procured lodgings for Marie de Solase, and promised her his advice and assistance, whenever these should be necessary, returned to his house in Berkshire with Julia. The day after their arrival they were joined by *Mademoiselle de Sagoné*, who having visited England in consequence of a fortune bequeathed to her there by an uncle, came to reside at Bolton-hall till she should receive the amount of it.

Time, the softener of sorrow, abated in some months the violence of Julia's grief, but *Mademoiselle de Sagoné* became extremely ill. A malady that had for some time affected her, gained strength daily. It was one that gave her not more pain than apprehension. It baffled the skill of the most eminent physicians, and in its symptoms was as extraordinary as its cause was unaccountable. The horrid night she had passed in the *chateau* was ever present to her recollection, and with it she combined, by an instinctive association, her present illness, for Miss Bolton had told her all she suspected of Count Egfryd.

"My God!" she would say to Julia in agony and terrour, "is it possible that I have been the victim of his profligacy? Have I, whose conscience is clear and immaculate, received a stain from audacious depravity? Is the blot of infamy to blacken my reputation and my name? and am I to afford a proof that female honour may be endangered, without any violation of innocence, and even without a consciousness of the forfeiture? Am I, alone, of all the daughters of Eve, to deplore a misfortune without precedent and without name? am I, alone, without being vitious, to suffer the vilest penalty of vice? Good Heavens! Do I bear, even now, the unhallowed and horrible triumph of the abominable Egfryd? Happy thou, whom Providence, by a manifest interposition, rescued from his snares!"

Sometimes nearly choked by her sobs, and shedding floods of tears, the unhappy girl would suffer paroxysms of frantick distraction. At other times, stupid with woe and horrour, she would spend hours and days in solitude. She felt all the punishment of shame without being sensible of a fault, and of guilt without being criminal. A fixed and cruel melancholy preyed upon her spirits. The thought of her unparalleled misfortune absorbed all other reflections, and she looked the living image of inconsolable affliction.

The attempts of the gentle and friendly Julia to soothe her were utterly unavailing. The agitation of her mind had a powerful and shocking effect on her constitution. A general relaxation enfeebled every muscle, and debilitated every fibre; each faculty was disordered, and each function of her frame felt the derangement of excessive and complicated disease. Her nerves became irritable to a degree that was truly piteous. The entire physical economy was vitiated and distempered, and a total and mortal revolution of the animal machine was hourly expected. But poor *Mademoiselle de Sagoné*, by the violence of her sufferings, escaped an evil that she dreaded more than death, and, satisfied of her escape from the most terrible calamity that an honourable female could experience, she bore the crisis which determined her good fortune with heroism, and in a short time she was out of danger. By slow degrees she recovered a portion of her strength, and at length was convalescent. In a few months she returned to the Continent, where she entered into a convent, in which she spent the remainder of her days.

To return to Theodore. The hook, attached to him by the assassin, had, in consequence of the weight suspended to it, torn through his coat, and been detached from it before he reached the water. As the vessel was under considerable way when he fell, he had not been able to make himself heard on board; but, fortunately catching at a coop that had been thrown out, he kept himself afloat. He remained in the water till the sun arose. He was almost dead with cold, but he still hung to the coop. He looked around, and at a distance, to windward, he descried a large vessel. The joyful sight gave him strength, gave him courage, gave him hope. His numbness, his fatigue, were forgotten, and in his anxiety to be seen by those on board, every impression of pain was lost. Unable to direct the motion of the buoyant instrument of his preservation, he was the sport of every wave, and with the means of preservation in his view, he found it impossible to approach them.

Sometimes he would imagine that in the irregular and disturbed rolling of the billowy surface, he was carried with horrible rapidity from the ship and towards death. At other times, hope equally illusive with fear, would persuade him that he was drifting toward the vessel. It was not long till this in full sail bore down. She went directly before the wind, which, happily for Theodore, blew her close to his coop. He was now to be seen or to perish. He waved his wet handkerchief about his head and roared for help. He was seen and heard and taken up, but no sooner was he on the deck than he fell into a swoon. The Captain humanely ordered him to be put into a warm bed, and continued to treat him with all possible attention till he was perfectly recovered.

Captain Jenkins was a kind-hearted, blunt, British tar. He sailed in his own vessel, the *Isabel*, and was now bound for St. Petersburgh. Theodore told him ingenuously all his story, concealing only such parts of it, as, under Mr. Bolton's promise of secrecy to the Count D'Egfryd, were not to be disclosed. "Well, well," said Jenkins, "never mind till we return to England, and if I don't find out that murdering rascal that hove you overboard, say I'm no seaman, that's all. I'll see him tucked up on a lofty gallows yet, or I'll be d—d else." The character of the Captain was new to Theodore—it amused and pleased him, while his, in turn, gained the respect and regard of the honest tar. Each liked the other, and before they arrived in Russia, a friendship was formed between them which continued during their lives. Unknown to either of them was that artificial and unworthy principle, which forbids a man of the world to seek or to retain a friend. The restraint, that such a connexion is said to impose, is irksome; the confidence it demands, is dangerous; the obligations it confers, are painful—only to the licentious, the dissolute, and the depraved. They remained in Russia about six weeks, and then they embarked together in the *Isabel* for England.

It may be imagined, but cannot be described, what astonishment, what rapture, Theodore's presence excited at Bolton-hall. With him came happiness, content and hope, while his escape, or rather his resurrection, was piously attributed to the supernatural and benign interference of protecting Heaven. The terms on which he had consented to come to England, were that he was to receive two hundred pounds *per annum*, for which he was to act as secretary to Mr. Bolton, and as preceptor to his daughter. He now entered on the duties of his new situation, and made an arrangement to send his mother in Bourdeaux one hundred pounds a-year. His wants were few and simple, and the remainder of his salary was quite sufficient to satisfy them. By his instructions Miss Bolton soon acquired such a knowledge of French as is seldom attained in England; she might, with truth, be said to speak and write with purity and elegance. Her advancement in Italian was likewise considerable. Love is as quick in learning as it is patient in teaching. But words were not her only study. Guided by his refined and classick taste, and improved by her sedulous imitation of his eloquent and copious style, her language acquired propriety, fluency and force, and her powers of literary composition became excellent and admirable.

In this state of things was the family at Bolton-hall, when Mr. Alcot, a neighbouring gentleman of large possessions and of ancient family, presented himself as a suitor to Julia. He was young, sensible and prudent, but reserved, sullen and malignant. He was not handsome and he was not amiable. His figure was clumsy and ill-proportioned. His face was harsh and irregular, and his manners were coarse and unfashioned. He was treated with politeness and respect by Miss Bolton and her father, but he found that all his assiduities had no effect in gaining her affections. He did not want for penetration, but he was not sensible of his own deficiencies. He therefore looked for the cause of her indifference and coldness beyond himself. Theodore was too prominent and too alarming an object to be overlooked. Jealousy, sharpened by pride, rage, and self-love, viewed with microscopick minuteness, and measured with more than hydrostatic exactness, every action, every look, and every word, that passed between the lovers. No doubt remains. Their mutual attachment appears from proofs crowded on proofs, by demonstration pressing on demonstration. Scepticism itself must shrink before the overpowering evidence collected by his industry and treasured in his memory. But this attachment, in his malignant eye, takes the appearance, the shape, the hue, of a clandestine and criminal connexion. Mr. Alcot was too artful and too reserved to let his suspicion or his hatred appear. He endeavoured to conceal both, and by degrees he removed himself from the society at Bolton-hall, without betraying either.

It was now summer, and Mr. Bolton prepared for the experiment on the kindness and liberality of General Dalbert, that he had projected when he became acquainted with Theodore. He would have gone to him before, but that the old gentleman had been confined with a severe fit of the gout. Being now, however, nearly well, further delay was not only unnecessary, but it might be dangerous.

Mr. Bolton was not unacquainted with the mutual sentiments of his daughter and her preceptor, nor was he displeased with them; but it was only an act of prudence and decorum, he thought, to wait on the General before the marriage ceremony took place, which, he was determined, should, at all events, be performed. He wished much to have it in his power to surprise the young people with the agreeable intelligence of a successful visit to the old gentleman, and therefore spoke of his journey to Holtham, where he lived, as a circumstance not likely to happen for another month.

True love, allied to content, demands little besides the presence of the beloved object. This delay, therefore, was a matter of trifling moment in the estimation of his daughter and Theodore. They were happy in each others society, and seldom thought of futurity. A proud and honourable sentiment on his part, and on hers the amiable and timid modesty of her sex, her age and her character, prevented them from bestowing a thought on matrimony; and when the idea of Julia, wedded to another more rich and more respectable than himself, would obtrude upon his mind, it was treated as an unwelcome visitor, and banished with all possible expedition. At some moments he thought and believed that Mr. Bolton wished to see him married to his daughter, but such an opinion he would not encourage, dreading that it was merely the illusive errour of hope and love.

There were moments of gloom and solitude, when Theodore, who was by nature thoughtful, would brood over his prospects in silent mournfulness. He would say to himself: I have attained my twenty-fifth year. Ere long my hair will change from healthful and glossy black, to dull and sober grey; my teeth, now so white and sound, will betray marks of decline, and my skin will be roughened by innumerable wrinkles. The early sportiveness of my disposition will no longer brighten my features; gravity and care will appear in my countenance and my gait; all, all will remind me of mortality. The springiness, spirit, and vivacity of youth will be succeeded by heaviness, inactivity, and relaxation. The warmth and sensibility of my nature will feel the exhaustion of use and time. Cold, decayed, feeble, it will be my miserable fate to perceive and measure the awful and slow, but inevitable approaches of death, without the endearing alleviation of a wife, or the consoling reflection of leaving behind me any legitimate offspring. Ah! who is there to smooth a pillow for my age? I shall die and be forgotten, no virtuous partner of connubial tenderness to bedew my grave with a tear, no son to retain my name, no daughter to bear my image into another family, and to talk of me to another generation: The comfortless and despised state of bachelorship awaits me; and when I die what shall I leave behind? Oh! wretched, wretched state! what avails it to me to know that marriages are too frequent and should be discouraged, that there are too many people in the world for their happiness or their support, and that wedlock always increases the cares of life? Alas! what has abstract reasoning to do with matters of the heart, with sentiment, with feeling? I must remain a solitary creature, miserable in an independence that selfishness only could desire, and cursed with privileges that libertinism only could hold important! Having no connexion of the soul with any female, and no reciprocalness of wants, duties, or affections; living solely for myself, and shut out for ever from the communion of virtuous love, from the pure, the holy, the mysterious delights of marriage, I shall be attached to society by no tie; I shall be isolated in nature; I shall be separated from mankind by the contemned and worthless individuality of my forlorn situation! When age shall wither my frame, and load me with infirmities, I shall think with bitterness of the amusement, sweet to an old man, that prattling grand-children would afford; and with agony shall say to myself, how much beauty, how much vigour, how much gallantry, how much affection, might have surrounded, and adorned, and supported, and cherished my existence, had I married! But now I look among all the inhabitants of this extensive world, and not a living creature owes to me its being, or can call me father!" Too late shall I then repent, in the anguish of my heart, that my pride, my indolence, or my weakness, should have tempted me to disobey the first dictate of our nature. Pride, indolence, or weakness, let it be. Come, contempt, misery, solitude, and despair, shower on my devoted head all your accumulated evils! but never, never shall woman receive my vows of fidelity and love. She whom I prefer to all others I will love till death, but her I must not wed. Of illicit connexions and an illegitimate offspring I shall never be accused. My prior attachment, my delicacy, and my morality, will ever preserve me from the former, and from the latter my humanity. Never shall child of mine be ashamed to call me father. Never shall the reproach of bastardy receive from my indiscretion its sting or its application.

To remain any longer at Mr. Bolton's, and trifle with Julia's affections, was what neither honour nor propriety could sanction. But he could not leave it without declaring that such was his intention. This he had done. From her father the declaration had drawn a serious rebuke, accompanied with a positive injunction not to quit him, and a promise of something undefined, but important to the last degree, provided he remained. As for Julia, it had made her so miserable and had so alarming an effect on her health, that Theodore literally had neither courage nor power to repeat the attempt. He was therefore, in a manner, compelled to stay.

The better to conceal his visit to General Dalbert, Mr. Bolton insinuated that there were some affairs of consequence which required his immediate attendance in London. His family, accordingly, entertained no doubt that he was going to town. They were now in England about a year, and, since Theodore's arrival, Mr. Bolton had employed all possible means to discover the name or the retreat of the assassin who had thrown him into the water, but hitherto without effect. That wretch had, as the reader must have suspected, been sent by the Count on the murderous commission. He had been paid a large sum on leaving France by Gaspar Pontgebre, and he had been promised that the remainder of his vile wages should be given to him by the same agent, as soon as an authentick account of Theodore's death should reach

Bourdeaux. Neither of them knew for whom he acted, and, while their employer continued to pay them liberally, neither of them felt any anxiety to know. Of Gaspar I have spoken before. The other was a native of England, and a miscreant covered with innumerable crimes. But more of him hereafter.

Marie De Solase being totally neglected by the Count, tired of solitude, utterly ignorant of the language of the country in which she was, and entirely dependant on the charity of Mr. Bolton, conceived an unconquerable disgust and hatred to England, and was seized, notwithstanding the dangers which awaited her in France, with the *maladie du pays*, that mental complaint which urges the patient with irresistible force towards home. How often does Providence, by an Almighty hand, impel the murderer to quit the concealment of craft and terrour, and to advance even beneath the sword of justice! She was, moreover, stimulated to return by her resentment of the Count, whose desertion of her had roused in her breast all the implacability and wickedness of her character.

Having procured from Mr. Bolton one hundred pounds sterling, she equipped herself in male attire and embarked for France. She obtained artificial whiskers, spectacles of green glass and a large wig, and used every other precaution that fear or cunning could suggest to disguise her person. Skilled in the composition of poisons, and experienced in the application of them, she purchased some Tokay wine, and added to it a mixture of the most deadly power, but free from taste, smell or colour, it being nearly the same as the horrible preparation called *aqua tofana*.

Having filled two small bottles with the deleterious liquor, she packed them in a case and sent them to Bourdeaux, accompanied with a note to the Count Egfryd, purporting to be written from Paris by the Baron Bikwaros, stating that the two bottles, one green and the other white, contained different wines, and that on the Count's opinion of the flavour of each depended a large wager. The infamous Marie had fabricated the note, and such was the unfeeling atrocity of her disposition, that she was utterly regardless, provided she poisoned him, how many beside might taste the mixture and die. To make her vengeance complete, she wrote to him, on the day after its departure, a letter, in her own undisguised hand-writing, of which the following is a translation.

To Count Egfryd.

"Ere this arrives my revenge shall have overtaken thee. Ere this reaches thee, the springs of thy life shall have been poisoned, and by me. Ungrateful, perfidious man, couldst thou think that I was to be neglected and despised with impunity? Proud, depraved and puerile character, wert thou to take advantage of my misfortunes, and to compel me under the fear of famine to submit to thy detestable arrangements? Wert thou to extort my compliances under the dread of hunger? Wert thou in the horrible slavery to which thou hadst doomed me, to triumph over my misery and to outrage all my feelings? Wert thou afterwards to desert me in a foreign country, a prey to poverty and spleen? and couldst thou hope to escape the terrours of my vengeance? In vain thou seekest the aid of physick. Thou art beyond the reach of mortal help. Thou shalt die, and that speedily, and in torture.

Where is now thy boasted art? How wilt thou preserve thy reputation from the infamy I shall stamp it with? Where is thy precaution, on which thy vanity taught thee to depend against every accident? Where is thy courage, or what avails it? Writhing in agony, thou diest by a woman's hand. Covered with reprobation thou sinkest in the flower of thy age, and in thy last moments let thy favourite doctrine of materialism, and thy contempt of futurity, yield thee all the happiness, and hope, and consolation, that thou deservest. But then, even then, surely thou wilt not forget

"Marie De Solase."

This letter she knew would reach him before his death, for the poison was of such slow operation as not to kill for forty hours after it was taken. It happened that Marie, on the day after despatching the letter, was recognized and apprehended; she was transmitted to Bourdeaux, identified as the convicted murderess of her husband, the advocate De Solase, and executed according to her sentence, impenitent and unpitied.

Mr. Bolton having fixed a day for his departure to London, every necessary preparation was made for his journey, and about nine o'clock in the evening, he left Bolton-hall accompanied by Theodore, with an intention to walk to Newbury, through which a stage-coach passed to London. A *valise*, containing a few necessaries, he had sent by a servant to the hotel the day before.

Here might I pause! When the Persian courier, travelling on foot from Betzurvan to Kehemend, arrives at Kasimadab, he stops for awhile and casts his eye upon the mountains he has traversed, thinks of the precipices he has passed, and looks forward, dejectedly, to the dreary and tedious journey that he has still to run. When the industrious Indian, in want of a vessel to navigate the ocean, whether to ensnare its finny inhabitants, or to attack the savages of some neighbouring island, fells the largest tree of the forest, and proceeds to convert with patient industry its trunk into a boat; he cuts, and scrapes, and scoops, until the external shape of his canoe becomes apparent; he has already employed months upon his work, and still it is to be hollowed, and his only tool is a hatchet of stone. He reflects on what he has done, and what he still has to perform. He utters a sigh of apathy, resignation or despair, and with sunken head renews his labours. When the chymical professor, intent on the establishment of a new theory, or prompted by the glory of tearing down an ancient system, commences a course of experiments, each of which must be pursued with care and with minuteness; every step he takes is noted, every observation written down; but unthought-of facts occur, unexpected phenomena present themselves, and in the midst of crucibles, furnaces and retorts, tired, oppressed and stupified, his success uncertain, and more than half his labours unaccomplished, he throws himself on a bench in his dusky laboratory, and with folded arms laments that the love of science or the fire of ambition should have ever urged him to the arduous enterprize.

Here might I pause! I have already passed over many leagues of land and water, my personages have suffered sundry misfortunes. Scenes of horrour and events of mystery have employed me. I have travelled through France, and I have brought my hero and my heroine back to England, but the most difficult part of my performance is not yet begun. My hero and heroine, do I say? Ah! let me not be misunderstood. They are not creatures of fiction. The incidents I relate are not imaginary. Too old and perhaps too dull for invention, I narrate nothing but what may be proved. With facility, with fluency, I have described a *chateau* and a cavern; the sufferings of virtue, and the stratagems of vice; but how many pages are still to be written? What heart-rending scenes remain still to be related? Oh! great is the labour yet before me. I have to record a true history, which equals if it doth not exceed all that the fertility of invention has ever produced, whether to rouse attention, to touch the feelings, or to surprise the fancy. I have to divest it of all that might seem incredible, and to make it appear as probable on perusal, as it is authentick in reality. What I have performed has been easy, it is but as a preface to the subject which first engaged me to write. That horrible and mysterious subject is now to be disclosed.

Here might I pause! but the uncertain tenure by which I hold existence forbids repose. Therefore have I hurried through the last chapter, and dismissed with such rapidity the Count and his agents, Mr. Alcot and Marie; and therefore have I fled with precipitation from St. Uldrich and *the grave*. I have already written more than my infirmities could well permit, but what remains to be described (alas! is such a description for my years?) fills me with dismay, and much, very much I fear that I shall never live to accomplish the arduous undertaking. But while I have strength let me proceed.

CHAPTER IV.

Who finds the heifer dead and bleeding fresh,
And sees fast by a butcher with an ax,
But will suspect 'twas he that made the slaughter?
Who finds the partridge in the puttock's nest,
But may imagine how the bird was dead,
Altho' the kite soar with unbloody beak?
Ev'n so suspicious is this tragedy.

....

————Foul deeds will rise
Though all the earth o'erwhelm them to man's eyes;
And murder, though it have no tongue, will speak
With most miraculous organ.

Miss Bolton and Theodore were sitting together at dinner, the day after her father's departure, when a servant, whose countenance and manner denoted excessive agitation, entered the room. "What is the matter, William?" said she.—"Oh! Miss, there be such a stir below stairs. There be all the sheriff's officers, and the coroner himself, about my master, they say, that's killed by his honour, Mr. Dalbert."—"Your master! is it my father killed?" cried she, trembling and growing pale.—"I beg pardon, my Lady. I'm sure I'd never think for to say whatsumever might flurry your Ladyship, but here is Mr. Alcot's steward, Mr. Derrill himself, who knows it all."—"How is this, Sir? pray can you explain the meaning of this liberty and this noise?" asked Miss Bolton.—"The meaning, Madam, is shortly this, your father is shot by that *munseer* at your side, and my master has sent us with this warrant to take him."—"My father shot!" shrieked she.—"Yes, shot and dead. He now lies at my master's, waiting for the coroner's inquest." Julia replied not. Such a shock was more than her frame could support. She sunk lifeless in the arms of Theodore.—"Villain!" cried he, in a voice of thunder, and his eyes flashing fire, "what have you done? See what your cruelty and folly have produced! Leave the room, fellow, instantly, and wait for me below." There was something in his manner as he said this that commanded obedience. Mr. Derrill muttered and retired.

Julia in a short time revived, and resting her arm, unconscious of what she did, upon Theodore's shoulder, tried in vain to give utterance to her words.—"Be composed, my Julia, my friend, my love," said he, little less agitated than herself.—"Your father and I were stopped last night by a robber, who held a pistol in his hand, which, as I attempted to wrest it from him, went off, and killed him on the spot. It was an unpleasant accident, I confess, but it troubles me little. I should have mentioned it to you before, but I feared to alarm you. Your father seemed to know the person of the deceased, and was so shocked at the recognition, and so wretched at the thought of the circumstance becoming publick, for what reason I can't conceive, that, to pacify him, I promised to inter the corpse in a retired spot, where no one should find it. In some measure quieted by my promise, he went on to Newbury, and I returned for a spade, with which I buried the body before morning. This they have discovered by some means, and hence the blundering impertinence of that fellow. But I will go and explain all the circumstances to the coroner, and will return to you before supper." He then left her, and proceeded with the officers of justice to Alcot-abbey.

His manner was firm and unconcerned, and though treated as a murderer by those who accompanied and guarded him, he entered the room where the coroner's jury was assembled, with composure and with dignity. Mr. Alcot, as a justice of the peace, assumed the privilege of making a speech. It was tedious, virulent and formal. He commenced with a panegyrick on Mr. Bolton, "whose murder," he said, "was the melancholy occasion of bringing them together." He then stated with minuteness the manner in which the body had been discovered buried in the ground, and asserted, as the truth was, that Theodore was the person last seen in company with Mr. Bolton the preceding evening; that, moreover, the prisoner had been heard to cough during the night in a hut into which he had entered by stealth, and in which the garden implements at Bolton-hall were kept, and that a spade placed among them had been found marked with blood, though it had been put by the night before with no such stain. That this was the spade employed to bury the murdered man, no doubt, he said, could be entertained; and thus by a short and simple chain of circumstances, the prisoner must, he contended, be judged guilty of murder. But to banish, as he said, the possibility of doubt from the minds of his hearers, "here," continued he, "is a bundle which arrived but a few minutes before the prisoner, containing the clothes worn by him yesterday, which were found locked up carefully in a secret drawer in his bed-chamber, and spotted thus with blood, and with them was this pistol, that has all the appearance of being recently discharged, and with which I am sure the unnatural deed was perpetrated."

Mr. Alcot in his speech omitted nothing that might induce a belief of Theodore's guilt, and having concluded it, he produced one of the gardeners from Bolton-hall, who, upon oath, confirmed his statement. This was the man who, lying on a loft in the hut, had heard the prisoner cough as he searched among the garden implements, who in the morning had found the spade marked with blood, and who had afterwards discovered the dead body. Mr. Bolton's butler, James Taylor, was then examined. He swore that the deceased had left home at nine the preceding night, intending to walk to Newbury, accompanied by the prisoner; and the witness further deposed that he was present when the prisoner's clothes were found, spotted with blood, in a drawer in his apartment; that the pistol was locked up with them, and that these were the clothes Mr. Dalbert had worn the day before.

The evidence being closed amid much bustle and confusion, the coroner desired to hear what the prisoner could advance in his exculpation. Theodore was about to speak, when, obtaining a view of the corpse, till then concealed from him by the crowd, what must have been his horrour on perceiving, not the body of an unknown ruffian, but the dead and mangled remains of his friend and benefactor Mr. Bolton? His senses failed, his blood grew cold, its circulation, as it were, ceased, his limbs shook, and he sunk inanimate upon the floor. When he returned to life, he seized one of the cold hands of the corpse, and kissing it with much emotion, burst into tears. He would have repeated, perhaps, what he had before said to Miss Bolton, but the shock he had received left him apparently only the power to declare, in weak and faltering accents, his innocence, and his total ignorance of the manner of Mr. Bolton's death. But this appearing to the jury, as it reasonably might, a mere evasion, they found a verdict of wilful murder against him.

The convicted wretch, execrated by all who attended the trial or heard of it, was with difficulty saved from the fury of the populace, and he was that night committed to Abingdon gaol. The assizes were to commence immediately, and a day for his trial was appointed. The news of Mr. Bolton's melancholy fate spread immediately throughout the kingdom, and excited universal horrour.

Miss Bolton passed some hours (after Theodore's departure from her with Derrill) in great uneasiness. There was something in the nature of the frightful intelligence she had received that must have disturbed the most unfeeling, but to her it was truly terrible. Her impatience and anxiety every moment increased, when at ten o'clock Mr. Alcot was announced to her. When he entered the room, she could only point to a chair for him.—"Miss Bolton," said he, heedless of her agitation, "I have a very shocking business to communicate to you. Would that some one else had apprized you of it!"—"My father"—"Your father, Madam, is no more."—"No more! my father no more! Ah! is my father dead? Where, where is he? Let me fly to him immediately!"—"He is at my house, but really you cannot, must not see him."—"Not see my father, and he dead! Nothing, nothing shall prevent me."—"You are yet to learn, perhaps, Miss Bolton, that he has fallen under the hands of an assassin; my good and worthy friend has been murdered."—"Murdered! and by whom? say, who could have the heart to murder my father?"—"Theodore Dalbert."—" 'Tis false! Theodore Dalbert is incapable, utterly incapable of such a crime. His nature is too mild, too noble, to harbour even a thought of such guilt. But let me fly to see my father, if I cannot save him." Saying which she hurried down stairs, ordered her chariot to follow her, and ran towards Alcot-abbey. She was soon overtaken by her servants and the carriage, and having entered it, she desired them to drive with all possible speed to her father. They already knew by report where he was to be found. Ellen, the faithful Ellen, accompanied her. Arrived at the house, she flew to the room where the corpse lay. "Ah! my father, my loved, my dear, my honoured father, friend, parent! Is it thus I see you? Oh! piteous, lamentable, shocking sight! Let me once again embrace you! Your Julia, your child, your darling, once again will kiss you, and never, never shall they tear me from you more! Here will I grow, here will I die!" In a paroxysm of grief the unhappy girl threw herself on the body, glewed herself to its shattered head, sobbed with convulsive agony, and dropped back motionless.

Removed to a chamber, undressed, and placed in bed, she was, with the assistance of Ellen and another woman, after some time restored to life. When sufficiently recovered to be able to speak, she begged to be permitted to see her father once again, but this was positively and peremptorily refused by her attendants. She then requested to see Mr. Alcot, to whom she made many apologies for the abruptness of her behaviour. Her apologies were not the result nor an act of ceremony. Even in the anguish of her heart she could think with uneasiness of the vehemence of her language to him. Her gentle mind could not bear the reflection of having given offence. "Mr. Alcot," said she, "can you forgive me? I have been guilty of rudeness, ingratitude and unkindness to you. My unparalleled wretchedness must be my excuse. To your generosity I sue for pardon." It was impossible even for Mr. Alcot, to retain displeasure against Julia. He entreated her to be assured that he had banished from his recollection the expressions to which she alluded, and that in his pity for her and his admiration, every other sentiment was lost. She desired to know the particulars of her father's melancholy fate, but a physician who had been sent for arriving at this juncture, prohibited any conversation, and desired that Miss Bolton should take a composing draught and be left alone till morning. The next days she repeated her request for permission to see the corpse, but her physician expressly forbade the attempt, and in a few hours afterwards it was buried. She insisted, however, though still extremely unwell, upon hearing the whole account of the murder, and was lost in utter astonishment at the relation that was given her. She could not believe that Theodore was guilty, and yet the circumstances were strong to incriminate him.

Mr. Alcot, with whom she conversed on the subject, in vain argued against him, in vain contended that the bloody clothes and the pistol found in his room, and his admitting to her that he had killed an individual, and buried him with a spade (found at Bolton-hall) in a retired spot, were such a confirmation of the gardener's testimony as must satisfy the most scrupulous and sceptical of his guilt. She, nevertheless, had no more doubt of his innocence than of her own being, and not knowing what to advance in his vindication, from thenceforth preserved a mournful silence, and sunk into profound melancholy. The next day she called for pen, ink, and paper, and wrote the following letter, which she committed to the care of Ellen.

To Theodore Dalbert, Esq. &c. &c.

"From my bed I write to you. Were I not confined by illness, I would visit you. You are now my first, perhaps my only friend. You are innocent I am sure. You are unfortunate I know. You must be my debtor for fifty pounds that I enclose. At this moment I can command no more. You will want money, and you may draw on me for what you will require. You have enemies who wish to ruin you. You must therefore lay aside that mistaken pride which would prompt you to silent contempt and scornful inaction. At this moment of sorrow and distress, shall I be excused for harbouring any sentiment but that of affliction, of using any language but that of lamentation? But if I loved my father, should I not be interested for him whom he loved? Your life and character are at stake. Preserve them and I may be, once again, happy. Forfeit them and I expire.

"Julia Bolton."

On the morning of the trial the court was crowded at an early hour, and Theodore, who refused all professional aid, having been arraigned, the indictment read, to which he was directed to plead not guilty, and the jury sworn, counsel for the crown arose and addressed the court thus.

"Gentlemen of the jury, you are this day called upon to acquit the most injured of mankind, or to convict the most atrocious of criminals. The prisoner at the bar is to receive from you life and honour, or death and infamy. How important, therefore, is your duty! Would to Heaven I could hope, for the character of my species, for the dignity of human nature, that your sentence would restore him to the esteem and affection of the virtuous! But if I am informed rightly, who among the bad is half so vitious? If I am informed rightly! Ah! too faithfully, too truly have I been instructed! A series of proofs as simple as they are convincing, as certain as they are probable, the evident interposition of Almighty Providence, and the confession of the culprit himself, all, all, authorise and urge me to hold him forth to your view and to the publick execration, as a monster of unexampled perfidy, of unparalleled ingratitude, of matchless cruelty, as a felon of the blackest stamp, as a murderer, and, I might add, a parricide.

"It is my duty to state the circumstances of the case, or my respect for your feelings, and the pain that I shall myself suffer at the recital, should impose eternal silence on so horrible a subject. For two and twenty years have I had the honour of attending this court, and of practising at the bar. For this period of time and some years longer have I studied the laws of my country, and the history of its criminal jurisprudence. But neither has chance brought within my observation, nor has reading furnished from past experience, a case at once so clear and so barbarous; a delinquent so specious and so dangerous, as this case and this delinquent. The needy villain who shoots the object of his cupidity, who happens to oppose him in committing an act of robbery; the sanguinary assassin, who, prompted by revenge, penury, or jealousy, deprives of life his fellow creature, can offer in their behalf some plea, some excuse. Passion blinded, anger provoked, or despair urged, or the object of their violence was unknown, or had never conferred a benefit. But here is a wretch to whom subtlety itself, or sophistry, or eloquence, or ingenuity, cannot afford the slightest semblance of extenuation.

"Released from a state of the most abject poverty in France by the good, the worthy man, whose loss we all deplore; brought over by him to this country upon terms of unexampled liberality; introduced to his friends and relatives as an equal and a friend; treated in all respects as his child: What return does he make? Admitted into the garden of innocence and happiness, this viper, this foreign miscreant, this second Satan, with a flagitiousness and atrocity happily unknown to our favoured island, plots the destruction of his benefactor, and contrives by some false pretences not well known to us at present, to seduce him to undertake a journey to London. On Friday the 27th of last month, they left Bolton-hall, about nine at night. It will appear in the evidence that the prisoner at the bar undertook to see the deceased safe from his own house to the town of Newbury, through which a stage-coach passed that was to carry Mr. Bolton to town. Mr. Bolton had, before he left home, expressed an intention to sleep that night at the Mitre-inn, where the stage-coach stopped, but it will be shown that he never reached this inn, which is the principal one in Newbury.

"Before I proceed to state to you, gentlemen of the jury, the substance of the evidence that will be adduced, I cannot help remarking for a moment on the wonderful wisdom and justice of Providence, that never suffers the crime of murder to escape undiscovered or unpunished. I may indeed with truth declare, that but for a miracle this nefarious offender would not have been discovered. Discovered, do I say? nay, would not have been suspected. How could suspicion rest on him? Could the hand which was loaded with benefits be supposed to wield the weapon that was to destroy its benefactor? Could a heart be found so depraved, a head so corruptly suspicious, as even to imagine that the creature of bounty, the object of beneficence, the beloved child of adoption, would be the treacherous assassin of his more than father? Every ennobling sentiment of our nature would spurn, in honour to humanity, so foul an imputation. To harbour it unjustly would betray a mind nearly as replete with atrocity as that which instigated the commission of the crime, and the very arraignment of the prisoner at the bar, amounts almost to a confirmation of his guilt. At what hour he returned to Bolton-hall that night is not known, as he always kept in his pocket the key of a back door, which permitted him to enter when he pleased, but it is certain that he appeared at the breakfast-table, in the morning, with apparent unconcern; and this consummate hypocrisy on his part, is, in my mind, no small aggravation of his crime.

"It will appear to you, gentlemen of the jury, that one Thomas Andrews, a gardener in the employment of Mr. Bolton, was accustomed to sleep upon a loft in an out-house near the garden, on the ground-floor of which he kept all the implements of his occupation. This man knew the prisoner at the bar, he had frequently attended him on botanical excursions, and had as frequently conversed with him. He knew his person, was acquainted with his voice, his foreign pronunciation of English, and with the sound of a cough that had never parted him since his arrival in this country. On the night of the day laid in the indictment, Thomas Andrews was asleep in his bed, when he was awakened by the noise of some one entering softly into the out-house where he lay, and (listening attentively) he heard the person who had entered cough (in such a manner as indicated a wish to suppress the noise of it), and search among the garden implements, which were in a particular corner. Andrews knew the cough to be the prisoner's and therefore he made no alarm. He and all the servants of Mr. Bolton had been taught to look upon the prisoner with the greatest respect, which, had his moral character been equal to his manners and his accomplishments, I confess would have been well deserved. Andrews from his respect to the prisoner, therefore, made no noise. He heard him depart in a few minutes, closing the door of the out-house after him, and just then the great clock at the stables struck eleven. Immediately upon this he fell asleep again and did not awake till six the next morning, when he got up. The habits of such a person are simple and uniform. He was accustomed to visit the gardens at this hour, and it happened that this morning he required a spade to assist him in his work. He had but one. This he had placed the evening before, without any particular mark or stain upon it, among the other garden tools, but now he found it spotted with blood. Surprised at this he repaired to his work, but happening, in the course of the day, to pass through the shrubbery, he perceived the mark of blood upon the ground. The stains upon the spade instantly occurred to him, and influenced by suspicion, he followed the track of the blood till he arrived at a retired and unfrequented spot, which had the appearance of having been newly turned up. The man, at once curious and alarmed, as it was natural he should be under the circumstances, lost no time in raising the recently stirred earth, and in a little while he found, about a foot below the surface, the body of the deceased. Terrified and shocked he instantly ran towards the house, but within about two hundred yards of the fatal spot, he chanced to meet Mr. Alcot of Alcot-abbey. He returned with him, and that gentleman, whose activity as a magistrate, whose humanity as a man, every one is acquainted with, had the body immediately removed to his own house, and having heard the gardener's story, he sent some people to apprehend the prisoner and to search his apartment.

"It is happy for the peace of civil society that the wicked never possess foresight and cunning equal to their depravity. This observation is forcibly exemplified in the case of the prisoner at the bar. He whom neither affection, gratitude, religion, nor compassion could influence, he, who was insensible to every social, every human affection, had not the sense, or had not the cunning, to destroy his clothes. Probably he thought that the body would never be found, and that he might, at his leisure, burn the bloody witnesses of his guilt. In one of his drawers were discovered the dress he had worn the night before, covered with blood, and the pistol with which he had effected the horrid act; and to Miss Bolton, the afflicted and amiable daughter of his victim, he confessed, in a moment of terrour and surprise, that he had taken the spade with which he had buried the body of an individual, whom he had killed the night before: but with impudent absurdity he added that the person killed was a robber, who had been shot accidentally by his (the robber's) pistol, which he had presented against her father. This happened, the prisoner asserted, as he (the prisoner) endeavoured to wrest the pistol from the pretended footpad.

"Such, gentlemen, is the conclusive and incontrovertible evidence that shall be adduced to you, and such is the evidence on which the coroner's jury convicted the prisoner of wilful murder. In addition to this, it will be shown that since he was committed to the gaol of Abingdon, there was found in his pocket the key of Mr. Bolton's cabinet, in which was personal property to a large amount; and the last will of the deceased, in his own hand-writing, will be produced, wherein is contained a bequest of three thousand pounds sterling, to his unnatural and cruel murderer. Fatal bequest! Unfortunate legacy! The very kindness of the worthy man was probably a chief cause of his destruction. It is also clear that another object of the prisoner was to possess himself of the property in this cabinet, to obtain which he did not hesitate to commit the most atrocious of crimes; and which, but for his speedy apprehension, he, doubtless, would have seized.

"You are assembled, gentlemen, on an awful occasion. The life of a man is in your hands. Save him if it be possible. If it be possible! Alas! it is not. You are assembled, this day, to give by your verdict the vengeance due to the outraged laws of society. Oh! if in the tissue of this woeful subject, one thread could be found that might lead even to a doubt, would not I be the first to seize it, and pursue the clue of mercy? But, here, all is conviction, all is murder, all is hell; and there the fiend, who must expiate his barbarous and infernal crime, by a publick and ignominious death."

Thomas Andrews the gardener, and James Taylor the butler, were then severally examined, and in every particular corroborated the statement of counsel.

Mr. Alcot deposed that he met Andrews in great agitation, about two o'clock in the afternoon, that he returned with him a short way, and that he saw the deceased lying, partly covered with earth, and in a shallow grave, according to Andrews's description. He added that the gaoler of Abingdon had, in his (Mr. Alcot's) presence, found in the prisoner's pocket, a key, which afterwards proved to be the key of Mr. Bolton's cabinet, wherein was negotiable property to the amount of six thousand pounds, together with the will of the deceased, in his own hand-writing. The will was identified, and the writing proved, by Mr. Alcot, to be that of Mr. Bolton. It contained a bequest of three thousand pounds to the prisoner.

The innkeeper at Newbury was the next witness produced, and he deposed that he well knew Mr. Bolton who had been his landlord, but that he had not seen him for some months, and that on the night laid in the indictment, the deceased had not visited the Mitre-inn, though his *valise* had been sent thither the day before, nor had he left Newbury the next morning in the coach.

The clothes, the pistol, and the spade, were all produced and identified. The gentleman who conducted the prosecution now stood up and said, "We might close here, my Lord, on the part of the crown, certain that the enlightened and respectable gentlemen who compose the jury, would, without quitting their box even for a minute, unhesitatingly convict the prisoner. But to demonstrate his guilt beyond the remotest possibility of doubt, we shall examine one witness more. It has been already shown that he left Bolton-hall with the deceased, who intended to sleep that night at the Mitre-inn in Newbury; that the deceased never reached that inn; that the prisoner at the bar, some time after their departure, took a spade which he returned to its place before morning, but which, while in his possession, received the stain of blood; that the body was buried in the ground, an operation that required a spade, that the clothes worn by the prisoner that night, were found concealed in a secret drawer and spotted with blood, and that along with them a pistol was discovered. Why take the spade, unless to bury the body? He took the spade, it was marked with blood. He wore the bloody clothes, and they had all received their sanguinary marks on the night when the man was killed and when the body was buried. Is not this damning proof? That the murder was perpetrated in order to commit a robbery, appears by the key of the cabinet having been found in the prisoner's pocket, whose cruelty and ingratitude are confirmed, if confirmation were necessary, by the will of the deceased bequeathing to him a sum of three thousand pounds. But one witness remains to be examined, whose evidence will strengthen all that has been said, and will terminate this tragick tale. Let Miss Bolton know that his Lordship begs to see her."

Miss Bolton, pale, trembling, emaciated and almost insensible, entered in deep mourning leaning on two ladies. She had been confined to her bed till this morning. A more interesting figure cannot be imagined. Silence was called and obtained.

The judge, in the most soothing and polite terms, said he hoped she might be able to compose herself, assured her that nothing would be permitted which might in the most remote degree wound her feelings, and advanced a few steps to conduct her to the bench whereon he sat. It was a solemn scene. It was a daughter accusing the murderer of her father: but that murderer was her lover, and that father was, oh! such a father! How dear was each of them to her heart!

"Miss Bolton," said his Lordship, "this is a sad and trying hour. The laws of our country call for justice and an example, and it happens, unfortunately, that your testimony has become necessary. You shall be asked only a few words. These I will have the honour of addressing to you myself, and your answers it shall be my care to repeat aloud. But first according to our forms, (with which I would in this instance willingly dispense, if it were in my power) it is necessary that you should be sworn. Be pleased, therefore, to hold this bible. 'You will true answers give, Madam, to all such questions as shall be put to you on this trial; so help you God.' Now, kiss the book, and, in order to prevent any doubt or misconception, you will be so good as to try to identify the prisoner."

Julia, who till now had not raised her eyes, encouraged by the gentleness and suavity of the judge, turned them towards Theodore. His looks met her's—unfortunate man! Didst thou see in that glance the malevolence of a prosecutor, the estrangement of inconstancy, or the coldness of insensibility? No, kind, compassionate and tender, those lovely eyes viewed thy miserable condition with a tear of pity and affection, and thou feltst at that moment that at least one sincere friend was still left thee in a strange land and among a host of enemies.

The dejected, sickly appearance of the prisoner, so lately her preceptor, added to the anguish Julia already felt, and increased her perturbation.

"That is *Monsieur Dalbert*, my Lord," said she, in a voice scarcely to be heard. "You recollect, perhaps," said his Lordship, "the 27th of last month."—"I do."—"Had he any conversation with you then upon this melancholy affair?"—"Yes, my Lord."—"Pray, relate the conversation."—"He said that he had taken a spade the night before, from Bolton-hall, for the purpose of burying a man who had stopped my father and him. The deceased, he said, intending to rob them, held a pistol in his hand, which in Mr. Dalbert's endeavour to wrest it from him, accidentally killed him. But for——"—"Miss Bolton, I shall ask you no further questions; and if the prisoner has no interrogatory to put, you may retire."—"Then Miss Bolton, you, too, believe me guilty?" said Theodore. The look that accompanied these words, which were the first he spoke during the trial, penetrated to her heart. It conveyed all the bitterness of reproach, but the expression itself was uttered with that softness of manner, that melody of tone, which love alone and Julia could teach.

Animated, roused, she forgot her timidity, and, for a moment, her distress. "Believe you guilty of my father's murder! No, Theodore! Of your innocence I never entertained a doubt. I know you to be too good, and too grateful, for such a crime. I know you loved my dear and honoured parent as sincerely as I did myself; and I have attended here this day from a desire to utter this, which I hoped might serve you on this dreadful trial, and not to assist in your prosecution. To serve you I would do much, to save you I would willingly lay down my life." She uttered this with rapidity and fire. It was the last exertion of pity and attachment. It was the passionate effusion of love, too powerful to be checked. A deadly whiteness suddenly overspread those cheeks, which a moment before glowed with crimson. A universal tremour seized her frame, and she would have fallen to the ground, but for the assistance of the judge.

Wonder and curiosity were expressed in every countenance. Theodore in the contemplation of her illness and danger, no longer remembered that he was a prisoner. "My Julia," said he, utterly unmindful of the surrounding crowd, "let me assist you. Let my arms support you. These unfeeling men shall not pollute you with their touch. Thou sayst true, admirable girl, I am innocent; but not more innocent, than grateful to thee for what thou hast done and said. Let my gratitude now appear." His words were uttered with gestures of frenzy, and were accompanied by an effort of prodigious strength and activity to advance to her; but the gaoler and his assistants overpowered him. "Barbarians, ruffians, assassins!" cried he, "unhand me! Behold the fairest and sweetest of her sex, whom you have reduced to that extremity, and let me bring her back to life!" As he said this, she was carried out of court senseless and without motion, and he was forced back in a state of indignant desperation.

The scene was new to the judge. He was a man of feeling and it moved him. He desired silence to be called, and then addressed himself to the prisoner.

"Mr. Dalbert, the evidence for the prosecution is concluded, and it now remains for you to examine your witnesses, to prove your innocence, and to address the court. The laws of England are not in heinous cases unmerciful. You might have had the aid of counsel, you declined it. You might have cross-examined each of the witnesses, but this, likewise, you declined. The proofs against you are few in number, but strong, and I fear convincing. But philosophy, and I will add christianity, justify me in thinking that it is possible you may be innocent. Show that you are not guilty, Sir, and you will have contributed much indeed to my individual happiness. Be cool, be collected. No person shall interrupt you, no noise shall disturb you, and no impatience will be felt by me or by the jury."

Such a speech was well calculated to calm the disorder of the prisoner. His agitation gradually subsided, and he became firm and undisturbed.

CHAPTER V.

If ever you have look'd on better days;
If ever been where bells have knell'd to church;
If ever sat at any good man's feast;
If ever from your eye-lids wip'd a tear,
And know what 'tis to pity, and be pitied;
Let gentleness my strong enforcement be.

....

No ceremony that to great ones 'longs,
Not the king's crown, nor the deputed sword,
The marshal's truncheon, nor the judge's robe,
Becomes them with one half so good a grace
As mercy does.

"Who, among the various wretches," said the prisoner in a graceful attitude and with a low but distinct delivery, "doomed by an incomprehensible and cruel destiny to misery, is most miserable? Who suffers most affliction and receives least pity? Who of the innumerable inhabitants of the wide globe has the dreadful distinction of prime and pre-eminent pain? I am he.

"Oh! for the nervous tongue that might convey my piteous tale into your inward hearts, then would your bosom send forth sighs of commiseration and your tears bear witness to my wrongs! Poverty, disappointment, corporal suffering, death, what are these? the inevitable portion of mortality. I regard them not, I fear them not; but universal reprobation, ignominy and the gibbet—these, these I confess, fill my soul with terrours: yet these are evils that many suffer; but where shall we find an honourable and innocent man publickly accused of treachery, ingratitude and murder? where shall we find a man conscious of his own purity, and yet incapable of controverting any part of the evidence that convicts him of these crimes? Alas! I am he.

"The black and detestable calendar of capital delinquents will transmit my trial and my condemnation, with those of the vilest and most abhorred of miscreants, to the latest posterity. The moralist will quote me as a rare and tremendous example of depravity, and a striking instance of the divine vengeance. The misanthrope will adduce my horrid story to justify his distrust and hatred; and nurses, with my name, will affright their wayward babes. On the gallows I shall be hanged, like a dog, loaded with the maledictions of the populace. No consecrated spot will receive my corpse. To the barbarous knife of the surgeon will my body be consigned; and yet, I am innocent.

"Almighty Creator! Thou whom I have been taught to worship with love and fear from my infancy! Thou, oh Lord! knowest the wrongs I suffer. Thou knowest my integrity, and the filial affection that I bear to the best of women. On thy divine justice my heart relies. Thy inscrutable wisdom I adore. Thy unspeakable goodness I have experienced. Father of mercy! support, I beseech thee, my honoured mother under the heavy affliction of my ignominy, and breathe into her bosom a certainty of my innocence. Open the exhaustless fountains of thy mercy, and mitigate, oh God! her maternal sufferings! Men of Abingdon, by that Being whom I have supplicated, I utter truth! May his Providence utterly forsake me; may his utmost wrath eternally pursue me, if I be not guiltless of the crime alledged against me!

"Gentlemen of the jury, though you will not, and perhaps cannot, believe me, let me solicit your attention for a few minutes. What I say will be remembered. I perceive it is noted down. It may hereafter prove useful, and if in the course of succeeding time, this mysterious and horrible affair shall by any means, inconceivable at present, be developed, it will be seen how the much-injured Theodore Dalbert thought and spoke in the hour of unprecedented anguish. This is the last breath of my vanity; will you pardon it? I expect not your acquittal. Hope has fled from my bosom, and in her place sits despair.

"To you, my Lord, I owe the warm tribute of gratitude. Your patience and your mildness have touched me sensibly. Wretch as I am, and overwhelmed with calamity, I can feel your condescension and benevolence. Such power have politeness and humanity, over the heart of man.

"Called upon for my defence, invited to prove my innocence, what shall I say? How shall I begin? endowed with no eloquence, instructed by no preparatory study, practised in no declamation, in vain would I oppose the industry with which my prosecution has been conducted. But at least let me describe all that passed on that fatal night, and a few circumstances which happened previously.

"My Lord, and gentlemen of the jury, my family is well known to you. General Dalbert is my grandsire. I was born and educated in France, but my father, who was an Englishman, instructed me early in the language of this country. He is dead. It is now more than a year since Miss Bolton visited me in Bourdeaux. I had for some time prior to that period supported my mother and myself by my pen. I wrote for the stage and I wrote novels. My works were not unsuccessful, but I was poor. Mr. Bolton kindly invited me to England, hoping, as he said, that my grandfather, who had then no child, might be prevailed upon to take me under his protection. I was not in circumstances to travel, and Mr. Bolton, I believe to conceal his generosity, offered to engage me as his secretary and his daughter's preceptor, at a salary of two hundred pounds a-year. I accepted his offer with gratitude. Half of this sum was sufficient to support my mother, the remainder was enough for me. Some accidents happened afterwards that separated me from my new friends for a time, but these I need not now mention.

"Mr. Bolton, in consequence of a tedious illness under which my grandfather laboured, was obliged to postpone his intended visit to him: but having some business, of the nature of which I am totally ignorant, to transact in London, he made preparations for a journey. He expected, he said, to be detained there for a few days, and on the evening of the 27th of last month, he committed to me the key of his cabinet, in which were papers that I had to arrange and copy. On this same evening he expressed an inclination to walk to Newbury, where he was to take the coach next morning, and I accompanied him on his walk thither.

"It was about nine o'clock, and we had passed through part of the shrubbery, along a winding path, when suddenly I heard, as I followed him, (there was not room for two to walk abreast on the path) a loud cry, before me, of 'Stop!' The winding of the path and the thickness of the surrounding foliage had prevented me from seeing the person who spoke, and consequently had prevented him from seeing me. But the moment I heard the sound I rushed forward, and found that my friend had been stopped by a person with a pistol in his hand. I immediately threw myself on the man and endeavoured to seize it. We were nearly of equal strength. Our contest continued for a minute, when, by accident, in our struggle the trigger was pulled, and the robber was mortally wounded in the face.

"Mr. Bolton had been a long time infirm. He was always nervous, and at this moment his agitation was excessive. He advanced to the body, now lying on the ground, in order to examine it. The moon shone brightly upon it. 'It is, it is he, oh! oh! lost! undone! unfortunate! reprobate!' cried he. He knew the person of the deceased, and in the contemplation of the body, and his distress and sorrow for what had happened, he seemed to have totally forgotten both me and his journey. The hurry of my spirits diminished, perhaps, in some degree, my sensibility, for I confess I looked at the corpse without feeling the least contrition. But I could not be so indifferent to the apparent misery of my friend, the agony I should say. I really want words to describe his extreme grief, his violent emotions. I saw plainly that the deceased had been dear to him, and that they had been united by no common ties. The circumstance was extraordinary and mysterious, and it therefore was not for me to inquire into it.—'Is it thus,' exclaimed he, 'I see you, is it thus you perish?'—'Sir,' said I, 'be pleased to moderate your affliction: the deceased was a robber, perhaps a murderer. The pistol went off by accident. The law of self-defence justifies us in what has happened; and upon no principle of reason or justice, is he worthy of your pity or regret.'—'Oh Theodore!' answered he, 'if you knew who he was, how dear, how very dear to me, you would curse your rash and cruel hand that caused his death. A terrible tale is attached to his appearance here. I am filled with horrour and alarm; and when it is known that he has fallen in this place and by your means, the universal detestation of mankind will attend me. Shame and disgrace will follow my steps, and tears, bitter reflection and remorse will evermore await me. Oh God! oh God! what shall I do, whither shall I fly?' Saying this he knelt by the dead body, and burst into tears. Moved and shocked by the vehemence and agitation of his manner, and the obscurity of his expressions, I entreated him to arise. 'I perceive, Sir,' said I, 'some mystery in this affair: I seek not to develop it—Let us continue our walk to Newbury. In my faithful bosom the transaction shall be for ever buried, and in a retired spot I will this night deposite the dead body. No one shall see it; no one shall ever find it; and father Lanesby, your pious and venerable confessor, shall privately consecrate the ground, and perform over the corpse every necessary ceremony. Be composed, dearest Mr. Bolton; you make me excessively unhappy to see you thus. I repeat it, you are blameless. The fault, if any, is mine. Be persuaded, therefore, and let us proceed.'

" 'Well, be it so,' replied he, somewhat relieved by my words. 'To you, my dear Theodore, I commit the management of this shocking business. Oh! when you hear the name of the deceased, you will wonder how I can survive him. Know that'—'Hold, Sir,' said I, 'you will only irritate your grief by dwelling on the subject any longer. Another time we shall speak upon it at our leisure.' Alas! had not my regard for his feelings prompted me to recommend silence to him, I should now be enabled to vindicate my innocence in some other manner than mere assertion. But I am a child of misfortune, and at my birth the planet of malignity presided, and shed upon my hopeless head its most baleful influence. We proceeded to Newbury without exchanging another word. Arrived at the entrance to the town, he took both my hands, squeezed them affectionately, and pointing to me the road we had come, left me with precipitation.

"It was now past ten, and I had a solemn promise to fulfil. I returned with speed to Bolton-hall, which is about three miles from the spot where Mr. Bolton parted from me. I admit that I entered the hut wherein the garden implements were kept, and that I took from among them a spade. I do not recollect, now, whether or not I coughed while in the act of searching for it, but I suppose I did, as Andrews has said it. With the spade I returned to the body, which I dragged to a retired spot, about a hundred and fifty yards from the place where the shot had been fired; and having dug a grave, I put the corpse into it, dressed as it was. I then covered it with the earth I had raised, and returned to Bolton-hall, taking care to deposite the spade where I had found it. I admit that it might while in my possession have received marks of blood, and I must believe that in the place where I had buried the body of the robber, Andrews found that of Mr. Bolton. It was day-light when I entered my own apartment, and having stripped myself, I put the dress I had worn, together with the pistol, into one of the drawers. I acknowledge that the blood upon my clothes was my motive for doing so, and that it was my intention to burn them when an opportunity should offer for that purpose.

"The next morning when I heard from Derrill that Mr. Bolton was murdered, and that I was accused as the assassin, I conceived that the body which I had buried had, by accident, been discovered; and that from some resemblance in the dress and shape, they had stupidly mistaken it for the body of Mr. Bolton. With this persuasion I attended the coroner's inquest, not doubting that

I could, in a moment, cover my accusers with confusion and disgrace. I therefore felt during the trial, more of exultation than apprehension, and it was not until it was concluded, and that I turned about to prove to them their blunder and impertinence, that I had the most distant idea of Mr. Bolton's death.

"It is not within the scope of language to convey—it is not in the power of the imagination to conceive, what I then felt. To see his murdered body were alone enough to produce dismay and woe; but to have these painful feelings aggravated by the reflection that I was charged and believed to be his murderer, and that as such I would probably suffer an ignominious death.—Oh what a situation was mine! And what was the conflict, what the confusion caused in my mind, by viewing his mangled remains where I expected to see the corpse of another? and then each of the two bodies to be wounded in the same manner and in the face! No, I cannot describe what fills me, even at this moment, with perplexity, horrour, and consternation. For a moment such was my stupefaction that I actually thought I had killed my benefactor, and in consequence I felt all the remorse and self-abhorrence that such a crime may be supposed likely to produce. Never since the human heart beat with sorrow, never since the human mind experienced surprise, never since the human frame trembled with fear, was terrour, astonishment, or anguish equal to minc. That I who would have devoted my whole life to promote the happiness of the only man on earth I loved, who would have hazarded my existence to preserve him from danger, should be thought his murderer, his treacherous, base and mercenary murderer, the murderer of Mr. Bolton! Oh! it was too horrible! Had the means of self-destruction been within my reach, I fear I should not now be here. I threw myself on the body, I kissed its cold hands, and I thought I should have expired with grief and agitation.

"Convicted by the jury, I was conveyed on foot to gaol, a distance of some miles. It was with difficulty that the officers of justice could preserve me from the fury of the people, and my arms being pinioned, I could oppose no resistance. An immense crowd was soon assembled about me, all hissing and reviling, and all willing to tear me to pieces. Defiled with the dirt they threw on me; stupified by the blows they gave me; pale, wild, and tottering, I prayed for death to release me from my sufferings; and *'Dalbert the murderer'* was so often reiterated around me, that in a short time I could scarcely dare to believe myself not guilty. At length I gained a refuge from my persecutors in my solitary cell, where, bound by heavy fetters, I have since remained.

"I have told you, my Lord, and you, gentlemen of the jury, all that has passed within my knowledge. I have told you nothing but the truth. This, as I hope to enter the mansions of the righteous, and as I value the promise of an hereafter, I assever. It is my singular and unhappy destiny to stand in a situation wherein exculpation is impossible, and in which I myself am confounded with the extent and magnitude of my apparent guilt. But I am innocent.

"If it be asked, how came Mr. Bolton to be murdered, and his body placed where that of the robber had been buried, and what has become of his? I know not how or what to answer. A mystery that I can neither develop nor comprehend, involves the transactions of that horrible night in utter and irreconcileable obscurity and contradiction. At times I think that some miscreant, associated with the footpad, had been an unobserved witness of the scene in the shrubbery, and that immediately after I parted from Mr. Bolton, he murdered and then robbed him; but why incur the risk or take the trouble of carrying away the robber's remains, and placing in their stead those of my benefactor; or how discover the spot that I had chosen for the interment, I can neither explain nor conjecture. Perhaps he overheard me say to Mr. Bolton that I would bury the unknown, and, having effected the assassination of my friend, returned to the shrubbery in time to observe whither I conveyed the corpse; and perhaps his intention in exchanging the bodies, and shooting Mr. Bolton in the face, was to found a criminal prosecution against me. But I am so bewildered, so lost in the distraction of my vague surmises, that upon this impenetrable secret I must not be more diffuse, as I cannot be satisfactory.

"The proofs brought against me have been I confess clear and convincing, but whether the gentleman who stated the case, in the decisiveness of his manner, the violence of his invective, and his premature condemnation, complied with his express instructions, or followed the ordinary course of his profession, I know not. I should be sorry to call his profession a trade, or to think that that trade had tricks. He spoke from a written document, and therefore much of what he uttered was doubtless the substance of his brief; but as that brief could merely convey intended proofs, and therefore could not convict me, and as every man is considered innocent by the enlightened, until he is found guilty on being tried, I shall not pretend to say whether the learned gentleman evinced his knowledge, his logick, or his humanity, *by holding me forth to the publick execration*, to use his own words, *as a monster of perfidy, ingratitude and cruelty; as a felon, a murderer, a parricide.* Is it liberal or generous in an advocate, enjoying himself the sweets of independence and liberty, to exhaust his borrowed rhetorick, to employ the mechanical and little-meaning common-place substitutes for eloquence, the vulgar fluency of ignorance or vacancy, the artificial and undignified cant and pertness of forensick pleading, with unfeeling flippancy, obstreperous utterance, and grotesque gesticulation, against a wretch, trembling for his life, guarded by gaolers, and just led forth from his dark and dreadful dungeon, where bread and water had been his only support, and a little straw his only comfort? If the coarseness and vulgarity of such a speech disgust every person of taste, sense or information that happens to hear it, what must be its effect on the object of its virulence who is compelled to listen to it, or would you be surprised if it should irritate his terrour and anxiety even to frenzy?

"In what school the gentleman learned his philosophy I am ignorant, but I fear his position is more useful than true, that *Providence never suffers the crime of murder to escape unpunished.* Equally enlightened is his declaration, that *but for the miraculous interference of some supernatural agent, I should not now be in custody.* These are the mistakes of judgment or the errours of ignorance; but, gentlemen of the jury, was it right, was it decent, was it humane, was it just, to anticipate your conviction, and to tell you that you could not but inflict on me the punishment of death? Should he, whose rank in society, whose knowledge of the laws, whose superior education, whose extensive influence, give him an authority over your minds, presume to declare to you, before a single proof was adduced, that your mercy would be injustice, and that you must do what—deprive him of life, whom at that moment you were bound to consider as innocent as yourselves? Was it becoming, was it manly, to cover me with reproach, and to pour on an unprotected and wretched foreigner and prisoner, a torrent of vulgar vituperation? How much more decorous, how much more worthy of a gentleman, a scholar and a christian, would it have been to have conjured you to divest your minds of all passion and partiality, and to suffer no intemperance nor prejudice to disturb or bias your understandings; and then to have stated the case, as it was described to him, with moderation, quietness and simplicity; to have shunned all exaggeration and scurrility; to have banished from his language every thing turgid, every thing superfluous; and to have deplored the loss of the deceased, but to have wished, at least, if not to have hoped, that the unhappy prisoner might prove innocent? But I dismiss the speech and the speaker from my thoughts.

"I am now on my trial for a capital offence, and my conviction is to be followed by death. But by what authority are you armed with the power of depriving me of life? This is a solemn question. My Lord and gentlemen, there is an essay on crimes and punishments written by the Marquis Beccaria.* It may not have been generally read in this country, and I shall be excused, I hope, for stating the outline of his arguments against the justice, and against the policy of capital punishment in any case. It is a book which I read when very young, and I have since studied it with much attention. The drowning wretch will snatch at a straw, and I take the liberty of conveying to you, gentlemen, his reasonings on this subject, not hoping, but not despairing, that it may convince you.

"He says that men are by nature free. To unite themselves in society they were obliged to surrender a portion of their independence, and the conditions on which they did so were what are called the laws. Natural liberty is of little value from the precariousness of its duration, and the number of evils attached to it, and therefore men willingly sacrificed a part of it to secure the quiet enjoyment of the remainder. The sum of all these portions of liberty or power, constitutes the power of every government. To prevent the infraction of this social compact, some motives that might strike the senses were necessary, and it was found that the only effectual motives were punishments; but as no man ever resigned a portion of his natural liberty for the good of the publick, but merely for his own security and comfort, it follows that any punishment which is unnecessary is unjust. It is likewise certain that every individual would decline to put into the publick stock more than the smallest portion possible of his freedom, and merely as much as might be sufficient to engage others to defend him, or in other words to extend to him the benefits of society. The right of punishing is to be found in the aggregate of these the smallest portions possible of individual liberty, and all that extends beyond this is injustice.

"Each punishment has two objects, one is to prevent the criminal from doing more injury, and the second is to prevent others from committing a like crime. But who shall say that any community has a right to sacrifice one of its members? Did any one of their number give to them the right to put him to death; or in the smallest portions possible of liberty, can there be contained the greatest of human advantages, life? God created man in his own likeness, and breathed into him an immortal soul. Who but God, then, shall dare to rob of life the image of our Maker? "*Take not away that which thou canst not give.*"

If no individual has the right to kill himself, how can he give such a right to others? The punishment of death therefore is a murderous act of a whole nation against an individual.

"It is not the intenseness of the pain that has the greatest effect on the mind, but its continuance, for the sensibility of man is more powerfully excited by weak but repeated impressions, than by a sudden violence. A punishment, to be just, should be severe enough, and only severe enough, to deter others from offending in the manner in which the punished person had offended; and solitary confinement for life is sufficient, and has been found to be sufficient, to deter the most reprobate; nay it is more effectual for this purpose than death. The mind, by collecting itself and exerting all its strength, can, for a while, repel grief and dread, but its most powerful efforts are insufficient to resist the horrours of perpetual confinement in solitude.

"The punishment of death, moreover, has a bad effect on society from the spectacle of cruelty it presents, aggravated by the solemnity of the trial, and the terrible pageantry of the execution. Let us look to the kingdoms and ages most notorious for capital punishments, and it will be found that they have been invariably those in which the most atrocious crimes have been perpetrated, and on the contrary, in those countries where mildness and humanity prevail, (as in Pennsylvania) there are fewer heinous offences committed, in proportion to the number of the inhabitants, than elsewhere.

"As punishments become more cruel, the minds of men, like a fluid which always rises to the height of its source, grow more callous, and the force of passions still continuing, the wheel in some years terrifies no more than formerly the prison. In some regiments there is no corporal chastisement applied; in others not a day passes that one, at least, of the few hundred men composing the ranks, does not receive the torture of the lash. Is the gentle discipline less efficacious than the bloody? Universal experience proves the contrary. Men regulate their conduct by the repeated impressions of evils that they know, and not by those with which they are unacquainted; and it is possible to make a man as much afraid of solitary confinement for a month on bread and water, as of a flogging that should tear all the flesh from his back.

"Let us suppose, argues further the philosophick Beccaria, two nations, in one of which the greatest punishment is perpetual imprisonment, and in the other the wheel. Each of these punishments will inspire the same degree of dread, and there can be no reason for rendering the former more terrible than it is, which will not be equally valid for augmenting the latter. But who can think the rack too lenient? Capital punishments, then, are unnecessary, useless, unjust, and cruel.

"This, gentlemen of the jury, is a mere sketch of that great man's reasoning; but hasty and superficial as it is, perhaps it will make you doubt the justice of the English criminal code; and if it should convince you that society has no right to take away the life of one of its members, how will you reconcile to your consciences the conviction of a person capitally indicted? To this you will say, is the criminal, proved to be guilty of the offence alledged against him, to escape all punishment, because no punishment but death is inflicted by our laws for his crime? and are we (ignorant of this abstract and recondite doctrine when we entered our box, and swore to give a true verdict according to the evidence) to perjure ourselves by acquitting the prisoner whom we think guilty? To this I answer shortly, that as it is a less crime to commit perjury than murder, you are bound, as conscientious and honest men, to acquit me, though you should be convinced that I am really guilty; and here I suppose you think that the breach of your oath would be perjury. But it would not. A perjurer is he who wilfully takes a false oath; but you, summoned under pecuniary penalties to try a prisoner, have been seduced or compelled to take your oath; and its violation, where the life of a fellow-creature would be lost were it observed, becomes a virtue. To observe it were to commit murder; because, on your conviction depends the condemnation, and on the condemnation the execution of this individual.

"If an oath were to bind under such circumstances, there is no cruelty that might not be accomplished under the semblance of justice. Twelve men are forced, by the fear of fines, to assemble, and to swear that they will *give a true verdict according to the evidence* to be adduced to them. If they acquit the prisoner they save his life, or preserve him from torture; but they find him guilty, and expose him unjustly to death or torment; why? because, if they do not, they will have perjured themselves. Silly reasoning! wretched logick! Their acquittal hurts no one, and saves the prisoner; their conviction murders him; but they hesitate not to pronounce it, for they have been trepanned into an oath to do so. What a trick upon the conscience, how puerile, how preposterous, how barbarous, the practice!

"But is the prisoner, though guilty, to escape all punishment? Yes, if he be arraigned in such a manner as that he cannot be punished at all except with death, which is my case, inasmuch as no human power has a right to inflict death. To pronounce a capital conviction were to commit murder, and the Lord saith in the decalogue, 'Thou shalt not commit murder.' To produce an amendment in the laws, it is only necessary to act in three or four cases according to philosophy, good sense and humanity, by acquitting notorious malefactors, and the legislature must soon, from necessity, correct its bloody code. Gentlemen, I seek not to deceive you. I avail myself of no sophistry. I utter the dictates of reason. The doctrine I have delivered may surprise from its novelty, but it is just. It has convinced me, and it has converted thousands.

"In future times, when there will be no executioners and malefactors will be fewer, with what disgust, with what repugnance will not the studious inquirer peruse the system of English jurisprudence as it respects crimes! How shocked must he be at the continuation, among a nation of poets, philosophers, legislators and lawyers, of a bloody code founded on cruelty, supported by ignorance, and extended by tyranny! Will he not shudder to find, that of the actions which a man is hourly liable to commit, there are near two hundred, which in this country are now punished with death? And what will be his reflections when he casts his eye over the indisputable lists of the thousands who suffer under such laws? Alas! How weakly do reason and virtue oppose, how slowly do they conquer prejudice and violence? If we look into the page of history, what does it disclose? A tissue of craft, rapine, slaughter and imbecility. Each revolution has discovered, and published, and derided the errours and the absurdities of the age preceding it: and we, at this day and in this kingdom, wonder at the laws of Draco,* the existence of slavery, the institution of the Holy Office, at the use of the rack, at the trials by ordeal and by battle, at the acquittal by compurgation, and at the mortal penalty of witchcraft. We wonder at these excesses of superstition, at these mistakes of polity, and we deplore their evil effects; but we are blind to the barbarism and savageness of our own institutions, and we know not, or we forget that each capital convict in England is cruelly deprived of that to which society has no right, and that he is murdered—murdered without the plea of necessity even, for it is demonstrable from facts that a juster punishment would be more efficacious in deterring others.

"But let it not be supposed for an instant, that in the arguments which I have used, I have even by implication insinuated my guilt. I have only said that were I guilty, you would be bound notwithstanding your oath, to acquit me; but while I have breath I will assert my innocence, the consciousness of which only could support me under the heavy pressure of my affliction. The case against me is mysterious. My guilt I confess is probable. I can offer no proof in my defence, I have only to advance naked, unsupported assertion; but were it not better that ninety-nine criminals should escape than one innocent man suffer? Have I said that my guilt is probable? It is not. Nothing was ever offered to the consideration of a court more remote from likelihood. Ask your hearts if it be probable, if it be possible, to banish by one effort religion, gratitude, mercy and affection, and to fill the place which they had occupied in the breast with the black, corroding, horrible stratagems of murder. To possess the happiness of an unspotted reputation, and to resign this inestimable treasure for the execrable character of an assassin. To walk during life in the peaceful and flowery paths of innocence and virtue, and suddenly, without provocation and without incitement, to plunge into the infernal gulf of parricide. No! great crimes have ever been preceded by slight transgressions, and it is yet to be shown that our nature is capable of passing, at once, from rectitude to atrocity. My past life should acquit me of the charge that is now alledged.

"The most beneficent act of the Deity is the creation of man, and the most acceptable service we can render him is the preservation of our species. Respect his work, then, and destroy not his creature.

"Gentlemen of the jury, I fear it is impossible that your minds can have escaped some impression against me, from the number and the nature of the calumnies that have been within a few days past so widely circulated. Are you sure that your passions are not inflamed? are you sure that you can weigh the evidence and my reasoning with coolness? are you sure that you are entirely free from prejudice? It has been said that I had an interested motive for perpetrating the crime. Oh! was it not my interest that my only benefactor should live, to realise his noble intentions towards me, and to procure for me from my grandfather a settlement of thousands of pounds by the year? By his death I lost an honourable and a secure asylum and a yearly stipend. But in losing him did I not lose my only friend on earth? The only friend who could restore me to my family, to an elevated rank in society, and to all that my utmost ambition could desire? How then did my interest demand so horrible a sacrifice?

"Were I the murderer of Mr. Bolton, would his daughter have declared that her only object in attending this court was to express her conviction of my innocence? Is it probable that she would screen the assassin of her beloved parent? or does she feel less poignantly his irremediable loss than the learned gentleman who so humanely anticipated your conviction? Gentlemen of the jury, nothing but my innocence could have caused such a declaration by Miss Bolton. Who can deny that it is possible I may be innocent? Let us then suppose that I shall be unjustly executed under your conviction, and that my innocence will in some time appear unquestionably. What, I ask you, will be your feelings on this discovery? Will you not say to yourselves—'Precipitate and presumptuous that we were! To keep an oath that we should not have taken, we have committed the most atrocious of crimes. We have wantonly sacrificed that which no earthly power can restore. How useful to society, how respectable, might not our wretched victim now be, had we deigned to hearken to his supplications! Blessed probably with a wife and smiling babes, how happy, how delighted should we be, to witness their felicity—creatures of our wisdom and benevolence! Barbarians that we were! never to recollect any of those numerous cases where the innocent suffered, as proved by events that occurred after their execution!' Will you not, I ask you, suffer the stings of remorse and guilt? will you not shudder to think of your callousness and cruelty? will you not be pointed out as the butchers of a helpless prisoner? and will you not sink into the grave, loaded with the contempt and abhorrence of all the wise and virtuous, and condemned by your own consciences, as inexorable and merciless murderers?

"But alas! should you be insensible to my reasoning, should you be blind to my misery, should you be deaf to my entreaties, should you exert your tremendous authority, what evil, what suffering, what wretchedness, will you not inflict? my ancient family disgraced, my venerable mother broken-hearted and deprived of all support, and myself exposed on an ignominious gibbet!

"Among the diseases which afflict our species, some

there are which spread from individual to individual, and some which descend from one generation to another, first torturing the original sufferer in his own person, and afterwards inflicting their penalties on all his posterity; but the ignominy of my death, more horrible than gout, scrofula or plague, not only will descend a foul and contaminated inheritance to hundreds yet unborn, but with active sympathy, equally peculiar and pestilential, will go back in the scale of being, and brand my mother, my grandfather, and every human being connected with me or them, with shame and dishonour, never, never to be obliterated.

"The tyranny of opinion sometimes produces in the moral world disasters, which, like the liquid circles on the surface of a lake, extend from a point, and increase on every side in proportion as they retire from it. It is not enough for the pitiless eye of society to see me suffer death in pain and disgrace. It is not enough for its obtuse ear to receive my groans and lamentations; but the infamy which its barbarous sentence shall have heaped on me, must be conveyed, with the ingenious industry of elaborate and artificial cruelty, to every corner of the earth where a Dalbert may be found, and spread through his entire offspring for centuries to come. Must that name, heretofore unsullied and respectable, be henceforth synonimous with murderer? or must it become, by any means, extinct? I who should have guarded the sacredness of its character with the vigilance of an eagle and the fury of a lion! ah! who will bear it, henceforth, that can change it for any other?

"My dear and honoured parent, what will be thy fate! an aged, an infirm, a venerable matron, in whose breast time and disappointment have left no earthly affection, save maternal love! For my happiness all her prayers are directed, on me and my former hopes all her thoughts are employed. Of my success entertaining no doubt, doting on me with more than a mother's love, and expecting intelligence from me with more than a mother's anxiety. A letter arrives, it is from England. She opens it in haste, expecting to read of my advancement in life, or my introduction to my grandfather. The tide of pleasure already flows through her aged veins, and joy intoxicates her soul. But what does it contain? it gives my short, heart-rending story. The nectar of her hope is converted into aconite! The fond and airy dream of maternal love, of maternal pride, is for ever banished. The letter that was hailed as the harbinger of bliss, blasts her fond, her dearly-cherished expectations. It tells her that I, whom she had educated with so much care, and whose morals and humanity she had established by early precept and example; that Theodore Dalbert, her beloved, her son, had—my tongue falters in expressing it—murdered his friend, his benefactor, his father; had basely and cruelly murdered—Mr. Bolton! That no doubt of my guilt was entertained by the most incredulous, and that for this hellish crime I had been—Oh! I cannot finish the sentence! Indeed I cannot.

"Picture to yourselves, if it be possible to do so, what her situation, what her emotions, what her horrour, what her agony will be then. In one fatal moment, all of mankind that she loved, all that on earth she cherished and esteemed, to be at once torn from her sight for ever, and given to her amazed conception, by infernal transformation, as a villain to be abhorred, as a reptile to be loathed! Her Theodore, her only child, whom she had lately seen in the pride of manhood and the dignity of virtue, exhibited, as the vilest of miscreants, on a loathsome gibbet! Oh! gracious Providence! was ever disappointment charged with such poignant anguish? Forgive these tears, gentlemen, they will flow.

"A youthful conqueror made prisoner, and yoked to a victor's chariot; a nabob returning to Europe with his health, more than a kingdom's purchase, and cast pennyless on a desert island; an African monarch, perfidiously betrayed into the hands of a Guinea captain, and conveyed, naked and in chains, a slave to the West-Indies—will afford but a feeble idea of the intolerable shock. Fatal as the stroke of Heaven's lightning, it will, perhaps, carry with it instantaneous death! Immortal powers! and shall the death of my mother be caused by me? Wretched woman! little didst thou think I would bring thy silver locks with disgrace and sorrow to the tomb. Little didst thou think that when thou suckledst thy darling, thou wert nourishing a creature who was to tear thy very heart-strings. Better, far better, hadst thou given him poison than thy milk, or hadst strangled him at his birth! Then wouldst thou not know the throes that now await thee.

"But should she, should my mother, survive the dreadful blow, what will be her lot? Deprived of all support, shut out from all society, she must shrink into the narrow and lonely recess of poverty. For the first time in her life, ashamed to meet the look of an acquaintance, her dim and humid eye will seek for those she knows, in order to avoid them. Disease, hunger, and despair will fasten on their victim, and will torture her with unceasing pains, till death, impatient of their dilatory torments, shall terminate her sufferings.

"Oh! were I gifted with the powers of oratory, what sympathies should I not touch, what pity should I not excite? I would compare, with the situation of this miserable matron, that of the happy mother of one of you. The tears, the sighs of the one should be opposed to the smiles, the chearfulness of the other, and content, happiness, and hope, should lend their aid to represent, with greater intenseness, their contraries, disappointment, anguish, and despair.

"Ah! can I hope that you, placed at your ease, enjoying affluence, content, and peace; respected by your neighbours, surrounded by your families, and at liberty to go whither you will, to do whatever you desire; that you, armed with the awful power to save my life, or deprive me of it, will deign to look down from your enclosure of independence and security, on the most wretched among the sons of man? Oh! will not the apparent impossibility of your ever suffering what I now endure; will not my remoteness from your happy state; will not the very extremity of my woe extinguish your commiseration, and make you even forget that I am of your species?

"What a dreadful vicissitude is mine! a few days ago I was as free as air, enjoying felicity to the extent of my utmost wishes, and even beyond my fondest hopes; expecting the immediate protection and liberality of my grandfather; possessing no small reputation as an author, and dear to all those whom I regarded. From this high and brilliant seat have I in an hour been degraded to the dust, loaded with chains and infamy, thrown into a deep and dreary dungeon, charged with a crime at which my very nature revolts, deprived by fate's impenetrable decree of the possibility to show my innocence, believed guilty by all the world, and looking on the meanest of mankind as my superiour, at least in happiness; my fears all awake, my feelings all tortured, my hopes all blasted.

"This, and worse than this, with burning words should I convey, had I the talent of ready rhetoric, and no breast so obdurate that would not melt, no hatred so inveterate that would not subside, no justice so inflexible that would not relent. Insensibility should shed tears, and cruelty learn pity. From these hard and frigid walls, that have so often returned the sounds of accusation and conviction, should be heard, for the first time, a murmur of compassion. Death that now waits impatiently for your verdict, should fly, disappointed, to some more barbarous tribunal. The very stones should hear me and be moved. Without quitting your box you would pronounce me *not guilty;* the approbation and applause of all the world would await you, and I, joyful as the soul that is transferred by the prayers of the good from utter perdition to the regions of ineffable bliss, should fall at your feet, should implore the blessings of Heaven on your heads, should kiss your knees with gratitude and affection, and should weep from very ecstacy. My name should escape a blot, and my mother should still live, and still be happy.

"But, now, what remains but to hear my sentence, and to die? To die! oh! must I, then, must I die upon a gallows? No! let it not be said that an innocent man perished by your verdict! You can save me from infamy, and will you not? Think, oh! think of that last dread day, when the seas and the sepulchres shall give forth their dead, and we all shall cry for mercy! As you hope for pardon at that awful hour; as you would shun the agony of unavailing repentance; as you respect the example of our Blessed Saviour; as you will deserve salvation yourselves, look with an eye of pity on a wretch, who is unfortunate but not culpable, and whose existence and honour are in your hands! Oh save me from infamy! Oh save my mother's life! Oh let us live to bless you!"

The prisoner concluded his speech, and sunk back almost exhausted.

END OF VOL. II.

The Mysterious Hand

Volume III

THE

MYSTERIOUS HAND.

CHAPTER I.

Yet show some pity.—
I shew it most of all when I show justice;
For then I pity those I do not know,
Which a dismiss'd offence would after gall:
And do him right, that answering one foul wrong,
Lives not to act another.

....

With that he gave his able horse the head,
And, bending forward, struck his agile heels
Against the panting sides of his poor jade,
Up to the rowel-head; and, starting so,
He seem'd in running to devour the way.

....

Je vous revois enfin, cher objet de mes vœux!
Momens tant souhaités! ô jour trois fois heureux!

The silence that had been observed during Theodore's speech terminated with it. A murmur of compassion and admiration spread through the entire court as he concluded, when the judge, rising from his seat, thus addressed the jury:

"Gentlemen, you have heard the evidence offered to prove the prisoner's guilt, and you have attended to his reasoning against the right of pronouncing a capital conviction in any case. The former was clear and short; the latter able and ingenious. No point of law has occurred, and it is for you to determine on the prisoner's guilt or innocence, and on the justness of his arguments. You stand in a situation that requires delicacy and judgment. I believe you possess both, and I am sure that your verdict will be the result of good sense and humanity. It is unnecessary for me to recapitulate the evidence; it must be deeply impressed on your minds. I willingly avoid so painful a task. The law of England has made you judges of matters of fact, and nothing else is here to be considered. If I were required to give my opinion of the case, I would say, without hesitation, that a clearer one I never heard, and that it is impossible to believe the prisoner innocent. But herein you are to decide, and therefore I shall be silent. With respect to his arguments against the punishment of death, it might be supposed that it is my duty to refute them, if they be refutable; but such a supposition would be erroneous. I am here to interpret the laws, and to enforce them. It is not for a judge to moot points of philosophy, or to argue on topics not known to, or not admitted by, his predecessors. I repeat it, therefore, gentlemen, you are to decide on the evidence that has been produced, and you are, or are not, as your wisdom shall govern you, to be influenced by the eloquent and persuasive defence that you have heard. You now know my sentiments, gentlemen, and you may retire."

The jury accordingly retired, and during their absence, which continued from four in the afternoon until eleven at night, suspense and anxiety were pictured on every countenance in the court. A noise from the room to which they had gone would sometimes produce a whisper of "Are they coming?" or, "They are coming," and instantly every eye would be directed towards the door through which they were to pass, and from that to the unfortunate prisoner at the bar. "How well he spoke!" one would say.—"How nervous his language!" another.—"How handsome he looks!"—"What an interesting man!"—"I am sure he is innocent."—"If I were on the jury, I would starve before I would find him guilty." These, and a thousand other observations, were made by the by-standers, while Theodore sat, almost all the time, with his face resting on his hand, and this supported by his knee. At last the door opens, and the jury advance to their box.

Clerk of the Arraignments. Gentlemen, are you all agreed on your verdict?

Jury. Yes.

Clerk of the Arraignments. Who shall say for you?

Jury. Our foreman.

Clerk of the Arraignments. Theodore Dalbert, hold up thy hand. Gentlemen of the jury, look upon the prisoner. How say you, is Theodore Dalbert guilty of the felony and murder whereof he stands indicted, or not guilty?

Jury. Guilty.

Clerk of the Arraignments. What goods or chattels, lands or tenements, had he, at the time of the said murder and felony committed, or at any time since, to your knowledge?

Jury. None.

Clerk of the Arraignments. Hearken to your verdict, as the court hath recorded it. You say that Theodore Dalbert is guilty of the felony and murder whereof he stands indicted, and that he had not any goods or chattels, lands or tenements, at the time of the said felony and murder committed, or at any time since, to your knowledge; and so say you all.—Theodore Dalbert, hold up thy hand. You have been indicted of felony and murder. You have been thereupon arraigned, and you pleaded thereto, not guilty; and, for your trial, you have put yourself upon God and your country, which country have found you guilty. What have you now to say for yourself, why the court should not proceed to give judgment of death upon you, according to law?

Crier. Oyez; my Lords the King's Justices do strictly charge and command all manner of persons to keep silence, whilst sentence of death is passing on the prisoner at the bar, upon pain of imprisonment.

The wretched convict had heard the tremendous word uttered by the foreman, with the wild and vacant gaze of extreme and hopeless suffering, his cheeks pale, his mouth unclosed, his lips trembling, his arms advanced, and his head thrown back. But this agony of despair was soon succeeded by coolness and apparent resignation. He sunk his head slowly, and spoke not another word.

The judge was still to pass sentence. He expatiated on the heinousness of the crime, aggravated, he said, in this case, by treachery and ingratitude. He declared that, in his recollection, no accusation of murder had been so fully proved as this one had been; that it was impossible to entertain the slightest doubt of the prisoner's guilt, or of his malice prepense; that his arguments against the justice of capital punishments, though strong and specious, should not prevent him, as a judge, from doing his duty, as prescribed by the laws; and that, accordingly, he should pass sentence on him. "If jurymen and judges were to yield to such reasoning, and acquit the guilty offender, or refuse to condemn him, what," he said, "would become of society? The worst of evils would ensue—confusion, disorder, anarchy, and perhaps revolution; evils much greater than that of robbing the community of a vicious member.

"*You, Theodore Dalbert, therefore,*" continued he, "*shall be taken to the gaol of Abingdon, from whence you came, and from thence, on Monday next, to the place of execution, and there hanged by the neck until you be dead, and afterwards your body is to be dissected and anatomized. May God, of his infinite mercy, receive your soul!*"

Theodore was conveyed back immediately to gaol; and, as his fate was no longer uncertain, his native fortitude prevailed, and restored to him all his calmness. He slept well that night, and the next morning, having dressed himself in black, he sat down, at an early hour, to write to Miss Bolton. He had now purchased the luxury of candles, requisite, even in the daytime, in his gloomy dungeon, and the use of a bed, a chair, a table, and writing materials. For these, and the privilege of having his hands and feet unconfined, he paid the gaoler forty pounds. Previous to his trial, his agitation had rendered him, in a great degree, insensible to his present wants, and by a strange incongruity, until he lost all hope, he sought no comfort. He had just begun his letter, when he was disturbed by the loud and alarming sound of some one opening the doors of his cell. These were two in number, and placed in a small door-way that passed through a stone wall of eight feet in thickness. Each of them was plated with iron, and fastened by a chain, a massy bar, and three immense locks. He laid aside his paper, and looked up. "You must stoop, Ma'am, as you enter this cell," said the turnkey. "There," added he, "you see your man." It was Miss Bolton.

Theodore started up. His graceful figure but ill accorded with the wretchedness of his dungeon. A glow of gratitude and joy overspread his face. "Dearest Miss Bolton, is it you? can it be possible? what do I not owe you for this visit? what unparalleled goodness and humanity are yours? But you are alarmed and unwell. Will you sit upon this chair?" The man who had conducted her in now retired, telling her that it was permitted to none but the clergyman to remain longer than a quarter of an hour. On quitting the cell he fastened the two doors after him.

Julia, heaving a profound sigh, threw herself on the chair, rested one arm on the table, and extended the other to her unfortunate preceptor. He knelt by her side, and kissing her hand with unutterable tenderness, hoped that *she* did not believe him guilty. "Let me," said he, "believe that in you, at least, I see a friend who thinks me innocent."—"Oh Theodore! is it thus I meet you? Would to Heaven you had never seen me! then might you have escaped this dreadful situation. Believe you innocent? Ah! could I think *you* guilty of my father's death? you whom I love, you by whom I am loved?" The gentleness of her manner and the sweetness of her voice received, at this moment, an interest from her terror and anxiety, and from her declaration of attachment, that brought a tear into his eye. It was a tear of tenderness, not imbecility. She never appeared so amiable to him or so lovely. "But rise," added she, "this is not a moment to practise the submissions of gallantry. Here are a thousand pounds. Employ them to procure your escape, if escape be possible, or in any other way you please. You must not refuse this money. I have no use for it, and I am determined you shall keep it."—"Admirable girl! why cannot I return your goodness by a long life of devotion to your service? but," said he, rising, "it must not be! It were vain to seek to save a wretch whom fortune has deserted, and who must perish. Take back the money, escape is impossible, and if it were possible, should I in honour attempt it? To fly like a felon! No, no! take back the money, it must not be!"—"Oh!" cried Julia, bursting into tears, "did I want this to complete my misery? Theodore, if you do not wish to see me die at your feet, lay aside your haughtiness and your despair. Hope yet to live. Hope yet to call me yours. Keep the money, try to escape this night, and in the mean time, call me your wife, your true and loving wife."

"Adored and delightful Julia! Call you wife! That transporting word presents to my soul visions of endless bliss. Yes, I will live. I will try to escape. Give me the money, and pray for my success."—"Thank you—thank you—dearest Theodore—this is kind indeed. They will soon force me from you. I shall leave you in a horrible place, but let the remembrance of this embrace support you in my absence." With the eagerness of genuine love, Julia threw herself into the arms of her lover, and suffered her mouth to be pressed by his. For some minutes not even his misery could rouse him from the trance into which her action had thrown him. Soon, however, the noise of the turnkey's entrance announced the sad necessity of separation. Locked together in a mutual embrace, each viewed the other with a mixture of grief and rapture, and then again advanced their meeting lips, and again exchanged the ecstatick pressure and the very ravishment of love. How willingly, were it permitted her, would she not at this moment have exchanged situations with him, and have given her life to save his! But inevitable necessity forced her to part from him.

"Go, best, fairest, fondest of your sex," said he, "and think of a man who loves you with all a husband's tenderness, and with more than a lover's ardour." The gaoler having just entered, he added, that he had been writing to her when she entered, and that his letter should have been to entreat that she would extend her protection to his mother, and, with all possible expedition, convey to her an account of his horrible fate. Having promised to comply with these wishes, Julia, being pressed by the turnkey, departed, unable to speak, and with scarcely the power to walk.

As the man was retiring, Theodore told him that he wished to converse with him for a few minutes, and begged he would soon return. In an hour he appeared again. "My friend," said Theodore, "I shall not detain you long. You are, it seems to me, placed in a very unpleasant situation here. You are, in fact, yourself a prisoner, and but poorly paid, I fear, for enduring so much gloom and confinement, together with the contempt of the world. You have much authority in this prison, and it is in your power to effect my escape. Do this, and you shall have a thousand pounds sterling paid to you immediately, and a hundred a-year during your life. I will pay you the thousand pounds before I leave this cell, and I will bind myself here in writing to pay you the annuity regularly."—"Why, Sir, your offer is fair enough, and, do you see me? I agree to it. I know you are a gentleman, every inch of you, and, as you say, it is in my power to let you off. But I must be first sure of the thousand—do you comprehend? It's my way always."—"Then you promise to assist me in my escape, my worthy benefactor, my honest fellow!"—"I do promise, but on one condition howsomdever, that is to touch the shiners—do you take? to finger the mocuses, the brads, the shiners, the dust, the corianders, as a body may say."—"You shall have them. Here is one bank-note for a thousand pounds. Here, take it, and to your contrivance I commit my deliverance."—"Let me see, a thousand pounds—so it is, by my conscience! thank you, Sir; I'll take this money from you, as you have no use for it, and I wish you good-by, Sir."—"What! is it thus you treat me? Is it thus you act under our agreement?"—"What agreement is it you are bothering about? Sure you would not have me join in jail-breaking? The thing is felony, and if once you got out, to the devil you'd pitch me, so the hundred a-year would be all in my eye, and my thousand might be taken from me, and myself confined for life in your place. No, no! my darling, you never will catch Jemmy Philips at so young a trick as that neither. Besides, it would lie on my conscience to save a murderer from being hanged."—"Villain! lay down my thousand pounds immediately!"—"Oh! none of your hoity toitys, my man, or we'll soon clap the darbys on you, the neat fetters and decent hand-cuffs, you know, and thumb-screws and neck-yokes, do you see me? Your servant, Sir. Good-by to you, my hearty. Oh! what a cake I wasn't!"—"Infernal miscreant! do you trifle with my misery? do you rob and then mock and abuse me? Merciless rascal! take this!" So saying, the prisoner aimed a blow at his head with an iron candlestick, that brought him to the earth speechless. Theodore instantly took from him the keys and thousand pounds, and having exchanged clothes with him, and locked him into the cell, proceeded with a beating heart through the prison, hoping to make his escape in this disguise.

He had already passed to the outer-door, when the head gaoler called out, "How, Jemmy, are you going out with the keys in your hand? Please to lay them by in their proper place in my room." The fictional turnkey grew pale at these words, and knowing that if he turned about he must infallibly be detected, thought it better to attempt sudden flight; throwing down the keys, therefore, he hastily unbolted the door and ran out; but the alarm being given, he was pursued by the gaoler and his attendants. Not knowing the streets of Abingdon, he entered one where a house had lately fallen, and a crowd having been assembled at the same spot by some accident, he was compelled to stop, and his pursuers coming up, and calling him *murderer*, every one was inclined to assist them in his apprehension. Out of breath, but in a state of excessive desperation, he seized on a piece of timber, part of the ruined house, and with it attacked his enemies. He had knocked down six, made the greater part of the remainder retreat, and was preparing to continue his flight, when a stone, flung by the gaoler, struck him on the forehead, and deprived him of all sense and motion. He was brought, or rather dragged, back to the gaol, and abused, on his way thither, with innumerable indignities and blows. Conveyed a second time to his dungeon, he was loaded with an unexampled weight of irons, and left on the bare stones to perish or live, as chance might direct, till the hour of his execution should arrive. But his pockets were first emptied of their contents.

Julia, meanwhile, had, the moment she had parted from him, set out for Windsor, whither she travelled with as much expedition as English posting, with four horses, would permit. Ellen attended her. Her intention was to apply for a pardon for Theodore. Colonel Tennant, one of the equerries, and who was likewise her cousin, readily undertook to procure for her an opportunity of making the application.

The King* was taking his evening walk on the Terrace, when she advanced towards him. Her dress was disordered, her hair dishevelled, her face pale, her manner and her motions hurried, eager, and agitated. Having been at Court three or four times, she was not unknown to his Majesty, who, seeing her approach at a distance, and, being told her name, walked a few steps to meet her, and endeavoured, in vain, to prevent her from throwing herself at his feet. "Miss Bolton, pray don't kneel on the ground," said he, in the kindest and most affable manner. "I condole with you sincerely on your father's unhappy fate, and I shall be happy to do any thing that may alleviate your misfortune. But, prithee, rise."

"Sire, an unfortunate, innocent man is to suffer to-morrow at Abingdon. Mercy, mercy! At your knees I must remain till I know his doom."—"To-morrow—who is he?"—"Theodore Dalbert."—"What! the murderer of your father?"—"He has been condemned as such, but he is innocent. Some malignant demon, envious of his goodness, has contrived to overwhelm the most virtuous of mankind with apparent guilt. To you, Sire, he sends. Spare his life, great King! oh spare an innocent life!"

There was a softness as well as energy in her address, that gave to her words much of the power of persuasion. The music of her voice received from her immoderate grief a pathos that touched all the finer strings of the heart. A shower of tears completed the interesting expression of her sorrow.

"Miss Bolton, you must rise, indeed you must—your request is a serious one. The case of Theodore Dalbert, his trial and his condemnation, I have already learned, by express, from Baron Kellet, who presided at Abingdon, and I am sorry, very sorry, to say that I think my duty as a man, my honour as a sovereign, and my conscience as a Christian, all forbid the exercise of my prerogative on this occasion. It is the lot of kings to appear to have most power when they are in truth the least independent. How willingly would I grant your petition! How reluctant am

I to refuse it! How difficult is it to deny you any favour! but I cannot interpose between the laws and Dalbert. No circumstance of extenuation, I understand, appeared on the trial, and no doubt of his guilt is entertained by the judge. Under these circumstances, how could I excuse my mistaken clemency, to the relatives of all those who have suffered, during my reign, for crimes infinitely less atrocious than his, and who were convicted on evidence infinitely less conclusive than that which was produced against him? I regret, therefore, Miss Bolton, to say that the law must take its course. But, how are you his advocate? you, whom he has injured irreparably?"

Julia could not answer. Her hopes were blasted; despair usurped their place, and, no longer capable of resisting the effects of fatigue, hurry, grief, and anxiety, she sunk into the arms of the attendants. His Majesty ordered every possible care to be taken of her, had her conveyed into a chamber of the palace, and sent for his own physician to attend her.

On the following day, at one o'clock, Theodore, with a rope round his neck, and a fillet round his wounded forehead, was led to the front of the gaol by the executioner. His hands were tied behind his back, and Father Lanesby and the sheriff attended him. His countenance was severe and his step firm. The rope having been passed over a pulley in the gallows, he begged to know if he might speak. The sheriff answered in the affirmative. The place was crowded with a multitude of people, whom the convict then addressed in these words:

"You who are assembled on this melancholy occasion, perhaps think me guilty and abhor me. But the hour will arrive when you will learn my innocence and pity me. People of Abingdon, I am innocent. I am prepared to die; and I look at all these preparations for my death without terror. But I confess I cannot think of the shock that my aged parent will receive, when she shall hear of my execution, without feeling a dreadful pang. But God's will be done! I forgive all my enemies. At the moment of my departure for the world of spirits, I would not let a falsehood defile my lips, and, with my dying breath, I now repeat that I am innocent. So help me, Jesus!"

He now dropped a handkerchief, the signal for the executioner to lower the cap and terminate the tragic scene. The pangs of death, for a few minutes, convulsed his limbs; for a few minutes only, and then all appearance of life completely vanished.

Among the immense crowd that was assembled a universal and perfect stillness prevailed. The lowest sound that had escaped him had been heard with awful distinctness by the remotest of the multitude. Every eye was fixed on the swinging body, and every heart beat with pity or anxiety. Not thicker, on the sea-shore, are the stones, rolled by the tide, than seemed the faces directed toward the now inanimate Theodore. He was a fearful spectacle. It was a terrible and tremendous scene.

A faint murmur, like the low echo of a distant tumult, is heard. It is obscure, but it disturbs the silent solemnity that prevails. It grows in the wind. It swells upon the ear. It becomes articulate. The words, "Mr. Bolton!"—"Alive!"—"Make way!"—" 'Tis he!"—"What?"—"Hush!"—"No!" can be distinguished. The swarming mass of life, the incorporated thousands, till now motionless, seem to stir. Some strange or terrifying cause has produced so sudden and remarkable an effect. The noise increases; the agitation spreads. What can that be which rushes through the crowd? It occupies a small circular space, and that space seems to fly through the congregated multitude! So, when in northern latitudes, a grampus, wandering amid the deep, encounters and penetrates a herring-shoal, filling leagues upon leagues with its migratory millions; impatient of the interminable throng, he pursues his quickened course to the south, but is still surrounded on every side by an ever-changing mass of moving myriads.

At length the cause of this agitation in the crowd appears: a man on horseback is seen galloping at the top of his speed towards the gaol. "A reprieve! a reprieve!" is shouted from mouth to mouth: "A reprieve! a reprieve!" is echoed by the surrounding hills. The man flies to the fatal tree, throws himself from his horse, cries "Save him! save him!" and then falls speechless.

It is Mr. Bolton! he that had been believed to be murdered, it is he himself! "How is this?" said the sheriff. "Surely this is Mr. Bolton. Instantly cut down the man. There is some strange and wonderful secret in this affair." Theodore was cut down and liberated from the rope, and brought, together with Mr. Bolton, into the gaol. All proper means were employed for each. Mr. Bolton in a short time revived; but it was an hour before Theodore shewed signs of animation. By bleeding in the jugular vein, and other remedies, he was, however, gradually recovered.

"Oh, Theodore!" said the good man, "what horrors have you not endured! but I am not to blame. You will think so when I explain this mystery. About two months ago, I received a letter from Plymouth from my only brother. He had been compelled to fly from England, when a young man, for his reprobate conduct, and I thought he had been dead for many years. He represented himself as suffering under the most urgent distress, and even in want of food and raiment. By the return of the post I remitted him a bill for one hundred pounds, and I sent him, by the mail-coach, a complete suit of my clothes. In a week afterwards I received another from him, informing me that he had lost the hundred pounds at a gaming-table, and demanding a further remittance. This letter I did not answer. The robber, that was shot accidentally in the shrubbery, was this brother, who, as it was my practice to walk out at night alone, had, doubtless, expected to meet me unprotected. As he wore my clothes, as his figure resembled mine, and as part of his face had been shot away, it is no wonder that his body was thought to be mine."

Mr. Bolton added, that he had consented to the secret burial of the body, from his dread of the disgrace that would attend a discovery of it; and that he had not stopped in Newbury that night, in consequence of his extreme agitation, which took from him all self-possession, and disinclined him entirely to rest; that he had, therefore, walked on to Great Bedwin, which was a town still nearer to General Dalbert's residence, and in which town he was not known, and where, for want of his *valise*, he was obliged to purchase some articles of dress; that he had not intended to go to London, but had spoken of a journey thither, in order to conceal from the young couple his visit to the General, with the successful result of which he wished to surprise them; and that having, that very morning, at breakfast with the General, seen, by mere accident, in a provincial paper, an account of the trial, he had immediately mounted a fleet hunter, and galloped to Abingdon.

"And now," said he, "I feel not only the indescribable happiness of having saved your life, but I have the pleasure to assure you of your grandfather's protection, who has consented to settle on you an estate of three thousand pounds a-year, provided Julia will consent to marry you. Her fortune is, you know, twenty thousand pounds."

Theodore could make no reply. The agony of his mind and body he had so lately suffered, and the transport he now felt, deprived him of utterance, and he could only throw himself into the arms of his worthy benefactor.

When it was dark they left Abingdon, (Theodore having got back the thousand pounds); and they proceeded to Bolton-hall, where, in a few days, they were joined by Julia and General Dalbert.

The General had now attained his grand climacterick. At fifteen a commission had been purchased for him, and in thirty years he had been able to retire with a fortune of forty thousand pounds sterling. His paternal estate of Holtham produced three thousand *per annum*; and, within the eighteen years which had elapsed since his retiring from the army until the present period, he had accumulated a considerable accession to his wealth. When young he had been handsome, and he still retained some traces of strength and beauty. His manners were plain, and his conversation was unadorned, but in all that he did and said, there was a certain air of dignity, that gentlemanly something, which men of good birth, and accustomed from their infancy to good company, are often found to possess. His disposition was cholerick to an extreme, and this fault, by early and long command in the army, had become an unconquerable, and, to many, an intolerable vice. He was, nevertheless, kind and compassionate, and by all to whom the General was known, he was considered a hasty, but a hospitable, honest, friendly character. He had hardly seen Theodore when he felt for him the affection of a parent; and in a few days the old man was proud to declare, that, in his grandson, he saw the first of the Dalberts.

CHAPTER II.

I will sooner trust a crocodile,
When he sheds tears; for he kills suddenly,
And ends our cares at once; or any thing
That's evil to our nature, than a man.

....

Methinks, already in this barbarous isle,
Like a benighted traveller, I stand,
Viewing with wat'ry eyes the sinking sun,
And night displaying her sad ensigns round:
No friendly visage near me, all before
A horrid maze of death; without a hope
Of help or of escape. Despair, darkness,
Death, and everlasting horror round me.

....

Dans des antres profonds on a su renfermer
Des foudres souterrains tous prêts à s'allumer.

THE miscreant who had attempted to drown Theodore, was he who lost his life in the shrubbery at Bolton-hall, the execrable brother of the respected and worthy Mr. Bolton.

Mr. Bolton and his wretched brother, who was a year younger than he, were the only children of the famous Colonel Bolton, who, in his time, had been the most noted gamester in England. Their mother died when they were infants, and their father neglected them. Committed to the care of mercenary attendants, the two boys grew as nature and chance directed. The elder was mild and docile, but Edward, on the contrary, was sulky and mischievous. His associates were gipsies and jockies, and at the age of twelve there were few of the vices of low debauchery with which he was unacquainted, and none to which he did not incline. Even then he was often intoxicated with ardent spirits, and it frequently happened, that by the scientific shuffling of cards, he won the wages of his father's servants. At the age of sixteen he was a rake, and at eighteen a notorious swindler.

About this period, having defrauded a tradesman in London of some money, he was apprehended and committed to jail, from which Colonel Bolton, with considerable difficulty, had him released. After this, being poor, and shunned by all the world, he was glad to accept of a situation under the Hudson's Bay Company,* obtained for him by his father. But industry was too foreign to his nature, and the seeds of dissipation, extravagance and debauchery were too deeply sunk in his corrupt heart, to permit him to apply long to any honest employment. Having committed as many frauds as it was possible to practise in his new situation, he fled into the United States of America, where he got acquainted with a family of the name of Harold. Miss Harold, being pretty, received much of his attentions, but as he had a rooted aversion to matrimony, she soon discovered that she was not to be Mrs. Bolton. She was long impatient of celibacy, and this new disappointment exasperated her to fury. She complained to her brother of the base man who had, she said, engaged her affections without any intention to marry her. "Why," urged she, "should he gain my love when he himself was indifferent? Such conduct is dishonourable and ungentlemanly, and the credit of our family and my happiness demand that you should horsewhip him." The brother was as violent and unreasonable as the sister, and he actually carried her wishes into effect. The other, who always carried pistols, shot his assailant in the neck;

and, immediately afterwards, thinking he had killed him, though in this he was mistaken, departed for the Spanish territory in the south.

The vigilance and strictness of this government not according well with the laxity of his principles, he, in a few months, took his passage for Cadiz. There he associated with cheats and sharpers, and passed rapidly through many of the gradations of rascality. Grown bold from practice, and desperate from necessity and danger, he next became a bravo and an assassin. As such he travelled into Italy and France, and as such he became acquainted with Gaspar Pontgebre. From him he had received a considerable sum of money for the murder of Theodore, of whose death, by drowning, he had brought to Bourdeaux satisfying proofs. A run of bad luck at play had stripped him, in a few nights, of his ill-gotten gold; and, as had often happened to him before, distress and hunger approached sufficiently near to be seen and felt by him. Under the pressure of urgent want he thought of his brother, and determined to practise on his benevolence. With this view he returned to England, where he met, from the hand of Theodore, a fate that he had long deserved.

Theodore was still unwell. It was necessary, therefore, to delay the intended marriage; but the General, in contemplation of it, settled on his grandson three thousand pounds a-year. The old gentleman determined that the wedding should take place in a few days, and Mr. Bolton and Theodore purposed to return, immediately after the ceremony, to France. To live in England, after what had happened, would be to expose themselves to perpetual mortifications, and it never occurred to them that Julia could have any objection to the removal. They were all perfectly happy except her. She, without any apparent cause, was absent in her manner and pensive; and, as the day approached that was to see her united to the only man she had ever loved, her dejection increased. Her father considered this as the effect of maidenly timidity, and of the horrid events that had lately happened; but Theodore, more discerning, penetrated further into her mind, and ascertained the existence of some hidden grief.

One morning that she was sitting with him in the summer-house, he took one of her hands in his, and begged, with tender anxiety, to know what it was that caused her melancholy. "No impertinent motive prompts me," he said, "to make the inquiry; but my happiness is now connected with yours, we shall soon have only one interest, and therefore, even now perhaps it is my duty, as it certainly is my inclination, to participate in your sorrows." She blushed—a tear trembled in her eye, and a general agitation disturbed her frame. "Theodore, a secret lies concealed in my bosom. It preys incessantly upon my spirits, and that which should contribute most to my happiness—a union with you, but aggravates my distress." Theodore fixed his eyes on her with astonishment. "You may well be amazed," continued she, "but your honour forbids a longer silence on a subject which I shudder to disclose." The look with which he viewed her, as she uttered these words, beggars description. "The wife of Theodore Dalbert," proceeded she, "should be not only perfectly unsullied, but should have ever been beyond the defilement of aspersion. No human being should be able to say of her—'That is she whose innocence I doubt.' But, alas! such a wife, perhaps, I should not be."

Her sighs and sobs interrupted her utterance, and it was only by broken words and disjointed sentences that she conveyed to Theodore the tale of that fatal night at the *chateau*, and the horrible misfortune of *Mademoiselle de Sagoné*. As she spoke she hid her burning face behind his neck, while she rested her hands upon one of his shoulders. "That misfortune," said she, "was intended for me, and it is to the goodness of Providence that I am indebted for my preservation."—"Could I have supposed," returned Theodore, "that my affection for you was capable of increase, my dearest, my beloved Julia, your present narration was wanted to make my passion perfect; but seek not to improve it further, or I shall expire from excess of love. Come to my arms, fairest—chastest creature, and re-assure me that you will be mine."

Her light and elastic figure, by a magical movement, was instantaneously placed upon his lap. She sunk her head upon his bosom in gentle agitation; a sigh from his heart came warm on her cheek; its odour was the freshness of health; its lengthened cadence was the eloquence of love. "Banish from your mind, my Julia, all recollection of this terrible occurrence. I lament it because it has made you unhappy, but it has not lessened my esteem for your virtues, my confidence in your goodness. What you have communicated to me has awakened a new interest in my bosom, which, joined with my admiration of your candour and your delicacy, has exalted my passion for you almost to idolatry. Believe me, love, the intrinsic virtue of your friend, the unfortunate *Mademoiselle de Sagoné*, received not the slightest stain. What is chastity? Not a dubious distinction—not the ignorant idol of barbarians or debauchees—not the vain virginity of visionary vestals, but that mental immaculateness—that intellectual fidelity—that modesty of disposition and unchangeable devotedness to one preferred object, which philosophy approves, morality teaches, and religion sanctifies. But come, chace from that lovely brow those little clouds of uneasy recollection, and let us speak of our approaching wedding. My wife you will soon be, and never, Julia, never while we live, shall I love you less than I do now."

Julia raised her head. No human felicity could exceed that which she enjoyed at this moment. Pleasure, too abundant to be concealed, sparkled in her eyes. She could not speak, but her lips involuntarily approached his. Pressed to his heart with fond violence, she received and returned the sweetest of kisses; and yielding gently to his legitimated ardour, moderated as it was by delicacy and respect, closed her beauteous eyes in timid and blissful perturbation.

On their return to the house, Theodore received a letter from France. It announced the expected death of his mother, and conveyed to him her wish to see him before she should depart from this world. The intelligence affected him extremely, and as his affection for her was unbounded, he determined to set off that evening for Dover, and to postpone his marriage until he should meet Julia in France. She and her father agreed to this arrangement. He departed from Bolton-hall in a few hours, they followed him in four days. The General returned home. Theodore, though he used all possible expedition, did not, however, receive his mother's last breath. She had been buried three days before he arrived in Bourdeaux.

The *Comte D'Egfryd* still lived at the *chateau de St. Uldrich*, and was still loved and respected. Strange to relate! the apprehension of *Marie de Solase* had not publicly exposed any of his villainy. She, it is true, had, before her execution, told the turnkey who guarded her, in answer to some questions put by him, the mode of her escape from justice, and her retreat in *the grave*, procured for her, as she said, by the Count. But in this, the brutish and profligate gaoler discovered nothing worthy of censure or of repetition. It therefore had not transpired. From the want of time, or strength, or recollection, she had, luckily for the Count, uttered no formal denunciation against him, and therefore he continued to enjoy and to abuse the confidence of the world. He possessed extensive popularity, but he persevered in all his accustomed vices. Gaspar Pontgebre and Pierre Dontache, he who had seduced Theodore from the *chateau*, under the pretence of a message from his mother, were still the instruments of his iniquity. He had been preserved from the poisoned tokay by an accident that had happened on the road to the case containing it, the consequence of which accident was that both the bottles had been broken. By Marie's death, one of the four persons who could criminate him was removed, and the destruction of the other three now occupied all his thoughts. Those three were, Mr. Bolton, Julia, and Theodore.

Accustomed to state and magnificence from his infancy, and profuse from disposition as well as habit, he required, and had always possessed, a princely fortune; and if he had been compelled to chuse death or pecuniary distress, he would not have hesitated to prefer the former. To such a man the prospect of poverty has greater terrors than those can conceive whose wants are few and simple, and who are accustomed to earn their subsistence by the unremitted exercise of industry. The remotest probability of having a wish which he could not afford to gratify, or being applied to for a debt which he might not have the ability to discharge, would fill the mind of such a man with grief and anxiety; but what must have been the tortures of the Count on the rack of insolvency itself?

Shortly after the providential discovery of the cavern by means of the goldfinch, judgment had been pronounced against him in a lawsuit of thirty years standing, and which involved the greater part of his paternal inheritance. By this judgment he was compelled not only to deliver up the possession of the estates in dispute, but to pay, within twelve months, the accumulated arrears of the rent for fifty years. For this purpose he was obliged to mortgage the remainder of his property; and, having paid the arrears, he found, that instead of eight hundred thousand livres* of rent per annum, he was reduced to ninety thousand livres† per annum; but it was not permitted by his pride to make any retrenchment.

"What!" it is probable he thought, "have I divested myself of all prejudice; am I possessed of coolness, craft, caution, and contrivance; do I love only myself, and hate or despise the whole world besides—all to no end? In society there is a perpetual struggle between the few who seek to monopolize riches and power, and the many who wish to wrest from their oppressors a portion of their superfluities. The needy wretch, who, obeying the voice of nature, endeavours to relieve his distress by seizing part of the property of his tyrants, is hanged for his crime, as it is called, and it is fit he should be executed. I, as one of the privileged order, am interested in supporting their authority, and defending their despotism and their luxuries. What are the sufferings of others to me? My comforts and my pleasures demand slaves, and are protected by laws, judges, gallies, gibbets. These, therefore, have my support. But why is he hanged? Because he is needy, because he is ignorant, because he is timorous, because he

* About 40,000l. sterling.

† About 4,500l. sterling.

is stupid. His imbecility demands the aid of a confederate, and that confederate, for a reward, betrays him. His prejudice, which he has been taught to consider as the supernatural warning of conscience, makes him tremble at the thought of removing any one of his enemies, and at that of relieving any of his wants; and, to the dread of the executioner is added, in his mind, the insensate and fanatic horror of everlasting torments. His poverty forbids the expensive instrumentality of prompt desperation and blind obedience; his stupidity allows him neither foresight, invention, nor ingenuity; and his ignorance exposes him, at every step, to the danger of falling into some of the numberless ambuscades that experience, cruelty, and avarice have placed round property, exclusive and forbidden by the laws, though, by right, common to all mankind. But shall *I* cast a longing look at this inviolable treasure and not be gratified? Shall *I* want a portion of it and not obtain it? No; it suffices for me to know that there is wealth and I stand in need of it, and I will possess it. Yes, I will possess it, without incurring either danger or suspicion, although it should be guarded by all the terrors that cunning can devise, fear suggest, or power employ."

But I return to Mr. and Miss Bolton, who had now arrived in France. They travelled unattended by any servants. These and their heavy luggage were to follow them. Without hurrying themselves on their journey, they proceeded with uniform diligence through the provinces of Artois, Picardy, Isle de France, Orleannois, Touraine, Poitou and Angoumois, towards Bourdeaux. But, previous to Mr. Bolton's departure from England, he received the following letter from Father Lanesby.

"MY DEAR FRIEND,

"You have heard, to be sure, of the severe complaint with which it has pleased God to afflict Mr. Alcot; but he is now better, and the physicians are not without hopes of his recovery. He sent for me yesterday, in order to make a confession to me, which, he said, regarded your family materially.

"I attended him, and found him absolutely in a state of despair. 'Mr. Lanesby,' he began, 'I am the basest and wickedest of men, and I cannot die in peace without repairing, as much as in my power, by an ample confession, the greatest crime that was perhaps ever committed against an innocent man. What I tell you, Sir, you may repeat. I well deserve reproach, abhorrence, and humiliation. Mr. Dalbert's innocence, that is now proved to all the world, was known to me, Sir, from the first. In the pocket of the deceased, I found a letter which I suppressed. It was from Mr. Bolton, and I learned by it that the person killed was his brother, and that this person's conduct had been reprobate. In short, Sir, I had a conviction on my mind of Mr. Dalbert's innocence when he was apprehended, and of the truth of his declarations on both the trials. It was in my power, by a word, to save him at Abingdon, for, exclusive of the letter, I had the day before seen Mr. Bolton in the demesne at Holtham, as I rode along the high road. Notwithstanding this, I attended and assisted at the prosecution; and I heard the capital conviction of the unfortunate prisoner, not only without remorse, but with satisfaction. A malignant envy was the hellish passion that extinguished my humanity; but now, that death threatens to snatch me to a place of everlasting punishment, the agony and terror of my mind cannot be described.'

"I need not tell you, my worthy friend, that I was much shocked at this confession; but I felt, at the same time, pity for the unhappy man who had been guilty of such inveterate and unparalleled baseness. I said to him every thing that I thought could relieve the torments of his conscience, and finally I succeeded in restoring him to a state of comparative composure. I have seized the earliest moment of complying with his wishes, and I pray you and Theodore to forgive him. He is at this moment an object of compassion and of pardon. May Heaven have you and my amiable young friend in its holy keeping evermore! Amen. WM. LANESBY."

Mr. Bolton had shown this letter to Theodore and his daughter. They all shuddered at such unprovoked atrocity, but they forgave the wicked Mr. Alcot, and even prayed for his recovery. He did recover, but during the remainder of his life he was an object of contempt and hatred.

Mr. Bolton and Julia proceeded, as I have said, on their journey to Bourdeaux by easy stages. Approaching the town of Cognac, they were struck with admiration by the beauties of the surrounding country. On one side was a deep declivity covered with wood, at the bottom of which flowed the *Churente* in a serpentine course, between enamelled borders, and on the other, an abrupt and rocky hill ascended to the clouds. The distant prospect afforded to the view many objects, picturesque or beautiful, such as mills, hamlets, and vineyards; cottages, boats, and plantations. All courted observation, and invited inquiry, while the distant spire of Cognac promised, by grateful association, a good supper and sound repose.

"How happy is a country life!" said Julia. "Blessed with health and competence, who would desert the quiet security of innocence and simplicity for the tumult and perils of a city? Look at that snug little cottage among the trees, with the column of smoke rising from its chimney, and its vineyard so neatly planted on the left. My imagination pictures its inhabitants. It is occupied by a young couple who have fondly quitted the world to enjoy a little paradise of their own formation. She is young, pretty, modest, intelligent, and interesting; and he, manly, sensible, vigorous, and active. Each lives in the other, and both are but one. Anxious to please, she seeks no dominion but that of happiness. The sovereign of his soul, she holds her sceptre—the sceptre of affection, with propriety and grace; but her empire extends no further than the limits of their farm, and her only subject is her husband. She is his queen. He repines not at her power; he sighs not for liberty. Her power is that of virtuous love, and it were death to him to diminish it. A little prattler already emulates her mother's sweetness. It connects the fond pair by a new and sacred tie; and parental tenderness completes the amiable character of each."

Mr. Bolton was pleased with his daughter's sketch, and smiled.

From the high road a narrow, rough alley led down the declivity towards the river. Into this alley the driver suddenly whipped his horses. Mr. Bolton called out to him to know what he meant by doing so, and, receiving no answer, told him, in a loud and resolute tone, that if he did not instantly return to the high road he would shoot him. It was manifest that some treachery or violence was intended. The man turned about his head at the menace and laughed. Provoked to the last degree by such audacity, Mr. Bolton cocked and snapped one of his pistols at the fellow, but it missed fire; and on examination he found that the flints had been taken out of them. Pierre Dontache was the driver, and death, or worse than death, was connected with Pierre Dontache.

Meanwhile the horses were driven in full gallop down the hill, which, from its steepness, and the rough state of the road, rendered the situation of the travellers in no common degree dangerous, and prevented the possibility of their jumping out. Their rapid course was continued to a wooden bridge that had been thrown over the river, and this being crossed, the horses were urged with increased velocity along the water's edge until they came to a little creek, wherein was a boat guarded by two men. The creek was opposite to a romantic island that lay in the middle of the river. The carriage stopped, and, with imprecations and force, Pierre, assisted by the two men, compelled the father and daughter to enter the boat. She was speechless and almost inanimate from terror. He was at once irritated and alarmed. They, with the luggage, were immediately rowed to the island, and the carriage was soon driven by Pierre out of sight.

The boatmen were two of five outlawed smugglers hired by Gaspar Pontgebre, and paid largely for executing his orders. These, though given by him, originated with the Count, who, on the supposition that Mr. Bolton would have been attended by his servants, had calculated that the assistance of five ruffians might be necessary. An old woman, whose name was Garquine, and the wife of one of them, was their cook. The island on which they resided might be about half a mile in circumference, and it was called the *Isle de Peine*. On it was a ruined monastery which served to shelter these desperadoes. In about forty minutes the travellers were landed, and the boat securely moored.

To the questions of Mr. Bolton no reply was made. On the illness and distress of Julia no attention was bestowed. They moved on, the two men carrying the luggage, in suspicious and gloomy silence, towards the ruins, now forcing their feet through the matted brambles which choked the ancient avenue, and again clambering over some of the parapets that had fallen to the ground. At length they gained the gateless entrance of a venerable ivy-covered pile, and proceeded to what had been the refectory. There the other three ruffians and the old woman were sitting round a fire of wood.

The sun was set about a quarter of an hour, and there was therefore scarcely any light but what proceeded from the blaze on the hearth. Such a group and such an apartment would have suited the taste of John de Laer,* and demanded the pencil of Lucas of Leyden*—their faces fierce and squalid, their dresses gaudy and ragged, their figures mean and exotic, and their uncouth looks expressive of fearful anxiety and habitual desperation. The room was spacious, arched, and lofty, but time had torn away the windows, the stucco, much of the plaister, and a little of the floor. A sooty yellow stained the walls and the ceiling. There was no door, nor was there any furniture save a gridiron, an iron pot, and two forms. But there is in heat and light a virtue that subdues desolateness, and gilds even poverty. The flaming faggots diffused a portion of cheerfulness over this misery; and had not Julia been a prisoner among banditti, she could have found something here to approve.

"So please you, gentlefolks," said one of the men, "don't be alarmed; no danger will happen to you here; you shall have plenty to eat and drink, and beds likewise. Besides, you will have the liberty of walking about the island, and if you feel yourselves hungry now, we have a little fish and some bread and milk at your service. Though you be in the *Isle de Peine*, you shan't be starved neither." The travellers felt no inclination to eat, and having requested to be shown to their beds, Garquine lighted two small candles, with which she conducted them through the edifice. It was dismantled and ruinous in every part. The staircases, which were of stone, were filthy, broken, and slippery. There were no balusters, and the small number of the narrow casement-windows, that had not been removed, were broken. Having entered a corridor that was damp, dirty, and decayed, the old woman pointed out to Mr. Bolton a room without a door, which, she said, was allotted for him.

She gave him one of the candles, and was proceeding still further in order to light Julia to her room, when this affectionate daughter threw herself into her father's arms. "Had I not better remain with you here all night, Sir?" said she. "You will be very comfortless in such a place as this by yourself; allow me to stay with you."—"Your room is up higher," grumbled Garquine. "There is no use in opposing our fate," cried the good man. "Good night, my dear, I hope to see you in the morning." He then entered the doorless chamber, and waited not for a reply. Julia followed Garquine till she came to a low oaken door at the top of the building. The door was too strong and heavy to be removed without much difficulty, or it would, doubtless, have been carried away with the others. "This is your room," said the old woman, entering it with a candle. It was arched at top; the floor was stone-work; there were two loop-holes for windows, and it forcibly suggested the idea of a place of confinement. It was in truth a most dismal recess.

A rude bedstead, a *paillasse*, and some bed-clothes were its chief articles of coarse convenience. "This is your room," repeated Garquine. Julia looked at her, and raised her eyes to Heaven.

Garquine, who presented the appearance of incorrigible termagancy and extraordinary robustness, was, notwithstanding a stoop, nearly six feet high, and she was about sixty years of age. Her limbs were slender to an excess, but hers was the slenderness of indefatigable action. Her shoulders were broad and elevated; her arms long, red, rough, and hairy, and her hands, feet, and head enormously disproportioned; her legs were bowed, naked, and discoloured; her neck was long and scraggy; her hair wiry, short, matted, grey, and foul; and her voice discordant, loud, inarticulate, and abrupt; her eyes were large, white, staring, and far removed from the other; her nose was cocked and crooked, and her mouth was of a prodigious extent; the under lip touched her nostrils; her waist was large; her chest was flat; her skin had the hue of dirty copper; her forehead was low and projecting. She never walked; a trot was her gait; her look was savage; and, in short, her every motion, her every sound, her every feature, was not only rude and rustic, but ferocious and alarming.

" 'Tis very well," said Julia, surveying her guide with horror, "as this is my room I will not trouble you any more. But how will you be able to go down without a candle?"—"Oh! I am used to the building, and I want no light."—"Well, then, I wish you good night, and I thank you."—"Oh! good night to you."

Julia, when alone, looked about for something to secure her door on the inside, and fortunately found a strong wooden bar behind the bed, with which she effectually guarded against intrusion. The next morning, at an early hour, she arose, after a short and uneasy sleep, and found, outside the door, her trunk, dressing-case, and writing-box. She went immediately to visit her father, but he was still lying on his miserable couch and asleep. His luggage had likewise been brought up. She walked gently to his bed, sat at his side, and watched till he should awake. In a few minutes he stirred and extended his arms to his daughter. She kissed his hands affectionately, dropped upon his bosom, and joined her cheek to his. With surprise and terror they talked over their adventure; and it was soon determined by them, that, as soon as he should rise, they should inspect the situation of their prison. She returned into the corridor until he dressed himself, and then they proceeded to examine their ruinous habitation and the island.

The sun had just risen. It was the month of September, and all was involved in sleep and stillness, when they found themselves beyond the dilapidated fabric. It was a massy and picturesque object; but, as a human dwelling, it was abominable. It was impossible to connect the idea of commodiousness with it, and it seemed to totter on its foundations.

Mr. Bolton and Julia, in the hope of escaping, quickened their steps; but everywhere the island seemed encompassed by an impassable morass, on which a bird could scarcely stand, and through which no boat could be forced. The place where they had landed the evening before was the only spot in the whole circumference of the island that permitted a debarkation. It was the termination of a serpentine canal of rock. This canal, which was formed by nature, passed through the morass, and was always navigable, in consequence of the incessant agitation of the water forced into it by the current of the river. The morass was thus prevented from filling it. The canal, including all its windings, was nearly a mile in length, and nowhere more than twelve feet wide. One of its ends terminated in a small bason, where the boat had been moored, not far from the ruined monastery. The other end opened into the river, and beyond the morass. The upper surfaces of the sides of this canal were all under the water, and in some places at no less a depth than five feet. To call that a canal, the sides of which were always under water, may be considered a misapplication of the term; but it will be recollected that these sides, being of stone, stopped the growth of the morass, and therefore preserved an uninterrupted navigation.

From one of these sides, and near that end of the canal which entered the river, there arose a rude and narrow causeway of rock, which, widening and rising, advanced a considerable way through the morass, and then terminated, by a gradual descent and diminution, in the midst of it. It was impossible to arrive at any part of the causeway, except by the canal; but it well repaid the trouble of visiting it by the natural curiosity it presented. This was a sloping cavity within it, which penetrated to an immense depth, and was both dry and spacious. The entrance to the cavity was within a few yards of the spot where the causeway was connected with the canal.

Julia and her father having ascertained the only way by which an escape could be attempted, thought to avail themselves of the absence of their gaolers, and to take the boat; but, to their grief and mortification, they found that it was fastened by a strong chain and a large lock, the key of which had been removed, together with the oars.

Despairing, therefore, of being able to escape, at least for the present, and placing all their reliance on Providence, they turned from the boat, and seeing a sheet of paper pasted against a rock near them, they advanced towards it, and read, in French, to the following effect:

"Inhabitants of the *Isle de Peine*, now eight in number, read this paper with care, and know that your existence depends on your obedience. Last night, after the arrival of the two prisoners here, twenty barrels of gunpowder were, by Gaspar Pontgebre and Pierre Dontache, deposited in the cavity beneath the causeway. Across that part of the canal which is nearest to it, a number of strings and rods have been, according to my directions, placed, each of which strings and rods communicates with a spring, on the slightest motion of which the mine will be blown, and thousands of tons of rock will bury you all in instant and inevitable death. To navigate your boat, or swim from the island, through the canal into the river, must produce this tremendous effect. You will therefore remain here to obey the orders that shall from time to time be sent to you, and your wants shall be attended to.

"A rope, made heavy enough to sink in water, passes round a post, at the yellow cottage, on the left bank of the river, and round the stone pillar in front of your churchyard. To this rope, the ends of which have been spliced together, is tied a small water-proof vessel. In this vessel you will find my orders, and be supplied with necessaries; and in this vessel you will convey to me your letters. Every day, at twelve, let it be searched and returned to me. The strength of five men is more than sufficient to move it, though full, across the bottom of the river.

"The gunpowder I have mentioned is secured against dampness and surprise. No one can approach it but by the canal, and approach by that is instantaneous destruction. To prevent the possibility of your being blown up by the accident of any person entering the island, and, consequently, stirring the fatal spring, an immense stone, concealed by some bushes, is placed on the top of the causeway, in such a manner, as that any large body entering into the canal, will, by pressing against some ropes connected with the stone, cause it to fall with irresistible violence, and, by the death of the visitor, save you from the explosion of the powder, which would take place if he should advance a little further.

"All this was done last night by Gaspar and his associate, with the assistance of three men, whom the former had brought from Bourdeaux for the purpose. I was a spectator of their work, though they did not see me. They observed my orders strictly, though they know me not; and now they are all dispersed and sent to remote places. Be obedient for a few weeks, and hope for liberation and reward. Let the two prisoners be taken care of.

"Outlaws! your desperation might prompt you to attempt some mode, not conceivable to me at this moment, of crossing the morass, and thus quitting the island; but know that information has, by my means, been given against, and a reward advertised for the discovery of each of you. My wrath would pursue you should you escape, my power would apprehend you. In vain you would fly from the one—in vain you would conceal yourselves from the other. Keep these lines in your recollection; to-morrow they will have vanished from this paper. If you neglect my orders you shall perish; and recollect that I shall be sometimes among you, though you shall never behold me."

"Oh!" cried Julia, "this is the work of that monster Egfryd. We are his prisoners; these are his creatures, and this is his island." Scarcely had she uttered these words, when Jacques Ferrau, one of the banditti, joined them. They were still looking at the infernal scroll. "What is this?" said he. "Have you so soon found out an amusement for yourselves? This is now some copy of verses, I warrant, on the island and your confinement; and very pretty they are, no doubt. I should be glad to read them, if I might take that liberty. Might I be allowed?" The father and daughter turned aside. Approaching nearer, Jacques perused the paper, and his colour changed as he read.

"Damnable villain!" muttered he, "Gaspar described you well. The devil himself could not have planned a blacker scheme. So, here we are, compelled by hunger and necessity, to be your slaves! We cannot disobey; we cannot escape; no creature can approach us. We must do your hellish work, whatsoever it may be. You run no risk; we know you not; and when we shall be no longer useful, your security will, probably, demand the sacrifice of our lives, and we shall, perhaps, be all blown up. Oh! that you were now within my grasp, invisible, tremendous fiend!"—"But," said Mr. Bolton, interrupting him, "are you sure that there is no part of the morass fordable?"—"Oh! God bless you, Sir! fordable! it would swallow a steeple; and it is so broad in every part——"—"Then the canal alone presents any mode of retreat?"—"The canal alone—why, to be sure, Sir; but who would dare to approach the further end? Even a man swimming would disturb some of those strings or rods, and blow up the whole island; and if the morass could be crossed, do you think we would venture to attempt it? No, the gallows too surely would await us on the other side. I heard enough from Gaspar Pontgebre, who paid us handsomely enough for coming here, of his secret master, to convince me that every word in that paper is true; and I would not, for all the register-ships that ever left Manilla, venture within ten yards of the causeway. What his designs are, time alone will show. He is the prince of darkness, and our lives are not worth an hour's purchase while in his power. He says he will be sometimes among us, and I don't doubt it. He makes all nature bend to his purposes."

Julia laid her head on her father's bosom. "Ah! Miss," continued the fellow, "I pity you from my heart. I am not much given to compassion neither. But it is impossible to see so sweet a young lady in this terrible situation without feeling something; and, at this moment, damn me if I would not venture my life to save yours. While with my companions, I sometimes forget that I was once honest and virtuous; but I have my moments of bitter repentance."—"My good friend," replied Mr. Bolton, "I feel sincerely obliged to you, but it is in vain, from what you say, to look for any succour. To Heaven, therefore, be committed our deliverance!"

"You must have a terrible opinion of me, Sir," said Jacques, "seeing me in such a place, associated with such people, and married to such a wife, for I am the husband of Garquine; but I deserve at least as much pity as reproach. It is not four years since I was comfortably and respectably situated in Lyons. I carried on a stocking manufactory in that city. I was blessed with a gentle and affectionate spouse. I was the father of two lovely babes; and I enjoyed the confidence of my neighbours. But, unfortunately for me, a fatal passion took possession of my whole soul. This was the love of gaming; and the billiard-table had not only all my leisure hours, but also much of that time which should be devoted to my trade.

At length the propensity grew so strong that I became inattentive to every thing else. My affairs fell into confusion, and, in the vain hope of retrieving them, I grew venturous in my bets, and, finally, desperate.

"I was soon declared a bankrupt, which, with my misconduct, had such an effect on my poor wife, that she fell sick, and died of a broken heart, and my children became a burden on the public. In this state of misery I revolved in my mind the most horrible modes of relief; and one evening, with a cocked pistol in my hand, my only remaining property, I robbed a gentleman near Lyons. I thought no one was near me; but Garquine, who kept a house for the reception of stolen goods near the spot, was a witness of the transaction from an adjoining field. She knew me, and, having overtaken me, demanded half my prize. I was forced to comply; and I went with her to her infamous abode. A reward was offered for my apprehension; and, under a threat to inform against me, she terrified me into a marriage with her.

"By her means I became acquainted with smugglers, robbers, and villains of every kind; and my love of gaming and my distress continuing, I never had the resolution nor the means to fly from her; and, crime following crime, and misfortune treading on misfortune, here I am at last, an outcast from society, and probably the victim of a greater delinquent than myself."

Just as Jacques had concluded, the other outlaws appeared, who, being made acquainted with the contents of the paper, joined in execrating the dark and wicked monster that governed them; at the same time declaring, with the inconsistency of low dissipation and idle profligacy, that, provided their wants should continue to be supplied, they should not grumble at the confinement of a few weeks longer. They, nevertheless, felt respect for their two amiable prisoners, and did all that was in their power to alleviate their misery.

The father and daughter never separated except at night. They read, they wrote, they sang, they strolled, they conversed; and, were they not conscious of being in the power of Count Egfryd, they would not have been miserable. There were goats on the island. Upon the milk of those, and bread, they principally subsisted. Mr. Bolton kept the sheet of paper, but the writing on it disappeared in two days.

One of the bravoes had, in his youth, been a performer in pantomime. He was naturally a buffoon; and upon no occasion could he resign a certain dryness of humour, that often carried with it pleasantry and point. His education, besides, had not been so much neglected as that of the others. It chanced, on the third morning after the treachery and violence practiced on Mr. Bolton and Julia, that the former spoke to this man. Among other matters he inquired about Gaspar Pontgebre. The account he received was in these words:

"The father of Gaspar Pontegbre, Sir, had been a cooper, and his mother a washer-woman in Milan. Despising the reflections of a censorious world, or too innocent and too tender to acknowledge any laws but those of love, the simple pair had neglected, or had forgotten, to celebrate their union with the ceremony of wedlock. Strangers to formality, and enemies to ostentation, they had plighted their troth, each to the other, in secret; and the only witness to the blushes of Giacobba, was the enamoured and sympathizing Raolo. Cupid, proud of the triumph over his rival Hymen, stole from him, as he slept, his crown and his torch. With the latter he lighted the conscious couch, while, from the former, he scattered over the happy lovers marjoram and roses.

"Raolo was a social and merry fellow. He could tell a story; he could crack a joke; he could sing a song. His companions liked him; he liked them; and they all liked wine; but neither they nor the wine could be enjoyed at home. He found it necessary, therefore, to absent himself, at times, from his beloved Giacobba and their little prattler Gaspar. The activity and curiosity of the child were admirable. His mother thought it a pity to impose the slightest restraint on him. He was, in consequence, accustomed from his infancy to ramble about the streets, thus acquiring a stock of health and ideas; for what invigorates the constitutions of children so much as constant exercise in the open air? what is so conducive to their mental improvement as a multitude of objects? This little darling, the pledge of his parents' love, possessed, among other qualities, a nimbleness of finger, and a quickness of eye, that often drew from his exulting father this pleasant remark—'I don't think that that little rascal will ever be hanged;' by which, while he conveyed his anxiety for his boy's future destiny, he jocosely insinuated that such talents and such dexterity, as the child possessed, would always preserve him from so ignominious a fate. Never was a creature so lucky in finding small articles as Gaspar was, and whatever he found, he, with filial affection, invariably carried to his mother. Pocket-handkerchiefs, it was observed, he was most successful in discovering, and seldom a day passed that he did not find one or two. As he advanced in years his talents became much improved and more valuable. Not only handkerchiefs, but tweezer-cases, gloves, snuff-boxes, hats, and watches, were obtained by his acute researches.

"The adventures of childhood are interesting, so far as they represent unperverted nature. At the age of eleven, passing through the streets, his eye happened to be caught, one evening, by the window of a jeweller's shop. Within that particular pane were several toys of great brilliancy. The inquisitive boy stopped. 'Oh!' thought he, 'if I had all those fine things now in my pocket, what a race should I not take to my mammy!' He looked, he sighed, he considered. It was evident to him, young and inexperienced as he was, that he could not go into the shop and take them away, for several reasons, one of which was, that there were three men attending it, who would probably be unwilling to dispose of the bawbles generously. How then are the pretty things to be obtained? why, by removing the pane; and how is that to be displaced? with his knife. Such was the simple train of his juvenile reasoning. The exclusive right to property is, you know, Sir, among the last principles that the youthful mind receives. It never occurred to him (to what uneducated boy of his age would it occur?) that, in taking these trinkets, he would violate honesty and justice. These were abstract terms to which he had not yet learned to attach the proper complex ideas.

"With an industry, therefore, worthy of his birth, he proceeded cautiously to pick away the putty that secured the glass. Having removed it, he looked around, lest any meddling, impertinent person should have observed him. All was safe, he thought; but just as he was about to remove the pane, he received a box on the right cheek, that produced for some time within his head the music of a peal of bells. It came from the rough and avaricious proprietor of the shop, who, insensible to his ingenuity and his youth, had stolen upon him.

"The next morning, one of the magistrates of the town, aware of the long train of evils that results from want of exercise, benevolently sent him to a house where persons, under the influence of a morbid disinclination to regular employment, are often induced, by the prevailing arguments of some gentlemen who attend them, to exert themselves in the laudable occupation of preparing the valuable plant *cannabis*, which is sometimes distinguished among botanists by the name of hemp. As a vegetable regimen is found most conducive to health and morality, the diet of the persons residing in such houses is generally of bread and water.

"In this excellent abode the little Gaspar tarried three months; and it was thought by his parents, but herein perhaps they evinced some partiality, that he departed from it much edified.

"At the age of eighteen, he had the good fortune to please a young man, whose approbation was surely not a little creditable to him. This young man, though not a prince, had the spirit of one. He would have commanded armies if he had them, and have stamped metal with his own image, if, by so doing, he could have made it coin. He felt that he had talents to govern, but he lived in a country where the government was jealous of rivals. Consequently it was quite natural that a warfare should take place between him and it; but for want of forces on his side he was compelled to proceed secretly. The sinews of war are money; and as his enemies ungenerously kept this from him, he, like a great man, determined to make some for himself.

"By his skill in metallurgy, he was enabled to bestow on mere brass and pewter the appearance of gold and silver; and to his admirable imitations he contrived ingeniously, for the greater facility of negociation, to give the exact resemblance of the circulating medium employed by his foes. This was, it must be admitted, a masterly stratagem. Gaspar, whom he employed to purchase necessaries for the campaign, was unfortunately suspected of a hostile intent and apprehended. He exhibited a firmness on the occasion that would have done honour to a Roman; and such was the effect of his interesting appearance and of his eloquence, that, after a few preliminary ceremonies, he was carried in triumph to the market-place, and there elevated amidst an immense crowd of people, upon a frame, curiously fabricated for the occasion, and constructed with such an attention to his comforts, that it even presented proper conveniences to support his head and hands. It being a fast-day, the populace, according to the ancient and simple custom of the country, produced such a number of eggs for his use, that they might be said in a manner to shower around him.

"On a subsequent occasion, being in distress for some necessaries, he, in that frank and unceremonious manner which often marks the great, accosted a gentleman on the high road, and borrowed from him eighty *Louis d'ors*. Being determined in his own mind to discharge the obligation punctually, he thought it unnecessary to make any formal speech at the time promising payment; and it was a matter of no small surprise to him, some months afterwards, to find himself arrested at the instance of his ungenerous and hard-hearted creditor.

"Hearing that he had a taste for navigation, it was thought a pity to confine Gaspar in a jail, so the judges, purely out of regard for him, and to testify their sense of his merit, took the trouble of procuring for him a situation aboard a royal vessel. In this he remained five years, and in that time his manners and his morals were improved considerably. He afterwards entered into general trade, but, being naturally forgetful, he omitted, upon some occasions, to pay the duties imposed by the legislature on his merchandize, and his enemies, taking advantage of these inadvertencies, had the baseness to call him a smuggler, and as such to prosecute him; but he escaped their malice, and he has not yet been hanged."

CHAPTER III.

Miser chi mal' oprando si confida,
Ch' ogn' or star debbia il maleficio occulto;
Che quando ogn' altro taccia, intorno grida
L'aria, e la terra stessa, in ch' è sepulto;
E Dio fa spesso, che 'l peccato guida
Il peccator, poi ch' alcun dì gli ha indulto;
Che se medesmo, senza altrui richiesta,
Inavvedutamente manifesta.

....

——————————The tombs
And monumental caves of death look cold,
And shoot a chillness to my trembling heart.

....

My shivering blood, congeal'd, forgot to flow;
Aghast I stood a monument of woe.

THE time for the arrival of Mr. Bolton and Julia at Bourdeaux having expired, Theodore became alarmed for their safety, and, after twelve days of painful expectation, he resolved to travel towards Calais by the *route* which he knew they were determined on. Accordingly, leaving a letter for them, should they arrive in his absence, he set off, and by so doing escaped the violence of Gaspar

Pontgebre, Pierre Dontache, and other bravoes, who, on the night after his departure, were to have attempted his assassination. He thought himself bound in honour, by the promise of secrecy made to the Count by Mr. Bolton, and therefore what he knew and what he suspected of that monster, remained buried in his bosom; but, dreading the effects of his policy or his vengeance, he used the precaution of leaving Bourdeaux privately. He arrived at Cognac about noon, where he was told that no English travellers had passed for a considerable time.

Having ordered some refreshment, he walked out for a short time while it was preparing. As he sauntered along, a boy, whom he recollected to have seen at St. Uldrich, accosted him. "Ah! Mr. Dalbert," said the boy, "I am very glad to meet you, for I have had something to tell you, Sir, that is of very great consequence. Did you ever hear tell, Sir, of the *Isle de Peine*?"—"Yes."—"Mr. Bolton and Mademoiselle——"—"What of them?"—"Are now there, or at least I saw them brought to it eight days ago."—"How! brought to the *Isle de Peine*?"—"Indeed it is true, Sir. I was on the road going from this town to the village of Darsace, when, whom should I see rising the hill in a carriage, but *Monsieur* and his daughter? They were at some distance, and I expected to be passed by them in a minute, when suddenly they drove into a narrow, dirty little lane, off the high road. I thought it very odd to be sure, Sir, and I was tempted to follow the carriage, but it went so hard, that had I not taken a short cut, I should have lost sight of them. Knowing that this was only a by-road for the country-people, and that no carriage ever travels it, I was very curious to find out what brought *Monsieur* such a dangerous way; so there being a high rock near me, I climbed to the top of it, in order to have a wide view, and thence I saw the carriage pass the *Charente*, and gallop along the opposite bank for a good way. Immediately afterwards a boat, with some lady in white, and a green veil, passed across to the *Isle de Peine*: I am sure it was *Mademoiselle*, because I saw a green veil on her in the carriage. There were three men in the boat besides, and one of them, no doubt, was Mr. Bolton. What I had seen made me very uneasy, as *Mademoiselle* had been so good to me at St. Uldrich, and that *Isle de Peine* is such a terrible place. So, in order to make things sure, I went on to the village of Quardos, through which I knew the carriage must have passed, and there I heard that an empty one had gone through a little while before."

"Who lives in the *Isle de Peine*?" inquired Theodore. "Oh! Sir, nobody ever likes to go there. There is a ruined church on it that's haunted even in the daytime, and unless it is some murderer or other, no one, I believe, ventures into it. Only that my present master is in Languedoc, I should have asked him leave to go to Bourdeaux for a day, in order, Sir, to tell you all this, and now I think myself very lucky indeed to have the honour of seeing you here."

Theodore rewarded the boy with a few crowns, bade him be silent, and returned to his inn, musing on the intelligence he had just heard. Having ordered a horse to be saddled for him, he rode along one of the banks of the *Charente*, until he came to a spot from which he could observe the island. He had supplied himself with a good telescope, and he could plainly discover Julia in what had been the cupola of the monastery. His heart palpitated as he viewed her. "A romantick little island that, Sir," said he, to a decent-looking man whom he met. "Pray has it any inhabitants?"—"At present it has, Sir. I am told that within this fortnight some people have been seen on it, but for nine years past that I have lived in the neighbourhood, I can answer for it no human being was to be found there, save some coiners, who were detected in those ruins about a twelvemonth ago."—"Strange! surely the land might be turned to some account?"—"Why, Sir, none of our peasantry would enter that island for any consideration. They think that that old fabrick is haunted by evil spirits, and, besides, it is at all times extremely difficult to land there. Count Egfryd, whose estate it is, has never been able to derive the smallest advantage from it."—"Count Egfryd! Is he the proprietor?"—"Yes, Sir, and to him belongs the little yellow house you see on the opposite side of the river, and likewise the ruined castle near it, formerly the seat of the D'Auvignacs."—"You have been on the island?" said Theodore, seemingly unmindful of the information he had just received. "Yes, Sir, I have gone there to shoot, but it is so troublesome to get a boat through the morass that surrounds it, that a man pays dear enough for any sport he finds there."

"A morass surrounds it then?"—"Yes, Sir, except where a narrow canal, a mile long, I believe, winds with a thousand curves through it. I know nothing of fortification, but I do believe that two men, placed at the termination of the canal near the ruins, would be able to repel five hundred invaders, for the morass is so deep and so broad that it is absolutely impossible to cross it, and therefore there is no way to enter the island but by the canal."—"A picturesque, agreeable country all around," observed Theodore; "and if there were a cottage on this side of the river to be let, I believe I should be tempted to take it."—"Look," said the stranger, "at the little white one that appears to hang over the water, it is at present unoccupied, and you can have it with a few acres of land at a trifling rent."—"Nothing would make me so happy; but to whom am I to apply?"—"To me."—"Are you, Sir, the proprietor?"—"I am." In a few minutes the bargain was closed, and Theodore the next day, under the name of Mr. Froigné, took possession of his little farm.

He had brought a servant with him from Bourdeaux, a young man of the name of Guillaume, on whose fidelity he could depend, and to him he confided what he had discovered, and what he feared. It was clear that Mr. Bolton and Julia were prisoners on the island and in the power of the Count; but how were they to be released, or how was any information to be conveyed to them? A thousand plans occurred to Theodore, and as many to Guillaume. Each racked his ingenuity and invention. It was idle to think of violence, as the island was accessible only at one spot, where the slightest resistance would keep off a considerable force; and no force could be obtained so secretly, as that the vigilant Count, who was probably in the neighbourhood, would not be apprized of it. To apply to the magistracy, and thus expose him, were to urge him to desperation, and perhaps cause the murder of the prisoners. Stratagem alone, therefore, must be resorted to.

Among the accomplishments that distinguished Miss Bolton, was a perfect knowledge of short-hand. This art she had taught to Theodore, and it struck him that he might now avail himself of it to extricate her. Accordingly, that side of his cottage which was next the island, he painted black, and, in stenographic characters, as large as the wall would permit, he traced this sentence: *Theodore bids you be in the cupola at twelve to-morrow night.* Each letter was four feet long, and some of the characters were still longer, and two hundred and fifty lamps were nailed to the wall, along the lines traced, so that the lamps, placed as they were, expressed the sentence completely. This being done, he supplied himself with a large quantity of fireworks, and on the fourth evening after his arrival, all being then ready for his purpose, he, as soon as it became dark, began to play them off.

The outlaws, from the windows of the refectory, viewed with amazement the most brilliant exhibition they had ever witnessed. "What is the meaning of all this?" said one. "Some great festival, perhaps," answered another. "Or," cried a third, "maybe a marriage has taken place, and that this is a gallant contrivance of the bridegroom." A fourth thought it more likely to be the commemoration of the birth-day of the lord of the manor. "Whatever, or whosoever it is," observed Jacques, "we should be much obliged for the pleasure it affords us."—"Why obliged?" snarled Garquine. "What is it all but a little flame and crackling? Some fool, I warrant you, is throwing away his money, now, on this nonsense, and perhaps, before the year is out, will want wherewithal to buy his dinner. And all for what? To amuse blockheads and children; for there is no person of sense that must not laugh at it." Each gave a different opinion, while all, not even excepting Garquine, continued to observe with attention. The night was uncommonly dark, and, for two hours, rockets, wheels, stars, and various other inventions of pyrotechny, filled the air with illuminations and explosions.

In an instant the whole ceased, and all was black, but suddenly the two hundred and fifty lamps, which had been previously prepared with the essential oil of turpentine and flax, burst into one prodigious blaze, and the words *Theodore bids you be in the cupola at twelve to-morrow night* might, by any one acquainted with the system of stenography that had been employed, be read at the distance of a mile.

Theodore trusted that the attention of the two prisoners would be attracted by the fireworks, and consequently that Miss Bolton would be induced to examine the light of the lamps, and to read the sentence it conveyed. Nor was he mistaken. She and her father had been spectators of his brilliant display from the cupola; and when the steady lustre of the lamps had fixed their attention, Julia instantly comprehended its meaning. She read the burning words to her father, and each, at that happy moment, felt a transport of joy which banished every painful reflection. Hope once again, for an instant, animated their bosoms.

"What an admirable contrivance!" said Julia. "By no other means could we possibly have received that message. Oh, father! when we see Theodore, and my heart tells me we shall soon see him, all our danger and adversity will have terminated."—"You forget," observed Mr. Bolton thoughtfully, and dispirited by the sad and sudden recollection, "the danger of entering this island, and the impossibility of quitting it." Julia made no reply, but sunk on her knees, and, in silent prayer, invoked, for her beloved Theodore, the protection of her tutelary saint.

At twelve o'clock, the next night, the father and daughter were in the cupola. Not a star was to be seen, and not a sound to be heard, save the soft whisper of a gentle gale that blew from the south, and the gurgling of the river, where it rippled through the rushes. All was black and solemn, when the most interesting of females, and her excellent parent, looking toward the white cottage, observed a number of lights, apparently in a cluster, moving through the air. At first they seemed to skim the surface of the river, but soon they rose gradually to a considerable height. By degrees they approached the island, and at length appeared hovering above the ruined monastery. Still they continued to move, now to the right, then to the left; at one moment descending, and at another rising; sometimes in a direction down, and at other times up the river. They were about twenty in number, forming a luminous circle, and below them was a large but dim body of light, which appeared to have a motion different from that of the others, though connected with them. It was a strange and incomprehensible, but not unhandsome spectacle; and, to the two observers, it was, in a peculiar degree, interesting and important.

With their heads bent backwards, and their eyes fixed on the elevated moving lights, they waited silently and anxiously for an explanation of the phenomenon. For two hours they were kept in the most painful suspense, when suddenly, Julia cried out, in a tone of alarm, "What is that? oh, Sir! did you feel any thing pass across you?"—"Feel any thing! no, what was it?"—"There again! oh! something that hangs down from those lights—here it is!"—"Let me feel it," said he, in some disorder. "This! is this it? why, it is a silk string, and I will pull it."

He drew the string gradually, and when he had gathered about twenty yards of it, the motion of the lights appeared in a great measure to have ceased, and in a few minutes other strings fell on him, and some on her. These Julia collected, and all being joined, were pulled together. It was now evident that they were connected with the lights, which, as the cords were drawn, descended towards the cupola. Arrived within fifty or sixty feet of it, a large paper-kite was apparent, with a number of small lamps, being the lights that had attracted the observation of the two prisoners, burning in its circumference. A horn lantern, containing a light, was attached to the termination of its tail. Drawn nearer, the kite presented on its front, in red letters, these words—*a letter in the lantern.* "A letter in the lantern!" cried Julia. "Oh! let us draw it to us." The cords were pulled with redoubled activity, the lantern was seized, and the letter was found and read by the trembling girl to her father.

"When is our persecution to cease? When shall I clasp my best-beloved, my dearest Julia to my heart, never to part from her again? But the same Providence that rescued me from *the grave*, and from the barbarous effects of my unjust conviction, will guard your innocence, and deliver you from the power of the execrable Egfryd. Banish your fears. Believe my attachment to you unchangeable; and be assured that whatever love, money, courage, ingenuity and address can effect, shall be employed to liberate you. I occupy the cottage, one side of which was lately blackened, near the river. I am called Mr. Froigné, and I take care never to be seen by any one but my servant. *Adieu!* I could say much, but I must confine myself to what is indispensable. Make my most affectionate respects to my loved and honoured friend, your father. Oh! that you may not have been separated from him! Put your answer in the lantern. With what impatience shall I not expect it! *Adieu! Adieu!* THEODORE."

Julia, in speechless ecstacy, immediately wrote on a piece of paper, with a pencil:

"My father and I are well and together. Egfryd has not appeared. Six outlaws guard us. They are prevented from attempting to escape by gunpowder in the causeway, which any effort to pass through the canal would blow up, and whoever should enter it from the river would be crushed to death by a rock, placed for that purpose on the top of the causeway. Should the person attempting to enter by the canal escape the rock, and persist in advancing, then the explosion must necessarily ensue, which would involve us all in sudden and utter destruction. With what rapture do I not seize this opportunity to save you from danger. *Adieu!* ever, ever affectionately your JULIA."

This note she put into the lantern, and releasing the silk strings, the kite rose, and was drawn to the spot from which it first ascended.

With minds in a state far different from that which they had lately experienced, Mr. and Miss Bolton retired to rest, and the sun, which shone brightly the next day, saw them, if not contented, at least not miserable. It was twelve o'clock, and they were walking, her hand under his arm, in a gallery immediately under the cupola, when a sudden noise, like the feigned voice of a person speaking loudly, arrested their steps, and excited their fear and their astonishment. The word *hark!* was plainly articulated. Julia trembled. Mr. Bolton looked around. "Hark!" repeated the mysterious voice, after a little pause, "you have been brought hither to obey me, attend therefore to what I say. You, Mr. Bolton, possess a hundred thousand pounds sterling in the English funds, and you, Miss Bolton, twenty thousand. All this I must obtain, and I will obtain it without risk. To sell out this stock a letter of attorney from each of you to one Stephen Berland is necessary; and to receive it from him, when sold out, an order to him must be signed by you both, requiring him to pay it over. Two sheets of paper, stamped according to the English law, and a sheet of unstamped paper, are lying on the stone mantle-piece in the ruined dormitory, together with a precedent for a letter of attorney. Let each of you copy this precedent on one of the stamped sheets, and let the order to Berland be drawn by one of you, and signed by both, on the unstamped sheet of paper, according to the form subjoined to the precedent. Then leave the whole on the same mantle-piece. Let all this be done to-day, or you shall lose your lives—Shall lose your lives!—Mind these words. I must not be trifled with."

The voice ceased. It sounded as if spoken through a narrow tube. It was loud and hollow, but not indistinct. Uttered as it was by a hidden person, whose presence in the island was inexplicable, the amazement it caused in the mind of each auditor was mingled with no slight degree of horror. They stood motionless for some minutes, dreading a continuation of the mysterious address, when Mr. Bolton said to his daughter, in a low tone, "This is the Count. He said truly that he would be sometimes here, though unseen. Look at the six outlaws without the ruins on the grass. Who but he, then, can have spoken? But let us to the dormitory and do what is required. We shall else, certainly, fall a sacrifice to his disappointment and his fury. But perhaps," continued he, in a still lower tone, "before he can make use of the letters of attorney, we shall, with the assistance of Theodore, have obtained our liberation."

Julia, pale and shaking, accompanied her father to the dormitory, where they found all as had been described to them. They wrote the order to Berland and the letters of attorney in the manner prescribed, and then left the four papers on the mantle-piece. This was so high that a person standing on the floor could hardly see what was on it, and the ceiling above it had, in more than one spot, given way. The Count would probably have, with his own hand, fabricated the two powers of attorney and the letter to Berland, but no imitation, however excellent, of writing can escape detection, he knew, in the public offices in London. His only motive for suffering his two victims to live, was the possibility of some further act by them being necessary; and he concealed himself, lest, during his absence in England, on the perpetration of his fraudulent designs, the two prisoners might, by some unforeseen and inconceivable means, effect their escape, and be enabled to convict him.

The voice in the dormitory had, as Mr. Bolton suspected, issued from this formidable man, who had entered the island by an arched subterranean way, that led under the river, from the ruined castle on the main land near his yellow cottage, to the foundations of the monastery. A spiral staircase thence ascended to a small unlighted chamber, within the main wall of the building, from which chamber three narrow passages branched in different directions, through the partitions of the ruined fabrick. He had been long acquainted with these hidden avenues. They had been mentioned to him, under an injunction of secrecy, by his deceased father. The injunction was unnecessary. The mystery of such obscure recesses too well accorded with the darkness of his disposition, and the iniquity of his designs, to be confided by him to any person.

Miss Bolton's note, sent in the lantern, produced violent agitation in the mind of Theodore; but she and her father were well, and hope, which is ever inseparable from love, bade him expect to see them released in a few days. Their release, he knew, must depend solely on his exertions, and those he was not only willing, but anxious to employ. After much deliberation he determined to attempt the passage of the morass. The enterprize was difficult and dangerous, perhaps impracticable; but difficulties and dangers were unregarded by him in his ardour to save his mistress. With an alacrity, known only to those who are truly enamoured, he procured timber for the construction of a raft, and workmen for its formation; but he feared to send a second message by the kite, lest the suspicions of the Count should be excited, and the difficulty of the intended liberation increased.

While Theodore was employed on the construction of the raft, the Count was on his journey to England, whither he went when he obtained the two letters of attorney. These, from one of his hiding-places, he had removed off the mantle-piece, in a few hours after they had been placed there. He would, it is likely, have applied for and obtained them sooner, and perhaps immediately after the seizure of the two prisoners, but a hurt he had received by a fall, had disabled him from walking for some days.

Previous to his departure for England, he left orders with his servant Guiscard to learn the name of the stranger that had lately taken the white cottage, his business in that country, his connexions, and the object of those fireworks, which had been displayed with such apparently unmeaning expense.

It is at once curious and alarming to think of the present situation of the principal personages of this history. On one side of the river a decayed castle, communicating, by a subterranean passage, with the monastery, and possessed by Egfryd, the absolute master of all who breathe upon the island—by Egfryd, who has resolved that every individual of them shall perish. On the opposite bank Theodore, in his cottage, separated by an impassable morass, from all his soul holds dear, and endeavouring by some ingenious contrivance, to liberate her from dishonour and from death: while Julia and her father, joint inhabitants, with six felons, of the crumbling cloister, dare not even attempt to escape, and can scarcely hope for deliverance.

Mr. Bolton, on the day after the voice had been heard by him in the gallery, fell ill, partly from the agitation his spirits had sustained, and partly from his recent change of diet. Julia had watched by his side all night, and in the morning, finding he had fallen into a profound sleep, she retired to her favourite cupola, to enjoy the fragrance of the air and the freshness of the morning breeze, and to gaze on the habitation of her Theodore. She could not sleep, and the contrast between the close and wretched apartment she had left, and the magnificence and extent of the present scene, gave a new elasticity to her mind, and revived in her heart a portion of its latent cheerfulness.

She pondered a long time on the mysterious voice. It was Count Egfryd's she was certain—he whom her soul abhorred—he at whose name she trembled. But where was his concealment? how did he hide himself? A vague conception of the truth floated in her mind.

Surely, thought she, that impenetrable and tremendous reprobate has some passage from the main land, under the river, into these ruins. How otherwise can the presence of the invisible visitor be explained? for never would he expose himself to the possibility of a long confinement in a place where no enjoyment could be had, where his life would be insecure, and from whence, without such a passage, departure would be almost impossible. He is now probably on his way to England with the letters of attorney, and even were he not gone thither, there is very little danger, at this early hour, of his being here. Let me then, this moment, exercise all my courage and acuteness to save my father, and to see my Theodore.

With an eye, sharp as the inquiring glance of a nurse who seeks her stolen infant—with a step, light as the bound of the slender antelope, Julia traversed the dismantled apartments, examined the broken walls, sounded the rotten ceilings, climbed the tottering staircases, and inspected the fractured partitions. That which had formerly been the belfry, was a dark, arched, and lofty room. The floor exhibited sundry breaches, and below, at a considerable depth, might be seen the marble pavement of an ancient altar. It was an operation of no small peril to pass from one side of this belfry to the other, but Julia was urged by motives that gave her courage, and her courage was crowned with success. In an angle where a great portion of the wall had given way and tumbled down, and near to the floor, was an aperture five feet high, and nearly three feet wide. Into this she ventured, and within she found a passage to the left, leading directly to the top of a spiral staircase.

"God be praised!" cried she, piously, "I have discovered what I sought." Having fortified her resolution with a fervent prayer, and committed herself to the providence of Heaven, she descended the steps. They were of stone, and barely broad enough to admit one person. Perfect darkness surrounded her, but she still proceeded, using the precaution, however, of feeling on each side, lest she should cross any other passage that might bewilder her on her return. She had gone slowly, and with all possible caution, down one hundred and fifty-seven steps, when she found herself on an earthen floor. She ventured to make a little noise by coughing, and the echo at once terrified her almost to fainting, and convinced her that she was in a vault of immense extent. Dreading to lose, for an instant, her hold of the stone spindle, round which the spiral stairs revolved, apprehensive as she was that she should be for ever lost, and at the same time desirous to explore still further, she regretted that she had not thought to provide herself with a light, which would have enabled her to advance. It being useless to remain any longer in the dark, she returned to the ruined belfry, which, after her obscure and dangerous descent, appeared to her a cheerful and splendid apartment. Such is the powerful effect of contrast and comparison. Arrived in the belfry, she was glad to seat herself on a heap of stones, and having in a short time recovered from the effects of her fatigue and terrour, she returned to her own room.

Her father continued, during the morning, so unwell, that though she wished to communicate to him the discovery she had made, she could not do so, she thought, with propriety. At twelve o'clock he again fell into a gentle slumber, and at twelve o'clock, she, who was now urged by an irresistible desire to continue her researches, supplied herself with two candles, and proceeded to the belfry. From the belfry she descended to the earthen floor with safety; but such was her dizziness in consequence of her agitation and the many circular turns she had taken in the light, while wheeling down within the narrow stone cylinder that contained the winding stairs, that she was compelled to sit for some time on the bottom step. She put the candles on the ground, and rested her head on her knees. The vertigo, however, did not long distress her.

When recovered, she raised her eyes and saw a prodigious cavern, extending further than her sight could reach. The roof was about twenty feet from the ground, and arched, and several rows of rude columns supported it. The ground was wet and the air damp. Before her, as she sat, was an avenue between two ranges of the columns, and to the end of this she hoped to walk. Taking up one of her candles, and leaving the other on the earth to light her back in case any accident should happen to that which she carried, she advanced. She went about twenty yards when she thought she heard a noise behind her. With a ghastly countenance she turned her head, expecting to be appalled by an apparition, or, worse than any apparition, by the diabolical Egfryd. But her fears had deceived her. There had been no noise, save what had been caused by her timid steps, if that might be called a noise, which was scarcely audible even to her own now painfully sensitive organ. She made the sign of the cross upon her forehead, and walked on.

Arrived nearly to the end of the avenue, a black humid wall terminated her view. She cast her eyes along its gloomy length, and, at some distance, saw an opening. She deliberated whether she should venture to go to it. She knew that if she approached it she would lose the view of the lighted candle at the stairs, but if she should retire without looking into the opening, she would have effected nothing—she would have ventured much to no purpose.

Thus she deliberated, and with an intrepidity that would have done honour even to Theodore, she resolved to persevere in her enterprize. Marking attentively, therefore, the relative situations of the wall, the stairs, and the columns, so that she should not miss her way back, she went forward to the opening. It was high and narrow, and it ascended as it receded. She enters it. She goes about fifty yards. It then sinks. This, thinks she, leads under the river to the continent. Fresh ardour animates her. She walks with speed. She has already gone two hundred yards, when an insurmountable obstacle presents itself. This is a large iron door. She tries to stir it, but it is immoveable. It has no key-hole, and therefore it is, she supposes, fastened by bars on the other side.

Her disappointment bordered on despair. She returned, and, as she retraced her lonely steps, a part of the wall of the narrow passage attracted her attention. It was of a different colour from the rest of the wall, and it suggested to her mind the idea of a secret door. She stopped to examine it, and ascertained that it was a large piece of wood, which, in consequence of age, had fallen away a little from its ancient situation. She touched it, and found that it was worm-eaten and rotten. She pushed it, and it fell in pieces. A chamber appeared within. This was a temptation to curiosity that could not be resisted. She entered.

The side next the entrance was black, and on it was engraved, in a rude and grotesque manner, but legibly, though lightly, a multitude of letters, and in one place, near the door, a hand had been roughly sculptured in *alto relievo*, from the fore-finger of which was suspended a little ball. Julia cast a hasty glance at the engraving and the hand. "Is not this ball offered, as it were, to me?" said she to herself—"and should I not remove it?" She advanced her arm to it, took it off the finger, and put it in her pocket. No sooner had she done so, than she heard, or fancied she heard, an exclamation of detection and reproach.

"Hah!" was, she thought, the short but horrific sound. Fixed as the hand from which she had disengaged the ball, her eyes alone had motion. These she cast fearfully around, and, in the centre of the room, she beheld a spectacle, such as was never before seen. She dropped on her knees, implored, with her looks, the protection of the Virgin, and tried to support herself by placing one of her hands on a marble table that stood near. The other was scarcely able to hold the candle. Religion, that never denies its aid to the true believer, sustained her at a moment, when, but for the supernatural support of Divine Beneficence, she must have been struck lifeless with horrour.

The regions of night and death, into which she had with such boldness descended, had already, to her imagination, been rendered more gloomy, more silent, and more dismal than they were, by her recollection of the brilliant sun, which, a few minutes before, had enlivened and irradiated every object within her view—by the cheerful labours, still present to her thoughts, of the distant peasantry employed in their rural occupations—by the sweet warbling of the thousand winged inhabitants of the island—by the odorous gales and ripened charms of luxurious autumn—and by the enamelled plains, and waving woods, and flowing waters, that embellished every prospect from the cupola. The dreadful and intolerable solitude of these murder-menacing vaults had already acquired additional dreariness from the contrast it formed with her father's delightful society. The embittering remembrance of his animated serenity, his paternal attentions, and his calm and uniform tenderness, was now mingled in her mind with the painful reflections of a deep and rapid river flowing over her head—of a dilapidated cloister inhabited by banditti, among whom that beloved parent was languishing on a wretched pallet—of the monster Egfryd prowling amid its ruined chambers, stalking through treacherous recesses in its massy walls, or, perhaps, approaching with silent step and ruffianly intent to the very centre of human horrours, whither her temerity had led her, and not another being within hearing of her shrieks.

These, and similar reflections had robbed the hapless Julia of all her resolution when most she wanted it. Not for her freedom would she have dared to cast a second glance at the most dreadful of all dreadful objects; not to purchase the presence of her faithful Theodore would she have approached nearer to it by a single step. Almost petrified with fear, the pious girl, her eyes averted from the terrific sight, continued her fervid, though silent invocation. As she prayed she slowly recovered sufficient strength to stand, and she departed, tottering, from the frightful and appalling scene of mystery and murder.

Her knees sinking, and her steps as hurried as her faintness would permit, she gained the larger vaults and obtained a view of the columns. She began to breathe more freely, and her limbs began to tremble less violently, when a low and plaintive accent, uttered under some distant arch, reverberated upon her tortured ear. Her heart beat against her breast with painful emotion and a quickness that nearly deprived her of the power of respiration. Pale as the corpse of an unhappy maid, who has sunk under the deceitful stroke of slow consumption, her eyes starting from their sockets, her mouth wide open, her pallid lips moving tremulously, her tongue cleaving to her palate, her eyebrows raised, her hair erect, her face drawn to a state of preternatural elongation, her shoulders elevated, and her hands and arms shaking, the terrified girl stared around.

There is in all things that have life a principle, intended by Providence for their preservation, which is a capability of exerting extraordinary strength and unwonted activity in the moment of extreme peril. The fear of Julia had, upon the present occasion, the effect of resolution. She flew along the moist earth, and arrived in the avenue which she had first traversed. She looked toward the staircase, expecting to be guided by the light of the second candle, but dreading, at the same time, to behold some frightful object. Horrible to tell! the candle she could not see. It had been removed, and the one she carried in her trembling hand had now so long a snuff, and gave so dim a light, that she could not distinguish whether the staircase were before her. There was no time for deliberation. She proceeded according to her recollection of the way, and in a minute she saw the stairs, but there was no candle near them. Too much agitated to bestow much consideration on this strange circumstance, she ascended the steps and soon reached the belfry. There she dropped in a swoon, and it was an hour before she recovered and was able to crawl into her own room, where, having sat down, she viewed herself in the mirror of her writing-box.

Reader, imagine, if thou canst, her astonishment, when, on looking at the glass, she saw upon her bosom an amber necklace, which she had never beheld before, secured by a golden clasp. This circumstance, joined to what had occurred during her research, perplexed, and alarmed, and shocked her excessively. To the golden clasp was attached a slip of paper, on which were these words, written with a black lead pencil:—

"Never again be afraid to enter my palace. It is dark but spacious. I reign there, and you shall always have my protection. I have seen and I respect you. I have heard you converse with your father; you are a Briton, and I admire the English. Oh! how I loved a maid of your country! Eliza! I, Lonchiderimos! But no more! you shall never see me—my misery might terrify you. But still I reign, and who would dare to disturb me? Other monarchs delight in show, I find majesty in darkness. This necklace has hung on a royal neck, but never till now was it excelled by the beauty of the wearer."

On each bead of the necklace was a coronet. Julia looked at it, and then at the paper, looked again, and again, and the more she looked the more she was amazed. She then took the ball out of her pocket, and found, on opening it, that it was a square piece of silk, which had been wrapped up into that shape, and that it contained several words which had been worked in it. The silk had originally been white, but it had become brown from age, and the letters, in their present tarnished state, were entirely black, but they were still to be read. The language was Italian; the orthography was ancient, but the whole was, with a little study, intelligible. The following is a loose translation of it:—

"Whoever thou art that readest this, I conjure thee, if thou be a Christian, by our holy Saviour; or if thou be a Pagan or an Infidel, by the Almighty himself!—by thy eternal soul!—by all thou valuest!—by all thou fearest!—by all thou lovest!—do what I here require, and never, by word, or deed, or sign, or look, convey to mortal any thing thou mayest have seen, or read, or suspected, in these subterranean apartments! If thou refuse my request—if thou violate this injunction—may every ill that human nature can endure be thine! May thou commit some crime, new to the world, and horrible as new! May insatiable voracity and unquenchable thirst consume thee, without the means of procuring the vilest food or the foulest drink! May northern blasts, and drenching sleet, and starving frost, stiffen thy joints, and agonize thy every limb, and may thou want even the meanest rags to cover thy shivering frame! May sleep fly from thee! May thy parents desert and execrate thee! May thou dread the light of day, and the human countenance! May thou feel the cruellest pangs of never-slumbering remorse! May tumultuous and cursing crowds, urged by thy own children, hunt thee, whenever thou shalt appear, as a thing unclean, noxious, excommunicated, and abominable! May owls, rats, and other vermin of the dark, be thy only associates! May loathsome diseases attack thee, and may each of those diseases be incurable! May no beam of hope illumine thy festered heart! May fear and hatred be thy ruling passions! and may nought remain of thee, unimpaired, but thy memory, to envenom thy every pang!

"But grant my request, and preserve, undivulged, what thou shalt discover, and, if the prayers of a dying woman are heard, thou shalt be blessed with peace, content, and happiness, and crowned with unalterable felicity. Know, stranger, that the peace of a Christian soul depends upon thy exertions, and my salvation on thy active charity. Upon the wall of my prison is carved the story of my crimes and my sufferings. The nails of my coffin were my tools. It is unintelligible without a key to explain certain parts of it. That key is worked at the bottom of this silk. In a cavity, behind the marble table, is a box full of gold. Of this keep what thou mayest want; with the remainder pay for masses to redeem my sinful soul. But remember that thy compliance and thy secrecy are duties, not to be violated but at the risk of incurring the terrours of all the imprecations thou hast read. 14th June, 1583."

Under this were some marks, and dates, and names, each of which was followed by the word or words it was intended to express.

Julia laid down the silk. She thought of her father, of Theodore, of Count Egfryd, of the cavern, of the spectacle. Her mind, weakened by terrour, suffered pain even to anguish; but recollecting, at length, that her father might want her, she locked up the silk, the paper, and the necklace; and having bestowed some little care on her person, necessary after her explorement, she tottered to the invalid.

He was awake and expecting her, but as he was sick and heavy, her agitation escaped his notice, and the terrible and mysterious inhibition, she had lately read, enforced her silence. She remained with him until evening in a state of perturbation that few have experienced, and then she retired for the night, glad to conceal her disorder from his view.

CHAPTER IV.

'Tis now the very witching time of night,
When church-yards yawn, and hell itself breathes out
Contagion to the world!

. . . .

————Oh Hell! canst thou reserve
Still greater pains, or do I not indeed
Contain thee here? I do, I do, yes here! Within
This breast infernal furies dwell! No peace,
No calm content I taste; but sin, and shame,
And dread, confusion and dismay.

. . . .

O, my offence is rank! It smells to Heaven;
It hath the primal, eldest curse upon it.

. . . .

I saw a cavern black and fathomless,
Whereout foul steams exhal'd, and poisons flow'd;
Within its horrid womb, a blazing lake
Spouted sulphureous torrents through the gloom,
Tossing poor damned souls; whose shriekings rent
Hell's burning vault, through hell's entire extent.

The Count Egfryd, meanwhile, arrived in England, where he put in practice a plan, which enabled him, by means of the two letters of attorney, to draw out of the public funds one hundred and twenty thousand pounds sterling, without exposing himself to the possibility of suspicion. I should here develop the plan he practised, did not the well-being of society, and the security of private property, forbid so dangerous a disclosure.

Nature, how little dost thou require! but how difficult is it to obtain that little! Wherefore does the naked Esquimaux traverse the immense continent of North America even to the pole, encountering the savage violence of hostile tribes, immeasurable deserts, intense frost, and immoderate fatigue? Why labour, without intermission, from the beginning of the year till its termination, and year after year during their wretched lives, the degraded boors of Russia and of Poland? What urges the hapless beings who inhabit Friuli, Idria, Almaden and Guacamvelica, to expose themselves to the noxious vapours and volatile particles proceeding from the quicksilver which is found in these mephitick mines? Alas! hunger is the motive, and subsistence the end of all.

Is not the shivering author, scribbling in his garret, sensible of the pangs which await his temerity, from the insolence of booksellers, the severity of critics, and the contempt of the public; and alive to the present tortures that attend his violent efforts to invent incidents for a play, to fancy imagery for a poem, or to produce, amid penury and vexation, rich and lively descriptions of ease, luxury and pleasure? Ah! too sensible he is of those pangs and tortures, but—he must dine.

Placed between starvation and slavery, how many millions crave a little bread, of whom how many crave in vain? If old, feeble, or diseased, the wretch is left to perish, or is cast into that receptacle of human misery—a poor-house. If possessed of physical powers equal to long hardship and extreme fatigue, a paltry and inadequate pittance is mayhap scornfully dolled to him. For this he is compelled to sacrifice his liberty for life and his nature, and to become a brute part of that monstrous, murdering machine, an army. Nature, how little dost thou require! but how difficult is it to the innocent to obtain that little! How easy to gain it by crime! The vilest of mankind, the abominable Egfryd, by one atrocious act, has now possessed himself of one hundred and twenty thousand pounds sterling, the very interest of which would yield, for ever, all the necessaries of life to three hundred persons!

While he was thus employed, Gaspar Pontgebre was not idle. This villain never, for an instant, suffered himself to forget that if he could discover his unknown employer, he would be bribed to silence with independence and wealth. His reflections on this subject occupied his mind during the day, and often disturbed his rest at night. Between the turnkey of the gaol wherein *Marie de Solase* had been confined and him, such intimacy subsisted as congeniality of baseness and similar habits of sottish intemperance may produce between two wretches naturally vile, and inveterately wicked. In one of their drunken orgies the turnkey undertook to explain to the other, who, however, paid little attention to him, the mode of her escape; and then he proceeded, in the scarcely coherent talkativeness of inebriated vulgarity, to relate what she had communicated to him, after her apprehension, of her retreat in *the grave*, and of the Count.

The word "*grave*" roused Gaspar from his stupidity and inattention. Opening wide his horrible eyes, he listened till the other had concluded, when, starting up, he exclaimed: "By G—! I have him." The turnkey attributed this exclamation to drunkenness, as he did likewise Gaspar's departure, which was abrupt and precipitate. But he retired in order to deliberate in private. *The grave*, thought he, is not far from St. Uldrich. I carried Mr. Dalbert to *the grave*; Mr. Dalbert was a visitor at St. Uldrich; the Count D'Egfryd is the proprietor of St. Uldrich; he assisted Marie in escaping to a cavern in *the grave*; he is the richest and most powerful man in the country; and to him belongs the uninhabited *Isle de Peine*, whither the Boltons were lately carried. The Boltons were at St. Uldrich.—As I live he is the man!—now is the time to work on his pride and fear—now is the time to charge him with those crimes, and to demand a reward equal to his danger.

Gaspar accordingly lost not a moment in repairing to St. Uldrich. There he was told that the Count had, a short time before, travelled to his sporting cottage, in the province of Angoumois. This information confirmed his suspicions, and induced him to continue his journey even to the cottage. Being informed there that the Count had gone to England, he proceeded to Calais, where he waited until the object of his suspicion and his plunder returned.

It was about two in the afternoon when the packet arrived, and the first person seen by the Count on landing was the formidable Gaspar. A vague suspicion of danger instantly struck the crafty and suspicious Egfryd, and he feared, as the fact was, that nothing but an intention to watch or to insult him, could have brought Gaspar to Calais, as he had positive orders never to quit Bourdeaux without the permission of his invisible master. The Count was too great an adept in duplicity to appear disturbed, or to look again at the object of his dread. He repaired to his hotel, and seemed, to all around him, undisturbed and chearful. But in a far different state was his mind. He dreaded that he was discovered, and he revolved in his mind the immediate destruction of Gaspar and his associate. If his suspicions were well founded, he knew that the former would wait until an opportunity should offer of speaking to him in private; and he thought the best course he could adopt, at present, would be to walk out immediately into the country, and to saunter into some retired spot, where the fellow might accost him without being seen.

The Count, accordingly, about five o' clock, strolled into the suburbs, and, as he had conjectured, the bravo followed him. Having entered a little valley through which a rivulet flowed, the treacherous Egfryd seated himself negligently on a rock, and took out of his pocket a tablet wherein he pretended to write. Gaspar suddenly appeared before him. "Sir," said he, "I make bold to speak to you, but you will excuse me, for my business is of some consequence."—"My good fellow," cried the other, appearing surprised, and, as it were, interrupted by his address, "what would you have? I shall listen to you with great pleasure, but I am sure you mistake, for I don't know a creature in Calais. I am the *Comte D'Egfryd.*"—"Oh! my Lord, I know that very well, and it is because you are the *Comte D'Egfryd*, that I expect you will put me, for my life, beyond the reach of want."—"Because I am the *Comte D'Egfryd!* Explain yourself, friend."—"Explain myself, friend! why then I will, and that in a few words. *Marie de Solase*, Sir, was liberated from jail by your means, and concealed in a cavern in *the grave*; and by your means Mr. Dalbert was decoyed from St. Uldrich and left to perish at *the grave*—the same Mr. Dalbert whom I and another were commissioned by you to assassinate at Bourdeaux. You are found out, my Lord, and I will not be trifled with."

"My friend," said the Count, in seeming dismay, "surely you will not ruin me. Half my fortune is yours, and be discreet."—"Oh! as to that," replied the ruffian, "be you generous and I shall be discreet, I warrant you."—"Well, well, as an earnest of my liberality, in the first instance I will give you this." So saying, the perfidious man took out of his pocket what seemed a red leather case, tied into a cylindrical shape. "You shall have the contents of this," continued he, "for the present, and——"

What appeared a red leather case was the cover of a pistol of admirable workmanship. On the present occasion it shot a bullet through the brain of Gaspar Pontgebre.

The Count in a short time returned to his hotel, first placing a discharged pistol, of equal *calibre* with that one which had been fired, in the right hand of the deceased. The next morning Gaspar was found in this situation, and no doubt was entertained that he had committed suicide.

While the Count is on his journey, and while Theodore is engaged in the construction of a proper raft for the passage of the morass, let me return to Miss Bolton.

Timid by nature, and superstitious by habit, the mystery of the hidden chamber, the terrours of her late research, the necklace, the lost candle, the pencilled paper, and the denunciations of the embroidered silk, had presented to her imagination phantoms of horrour, and filled her mind with wild and gloomy reveries on supernatural operations. Her peace deserted her. Her anxiety for her sick father, her love for the absent Theodore, her apprehensions of the wicked Count, all were lost in dreadful conceptions of her fanatick, fear-fraught fancy. To utter a word of what she had discovered were, in her opinion, a profanation worse than sacrilege. On her obedience to the miraculous mandate she had received, depended, she thought, her future salvation; and on her promptitude and activity, her escape from the evils so solemnly imprecated. Peter the hermit* felt not more ardour to perform his mission, than the terrified Julia to comply with the adjurations of the unknown, whose soul was by her means, she believed, to be rescued from purgatorial fires, wherein it had already suffered for centuries. On no other subject could she think, and had not her father been confined to his bed and made dull by his illness, he must have observed the great alteration that took place in her looks and manner.

Fanaticism and superstition sometimes urge to acts which the cautious calculator would deem impossible, or the boldest warrior call rash. Resting her hopes of redemption on her implicit submission, and convinced that religion and Heaven demanded her agency, she was impatient again to explore the cavern. On the second night after she had made the discovery, leaving her father much recovered, she, at the eleventh hour, again ventured to descend. Warmed as she was by those new and powerful impulses, with her writing-box under her left arm, and a candle in her right hand, she reached the bottom of the stairs, where, instead of losing her courage, she seemed to acquire increased resolution.

With the enthusiasm of an enraptured candidate for canonization, she walked, after sitting on the bottom-step for a few minutes, to the end of the avenue between the columns, and turned to the right towards the opening. This opening she entered, and she continued her course until she came to the secret chamber, the door of which had before crumbled down. She entered undauntedly, and placed her writing-box and candle on the marble table, under which she searched for, and within a small cavity, found the box of gold. She put it on the table, and then, kneeling down, proceeded to translate the sculptured inscription into English on the leaves of her pocket-book. To translate was more easy to her than to transcribe, and she had brought her writing materials, lest any part of the promised history should escape her memory. The piece of silk with the embroidered characters was before her, to serve as a key to the obscurities of which she had been apprized. Thus she wrote:—

"Endow me, Almighty, with strength to complete my task. The victim of a mother's cruelty, the lost to happiness, the buried though yet breathing, the unnatural and justly punished Aminta, once gay, once proud, once beautiful, once great, carves upon her tomb the story of her woes. Ere my coffin shall receive my emaciated and half-famished frame—ere my loved, luckless babe, incestuous offspring! unbaptized, unsuckled, and unconscious of a mother's kiss, shall, within his infernal cage, be cramped to a cruel death; let me sculpture my horrid tale. I shall not, I wish not to survive him. Pride, pride, read here, and put away thy pomp! Poverty and pain, read here, and smile to think you know not my severer punishments! Gracious God! whether within thy heaven of heavens thou sittest, clothed in everlasting light and bliss, or from the living centre of creation sendest thy merciful and inquiring eye through the vast universe, the work of thy Almighty breath, Oh! hear my prayer! From this fiend who now gnaws my heart, and is never absent from my dungeon of death, deliver, for a moment, the most miserable of thy creatures. My guilt is undeserving of forgiveness, but let thy pity grant me some intermission from his fury. From hell he came, from that hell to which my eternal spirit is too surely doomed. Am I then, am I—damned! Oh! what horrible perdition is mine! Hell, hell! I know your torments, I see, I feel your terrours! your Stygian gulph yawns at my feet, and within I behold your grisly king on his fiery throne! A crown of blazing bitumen marks his dread state, and vice, envy, malice, anger, jealousy, fear, discontent, and hate, his progeny and his ministers, are at his feet. But the fiend within my bosom, prime pest of Satan, is a plague still more damnable than these!

"Yes, yes, I have looked into the bottomless pit! I totter this moment on its brink! now! now! now! A river of fire flows through the abyss; torrents, cataracts, and tempests rage within its dismal vaults! I see, I see the damned—whirled from punishment to punishment, from worse pain to pain still worse, from agony to agony, from rage to rage, through an inexhaustible and infinite variety of torments! But that flaming spot so intolerably red! Oh! that spot! and hark! those troops of demons! each of whom would make paradise a hell, how they shriek! how they shriek beneath the sulphureous concave! as with their brazen forks they rake the eternal, penal fires, and ring the accursed chaldrons! Hark their tremendous roar! which spreads dismay to every ghost in hell, and shakes the earth! Hark! Aminta! The devils' yell—incestuous fratricide! Lo! This spot is thine! This spot! This! This!"

These images of guilt and terrour were too horrible for the gentle Julia. Her enthusiasm was unequal to support her under their powerful impression. Her reliance on the divine protection was extinguished by the vivid and shocking phantasms of the frenetic Aminta. Buried in unknown and subterranean chambers, where eternal night, death-like silence, and withering desolation reigned; the very theatre, she believed, of mystery; the cave, she knew, of murder; the haunt, she suspected, of impiety and enchantment; the recess, she feared, of ruffianism and ravishment;—Who removed my candle? thought she. Who sighed in the dismal vault? who is Lonchiderimos? whence came the necklace? who cried "Ha!" when I removed the ball?

A universal shivering seized her. Were she at that moment possessed of the secrets of the philosopher's stone and *elixir vitæ*; were she endowed with the means of bestowing on her father and on Theodore immortality, inexhaustible riches, and eternal happiness, she would have willingly relinquished the wondrous powers to be once again within the belfry. Never, never, said she to herself, shall I see the light of day! A restlessness inseparable from excessive fear, caused her to turn her head. It was now, she knew, the hour of midnight, when all but the wicked sleep, and when charnel-houses and churchyards send forth their sheeted dead; when murderers steal on their victims, and when the murdered rise as bloody spectres. She turned her head. Good God! that spectacle! Protecting powers, preserve the unhappy girl! At such a time, and in such a place, to see that, which, in a crowded theatre, or on a market-day, in the open street of a populous town, might, like the head of Medusa, petrify a beholder! Incapable of motion, fixed as a statue, her blood congealed in her veins—her bosom heaving—she gazed upon it in speechless horrour.

On the floor was an open coffin, and sitting within it was a human figure, whose ghastly head rested on a stone bench. Its face was turned towards the quaking Julia. Eyes it had none; a corpse it was. Its skin, now of a dark brown, in part remained, but the flesh was gone, and many of the bones appeared. It was dressed in a strange and antique female fashion, and was attached to the wall by a long and massy chain. The teeth, the sockets of the eyes, and the jaw-bones were bare. No object could be more shocking save that which was on its right. This was the remains of an infant, within a cage, which had been forged of immense bars. The creature within had perished apparently for want of room. A part of its face still remained, and any thing so hideous, so pitiable, cannot be conceived. Such was the spectacle.

There, suspected Julia, is Aminta in the coffin, upon the humid floor of this black and abominable dungeon, and that is her infant in the cage. Misery in its worst shape—mortality in its direst form, never before appeared so dreadful. The total decay of human grandeur—the most disgusting effects of time and dampness on animal matter—the pains of a cruel death—the violence and concealment of premeditated murders, and all the mystery of crime, presented themselves to her mind. The terrible words she had just translated, and the imprecations on the silk, had filled her mind with the apprehensions of signal suffering on this earth, and of endless vengeance hereafter. They had revived in her memory what she had ever read or heard of future retribution, of hell-fire, of Satan, of his imps, and of damnation.

The skeletons before her connected her with the sepulchre that entombed them, and with the infernal regions of which it seemed the porch. Silence, darkness, and solitude, death, murder, incest, and eternal condemnation, all were here united. It was not within the scope of human daring to translate another word. Julia, the breathing picture of alarm, offered to Heaven a mental ejaculation, and withdrew her looks. She would have crossed herself, but she had not power to stir a finger. Her candle, she fancied, yielded a blue light, and the vapours of the cavern a smell, in part putrescent, and in part sulphureous. She was ready to sink to the ground, and expected every instant to see the arch-fiend himself, the very devil rise before her, lightnings to flash, and thunders to peal around. She bent her eyes fearfully on her writing-box.

It was open, and she chanced to look at the mirror which lay within its cover—when—Oh! how to relate it?

The reflection of a man's head and neck, both uncovered, and leaning over her shoulder, struck her tortured sight. Such a countenance! It seemed intently employed in reading what she had translated. Matted black locks and a shaggy beard, a squalid skin and gaping mouth, a rolling eye and frowning brows, a wrinkled forehead and hollow cheeks, gave to this mysterious head, which was moreover gigantic in proportions, all the appearance of brutal strength, invincible ferocity, and incurable madness. It was the head of a maniac whose insanity breathed the most alarming violence. Grinning hideously, and rolling with pernicious glare his black and baleful eyes, the madman seized the expiring Julia, and at the same time sent through all the arches of those accursed caverns, a shout, than which the roar of the famished tiger in the desert, sounds not to the benighted and unarmed traveller more loud, more terrible.

The skeleton, disturbed from its coffin by a kick from the lunatic, rolled frightfully towards the marble table. Its arms embraced the feet of Julia. The chain clanked. The iron cage swung across the vault. The bones of the child separated and fell together in a heap. The echoes of the shout reverberated among the distant passages. The crisis of horrour has arrived. Miss Bolton falls lifeless.

The sun had just risen from the eastern wave, dispelling with his chearful looks obscurity and sadness. The birds, awakened by his enlivening rays, had joined in tuneful symphony to hail his bright career. Night was no more, and all nature smiled, when Julia recovered from her trance, but the disturbance of fear and the colour of sickness still sat upon her countenance. As when a man, in appearance dead, is interred, and after his sepulture revives; he opens his eyes, but he is in utter darkness—he tries to move, but his limbs are bound in a cloth, and enclosed in a narrow box. He wonders where he is, and yet is instinctively unwilling to reflect on his situation; but the dreadful truth soon flashes on his brain. He knows he is in his winding-sheet, and buried in the church-yard. He cries—he shrieks. Alas! his cries, his shrieks are uttered in the grave. No mortal hears him. He exerts his strength—he lifts the lid of his coffin—he shakes the earth above, but already suffocation seizes him. No human force can raise the ponderous and smothering encumbrance. He falls back into—his coffin—he groans, and dies. So Julia, with a vague and undefined conception of some monstrous perils, feared to look, she knew not wherefore. The events of the night before passed like the fleeting images of a delirious dream through her disordered mind, and it was some time before she could summon courage enough to open her eyes. She thought, and she shuddered as she thought, that she was immured with Aminta, for ever, in the sepulchre. At length she ventured to steal a look. She was alone, and, oh blissful circumstance! in her own room. She was in bed, though not undressed. She tried to recall her scattered thoughts, and in the court-yard, beneath the loop-hole windows, she heard the uncouth voices of the outlaws.

Relieved from much of her perturbation by these sounds, and cheered by the rays of the sun that gilded a portion of her floor, she soon became composed enough to recollect all that had passed the night before. She trembled at the remembrance, and tried, in vain, to account for her removal from the cavern. Her writing-box was on the floor and closed, and near it were the worked silk and the box of money. She looked about. She was safe. She moved her limbs and her head. She was not hurt.

Extreme debility of body, and a painful anxiety of mind were the only effects of her adventure.

She arose. She opened the smaller box. It was full of gold coin, and its weight was about eight pounds. She then raised the lid of the writing-box, and within it she found all in proper order. Her pocket-book, in which she had begun to render the inscription into English, lay uppermost, and this she opened with a sigh of regret that she had not been able to translate the whole. But wonder and mystery were not yet exhausted. After her last line there was written:—

"Pour soul! to recompense you for the terrour I occasioned you, I shall complete the task that you began. The story of Aminta's sufferings, greater than my own, has for a moment dispelled my frenzy. I am a poor maniac, it is true. I know my brain is turned. My foster-brother and I inhabit the ruins of Count Egfryd's castle. He is a gardener. He is faithful, tender, and affectionate. Never in my most frantick moments have I offered him any violence. By accident I discovered the caverns communicating from the castle to the island. In them I live. Hunger alone has power to draw me from them. My food devoured, I return to them, and in their cold and midnight solitude my melancholy finds a horrible satisfaction. The necklace I gave you was my Eliza's. It was given her by the Queen of France, whose favourite she was. Love and religion made her mine, but violence and fraud robbed me of my jewel. Could I support the loss and retain my reason? No one ever sees me but my foster-brother, and he not oftener than once in the week. But now to finish your translation. May you continue insensible until I shall have placed it at your bed-side, and effected my retreat! To behold me a second time might cause your death. I am Lonchiderimos, king of the sable caves, formerly the Chevalier Du Lange. Ha! ha! but those times are gone. Now, mysterious marble, what sayest thou?

"Robbed by death of the fostering cares of a parent, I was yet an infant when my guardian, the cruellest of women, the barbarous *Duchesse D'Auvignac*, took me to this castle. My fortune was immense, my beauty was universally acknowledged, and my accomplishments were rare and estimable. I was the subject of general praise, and sovereign princes were proud to confess my power. Wherever I appeared, wealth and pleasure abounded, and my smiles, like the brightness of a morning in May, seemed to diffuse general content and pleasure. Gaiety and I were one, when, by the artful contrivances of the *Duchesse*, I was seduced to marry her son, the *Duc D'Auvignac*.

"I was then but sixteen, and I must acknowledge that my happiness continued undiminished for two years afterwards. The young, the gallant, the beauteous Albert, at this period came to our castle, and, for the first time in my life, a sigh of uneasiness escaped from my bosom. His reputation in arms, his noble carriage, his manly countenance, his dignified deportment, his insinuating manners, his eloquent conversation, fascinated my attention and won my respect and regard. He always looked at me, methought, with tenderness, and whenever he addressed me, the tones of his voice were softened into a cadence that penetrated to my heart. But it was not long till the colour deserted his cheeks. He sought solitude and retirement. Involuntary sighs would issue from him, and sometimes, as he would steal a glance at me, I could observe a tear start into his brilliant eye. I believed that he loved me, and I pitied him for the misery which I occasioned him. I thought incessantly of the amiable stranger.

I was agitated and unhappy. Sentiments before unknown to me were awakened in my breast, and I dreaded to reflect on the warmth of my emotions.

"Too well, too soon, he read my secret, and by a thousand little cares and artifices, invisible and unknown to all the world but myself, he kindled the spark of affection into a raging and inextinguishable flame. Love is fertile in resources, and I was ere long the most criminal of women.

"The *Duchesse* suspected our intrigue, and, in the absence of my husband at court, she obtained proof of my guilt. She immediately despatched a courier to him with the shocking intelligence. He, being naturally violent, was cast by the information into a state of unspeakable fury. Boiling with jealousy, revenge and rage, he arrived at this castle, and plunged a stiletto into the heart of my lover. He then stabbed me with the same weapon, and immediately afterwards he struck it into his own breast. The ill-fated Albert and he instantly expired, but unfortunately, my wound was not mortal.

"A livid mark, of a triangular shape, having been found on the neck of the amiable and now lifeless stranger when his vest had been removed, it occurred to my mother-in-law, that this might be Gonflair, my younger brother, who, at the age of two years, had, during an irruption of Bavarians, been taken away, and had never afterwards been heard of. Gonflair, she knew, had come into the world with a similar mark upon his neck; and the proper inquiries having been made by her, it was ascertained that the deceased had, in fact, been seized by a foraging party of Bavarians, some eighteen years before, in a country-house, which, by the description, proved to be my father's; that becoming a favourite of General Wolfskynk, he had been adopted by him under the name of Albert; and that he had been ushered into the world by the General as his son.

"The *Duchesse* having gathered these facts, flew to me with the countenance of a tigress. I was then pregnant. 'Oh! most infamous of women!' said she, 'incestuous and adulterous concubine of your own brother! murderer of him and of my beloved son, your husband! mother of a bastard, who is at once your child and your sister, if it be female; if male, your brother! a monstrous and accursed creature, that will be a reproach to our sex, and a disgrace to human nature!' She then, with malicious exactness, expatiated on the heinousness of my conduct, and, to my inexpressible sorrow, proved to me the certainty of my incest. I swooned away.

"On recovering I found myself in this cavern, chained to that wall, and sitting in this coffin. The *Duchesse* was at my side. 'Behold your prison,' cried she, in a voice that made me shudder; 'here you shall perish. That well in the floor will yield you water, and through that hole in the ceiling, your bread will every week be dropped to you. But, to aggravate your sufferings, you shall sometimes be liberated for a few hours. Twice in the year you shall appear in my banquetting hall. I will represent you to the world as a devotee employed incessantly in prayer. I have already caused it to be believed that your husband and your brother fell in a duel occasioned by a political dispute. But should you, when I shew you to my guests, disclose the secret of your confinement, the flesh shall be torn from your bones; and, that you should not deceive yourself by trusting to my pity, know that once in every month you shall be scourged with these hands.'

"Saying this, the inhuman woman inflicted on me a

discipline that caused me to swoon for very pain. Her threat has ever since been carried into execution with barbarous punctuality. The period of my delivery being nigh, she attended me herself, and placed my infant in the steel cage. She then, by means of springs, prepared in a particular manner, fastened the two bars which she had removed for its admission, so that all my efforts to liberate the poor innocent should prove ineffectual.

"The sufferings of the baby could not be seen, even by her, with indifference. Since his birth I have been compelled to ascend, by a ladder of ropes, to an upper dungeon, to receive my monthly castigation. To enable me to do so, she lengthened my chain. For two years I kept life in my child, but the straightness of his hellish prison at length killed him; and I, a prey to guilt, remorse, and terrour, have now survived him three years. With nought besides my bread have I, down to the present moment, been supplied, save a spoon, a knife, oil for my lamp, and the coarsest woollen clothing. The silk that I embroidered I happened to have accidentally in my pocket. Much longer I cannot live. The punishments I suffer, the privations I undergo, and the agony of my mind, must soon terminate my days, now too long protracted.

"Do thou, pious stranger, with the money which I found in the cavity behind the marble table, purchase masses for the redemption of mine and my infant's souls, and for the repose of my brother. May thy spirit, in return, enjoy eternal felicity! But remember to keep my story secret. The honour of a noble family demands this. Destroy the plaster on which these words are carved, and burn the silken ball. God and the saints preserve thee always! Amen, sweet Jesus!"

Julia, after reading this, felt herself so ill that she was

glad to return to bed. There she, in some time, fell into an unquiet sleep, during which her father (who, on awaking in the morning, had found himself much recovered) entered her room. Perceiving that she was asleep, he would not disturb her, but his attention being attracted by the wrought silk and the pocket-book, he took them up and read them.

CHAPTER V.

As when the Pyrenean wolf, impell'd
By hunger and by thirst of blood, doth rush
With horrid rage in quest of human prey:
So I, to feed my great revenge, with eyes
Inflam'd, and curses loud, shall dart on them,
My purpose cruel, fierce, and ravenous.

....

Angels of bliss! that help the weak, and guard
The innocent, assist our enterprise!
Or chains and death, or liberty and life
Await our bold attempt.

....

E'en as the thunder-strucken clown, who finds,
When day resumes his joyous face, and clouds
Retire, that what had lately scar'd his wits,
Innoxious pass'd, and left no trace behind,
And in his joy forgets his recent dread.

Mr. Bolton was some minutes before he could recover from the effects of his astonishment at the information he had acquired. As he sat musing and motionless his daughter awoke. The sight of her father tranquillized her speedily. She was delighted to perceive an amendment in his looks, and she was no less delighted to find that he had, by accident, learned the horrible secret. Reserve and mystery had been all her life unknown to her, and the concealment of her late discovery had given her the most painful agitation. They conversed for more than an hour on the subject of the subterranean passage, of the maniac, and of Aminta. They deliberated on the mode of proceeding that they had best adopt, and they resolved to disclose all to the outlaws, and to seek, by their assistance, to effect an escape from the *Isle de Peine*.

"I knew the *Chevalier du Lange*," said Mr. Bolton, "when I was in Paris, about twenty years ago. He was then young, gay, handsome, elegant, and accomplished. He moved in the first circles, and swayed the sceptre of fashion. The men imitated and envied him. The women admired and extolled him. Miss Stuart, a maid of honour to the Queen, received his vows and returned his passion; but their attachment was for a long time unknown and unsuspected. His family were Calvinists, and she was a Roman Catholick. His father was a man of immense wealth, and she possessed little besides beauty and noble blood. There were obstacles to their union that a man, less enamoured, and less ardent than the *Chevalier du Lange*, would have thought insurmountable; but he was not to be discouraged by any difficulties. He proposed a clandestine marriage, and she had not resolution enough to oppose his wish. She stole from her attendants. She fled from the palace. She met her lover, and the ceremony, which was to unite them indissolubly, had been already begun, when the persons sent in pursuit of her surprised them and prevented it. She was brought back a prisoner, and he was forbid by the king to enter Paris.

"All this the young man endured with patience, hoping, I suppose, to be able, at some future day, to effect the object of his wishes; but, in about six months afterwards, Miss Stuart was prevailed on to marry the Marquis Soulainviers, an old courtier and favourite. The unexpected event was immediately communicated to the unfortunate Du Lange, and the shock it gave him was so violent that it bereft him of his reason. All Paris was interested in his fate, and there were few who did not pity him and condemn his mistress. I recollect the circumstances perfectly well, but since that time having been principally in England, I have never heard more either of him or her. But now, my child, let us seek the outlaws, and obtain, if possible, their assistance."

Julia and her father, both weak and both unwell, descended to the refectory. The banditti were all there. "My friends," said Mr. Bolton, "I have something to communicate which I hope will prove of advantage to us all. I think I have discovered a mode by which we may effect our escape from this island. I require your assistance. Exclusive of the pecuniary rewards I shall bestow on you, if you effect my liberation (and among you I will divide twelve thousand livres*), I undertake to procure for each of you a full pardon from the Government. I have sufficient interest with it, I assure you, to obtain a much greater favour than this."

He then related, succinctly, the mysterious voice he had heard which demanded the letters of attorney; that his daughter and he had deemed it prudent to comply with the requisition; and that the papers had, shortly after they were placed on the mantle-piece, been removed from it. He told the manner in which Miss Bolton had discovered the circular staircase, and all that had happened to her during her first visit in the cavern. He omitted not to

* About six hundred pounds sterling.

narrate how the silken ball, the necklace, and the pencilled paper came into her possession. He had brought them down with him. He read the paper, and he translated aloud the words wrought into the silk. He mentioned the loss of the candle in the cavern, the terrifying noises his daughter had heard there, and the frightful spectacle she had seen. As he spoke of the spectacle Julia involuntarily laid hold of him and turned pale.

Mr. Bolton continued. He informed them of her second descent, and of what had passed during that dreadful visit. He then read to them the translation of the inscription, from her pocket-book. "This," added he, "is the box of gold, which you will share among you. I hesitate not to give it, nor to reveal to you the secrets of Aminta, because, without your assistance, her dying injunctions cannot be obeyed; and without a full disclosure to you of every circumstance that has come to my knowledge, I should not be able to obtain your assistance, nor perhaps should I deserve it. Her gold I bestow on you, because it will inspire you, I hope, with ardour in her cause; and because, once liberated, I shall apply the amount of it, more than doubled, to the purposes she desires. We have, I think, to fear none but the maniac, for I am almost sure that our persecutor, the Count Egfryd, is now employed at a distance with the two letters of attorney. He may rob us of a hundred and twenty thousand pounds sterling, but, thank God! I shall still have more than enough of property."

The outlaws heard him with attention, and swore to do as he should direct them. Having divided the gold among their party, each armed himself, as did likewise Mr. Bolton, with a cutlass, a dagger, and a pair of pistols. Garquine thrust a carving-knife into her girdle.

Mr. Bolton desired them to take nothing with them

besides their arms but lights, a heavy hammer, and a rope. They had, fortunately, a parcel of torches, which the gloomy and intricate passages of the cloister had rendered necessary, and a sledge. Hénoch Oguelauche, the strongest of the banditti, carried the sledge and the rope (which were merely a provision against casualties), and ten *flambeaux* were borne by the others.

The order of their march was this. Jacot led the way. Jacques Ferrau and Dissart followed him. The next was Garquine. Julia, leaning on her father, kept close to that abominable hag; and Hénoch Oguelauche and Marco closed the procession. They were eight in all. Having arrived at the belfry, they proceeded to the summit of the spiral stairs. These were too narrow to admit of more than one person. During their descent, therefore, they went singly. Mr. Bolton was the sixth, Julia the seventh, and Marco the last of the party on the stairs. Having reached the ground, they resumed their former order, and after a pause, occasioned by dizziness, they directed their course to the narrow passage which Julia had traversed twice before.

The blaze from the ten torches illuminated the cavern through its whole extent. They advanced quickly along the passage until they came to the iron door that had opposed the progress of Miss Bolton. As she crossed the entrance to Aminta's sepulchral chamber, she averted her eyes in dismay, and pressed against her father. Each of the banditti tried in vain to stir the iron door, or to find a key-hole in it.

"Hénoch, apply your sledge," said Mr. Bolton. Hénoch, who had been a smith, waited not for a repetition of the order, but with extreme violence hurled his ponderous instrument against the opposing metal. The noise of the mighty blow spread through the vaults like the sound of a *petard* discharged at a city gate. The iron door, however, yielded not in the least. It was of immense weight and thickness, and had been hammered into its present shape. Hénoch repeated his blows, but his assaults were useless. Miss Bolton's fears increased to a painful excess. Her father and the outlaws waited anxiously for the effect of Hénoch's exertions, but his efforts were unavailing. The door was not to be broken, and it could not be removed.

"Let us explore some other passage," cried Mr. Bolton; "this cannot be forced." They turned back accordingly, in obedience to his direction, and soon arrived at the entrance to Aminta's dungeon. "Hénoch and Ferrau, enter this vault," said he, "and ascertain if it present any mode of escape." The two entered, and whatever fears they might have felt, they had the strength of mind to conquer, or the prudence to conceal. They remained within it about five minutes, and on their return to the passage declared that they had been able to find no mode of departure, and that the opening into the upper dungeon, mentioned by Aminta, had been closed with a rough and immoveable block of stone. "A passage to the ruined castle on the continent there is somewhere," observed their respectable leader, "and probably there is more than one of them, let us therefore continue our research."

It were tedious to describe the course of each winding, the depth of each recess, the situation of each chamber in the caverns, the conjectures and the fears, the hopes and the disappointments, of the adventurous party. Suffice it that they met no living being, friend or foe, and that every secret passage of retreat escaped their observation. Vexed and dispirited, they returned to the belfry, extinguished their torches, laid aside their arms, and yielded their minds to wonder and discontent.

The Count had, the day before, arrived at his cottage

from England, and, on his arrival, he heard that *Monsieur Froigné*, about whom he had left orders to have inquiries made, was Mr. Dalbert; that a raft of singular construction had been prepared under his directions; and that it was to be launched that very night. The intelligence was not a little strange and perplexing to him. It was certain that Mr. Dalbert had, in some inexplicable manner, discovered the place where his mistress was confined, and the danger that would attend any attempt to enter by the canal. Hated and feared before, Theodore was now an object of aggravated terrour and detestation. As soon as it becomes dark, resolved the arch-impostor, I will visit the ruined cloister on the island, and will watch the proceedings of my enemy. Let him escape me if he can.

The moon shone brightly. He descended into the caverns, and passed without delay to the unlighted and unwindowed chamber where the spiral stairs terminated their windings. On treading the upper step, as he hasted forward, he stirred a board placed there by the banditti, which board they had made to communicate, by a thread, with a small bell in the refectory. The Count, not suspecting his danger, advanced, by a passage within the walls, to a distant room, from which he could command a view of *Monsieur Froigné's* cottage and the river, while the outlaws, warned of the arrival of a stranger by the ringing of the bell, stole silently to the belfry, with a fixed resolution to attack and seize the invader. Garquine carried a couple of flaming torches. Each of the others was armed. They entered the belfry and arrived at the windowless chamber. Having in the course of that evening strown some fine sand over its floor, they were now enabled to trace the marks of a man's feet, and to ascertain that the person who had entered had not yet retreated.

"My advice to you," said Garquine, "is this. As we have

got my gentleman here, snug and certain as I may say, let us close up this narrow passage with boards, which will prevent him, be him never so cunning, from getting away from us." The advice was approved of, and the narrow stairs were in a few minutes barred against all regress. The party then extinguished their *flambeaux*, and in a corner waited silently for their prey.

The Count was not long in his hiding-place till he saw, through a fissure in the wall, some large body that he conjectured was the raft, of which he had been apprized, approach the island. It appeared to come from the place where the fireworks had been exhibited, and ere long, to his infinite surprise, it moved slowly over the morass. The Count was pleased to see it advance. A diabolical satisfaction filled his breast. Now, said he to himself, I shall be able, by one act, to destroy all the people on earth whom I fear, save one. That one is Pierre Dontache, but he can easily be removed at any other time. Gaspar Pontgebre is no more; Marie de Solase is no more; the villain Bolton is no more; Conrad d'Aufrine is no more; and here are assembled the haughty Julia and her father, the six outlaws whom I employed to seize and guard them, and that abhorred Theodore. Here they all are, but never shall individual among them see the morning.

While these thoughts were revolving in his wicked mind, twelve persons landed from the raft and hastened to the ruins. The Count having viewed them for a few minutes, retreated rapidly through his secret passages, intending to descend to the cavern, there to prepare for the consummation of his iniquity. He arrived without interruption near to the circular winding staircase, and touched the upper part of the stone newel round which the steps turned. He expected in a few minutes to reach the subterranean passages, when, to his utter astonishment and alarm, he found the passage stopped up with pieces of timber. He now knew that his visit had been expected, and he feared that he was at that instant surrounded by his mortal foes.

His existence and his character were in the utmost peril. His presence of mind and his intrepidity did not forsake him upon the trying occasion. With the velocity of urgent need, quickened by implacable vengeance, he drew from his coat-pockets and cocked a pair of pistols, each of which contained three barrels. His blood boiled in his veins. Having thus prepared himself against surprise, he placed the pistols in his bosom, and proceeded impetuously to withdraw the pieces of timber from the staircase. He had already removed three when he heard the steps of persons approaching.

He again caught his pistols. In each hand he held one, and directing them to the quarter from which the noise came, he pulled the triggers. Four of the six barrels were discharged at the moment, and four bullets of lead shot forth with murderous intention. Being fired in the dark, the party in ambush escaped their killing violence. No wound was inflicted except one in Hénoch's side. It drew from him a roar, but he was not dangerously hurt. The flashes, which for a moment illuminated the chamber, enabled the Count to see the number of his enemies, who, unintimidated by the shots, and the cry of Hénoch, rushed furiously forward.

Egfryd, not having time to discharge the other two bullets, liberated, by moving a little spring, a bayonet which was attached to each pistol, but scarcely had he done so when he was rudely grappled by four of the ruffians. He exerted his utmost force, he kicked, he pushed, he strove, he stabbed, but their united strength rendered all his efforts ineffectual. A blow in the stomach completed his defeat. He was seized; he was disarmed; he was dragged to the refectory.

Theodore and his party, in the mean time, had crossed the morass. The mode he adopted for this purpose I shall relate for the instruction of any person who may hereafter be in similar circumstances. Having got a strong rope of sufficient length, one end of it was fastened to the gate of his cottage, and the remainder, being coiled up in a large eight-oared boat, was conveyed round the island even to the spot whence the boat had departed. The island being thus embraced, both ends of the rope were drawn, until no part of it was slack, by a powerful windlass erected at the cottage. This done, Theodore, his servant Guillaume, and ten other men, all well armed, embarked on a raft that had been previously prepared.

By pulling at that part of the rope which passed from the windlass to the eastern side of the *Isle de Peine*, they drew themselves to the island, and their vessel being peculiarly light, they found no difficulty in passing thus over a great portion of the morass. When they could go no further on in this manner, each of the ten men resorted to a contrivance invented by Theodore, which was simply an improvement of the snow-shoe of Lapland. Though broader and larger than the snow-shoe, it was lighter, and being strapped on each foot, a man could trust himself on the softest fen without any danger of being suffocated in it. He might gradually sink, it is true, if he stood still, but not more than five or six inches in a minute.

Thus provided, the ten could stand for a little while on the morass, and from their stations push the raft forward. The raft was formed of whalebone and varnished canvas.

It was twenty feet long, twenty feet wide, and eighteen inches deep. Its weight was only two hundred and forty pounds. When any one of the men found himself sinking too deeply, he had nothing more to do than to raise himself for a minute upon the raft, and clean his shoes from the mud they had gathered.

In this slow and laborious manner they reached firm land, when, taking up their arms, and laying aside their morass-shoes, they hurried to the ruins, leaving two of their party (hid behind a large rock, with six double-barrelled guns) to guard the raft.

They reached the refectory a few minutes before the banditti led in the Count. The first thing that attracted Theodore's attention was a heap of torches. He ordered some of them to be quickly lighted, and was going in quest of the two prisoners, his mistress and her father, surprised that neither they nor any of the outlaws appeared, when the latter entered with Egfryd. Each of Theodore's party had a scimitar and four pistols. They were all men of tried resolution. The banditti had been prepared by Mr. Bolton for some attempt, on the part of Mr. Dalbert, to rescue him and his daughter, and therefore the appearance of ten armed men in the refectory excited no great share of wonder or apprehension in their minds. Theodore's party waited in silence for his orders how to act, but he was satisfied on seeing the Count a prisoner, that the outlaws were not hostile to him. He looked at the miscreant without emotion, he thought only of Julia.

"You have, I see, secured the base and unmanly persecutor of Miss Bolton, and you shall be rewarded for it," said he; "but where is she? where is that much-injured young lady? where is my worthy friend, her father?"—"Both in their own rooms, or in the cupola, I dare say," answered Jacques Ferrau. "The occurrences of this morning must have rendered repose necessary to them; and, no doubt, the shots fired by our noble visitor here, just now, must have terrified them not a little; but I will conduct them to you in a minute." As he uttered these words he snatched a torch, and ran up the decayed steps. "Guard well your prisoner," cried Theodore to those who held the Count, "and wait in silence till Mr. Bolton shall determine his fate and declare your reward."

Indignation, wrath, and hatred convulsed the features of Egfryd. His artifices unsuccessful, his pride humbled, his vengeance frustrated, and disgrace and death impending over him, what must have been the tempest of his passions? Theodore deigned not to look at him. Mr. Bolton and Julia appeared. She flew into the arms of her lover, and her father, placing a hand on the head of each, bestowed on them his kindliest benedictions.

CHAPTER VI.

Meanwhile with rising rage the battle glows,
The tumult thickens, and the clamour grows.

....

Oh! that annihilation were a god
To hear my prayers! then should each living thing
Be straight involv'd in universal ruin.

....

Quasi ascosi avea gli occhi ne la testa,
La faccia macra, e come un' osso asciutta,
La chioma rabbuffata, orrida, e mesta,
La barba folta, spaventosa, e bruta.

....

Nulla Amazone mai su 'l Termodonte
Imbracciò scudo, ò maneggiò bipenne
Audace sì, com' ella————————

....

On voit en un instant des abîmes ouverts,
Des noirs torrens de soufre épandus dans les airs.

"Let us fly from this abhorred island," said Julia. "That vessel which we saw from the cupola, and in which, Theodore, I suppose you landed with those men, can convey us hence, can it not?"—"It can, and it was for that purpose that the raft you saw was constructed. Let us away—"—"Stay," cried Mr. Bolton, "a moment. I perceive that my acquaintances of the *Isle de Peine* have found and secured the enemy of us all. I promised to each of them, on my liberation, two thousand livres. I now repeat that promise. I undertake to procure for them a full pardon; and provided that they bring Count Egfryd a prisoner to your cottage on the bank of the river, I here pledge my honour to advance an additional gift to each of a thousand livres." The outlaws testified their pleasure by expressions of respect and attachment, accompanied with vehement gesticulation, and swore that that fiend of darkness, so they termed the Count, should never escape from them. "As soon as you have landed, Sir," said Jacques, "send back the raft to us, and we shall convey our prisoner on it from hence this very night."—"It shall be so," returned Theodore. "In three hours you may expect it back."

Theodore and his party of nine, with Julia and her father, were now retiring. Julia passed the Count without looking at him. She shuddered to be so near him though he was a prisoner, and though she was protected by her father and her lover. The villain's arms were held by Marco and Dissart. But his ingenuity and address were superiour to their caution and their strength. He drew, unobserved, from a concealed pocket, a small pistol, which, as the party were retiring (lighted by three *flambeaux*), he discharged at them. He intended the shot for Theodore, but it missed him. The bullet entered the neck of Mr. Bolton. "I am shot!" exclaimed the father of Julia. "The villain has shot me!" The fright and agitation of Miss Bolton on this occasion exceeded all that she had ever suffered. The rage of her lover amounted almost to madness, and the indignation of the outlaws was unbounded. They would have instantly put the perfidious Egfryd to death, but that the worthy Mr. Bolton desired earnestly he might not be hurt. "Justice will overtake him soon enough," said the good man, in the true spirit of Christianity. The treacherous assassin was spared, but the pistol was wrested from him, his pockets were searched lest he should have any more concealed arms, and his hands and legs were secured in a better manner than they had been before.

"Lay me down here," said Mr. Bolton, "I cannot stir. My wound is not mortal, perhaps; but motion to me at present would be death."—None present had the least skill in surgery. They could only apply a bandage of linen, and endeavour in this manner to stop the bleeding.—"We must send to Cognac for a surgeon," observed Theodore. "Do you, Guillaume, take seven of my men with you on the raft, and procure one with as much expedition as possible. He shall be rewarded most liberally for his trouble; and, my Julia," added he, "as you can be of no service here, had you not better accompany them, and escape from this scene of horrour? I shall not quit my friend."—"No, never will I leave my father!" cried the affectionate girl. "Here will I stay; here will I attend him."

Guillaume and the seven men did as they were ordered; and the banditti, with the other three men, forced the prisoner to an upper room, in order that the wounded gentleman might not be disturbed. None remained with him but Theodore and Julia.

Of Theodore's men there were now only three in the cloister, and it was manifest to the Count that this was the only opportunity he was likely to have for attempting his nefarious designs. To one of the outlaws who held his arms, he said in a whisper—"I will shew you gold that I have in the cavern to the amount of three hundred thousand livres,* and a secret passage to convey you thence, if you will assist me against my enemies." The villain to whom he whispered thought the offer eligible, and he whispered it to another. Thus it went round, and looks of acquiescence and approbation began to be exchanged, when Jacques Ferrau thus spoke aloud:—

"Look ye, Count Egfryd, it won't do. It is our interest

* About 15,000l. sterling.

to be honest on the present occasion, and I will prove it to all who hear me. In the first place, before we could stir in your service, we should have to secure or kill Mr. Dalbert below; and his men who are here present. Now, they happen to be all well armed, and it is therefore doubtful that we should succeed; but were we successful, it would be probably at the expence of half our number. Then we enter the cavern with you, where, for aught we know, we should perish under the blows of some party that you may have stationed there, or by some infernal contrivance that we could neither understand nor guard against. But supposing that there were no dangers of this kind, still we should run the risk of being tricked or deceived by you, in getting the gold you speak of, and afterwards you would employ your wicked arts, night and day, to find some mode of taking us off. Your interest and security would demand our deaths, and we should certainly be murdered. But, by keeping you a prisoner, we ensure our pardons; we gratify our hatred and revenge against you; we get a large and certain reward from Mr. Bolton or from Mr. Dalbert; and we incur no danger whatsoever; therefore, Sir, you will remain, if you please, in close custody where you are."

The ruffians attended to this address, and were so well pleased with it, that, as soon as it was concluded, they uttered a loud huzza, and at the same time twirled round their hats. He who held the prisoner's right arm did so like the others, and Egfryd, who was one of the strongest and most active of men, taking advantage of the circumstance, by a prodigious effort broke the cord which tied his hands, and disengaged himself from the men about him. One he knocked down, two he tripped backwards so that they fell, and another he pushed into the ancient fire-place. Then, rushing to an opening, that had formerly been a window, he threw himself out. The ground was thirty feet below him, but he broke his fall by catching at a projecting stone gutter. He alighted on his feet without hurt, and flew to the canal. Of the men who witnessed this action, not one had courage to leap from the opening. They fired their pistols at him, but without any effect, and they ran down the decayed stairs in order to pursue him.

Theodore hurried out of the refectory to learn the cause of the shots, and was informed of the prisoner's escape. "He is gone to the causeway," said Jacques Ferrau, almost out of breath, "to blow us all up." The conjecture of Jacques was well founded. The proud and vitious Egfryd could not support the opprobrium of his detection, and he wished to involve those whom he most hated in his final destruction. Theodore was acquainted with his character, and had no doubt that such was his intention. "Let us fly, my good fellows," said he, "to prevent his desperate intent!"

They took the nearest course to the canal. A person swimming through it was visible at some distance. Three, who were the best swimmers of the party, immediately threw off their shoes, coats, hats, and vests, and plunged into the water. The rest pushed out the boat, seized the oars, and rowed after the fugitive with all their might.

The Count had already arrived near to the spot where he might execute his hellish purpose. The three swimmers were far behind, but the boat gained on him. Arrived within twenty yards of him, six pistols were fired from it at the same moment. Two bullets reached him. One struck him in the hip, the other in the leg. He was disabled from swimming further. Six yards more, and he would have reached the fatal spot, where the strings and rods communicated with the gunpowder in the cavity beneath the causeway. Bleeding and in pain, but haughty and audacious, he was forced into the boat; and the three being likewise taken into it, they all returned to the little haven where it had been moored.

Theodore desired the Count's wounds to be attended to, and his clothes to be dried. "No," said the villain, "my wounds shall not be dressed, and I require no dry clothes." The other, shocked at the desperation and reprobacy that appeared in his countenance, ordered the men to guard their prisoner with particular vigilance, and they returned to the refectory.

Miss Bolton had felt excessive terrour during his absence, but her father seemed somewhat recovered. Both his daughter and Theodore entertained hopes that the wound which he had received in the neck was not dangerous. It had ceased to bleed. It produced at present but trifling pain, and he was able to interrogate his intended son-in-law about the pursuit in which he had been engaged.

In order to prevent the possibility of his escape, the Count was now tied in such a way that he could stir neither his hands nor his feet. The wounds he had received, though not mortal, were painful. On the bare floor of the room over the refectory, wet, bleeding, bemired, lay the degraded victim of licentiousness and vice. But no sign of repentance was visible in his looks; no sound of contrition escaped his lips. He looked a wretch and a villain.

The outlaws, six in number, including Garquine, to solace themselves after their dangers and fatigues, and to entertain their new guests, the three men of Theodore's party, produced a keg of brandy. The song, the toast, and the tale, went merrily round with the glass; loud laughter shook the walls, and jollity usurped, for an hour, the empire of dreariness. Theodore was a little alarmed lest their festivity should occasion remissness of vigilance. He ascended to the room where they were, cautioned them against excess, and examined the means that had been employed by them to secure their prisoner. Seeing that escape was impracticable, so securely had they bound each limb, he no longer felt apprehension, and he retired.

The party continued their debauch until they had emptied the keg, and exhausted their hilarity. They all fell asleep except Garquine and Hénoch. He was kept awake by the pain of the wound he had received in his side, and she had a project to execute which required immediate attention. This was to lead the Count into the cavern, and there force him to point out the place where his treasure was concealed. She whispered her plan to Hénoch, and he approved of it, but he declined lending any assistance unless the other four were consulted. This proviso was not agreeable to her, for she had calculated on effecting her design with his sole assistance, while the others were asleep, and consequently of procuring the gold without the knowledge of her husband; but Hénoch was inflexible, and she was compelled to submit.

She then awakened the other four, and told them how easy it would be to make their fortunes. Said she in whispers to them, "We shall promise him his liberty, but when we get the money, we shall bring him back a prisoner, so that our rewards from Mr. Bolton will be still secure; and, as to the danger of any party in the cavern, it is all nonsense. If there were any such party, would they not have made some attempt before this to liberate him?" The measure was unanimously agreed to, and the prisoner was told, in a low voice, that he now had an opportunity of gaining his liberty, if he would point out the spot where the treasure was concealed.

He readily agreed to the terms, and uttered many professions of gratitude and obligation. To enable him to walk they removed the rope that bound his legs, and Hénoch and Marco were stationed behind him, each with a cocked pistol in his hand, which, they swore, should be discharged into his head at the first symptom he should betray of an intention to escape. The party, consisting of seven, now mounted to the belfry, carrying two torches, and leaving Theodore's three men behind them asleep.

Arrived at the narrow stairs, the timber which blocked up the passage was removed, and they walked down, four preceding, and two following, the prisoner. They descended without accident, but within four feet of the lowest step, there stood on the floor of the cavern a figure, whose wildness and ferocity well accorded with the hideousness of the place. It was Lonchiderimos. He had gotten an immense club in his hand, and he stood as if guarding the entrance to his mysterious empire. Gaunt and haggard, of lofty stature, with frenetic gaze and outrageous aspect, the maniac brandished his formidable weapon. Egfryd, whose rapidity of thought and promptness of stratagem enabled him to draw advantage from the most untoward circumstances, saw at a glance that this madman might be induced to assist him.

"Sir! stranger!" roared he forth, "you see the most injured and abused of mankind! Rescue me from these villains, and my life and everlasting attachment are yours!" Lonchiderimos had scarcely heard these words when he levelled two of the banditti. Surprise seized the others. The shots which had been threatened were fired;

but they availed not. The miscreant felt a sudden accession of strength and energy, though his ear and shoulder were lacerated by one of the two bullets which were shot at his head. He tore himself from the grasp of those who endeavoured to hold him, broke asunder his manacles, and snatched a sword from Dissart.

With this he faced about, and exerted prodigies of strength against his enemies. The madman assisted him bravely. There were two opposed to five men and Garquine. Daring men they were, and a matchless virago was she. On one side was extraordinary skill, preternatural strength, courage, despair, and frenzy. On the other, numbers, boldness, exasperation, and dexterity. The maniac and the Count, the former with his terrible club, the latter with a murdering sword, gave a contusion or a scar at every stroke they aimed. It was death or a wound to come within the sphere of either of their weapons, with such killing and impetuous rapidity were they whirled through the hissing air. The two, thinking to effect their retreat from the cavern, retired as they fought, and were followed by the six.

A terrible blow, from the madman's club, upon Hénoch's temple, scattered his brains upon the earth, and a mighty sabre stroke at the same moment severed the head of Ferrau, the least odious of the gang, from its tottering trunk. Jacot pushed a rapier at the heart of Egfryd, and in doing so approached too near to his fatal blade: that blade, with horrible force, clove his scull in twain. Two only of the ruffians remained alive; Marco and Dissart with Garquine. Her eyes flashed fire; her mouth vomited vengeance; she danced with very rage; a fury from hell she seemed. The wary Marco and circumspect Dissart kept without the range of the whizzing weapons, and reserved four shots. One aimed at the maniac, the other at the Count. Each shot took effect. The ruffians levelled again, and the two great combatants fell to the ground.

Garquine rushed on them with her carving-knife, and cut, and slashed, and scalped her prostrate foes, with needless and wanton barbarity. "Hold!" exclaimed Marco, "don't kill the Count! let us get the gold!" The hope of plunder arrested her cruel arm. "Oh!" faintly cried the dying Egfryd, "don't kill me, and I will show it to you. See yonder vault with the step. Lead me thither, and I will point out to you where the coffer lies concealed." The vault was within a few paces of them. Having disarmed him and Lonchiderimos, they supported the former to the recess he had mentioned. He threw himself on the earth within it. He was a bloody and shocking figure. He was no longer to be recognized. "Beneath that board," said he, in a voice that was scarcely audible, "you will find what you seek."

Garquine, too late, was sensible of her imprudence. She saw in the vault an apparatus, containing a flint, steel, and springs; and she likewise saw some gunpowder. With the velocity of a tigress bounding on her prey, she grappled the wounded Egfryd. His arms she seized with her powerful hands, and in his face she fastened her terrible teeth. She endeavours to force him back into the cavern, but in vain she pulls, in vain she bites. He touches a spring, and a magazine of powder, placed there by him long before, receives a spark.

Tremendous were the effects of the explosion. The roof of the cavern was blown into the air, together with several of the massy columns which had for ages supported its enormous weight. A great part of the ruined cloister was tumbled to the ground; the whole island was shaken; and the Count and Garquine, the maniac and Marco, were not only blown out of the cavern, but cast, in the whirlwind of the fiery convulsion, upon the border of the morass. Marco was killed, but the others yet breathed. Garquine still kept her hold of the Count, and still were the teeth of the fury fixed in his face. Death alone could unlock her ferocious jaws.

The commotion of the elements continued, and a part of the causeway, distant as it was, loosened by the shock, fell into the cavity beneath it. The spring that communicated with the powder which had been lodged there, was touched and disturbed, and a second explosion took place, beyond comparison more awful than the first. The air was filled with water, earth, and mud. Rocks and splinters of rocks were shot into the clouds, and even to the extremities of the island. The cavern was filled by the river; the remainder of the cloister fell; the *Isle de Peine* tottered on its solid props; the *Charente* retreated towards its source, and nature trembled. A hurricane, an earthquake, and a volcano, now exhibited, for the first time, their united horrours. The silence of death succeeded.

During the convulsion, all was terrour, all was noise, all was flame. A fragment of flint, hurled from the causeway, reached the spot where lay Garquine and the Count. It struck that barbarous female in the head. It deprived her of life. She fell back. Her cannibal teeth relinquished their inhuman hold, and from them dropped a part of Egfryd's face. He had, happily, erred in his calculations on the effects of the two magazines of gunpowder; that at the canal, finding less opposition on the side next the water than in the direction of the cloister, had expended a great share of its force in blowing the softer part of the causeway into the river; and had the other one been smaller in quantity or weaker, it would certainly have been more fatal; but by its immoderate violence, unroofing as it did the whole of the caverns in an instant, it discharged much of its fury innoxiously, in the air.

The raft was on its return with a surgeon when these events took place. Luckily for those upon it, it had not reached the morass. The surgeon, hearing the two frightful explosions, and seeing the prodigious flashes, begged that they would put about in the now violently agitated water, and not venture to approach so dangerous a spot; but the faithful and intrepid Guillaume swore that they should proceed to the place of their destination, and that he would shoot the first person who should attempt to return. The men yielded to his persuasions, or were intimidated by his threats, and they all landed on the *Isle de Peine.*

The day began to dawn. The clouds of water, earth, and stone, that had obscured the air, were now no more, when Guillaume and his party ran to the heap of ruins, which, an hour before, had been the cloister. It chanced, providentially, that under the refectory there had been no vault, and that its roof had been an arch. The room above it, in which Theodore's three men had been sleeping, had likewise been arched. On the shock of the second explosion, this part of the building had been separated from its foundations, and prostrated to the earth; but such was its solidity, and the excellence of the ancient mortar which cemented it, that it still remained entire, and the persons within it, though some of them had been bruised and cut, were not killed.

Mr. and Miss Bolton, Theodore and his three men, saved thus miraculously, were taken out of the ruins, and the surgeon proceeded to exercise his art. He first dressed the old gentleman's wound, and without hesitation pronounced it to be not dangerous. Julia, in her joy at these words, forgot both her fright and her danger. She and her lover had escaped without any hurt. The three men were next attended to, and it was found that none of them had received any material injury. The whole party was impatient to quit the *Isle de Peine*. They advanced quickly to the raft, and were about to enter it, when the appearance of some bodies on the edge of the morass attracted the attention of Guillaume. He, with four of the men, ran towards them, and finding the Count and the maniac still alive, the two wounded combatants were carried to the raft, and embarked upon it with the party.

His loss of blood, his great exertions, his terrour, the strangeness of the adventure he had been engaged in, and the terrible shocks of the explosions, had dissipated the insanity of the *Chevalier Du Lange*. Every possible attention was bestowed, not only on him, but on the nefarious Egfryd, in Theodore's cottage, whither they all arrived safely. The wounds of the Chevalier were soon healed, as was likewise that which Mr. Bolton had received; but the Count's recovery was more slow.

He was at length declared out of danger, though a spectacle to excite disgust and dread. The officers of justice waited, meanwhile, in the neighbourhood, until his removal to prison could be effected; but, with returning strength, he seemed to acquire new desperation.

One day that the surgeon and Theodore were present, his depravity appeared in all its enormity. "You have taken me, Dalbert, and taken me alive," said he, his voice and looks denoting at once sudden alienation of intellect and inextinguishable wickedness, "but am I to blame that

I was not found a corpse? Am I to blame that you escaped from *the grave*, with the wife of my victim, De Solase? You intend me for the scaffold, but look well to it. You are about to marry a virgin too! Prithee question that virgin about the *Chateau de St. Uldrich*. Remind her of the night of her strange illness. On that night I occupied a place in the maiden's chamber. Marry her, sage young man, but, in espousing her, ally yourself to a beggar. One hundred and twenty thousand pounds sterling, the whole property of her father and herself, I am proud to tell you, was obtained by me out of the English funds—by me, whose death will rob you of all this property, and rob you, likewise, of your revenge. You escaped the hands of Gaspar (who fell by this arm at Calais), of Conrad, and of Bolton, all of whom I employed to murder you; you escaped the shot I fired at you in the *Isle de Peine*; but you lose your revenge, and you wed a beggar. Ha! ha! ha! ha! Excellent, Egfryd! you have robbed him of his revenge and a hundred and twenty thousand pounds! Admirably done! ha! ha! ha! And more—thus I prevent your cruelty—thus release myself from ignominy and a hated world." Uttering these words, he seized a fork that lay on a chair near his bed, and plunged it into his breast. The surgeon and Theodore were not quick enough to seize the arm before it struck the mortal blow. In an hour he died, raving and in convulsions, but in his raving he disclosed much of his iniquity.

Mr. Bolton, by the declaration of the Count, frantick though he was, was enabled to recover the property which that monster had so infamously obtained. The magistracy of Cognac being applied to, had his cottage searched, and in a *portmanteau*, that he had brought with him from England, bills drawn in London on Paris, to the amount of a hundred and twenty thousand pounds sterling, were found. These the French minister (as soon as he was apprized of the circumstances) ordered to be paid to Mr. Bolton. Pierre Dontache was soon afterwards prosecuted by Theodore for the attack on him when forced to *the grave*; and the ruffian was also prosecuted by Mr. Bolton for the treachery and violence he had practised towards him and Julia, on the day they were brought to the *Isle de Peine*. Pierre Dontache was, for these offences, condemned to the gallies for life. After his conviction, he confessed that he and Gaspar Pontgebre were to have assassinated Theodore in Bourdeaux, on his return thither from England, had he remained there another day.

Theodore and Julia were married, and masses were purchased for the unfortunate Aminta, her brother, and her son. Garquine and Marco were buried in Cognac, but the remains of the other four outlaws were never found, nor those of the caged infant in the cavern, or of its unburied mother.

Mr. Bolton lives with his daughter; and the *Chevalier Du Lange*, restored to his reason, is a partaker of their hospitality. Theodore and Julia afford a bright example of conjugal virtue and fidelity. They have two children, a girl and a boy, and their happiness is perfect.

I have arrived at the termination of my labours. I have lived to depict, in his true colours, the atrocious Count Egfryd, and to represent Theodore and Julia according to their merits. If the miserable end of the Count shall deter from vice, or the happiness of Julia and her husband incite to virtue; if any individual in society shall, by this Work, be saved from a bad action, or drawn to a good one, my object in writing it will have been accomplished.

Farewell, my Theodore; farewell, my Julia. Your

ancient friend and kinsman has now to attend to the important concern of dying. He has now to prepare for another world.

AUGUSTUS JACOB CRANDOLPH.

January, 1811.

FINIS.

NOTES TO THE TEXT

p. 20 Cesare Bonesano de Beccaria (1738-1794), Italian jurist. His book *Dei delitti e delle pene* (1764) in which he advocated the abolishment of capital punishment and the rack appeared in more than twenty translations and greatly influenced the development of the criminal law in Europe.

p. 29 Francesco Albano (or Albani), Italian baroque painter (1578-1660).

p. 30 Vertumnus was a Roman god of the seasons, of Etruscan origin. His successful amorous pursuit of Pomona, goddess of fruit trees, is related in Ovid's *Metamorphoses.*

p. 42 Hebe. The Greek goddess of youth.

p. 48 Joseph-Michel Montgolfier (1740-1810) and his brother Jacques-Etienne (1745-1799) owned a paper factory in Annonay and became famous as the inventors of a balloon raised by heated air. On 5 June 1783 they organized their first public demonstration in Paris, their balloon reaching a height of 2000 metres and covering a distance of four kilometres. The King, deeply impressed, raised them even further—to the peerage.

p. 56 Ceyx, son of Hesperus, was happily married with Aeolus' daughter, Alcyone. So happily, in fact, that they called each other 'Zeus' and 'Hera.' The gods were scandalized; Ovid relates in the *Metamorphoses* that Ceyx died in a shipwreck and that his wife, on seeing his corpse floating on the waves, plunged herself into them, whereupon both of them were changed into kingfishers.

pp. 99 William Godwin (1756-1836) was a clergyman until scruples led him to quit his post in 1782. In 1793 he published *An Enquiry Concerning Political Justice*, the anarchist views of which did not endear him to the establishment. His novels *Things as They Are; or, The Adventures of Caleb Williams*

(1794) and *St. Leon* (1799) have gothic overtones; Falkland is one of the first-named work's principal characters. Godwin's wife, Mary Wollstonecraft, a pioneer of women's rights, died in 1797 shortly after giving birth to Mary, the author of *Frankenstein* who married Shelley.

p. 104 Saint Teresa of Avila (1515-1582), founder of the Discalced Carmelites. She wrote mystical works such as *Camino de Perfección* ('The Way of Perfection,' 1565, revised 1570) and *Castillo interior* (1577), which compares the soul to a castle comprising seven chambers through which one has to pass to reach God. Teresa was canonized in 1622; her feast-day is 15 October.

p. 105 Dodona is a city in Epirus in the south of the Balkan peninsula where chthonic gods were being worshipped before the foundation of a Zeus oracle. Priests in the sacred grove interpreted the rustling of the leaves of a holy oak to determine the correct actions to be taken by those who came to consult them.

p. 108 The painter Charles Lebrun (1619-1690) was made director of the state-owned tapestry factory of the Gobelins in Paris in 1667.

p. 109 *Sultan*. A basket trimmed with silk in which ladies kept their gloves, fans, etc.

p. 109 *Ruelle*. Space between bed and wall.

p. 115 Endor is a place near Nazareth. According to the Old Testament (I Sam. 28) it was here that Saul requested a witch to raise the spirit of Samuel. She obliged, but the news that the ghost brought him was so bad that he fainted.

p. 187 Beccaria. See note to p. 20.

p. 192 Draco of Athens provided his fellow-citizens in c. 620 B.C. with a code of extremely harsh laws which, the Ancients said, 'were written with blood.'

p. 214 King George III (1738-1820) ascended the throne in

1760. In 1788 he became insane; about the time *The Mysterious Hand* was published he was excluded from all influence on the government, his successor ruling as Prince Regent. George's marriage with Charlotte of Mecklenburg-Strelitz was as happy as it was fruitful, for she bore him no less than nine sons and six daughters.

p. 222 Henry Hudson, born around 1565, was an English navigator who, while trying to find a north-western passage to China, discovered the river and bay that were named after him in Canada in 1610. On the journey home, a mutiny broke out, and Hudson, one of his sons and seven others were set adrift in an open boat, never to be seen again. The Hudson Bay Company was a joint-stock company founded in London in 1670. It relinquished its territorial rights to the Dominion of Canada as late as 1869, yet continued to exist as a fur trading company.

p. 234 John de Laer. Presumably a slip of the pen for the Dutch painter Pieter van Laer (1599-1642).

p. 234 Lucas van Leyden (1494-1533), Dutch painter whose engravings emulate those of Albrecht Dürer.

p. 278 Peter the Hermit (d. 1115) was a fanatic preacher from Amiens who led what may be called a preliminary first crusade. His 'paupers' army,' consisting mainly of French peasants, has been blamed for the massacre of thousands of Jews in Speyer, Worms and Mainz, but these atrocities were carried out under the supervision of Count Emich von Leiningen. Many of Peter's followers were made slaves by robber barons in the Balkans while the Turks slaughtered countless others, and Jerusalem was never reached, so the expedition can hardly be called a success.

www.ingramcontent.com/pod-product-compliance
Lightning Source LLC
Chambersburg PA
CBHW030810310726
48980CB00006B/449/J
9781934555361